Naughty
Two's
Three's

D0334382

Naughty: Two's Enough, Three's a Crowd

Brenda Hampton

www.urbanbooks.net

Urban Books
1199 Straight Path
West Babylon, NY 11704

ISBN- 13: 978-1-60162-180-1
ISBN- 10: 1-60162-180-9

First Printing February 2009
Printed in the United States of America

10 9 8 7 6 5 4 3 2

Distributed by Kensington Publishing Corp.
Submit Wholesale Orders to:
Kensington Publishing Corp.
C/O Penguin Group (USA) Inc.
Attention: Order Processing
405 Murray Hill Parkway
East Rutherford, NJ 07073-2316
Phone: 1-800-526-0275
Fax: 1-800-227-9604

ACKNOWLEDGMENTS

Always, a special thanks to my family, readers, book clubs, bookstores and friends. To Carl and Martha Weber, and the Urban Books family, your dedication to my literary career is truly a blessing. I can't think of any other team of people in this industry who I enjoy working with more. I owe all of you a heartfelt thanks.

An extended thanks to my Heavenly Father for not being with me only when times are great, but for looking over me when times are hard. I give all praises to You and look forward to the future that You have waiting for me . . . whatever it may be.

JAYLIN

Eeny, Meeny, Miney and Moe. I got Eeny and Meeny, now all I need is Miney and Moe. I love women; they're what make the world go round. So, the more of them I have, the better off I am. Settling down for me is out of the question. There's enough of me to share with as many women as I want—as long as they meet my standards. And standards, high standards, I do have. Any woman who wants to be considered must be not only bodacious, but she must have a degree, be able to cook, have job stability, drive a nice car, be African American, have no kids, and most importantly, she must be willing to cater to my every need. If not, then she ain't worth my time.

I'm dealing with two sistas right now who meet most of the above, but they're starting to slack on me. Slacking causes me to get bored, and when I'm bored, major changes have to take place.

Nokea is the kind of woman you can definitely take home to Mama, but since Mama ain't around anymore, there's no need for that. Nokea is a pretty, petite thing with curves in all the right places, and her skin is so smooth that sometimes I'm forced to call her Silk. She's got beautiful, big round eyes that go well with her luscious, soft lips. Her hair is shiny, black, and barely long enough for me to run my fingers through. But my true attraction to Nokea is her loyalty to me and her independence. She's a smart woman, and she ain't trying to reach into my bank account for nothing. Most of all, she got my back— and I have hers. She's my rock. I care about her more than any woman I've ever dated.

The problem I have with Nokea is she ain't upping no booty. She firmly believes a woman shouldn't give herself to a man unless she's married to him. And even though I respect her needs, I got needs too. Fucking needs. At least a minimum of three times a week. I expressed my concerns to Nokea, but she insists on depriving me. I don't play games, so I have never lied to her about my desires for other women. I guess she accepts it because other than that, I'm quite a catch. When she needs me, I've been there. When she's lonely, I hold her. When she calls, I'm there to talk. Since we've been together, I've only improved her life. I've shown her the qualities of a real man. A lack of sex is the only problem between us.

That's where Felicia comes in. Felicia's bad. She gives it to a brotha when, where, and however he wants it. Lay it smack dead on the table and pow-dow, brotha be all up in it! She's got a smooth, soft, and juicy dark-brown ass and nice firm breasts to match. Her long braids go well with her round chocolate face. And her smile, it's to die for. All she gotta do is lay one on me and I melt.

She works as an architect and makes pretty good money. Of course, her salary is nowhere near mine, but what the hell . . . there's not too many people kicking it down like me. The biggest problem with Felicia is she's fucking cheap. She never spends money on me, and if she does, it has to be a special occasion like my birthday or something—or if I've fucked her brains out and she wants to be generous.

As for Nokea, she buys me everything. Sends me encouraging cards when I'm feeling down. Takes me to dinner and pays. Even buys me clothes when she sees something I might like.

I just can't decide which one of them accents me better. That's why I don't choose one woman over the other. One woman can't give me everything I want, and for that matter, no two. So, now I'm on the prowl again. Looking for somebody to help fill this emptiness I've been feeling lately. Looking for somebody I can add to my collection.

More realistically, I need some more pussy. Getting sort of tired of the same stuff, and since my baby's mama, Simone, jetted with my child, I can't run to her anymore for a li'l something on the side. Things were just all right with us, but when she told me she was pregnant, I had to man-up and take care of my responsibilities.

I enjoyed spending time with my baby girl, Jasmine, and she brought so much happiness to my life. Then, one day, when Jasmine was almost one year old, Simone did the unthinkable and left. She had a boyfriend in the army, and according to the brief letter that I received in the mail, they were going to get married. The letter implied that her husband would now take my place, and Jasmine would be told that he was her father.

I could've killed Simone. When I jetted to her house to see what was up, it was vacant. I was so hurt, and as the weeks, months, and years have gone by, I feel as if a huge part of me is missing. Damn Simone for making me feel this way. This is another reason why I have a difficult time falling in love with women. No doubt, they can do some stupid shit!

In the meantime, Felicia be setting that pussy out for me, but I know she can do better. I've been trying to ease myself into Nokea too, but she ain't having it. So, a brotha gotta do what he gotta do to make sure his needs are being met. If I ain't happy, nobody's happy. And one thing Mama always taught me is to make myself happy before I make anybody else happy.

I miss Mama. A mugger robbed and killed her as she walked home from work one night. I was only nine years old and had to live in an orphanage until my Aunt Betty came to get me damn near two years later. Living with her was hell. She was a dope addict and treated her kids and me like shit. I moved out at sixteen, but kept my butt in school. Living on the streets wasn't no joke, so I quickly got a job at a restaurant. My charming personality brought in good tips, and that helped pay for my one-room apartment.

When I turned eighteen, my grandfather died and left me part of his estate. I didn't understand why because we never had a good relationship. Hell, I barely knew the man, but when my Aunt Betty told me about the money, I was ecstatic. I used some of the money to further my education, invested a large sum of it in the stock market, and outright purchased a million-dollar home in Chesterfield, Missouri. Now, I'm the number one stock broker at Schmidt's Brokerage Firm, and I rarely look back at my horrific past.

A few months ago, I got a call from Aunt Betty begging for money. She claimed she had kicked her habit and needed a new start, but I ain't no fool. The money I work hard for ain't never gonna be used for smoking no crack. I told her I was on my way to give it to her, but never showed. I hope she got the picture.

Unlike my rough relationship with her, I do have a close connection with my cousin Stephon. He's like a brother to me. He turned out pretty cool after being raised by my Aunt Betty. Got his own barbershop and makes decent money. He's the only person I consider as family, and the rest of them can go to hell, especially my father.

Before Mama was killed, my father and I had a pretty cool relationship. They weren't married, but he'd always come to the house to see me or take me with him. Aunt Betty said that Mama's sudden death took a toll on him, but did he have to run off and leave me behind? Who knows where he is now. The last time I saw him was at Mama's funeral. I was sure we'd leave together, but when I looked around, he was nowhere to be found. He left me without anyone in my life to love, and that was something I would never be able to forgive.

Now, I'm doing things my way. I'm very particular about who I let be a part of my life, and I only keep positive people in my company. If I feel some bullshit about to go down, I jet. Ain't got time for it. My main focus is my career, my money, my body—I work out every single day—and the gorgeous ladies in my life. Those things add to my confidence and allow others to view me as a well put together black man.

NOKEA

I've known Jaylin Jerome Rogers since we were kids, and during our elementary years, we became the best of friends. His mama worked with mine at a cookie factory in South St. Louis, and they too were good friends. Jaylin finally noticed me at twenty-one, and now at the age of twenty-nine, our relationship is going strong. He's a year older than me, and he has everything I want my man to have. Whenever he isn't too busy, he finds time to make me smile, to make me laugh, and to just plain old comfort me. I can ask him for just about anything, and without hesitation he delivers. Eventually, I think he's going to settle down, and when he does, I'll be waiting. I have a special bond with him—more than any other woman he's been with. And he told me that when the time comes, I would be The One.

So, my future is already in the making. Jaylin has a good job as an investment broker and makes about $500,000 a year. That doesn't even include the money he inherited from his grandfather's estate. The only reason that he works is to keep himself busy. He needs a beautiful, educated woman like me in his life, and if he thinks he can make it without me, he's crazy. I was there when his mama died and when his baby's mama, Simone, took off with his daughter. He cried on my shoulder. I promised to always be there for him, even when we were kids. To this day, I've never let him down, and I'm not going anywhere.

I'm well aware of his relationship with Felicia, but she doesn't have what it takes to keep him. I, on the other hand, do. She doesn't realize that a piece of booty isn't all Jaylin's looking for. He needs so much more than that, and since I've had years to observe him, I know what he needs versus what he wants. In the end, I'll be the one to give it to him. She's only temporary, and I'll still be there once she's gone, just like all the others.

See, while Jaylin makes it clear that he doesn't want a commitment, I make it clear that I'm saving myself for my husband. We've come close many times, but he knows I stand my ground. He respects me for not giving my body to anyone but my future husband. He also knows Daddy taught me well and I wouldn't do anything to dishonor his wishes. I know Jaylin has needs; that's why I try not to let his other relationships upset me. Besides, even though there have been plenty of women in Jaylin's life, after a while, they become history while I'm still around. Why? Because I'm connected with the most important thing on him. And that, of course, is his heart. No woman will be woman enough to take that from me. Deep down, even he knows it.

As kids, our parents said we were destined to be together, and there's no way he's going to forget what his mama told him. So, some day, hopefully soon, I'll be Mrs. Nokea Rogers and having the time of my life!

FELICIA

The first time I saw Jaylin, I knew he was the one for me. He stepped out of his black SL 500 Roadster convertible Mercedes Benz at Tony's Restaurant on Market Street and asked for my digits. Even though he was entertaining someone else that night, I didn't care and neither did he. His dark Armani suit and his curly black hair were what instantly attracted me to him. I could smell the money on him, and I thanked God for sending him my way. When Jaylin removed his tinted round glasses, I got a glimpse of his light-gray bedroom eyes and was hooked! I ain't never been excited about no light-skinned, tall brotha, but Jaylin had it going on.

After one day of talking, we were rolling in the sack. I held his broad shoulders and damn near broke my back trying to make sure this brotha called me the next day. I was successful, and he's been calling me ever since—mostly late nights, after he's exhausted from all the ups and downs of the stock market, which, by the way, can be a pain. His mood swings aren't anything to play with, but every time he starts to trip, I get up and go.

I know Jaylin loves me, but he has a funny way of showing it. This homely bitch, Nokea, thinks he's so deeply in love with her that he can't even see straight. But, I continue to deliver breaking news to her: Jaylin couldn't care less about a woman trying to cater to him like his mama. He tells me often that I'm the true happiness in his life.

When we come together as one, our salaries combined will speak volumes. Ain't a damn thing we'll want for. We've already been to Jamaica, to Paris, and even to Hawaii together. I paid my own way, but that's because I can handle my own, and . . . Jaylin can sometimes be cheap. Considering all of the money he has, I don't quite understand why he doesn't splurge on me. He spends just enough on me to get by, and that's only because he knows in order to get something, you've got to give something. He's lucky that I don't trip off the money thing too much. Only when he starts to slack on the "D" thing will I consider it.

Still, as far as I know, he hasn't even taken a vacation with Nokea. What man wants to be on vacation with a woman he can't touch? I'm the one who holds the key to his heart, and if he chooses her over me, he'd be a fool. She ain't even giving him no twang. Now, what kind of woman plays that crap in this day and age? How can she be foolish enough to even step to a brotha like Jaylin Rogers and play that "I'm saving myself" bullshit? All she's doing is saving up for a big disappointment, because I'm working him with everything I have. I'm the only pussy he's laying into right now, and hopefully that'll be forever.

He stressed that as long as I continue to give him what he wants, he'll make sure I play a valuable part in his life. So valuable, that one day, hopefully soon, I'll be Mrs. Jaylin Jerome Rogers, and feeling on top of the world!

1

FELICIA

Dinner was spectacular. Jaylin didn't seem to be his usual self, but since work always seemed to occupy his mind, I didn't push. No matter how tired he was, he almost always found time to make us dinner on Friday nights. I had offered to help tonight, but he wanted credit for the well seasoned porterhouse steaks and garlic potatoes.

I cleaned off the table and piled the dishes in the sink so I could wash them later. Jaylin went into his room to lie down because he insisted his head was banging. I peeked into his room to check on him, but instead of resting, he was on the phone. I knew he was probably talking to that bitch Nokea. He always acted like she was his mama or something, and every time something tragic happened, he leaned on her shoulder. It bothered me a bit, but I wasn't no fucking psychiatrist. I didn't have time to listen to his drama. My job was to satisfy his physical needs, and that's what I intended to do.

I went back into the kitchen and started on the dishes. Jaylin had a dishwasher, but he was a particular brotha. Real tidy. Neat as a pin. According to him, a dishwasher didn't do the job he wanted it to do. He had to scrub the dishes himself to make sure they were sparkling clean. Why buy a fucking dishwasher if you ain't gonna use it? Didn't make sense to me. He said he bought it just to blend in with the other stainless steel appliances in his kitchen.

He wasted a lot of money, and rarely used many of the items in his house, like the silver pots that dangled above the black marble-topped island in the middle of the kitchen floor. Never been cooked in at all. When he made dinner for us, he had another set he used. The hanging set was just for show, just like the furniture that he traveled the world to find. We'd never eaten at his dinette set, and if you'd dare take a seat in one of the soft white leather chairs, he'd have a fit.

We ate in his bonus room, designed specifically for his guests. It had a theatre-sized TV, a pool table, and a cocktail bar with every kind of alcohol you can think of. There was also a mustard-colored leather sofa that surrounded the room. We used it for fucking when we couldn't make it to his bedroom.

I dried the last plate and laid it neatly on the shelf. Soft music played on the intercom throughout the house, and I heard Jaylin open the kitchen door. When I turned, he stood naked, staring at me with lust in his eyes. The sight of his muscular body always weakened me, so I laid the towel on the counter to see what was on his mind.

"Jaylin, baby, are you okay?"

"I'm fine. I just came down to see what was taking you so long. My dick doesn't stay hard all night, you know."

With his hands, he tossed his dick from side to side and I watched it grow. No doubt, it looked delicious.

"I was just finishing up. Besides, I didn't think you were ready yet. The last time I checked, you were still on the phone."

"Well, I'm off now, so when you get finished in here, I got

something waiting for you up there," he said, pointing in the direction of his bedroom.

"I'll be up in a minute. Keep my spot warm for just a few more minutes."

Jaylin grinned and left the kitchen. I took a look at his tight, muscular ass and started to rush myself. Then I realized that if he came down later and saw something out of place, he'd throw a fit. I wasn't in no mood to hear his mouth, so decided to take my time.

When I was finished, I slid out of my sexy red dress in the kitchen and dropped it on the floor. Then I left my black bra on the banister at the bottom of the staircase, and tied my black lace panties around the rail when I reached the top of the stairs. I removed my hair clip and let my braids fall down my back. I followed Jaylin's scent to his room and opened the double tinted-glass doors.

Jaylin lay there asleep. He looked so handsome and peaceful I didn't want to wake him. My pussy had other plans, so I eased onto his California king-sized bed and lay next to him. I rubbed my fingers across his thick eyebrows to straighten them and kissed his cheek.

He slowly opened his eyes. "What took you so long?" he mumbled.

"I came right up, but you had already fallen asleep." By the time I finished speaking, his eyelids were already fading.

Friday nights were becoming a disappointment. Jaylin and I didn't used to miss a beat when it came to sex, but for the last three weeks, he'd been tripping. He used to wake up just to lay it on me; it wasn't like him to be too tired for sex. Something was wrong, but I couldn't put my finger on it. I fell asleep thinking about what was troubling him, only to wake up later to the sound of his loud voice.

"Felicia!" I heard him yell from downstairs. "Felicia! Why is your dress in the middle of my damn kitchen floor? And your bra and panties have no place being where they are. You of all people know I don't like that shit!" He stomped up the steps with my dress tightened in his hand.

"Damn, I'm sorry. But you ain't gotta get all upset about it at three o'clock in the morning," I said, standing naked at the top of the stairs. "It wouldn't have stayed there all day because you know I gotta wear something home, don't I? So what's the big fuss?"

Jaylin didn't say a word. He tossed my dress to me and cut his eyes, as if he wanted to tear me apart.

I wrapped my dress around my naked body and went back into his bedroom. I saw him bent over, while turning on the water in his Jacuzzi tub. I stood in the doorway and watched. Hot steam filled the bathroom, and after he stepped in the tub, he laid his head back on a contoured pillow.

"So," I said, removing my dress from around me. "Would you like some company in there?"

"No, not right now." He closed his eyes and appeared to be in deep thought.

"And, why not?" I asked with a slight attitude.

"Because, right now, I want to be alone. Before your mouth gets going, Felicia, I ain't up for a bunch of questions. So, either go to bed, or leave. Preferably, the door awaits you."

"Jaylin, look, I'm confused. What did I do to upset you tonight? I know the stock market is down but I don't want to be dumped on because you're losing your money."

He ignored me, got out of the tub, poured himself a glass of Moët, and got right back in. I know he told me to leave, but I had no plans to do so. I got right back in bed and turned on the flat-screen TV on the wall in front of me.

I started to nod off, but then I heard Jaylin on the phone again. This time, it sounded like it was one of his boys, because I heard him say, "Man, she be tripping." Since he was full of

Laughs and seemed to pick up a new attitude, I figured it had to be Stephon on the phone.

Stephon was cool. He wasn't as devious or arrogant as Jaylin, but they did have a lot in common. They looked like brothers; other than Stephon being bald and dark chocolate, they still resembled each other in many ways. When it came to their bodies, I couldn't tell which one was in better shape. Jaylin even treated Stephon like a brother. Bought him a barbershop in the Central West End, gave him half on the white 500-series BMW he drove, and recently gave him five grand to take this bitch he'd only known for two weeks on a cruise.

When I first saw Stephon, I considered getting with him, but by then, Jaylin had me hooked. Even Stephon's sexy hazel eyes couldn't sway me. But now that Jaylin was being difficult, maybe I should think twice.

Jaylin had the nerve to always call me cheap, but every time we went out lately, he was talking that "split the bill" crap. We could go through the drive-thru at McDonald's and he'd be having his hand out, asking for half.

It didn't used to be like that. I guess in the beginning, he did what he had to do to keep me; but now, if it wasn't for the good loving he was putting down, I would've been gone. I'd had plenty of brothas, but nobody set me out like he did, especially if the stock market was booming and he was making money. Brotha be working this ass all night long . . . sucking me dry. And then, we'd wind the night down with a bottle of chardonnay. That's the Jaylin I fell in love with. He'd better come out of this shell soon. If not, I would be looking for another brotha to give it to me like he used to. It would be tough, but sista gotta do what a sista gotta do!

I could hear the water running down the drain and watched Jaylin as he dried off. When he came into the bedroom, I pretended to be asleep. From the bottom of the bed, he lifted the satin sheets and crawled between my legs. I felt his thick lips kiss my thighs, and I trembled as his tongue lightly touched them. I interrupted him and lifted his head from between my legs.

"I thought you were anxious for me to leave."

He let out a deep sigh. "Felicia, why don't you just go? You've messed up my mood twice tonight, and my dick ain't even excited anymore." He moved next to me in bed.

"Would you like to talk about what's troubling you? Your attitude really stinks."

"I told you once I ain't got time to talk. If you want to talk, call up one of your girlfriends. They'll listen to you. All I was trying to do is get my fuck on. And since I can't do that, see ya." He turned his back to me and pulled the sheets over his head.

I'd had enough of Jaylin for one night, and put my dress back on. I grabbed my bra from the bottom handrail and jetted. I left my panties on the top stair for memories. Wasn't no telling when I was coming back. I'd have to try him another day, a day when he wasn't clowning like he was tonight. Knowing him, that day would probably be tomorrow.

2

JAYLIN

Felicia knew she be bullshitting. If I could have just gotten that woman to pick up after herself, she'd be all right with me. At five in the morning, she left me horny as hell with a dick that needed some direction. It was times like this that I hated being intimate with only one woman, and that shit had to change.

Instead of being alone, I called Nokea to come over and keep me company. She was an early bird and didn't mind coming over to see me. Before she got there, I slid in a porn movie and went to work on myself. Didn't make no sense for a man like me to have to get off like that, but a brotha gottta do what he gotta do to keep himself happy.

The doorbell rang and I ran downstairs to get it. My baby was nice enough to come all the way over here to keep me company. She knew how much I hated being alone and would always come when I needed her to. I opened the door, and the smell of Nokea's sweet perfume hit me.

"Thanks for coming baby," I said, giving her a tight hug.

"You sounded like something was wrong. Are you okay?"

"I'm cool. I had an awkward dream and couldn't get back to sleep."

"Well, I'm here. Do you want me to make you a drink or something?" she asked, walking upstairs to my bedroom. My mind left me for a minute as I visualized myself pounding the perfect little ass in front of me.

"I already had a drink before you came."

"That's not all you had before I came," she said, picking up Felicia's panties from the top handrail. "Who's been over here, Jaylin?"

"Baby, you know I ain't gonna lie to you; Felicia left not too long ago. She got upset with me because I didn't feel like having sex. Don't be upset. It ain't nothing but a fuck thang," I explained.

"Must you keep that trifling woman in your life? You act like you can't go without sex. If I can go without, I know you can. I'm just not sure how much more of this I can take."

"Don't go giving up on us, all right? I got needs, baby, and it's not that easy for me to go without sex. Since you're saving yourself, I have to make other arrangements. I know it's not what you want to hear, but it's the truth."

Nokea walked into my bedroom and pulled my Gucci sheets off the bed.

"Get me some clean sheets, Jaylin. I'm not going to lay my body on some sheets I know for a fact she laid on tonight."

Without a fuss, I went to the linen closet and got some clean sheets so I didn't have to hear Nokea's mouth for the rest of the night. She lay next to me and didn't say anything else about Felicia. As a matter of fact, she ended up falling asleep in my arms. I held her instead of her holding me, but I didn't mind. I knew what I put her through was wrong, but I needed more than just Nokea.

The next day, I found what I was looking for. I was going through my normal Saturday-morning workout, lifting weights at the gym, and she walked in. She asked if I was using a towel that was neatly folded on the rail beside me.

"No," I said, checking out her smooth, sweaty breasts as I handed the towel to her. "This towel is for anyone who needs to use it."

"Then, I guess that's me. I'm so exhausted from my new aerobics class and I don't think I'm going to be able to keep up." She wiped the dripping sweat from her curvaceous body and my eyes stayed glued to her. "So, what's your name?" she asked.

"It's, Jaylin . . . Jaylin Rogers. And yours?"

"Scorpio Valentino."

"Scorpio who? That's an unusual name."

"Valentino. My mother is black and my father is Italian."

"Oh, I see," I said while looking her over. She wasn't the type of woman I normally dated, but I couldn't deny my immediate attraction to her. Her eyes searched me over too. I'd seen that kind of look many, many times before. She wanted me between her legs, and I wasn't about to walk away from this one. I interrupted while she was speaking.

"Say, uh, I need to get back to my workout. Would it be too much trouble if I asked for your number?"

"I guess not, but I prefer that you give me your number. I'll call you."

I watched her wipe around her belly ring right above the good stuff. She didn't have a pen, so I whispered my number in her ear. She repeated the number to me and promised to call.

As she walked away, I watched her long, bouncing, curly hair move from side to side and her ass jiggle like it was calling my name. Now, that there was my kind of woman. She could definitely become number three in my life. And since she couldn't keep her eyes off my chest and the big bulge in my pants, it was obvious she liked what she saw too.

I was thinking about having sex with Scorpio, until Stephon came out of nowhere and smacked the back of my neck.

"Man, that shit hurt," I yelled.

"Fool, I saw you checking out that fine-ass woman with that bodacious body. I tried to grab her myself, but when I saw her step to you, I backed off. While you were lifting weights, I saw her staring at your ass like she wanted to come eat you alive."

"She was pretty nice looking, wasn't she? I gave her my digits. I hope she calls me tonight. I'd love to add those panties to my collection. If not, I'm gonna call and apologize to Felicia for last night and see if she'll come shake a brotha down."

"You know damn well she'll come. That pussy got your name written all over it. She hooked, and I mean bad. Shit, sometimes I wish I had it like that. These knuckleheads I be going out with just be looking for a damn handout. When a motherfucker gonna start handing me some shit? That's what I wanna know."

"What happened to that chick you took on that cruise? I thought everything was cool with y'all."

"Please. I got those panties on the cruise and that was it. When we came back, I had to let that ass go. Wasn't worth your money or my time. Besides, she was married. Her husband came to my shop and tried to punk me. I had to call the police to get his crazy ass out of there. Wasn't my fault he wasn't sticking it to her like I was."

"Damn, dog, that's messed up. You be careful messing with those scandalous-ass women. What you need to do is step up to my zone—start requiring qualifications and setting rules when it comes to your women. Don't just give your dick or your trust to anybody."

"I thought one of your rules was to only date black women. That cutie who stepped out of here just a minute ago wasn't black. She looked like she was mixed with something—if not damn near white."

"Yeah, I know. But there has to be an exception when it comes to a woman that fine."

"I hear you, my brotha, but don't go breaking all the rules unless you wanna wind up like me—with crazy women who seek a provider."

"Naw, dog. Never."

Stephon headed to the barbershop and I headed to Victoria's Secret at the Galleria to find Felicia something nice to make up for last night. I also picked up a dozen red roses at Schnucks in Ladue just to make her feel extra special. It wasn't often that I did nice things for Felicia, but after seeing Scorpio, I felt kinda horny, and Felicia was my only option. I figured I had some making up to do before she'd give me any.

Her gray GS 300 Lexus was in the driveway, so I knew she was home. I rang the doorbell and leaned against the screen door. I held the roses behind my back with one hand and held the bag from Victoria's Secret up with my finger so she could see it.

She opened the door and her eyes widened, especially when she saw what I had for her. She was all over me.

"Damn, woman, don't get too close. I'm still sweaty from my workout."

"I can't help it, baby. Is this for me?" she asked, taking the Victoria's Secret bag from my hand.

"Yes. I want you to go put this on for me. Now!"

She pulled the pink tissue paper from the bag and looked inside. Then she turned it upside down and shook it. There was nothing inside, as I'd changed my mind about giving her the negligee and saved it for another time.

"Jaylin, there's nothing inside of this bag," she said, standing with her hands on her hips.

"I know. That's what I want you to go put on for me: nothing."

"Cute. Really cute."

Felicia took the roses from my hand and went into the kitchen to put them in a vase she already had from my previous flowers. I stood and watched, as I thought about my plans with Nokea tonight. I told her we'd have dinner, but there might be a slight delay.

"I just wanted to tell you I'm sorry for the way I behaved last night. I'm losing money every day in the stock market and I don't like that. I don't mean to shut you out, but the less I talk about it, the better," I said.

"Jaylin, I understand." She wrapped her arms around my neck. "That's why I don't bother you about anything. I don't want my man stressing all the time, because you ain't no good to me if you're stressed."

"Well, I ain't stressing now." I rubbed my hands on her fat, juicy chocolate ass.

"And I ain't stressing either, so you know what that means."

"It means I gotta jump in the shower so I can get myself ready for some of your sweetness."

"Well, you know where to go, and after you finish, this here will be waiting for you over there," she said, taking off her clothes and pointing to her room down the hall.

I smiled and watched her prance her sexy ass to the bedroom. I had to be out of my mind tripping with a woman like Felicia. Sista couldn't give more than what she was already giving. But I still needed more than just Felicia. I couldn't stop thinking about that sweet little piece of ass I saw today, but was forced to focus on Felicia right now.

I hopped in the shower, and then made my way to the bedroom so Felicia could help me release the tension I'd been feeling lately. No problem there. She rode me like a jockey trying to win a race, and then placed those soft little lips on my goodness to finish the job. The feeling always had me on cloud nine, but after today, I wondered if our relationship would survive another woman joining my circle.

3

NOKEA

I waited patiently for Jaylin to come home, but it neared six o'clock in the evening and he was a no show. I hoped he hadn't forgetten about our plans tonight. Every Saturday, we'd go catch a movie or go to dinner. Sometimes we'd go see a play, depending on what was at the Fox Theater. It wasn't like him not to call me all day, but since I had a key to his place, I decided I'd go to his house and wait for him.

After sitting at his place for another hour and watching Wheel of Fortune, I decided to rummage through his belongings. I always did that when I was alone at his house. It was the only way I could keep up with what was really going on with him. Now, if I asked, he'd tell me; but I had to pretend like I didn't care.

I'd already seen some naked pictures of Felicia and some of his ex-girlfriends in a shoebox at the top of his closet and they disgusted me. I didn't understand how women could stoop so low by flaunting around naked pictures of themselves. Wasn't no telling what Jaylin did with these pictures. I knew his boys had probably seen them, and there was no way I was going to let his friends know what my goods looked like. Hell, Jaylin barely knew. Well, he knew what it looked like, but he didn't know what it felt like.

I was checking out this one disgusting picture of this chick with her leg resting on her shoulder when I heard the front door shut. I quickly threw the picture in the box and shoved it in the closet where it belonged. Jaylin jogged up the steps and I walked out of his bedroom to greet him.

"Hey, baby," he said, opening his arms to hug me. I didn't bother to hug him back, and instead stood with my arms by my sides.

Jaylin noticed my demeanor and gave me a quick peck on my cheek. "I saw your car in the driveway. How long have you been here?"

I folded my arms and followed him into the bedroom. "Uh . . . maybe just a few hours waiting on you to come home. Why didn't you call? And why are you so late?"

"I got caught up at the gym earlier, and then I went to apologize to Felicia for last night."

"Apologize for what? You said she was the one who left you."

"She did, but I wanted to apologize for my bad attitude, that's all. I don't like anybody leaving my house upset with me about my mood swings."

"And I'm sure you made it up to her. Just in case you didn't notice, it's Saturday. According to you, this is our day. So, what are you doing spending time with Felicia? You could've called and apologized to her over the phone."

"Nokea, what's been up with you lately? You know this ain't nothing new. I don't like nobody upset with me, and I'm always willing to apologize when I'm wrong. So, without the hassle, let me get out of these clothes and take a shower so we can go," he said, taking off his sweaty, pussy-smelling clothes.

I turned my back, seething with anger as I went downstairs

on the couch until he got ready. It was times like this when a huge part of me wanted to walk away from this relationship and never look back. Knowing that Jaylin had been with Felicia today was painful, and as I visualized the two of them in my mind, I wanted to get off the couch and run as fast as I could. I kept telling myself that I had a choice, but my decision had always been to hang in there.

Jaylin hurried down the steps wearing an off-white silk shirt and black wide-legged pants that fit him nicely around the waist. His shirt had a few buttons undone so I could get a glimpse of his muscular chest. He'd trimmed his beard and goatee so thin that I could barely see them, and his gray eyes shone as he walked into the living room and asked if I was ready to go.

"Yes, I'm ready. Been ready for quite a while now," I griped.

"So, what's the plan for tonight? If you don't know, I got a place in mind."

"Oh yeah, and where might that be?"

"There's a restaurant, The Hampshire, where we can sit on the terrace overlooking downtown St. Louis. The scenery is off the chain, and I want to share an enjoyable dinner with my number one lady this evening."

"Number one," I said with a shocked look on my face. What an insult. I wanted to be the *only* one. Maybe I was number one in his thick black book, but at this point, I couldn't take his words seriously. "What's the special occasion?"

"The special occasion is to show you how much I appreciate you being there for me. How much I know you want to kick my ass to the curb but you don't. Also, to show you how much I enjoy being with you."

"Jaylin, I already know that. It's just sometimes my jealousy gets the best of me. Felicia doesn't threaten me in any way. Of course I don't like the idea of you being with her, but this situation is only temporary."

Even though my words were the total opposite of what I truly felt, I didn't want Jaylin to know how much his relationship with Felicia bothered me. I placed my hand on the side of his face and he kissed it.

"Sex, Nokea, that's all it is. I have very little feelings for Felicia, and you have nothing to worry about. Don't you ever forget it, all right?"

He gave me a quick kiss on the lips and I pushed Felicia's drama to the side. Jaylin grabbed his keys, but as we got ready to walk out the door, the phone rang.

"Wait a minute, baby. Let me see who that is." He walked over to the phone. "Jaylin," he answered. "No," he said, smiling. "I mean, yes, I . . . I was on my way out the door. Why don't you give me a call tomorrow?" He paused. "Hey, no bother. Just call me tomorrow and we'll talk."

Jaylin hung up, and instead of looking at me, his eyelids dropped low. I knew him too well. That was a new woman. I didn't even have to ask him. But I wasn't tripping, because if anything, she'd replace Felicia, not me.

Our time together was fabulous. Jaylin was right; The Hampshire had it going on. The staff waited on us hand and foot like we were celebrities or something. As soon as our wineglasses were empty, they'd rush over to fill them. Jaylin ordered the filet mignon and I had a juicy New York strip steak. The food was to die for, and my time with Jaylin was truly the best. As the soothing jazz played throughout the restaurant, Jaylin asked me to dance.

"You feel so good in my arms," he whispered.

"So do you, baby. I love you so much, and the thought of us being like this forever is what keeps me sane."

"Yeah, me too. Promise me something, though?"

"What's that?"

"Promise me no matter how rough things might get for us,

you'll always be there. I know it's asking a lot, but you're the only good thing I got in my life. I'm very thankful for you. If I didn't have you in my corner for all these years, I don't know where I would be."

"That's an easy promise for me. I know it's going to get rough—it's already rough allowing you to do some of the things you do. But I have a reason for putting up with you. You are mine, and we were made for each other. Our parents always said we were destined to be together, so I'll wait. You'll come around, sooner than you think." I rubbed my hands up and down his back. He squeezed me tighter and kissed my forehead.

"Woman, that's why I care about you so much. Ain't nobody like you, and one day I'm going to make you all mine."

I wanted to believe Jaylin, but I had serious doubts. His actions didn't jive with his words, and I wasn't about to get my hopes up. We wrapped up dinner and then went back to his place for a nightcap. Like many times before, I wanted to give myself to Jaylin that night, but I couldn't. I didn't want to be on the other side with Felicia and the rest of his female companions. I wanted to continue to stay in a category all by myself. In his own words, he cared for me more than anyone else. I had to believe that.

But I also hadn't forgotten about his earlier phone call. My gut signaled more trouble for us, but only time would tell.

4

JAYLIN

Damn! Scorpio called and I didn't even get a chance to talk to her last night. I was glad when Nokea left. She hung around all day today as I waited for Scorpio to call back. As of yet, she hadn't, but I was anxious to speak with her.

Stephon and one of our longtime friends, Ray-Ray, came over to watch the football game. That took my mind off Scorpio for a while, and I was glad to be focused elsewhere.

"Negro, are you going against the Rams or what?" Ray-Ray said as we debated who'd go to the Super Bowl.

"You know ain't nobody in the league better than them right now. As long as we got the baddest quarterback out there, the Super Bowl is well within our reach," Stephon said, agreeing with Ray-Ray.

"All I'm saying is we need to quit with the turnovers and get back to business. Now, ain't nobody gonna beat us. I just think we got some work to do," I defended.

"Then stop talking that bullshit. You gotta have a little confidence in them, that's all. I don't care how many damn turnovers they make, no other team in the league can beat them."

As Stephon continued to rant, I walked over to the bar and poured another glass of Courvoisier. When the phone rang, I wondered who it was. I figured it wasn't Felicia because I fucked her well yesterday, and she knew I wasn't hooking up with her again until Friday. Nokea had left earlier and said she was spending the day with her parents. I knew it wasn't any of my clients because they knew better than to call me over the weekend. And my boys were here. I hoped it was Scorpio as I rushed to answer the phone.

"Jaylin," I answered in a deep tone.

"Hi, Jaylin. Hope I didn't catch you at a bad time again."

"No, you didn't. As a matter of fact, I wondered when you were going to call back." I walked off into the other room so my boys couldn't hear me.

"I would've called you earlier, but I took my daughter to Forest Park. We usually go there to spend a little quiet time together."

Damn, I thought, a kid. I particularly didn't want a woman with kids after the way I felt when Simone took away my daughter, but maybe this would have to be exception number two for Scorpio. *If I have to make any more, she's history,* I decided.

"To Forest Park, huh? That's cool. Gotta take time out for the kids."

"So, are you in the mood for company tonight? I've been kind of thinking about you and would like to see you."

Now she was really rushing things. I thought it was my job to ask her out. But then again, wasn't nothing wrong with confidence.

"Sure, Scorpio, I would love some company tonight. What time should I expect you?"

"Is eight o'clock okay with you? All I need to do is find a sitter and I'll be there by eight."

"It's on. I'll see you at eight."

I gave Scorpio directions to my crib. I wanted to screen her a little more, but her kid was bugging her in the background. I had my doubts about this one. But, what the hell? If anything, I'd get a good fuck and call it a day.

Ray-Ray's short, roly-poly self and Stephon weren't budging. They hung around just so they could check out Scorpio when she came. I went upstairs and changed into something comfortable—my silk burgundy pajamas—and turned on a song by Frank Sinatra that played on the intercom throughout the house.

"Man, what the fuck is that?" Stephon said, laughing at the song.

"Negro, it's my 'let me come make love to you' song that be having women jumping out of their panties, that's what it is."

"Sounds more like it'll have their asses jumping out of the window to me," Ray-Ray said, giving Stephon five.

"You know, y'all really be playa-hating. I got this nice-ass woman coming over here and you two insist on cock-blocking. Then when I put on something romantic, y'all dissing my song. I tell you what, why don't both of y'all get the hell up out of here? I'll share the gory details of tonight's events with y'all later."

Just then, we heard something that sounded like a loud truck with a rattling engine.

"What the fuck is that?" Stephon said, looking out the window.

"I don't know. I hope it ain't nobody's car," I said.

"It is a car," Stephon said, laughing. "And it's in your driveway. That pretty little thing from yesterday seems to be the owner."

"Man, what kind of fucking car is she driving?" I rushed over to the window to see for myself. This bitch had a raggedy-ass 1977 get-out-and-push Cadillac that I knew was probably dripping oil in my driveway. "Fuck that! This is it for her. I'm going right downstairs to tell her I got plans tonight and made a mistake inviting her ass over here."

"Man, now, you know you be too hard on the sistas. Everybody ain't got it like you, Jay. Give the lady a chance. She might have borrowed a car from a friend," Ray-Ray said.

"Which probably means she don't have a car at all. Man, I ain't even wasting my time."

I ran downstairs to open the door because she rang the doorbell over and over again. Ray-Ray and Stephon followed. When I pulled open the door, I opened my mouth but couldn't say nothing. Scorpio looked and smelled edible.

I moved aside and let her come in. I couldn't tell whose lip hung down the lowest—Stephon's, Ray-Ray's, or mine. She had on a white linen jumpsuit that criss-crossed in the back and tied around her neck. It draped in the front, where I could see just a sliver of her cleavage, and her long, curly hair hung on her shoulders. The bottom half of the jumper was kind of see-through. I noticed she wore a thong because of the string line on her upper hip. Her white-strapped sandals accented the outfit, and so did the red fingernail polish on her hands and feet.

"Hey, uh, Scorpio," I said, clearing my throat. "This is my cousin Stephon and one of my friends, Ray-Ray."

"Hey," both of them said in unison. They stood with pure lust on their faces. I nudged Stephon in his side to get his attention.

"Aw, wha . . . what's up, Scorpio? Nice to meet you." He reached his hand out to shake hers. She smiled and shook his hand. Stephon didn't let go. He held her hand and rubbed it with his other hand. "Smooth. Sweetie, you got some smooth-ass skin. What you putting on yourself these days to keep yourself so smooth like that?"

"No secret," she said, appearing unfazed by his comment. "I always bathe in baby oil, that's all."

"Hey, Scorpio, why don't you go ahead and have a seat? I'm gonna walk my cousin to his car."

"Okay, Jaylin, take your time."

Stephon and Ray-Ray waved goodbye to Scorpio and we walked to Stephon's car.

"Man, man, man! What you gon' do with all that in there?" Stephon said. "Sista might have a fucked-up car, but a woman like that, I'd buy her a new one. She is fiiiine. And if she doesn't meet your expectations, then pass her to me. She definitely meets mine."

"Negro, please. I'm gonna try to tap that ass tonight, and afterwards, you can have it. If it ain't Nokea, I ain't buying nobody shit. When Scorpio leaves, there better not be no oil stains in my driveway from that fucked-up car. If there is, I'm gonna ask your ass to correct it, since she'll be kicking it with you.'

"That's all right with me. I'll correct anything she wants me to. But you'd better watch out. She got an interesting look about her. I think she's gonna give you a run for your money."

"Please. I've had finer women than her chasing after my ass. Trust me; she'll be calling you tomorrow."

"All right, Jay. Don't say I didn't warn you. Something about that woman just doesn't sit right with me. And brotha, please strap one on tonight. I don't want you around here burning. You catch my drift?"

"Always, my brotha, always."

"Well, Ray and me gon' go get our roll on at Skate King in Pine Lawn. Are you sure you and Miss Sexy don't wanna come along?"

"Naw, man, I'm staying right here tonight. I'll roll with y'all some other time. Besides, I ain't in no mood to see you bust your damn head open tonight. Them cats be rolling down there, and personally, I don't think you can hang."

"Hang on this," Stephon said, grabbing his dick. "I'll holla at yo' ass tomorrow."

I went back into the house and saw Scorpio in the living room, looking at a picture of Mama on the fireplace mantel.

"Is this your mother?" she asked.

"Yes, it is," I said, taking the picture from her hand. "She's dead, though. I like to keep her memory around, you know what I mean?"

"Yeah, I sure do. My mother died of cancer when I was nineteen, and I still haven't been able to part with her pictures yet."

"So, can I get you something to drink? I haven't had time to cook any dinner because my boys had me tied up all day with the football games. Or, if you'd like, we can order some Chinese."

"I love to cook. Take me to your kitchen and I'll be more than happy to throw us a little something together."

I took Scorpio's hand and led her into my kitchen. Her eyes wandered. "Jaylin, this kitchen is immaculate. It's a woman's dream to have a kitchen this beautiful and clean. Are you sure you live alone?"

"Of course I do. I used to have a maid, but I got a few good friends who help me keep it clean every once in a while."

"Oh . . . I see. So, what do you have in the fridge?" She boldly opened it.

"I picked up some ground chuck from Straub's last week, and it's the only thing that's thawed. How about some Hamburger Helper? I got a box of cheeseburger macaroni on the shelf and it shouldn't take long at all."

I put everything on the counter for Scorpio and told her I would be back. I went to my bedroom to call Nokea back because I had seen her number on the caller ID. I guess she'd made it back from her parents' house and was calling to let me know. Surely, I didn't want her to show up tonight and mess up my action with Scorpio.

"Hey, baby, you call?" I asked as I sat on my bed.

"Yes. I just wanted to tell you what a wonderful time I had last night. It kind of got me thinking more about our relationship. How much you and I are meant for each other. How much I know you love me and I know some day you'll be my husband. So, baby, I . . . I think I'm ready."

"Ready for what?"

"I'm ready to give myself to you. I want to make love to you tonight."

After all this time, tonight she decides she's ready? I know I was anxious to get inside Nokea, but tonight wasn't the time.

"Baby, listen. I know how strongly you feel about saving yourself, and I want you to continue to stand your ground. Even if you're ready, I'm not. You're special to me, and I don't want to have sex with you while I'm involved with other females." I couldn't believe that bunch of bullshit had come out of my mouth.

"Once I give myself to you, hopefully your involvement with other females will stop. I thought you wanted this Jaylin, but—"

"I do, baby, but not while I'm having sex with other people. Tell you what; just give me some time to cut Felica loose. I don't want to make love to you until I'm free of these other women. That's fair, isn't it?"

"But—"

"But nothing, Nokea. Let me get off the phone so I can get me some rest. I'll call you tomorrow when I get off work. You can come by then and we can talk more about it."

"All right, Jaylin, but, do . . . do you have company? You seem to be rushing me off the phone."

I'd never lied to Nokea, but if I told her the truth, she'd

have more questions for me. I was trying to work on getting my thang wet, and now wasn't the time for questions.

"No. I'm just tired, baby. That's all. I promise I'll call you to-morrow."

She gave me a kiss over the phone and hung up. I hated to lie to her like that, but I guess there's a first time for every-thing. I just hoped she believed me. I wasn't in the mood for one of her unexpected visits.

When I got to the kitchen, I could have died. Scorpio had burned the hamburger meat, and grease was everywhere on my island. This was enough for me. Bitch couldn't even cook? I didn't care how fine she was, she had to go.

"Say, why don't you go in the living room and have a seat. Let me clean up things in here and I'll call and order us some Chinese."

"Jaylin, I'm so sorry. I searched for some seasoning salt in your pantry and when I turned around, the meat had burned. Let me make it up to you. I'll pay for the Chinese if you call it in."

"Okay, whatever. Just go have a seat in the living room and I'll be out in a minute."

She walked her sexy ass into the living room and out of my presence. As I cleaned up, I tried to come up with a good rea-son for her to leave so I could call Nokea back and tell her I changed my mind about waiting. Right about now, I'd rather be making love to Nokea than screwing this dizzy-ass broad.

I turned off the kitchen light and walked into the living room. Scorpio was leaned back on the sofa with her arms folded and her legs crossed, humming with the music on the intercom. I sat next to her.

"Scorpio, look. I think it was a big mistake asking you to come here tonight. I, uh, have a woman, and right now, we're having a difficult time in our relationship. I thought inviting you here would ease my pain, but it's not."

"How did you intend for me to ease your pain, Jaylin?"

"I don't know. Sex, probably, but I don't think it's in my best interest to go there with you. If my woman finds out, we'll probably never be able to work things out."

Scorpio reached over and twirled her fingers through my hair. "I'm so disappointed to hear that," she said seductively. "But what makes you think she's going to find out?"

"You know how y'all women are. Sooner or later, the truth always comes out."

She leaned in to whisper in my ear. "If you won't tell, then I won't tell."

Just that fast, her lips touching my earlobe made me want to fuck her.

"So, are you saying if you let me hit that, I don't have to call you tomorrow?"

"All I'm saying is I live for today and not for tomorrow. And right now, today, I want to see what this big bulge in your pants is all about. I'd love to feel it inside of me, and I want to get to know it, just for the night. If you have no desire to call me tomorrow, then don't. I promise you I won't cry, and I doubt that I'll lose any sleep."

Sounded like a motherfucking plan to me. Scorpio stood up and removed her white sandals. I scooted back on the couch, stretched my arms out and watched her. She stood right in front of me and untied her white linen jumper. She eased it down past her hips, until it hit the floor. When she turned around to walk over to my furry black rug, I noticed a tattoo of a red rose smack on the right cheek of her fat, juicy ass. She lay on the floor with her breasts facing me and her legs opened so I could see the neatly trimmed hairs that covered her pussy. My dick throbbed like I was about to explode. I stood up and got ready to remove my pajama pants.

"Jaylin, no," she said seductively. "Stay right there, baby. When I need you, I'll ask for you." She inserted her finger into

her goodness and my eyes were glued to it. She moved her finger in and out and then licked it. I sat filled with excitement as
she rolled her finger over her clitoris and her juices started to
flow.

"Now, it's your turn." She opened her legs wider and invited
me in.

I rose up and removed my pajamas while Scorpio anxiously
awaited me on the floor. When she got a glimpse of my nine-
plus inches, she smiled. My intentions were to go for the good
stuff first, but I also wanted to tease her ass like she had done
to me so well.

She held her finger out and I licked it to get a quick taste of
her. I eased my body between her legs and placed my lips on
her breasts. She sat up on her elbows and watched to make
sure I did a good job. As I teased her nipples with the tip of my
tongue, she closed her pretty eyes and leaned her head back.

I licked my way down her chest and rolled my tongue inside
her pierced belly button. The foreplay was getting intense, and
when she lay back and closed her eyes tighter, I went for it all.
My face brushed against her soft, pillowy hairs and I took a few
light licks up and down her moist slit. I stuck my tongue deep
within, and as she moaned, I could feel her body tremble. I
rolled my tongue around her clitoris and sucked the juices as
they rolled down my lips. Nothing but the taste of sweet
cherry lemonade hit me. When I finished, I found her lips and
shared the taste with her.

"Fuck me, Jaylin," she whispered in my ear. "Fuck me good,
baby." She didn't have to ask because that's what I intended to
do.

I stretched her legs out in the air and held them with my
hands while she lay back. I rubbed myself up against her to
make sure she was soaking wet. As I entered, I damn near lost
control. I dropped her legs and leaned down to gather myself

for a minute. Pussy felt so warm and good on my dick, I thought it had melted. I closed my eyes and tried to think about the St. Louis Rams football game today, about my job—anything to prevent myself from coming too quickly.

I was able to maintain my composure and get back to work. I worked her insides better than I'd ever done before. Turned her over and pounded her ass like a piece of meat. And just when she thought I was finished, I bent her body over my leather sofa, held her tiny waistline, and stroked her from behind. After all, she was the one who said "fuck me."

Scorpio and I took deep breaths as we lay on the couch. My legs were open and she had her slim, sexy body on top of mine. Her head was on my chest, and I couldn't help but rub my hands on her soft ass.

"Jaylin, I haven't had sex like that in a long time. It was so good to release all that energy with you."

"Same here. I haven't felt like that in a long time either."

"So . . . where do we go from here? I know you said you already had somebody in your life, but I kind of felt a connection between us. Tell me if I'm wrong."

I felt as if we'd made a sexual connection too, so there obviously had to be some changes in my original plans not to call her again. For now, her having a child, a fucked-up car and no cooking skills had to be put on the back burner. "All I can say is I'd be willing to take this one day at a time. First, let me tell you I ain't for being with just one woman. I have a lot of friends—good friends—whose company I enjoy a lot. If you don't mind being a part of my world, then sure, I'd love to keep you around."

"What's the need for so many women in your life? Can't you get everything you want from just one?"

I chuckled at the thought. "Honestly, no. Everybody in my

life accentuates it in a different way. It's necessary for me to have what I want, and if somebody decides to jet, I won't be left without."

"Oh, I see. So, in what ways do the other women accentuate your life? I'm sure I can fulfill many of those needs. It almost sounds like you're afraid of being left alone."

"Maybe you can accentuate my life and bring to the table everything I need, but now isn't the time to discuss it. As for me being alone . . . a man like me will never be alone. Still, I like my space and I don't want nobody in my life around the clock."

Scorpio lay quietly with her head on my chest. I got sleepy, so I suggested we go to my room for a drink. I took her hand and we moseyed up the steps.

"Jaylin?" she said, stopping me on our way up.

"Yes."

"I forgot something."

"Forgot what?"

"Sit and I'll show you."

I sat on the steps and Scorpio brought her lips to mine. She took my hand and put it between her legs so I could feel her wetness. Then, as soon as my dick gave her some attention, she swallowed it like no other sista had done before. I leaned back and enjoyed the sensation of the back of her throat.

Just as I was getting into it, she switched positions and put it on me. Stroked me so good, I couldn't think about anything else but being inside of her.

"Scorpio, damn, baby, please. Brotha tired," I said, suddenly feeling drained, which was quite unusual for me.

"Jaylin, you ain't fucking me," she whispered in my ear. "I need a man to fuck me."

I couldn't sit there like no punk who couldn't hang, so I quickly retrieved a condom from my nearby office, turned her ass over on the steps and tore into her from behind. She held onto the banister to keep still, and her long, beautiful hair dripped with sweat. I moved her hair over and pecked down the side of her neck. When I felt myself about to explode, I held the banister with one hand and gripped her butt with my other one.

"Woman, what in the hell are you trying to do to me?"

"I'm not trying to do anything. When I got something as good as you to work with, the best of me comes out. But, Jaylin?"

"What's up?"

"You're heavy. Do you mind getting up?" She pushed me back with her body.

"Aw, I'm sorry. I was just caught up in the moment." I stood and reached down to help her up.

We went into my bedroom. She seemed amazed as she looked up at the high coffered ceiling. I could tell she was impressed. I told her I'd had an interior decorator and paid her very well for her services.

Scorpio smiled and got her sexy self underneath my covers. I thought about the mess we'd left downstairs, and I went down there to pick up our shoes and clothes and then brought them upstairs to my room. Just the thought of my place being junky upset me. I neatly laid her outfit on my chaise and put her shoes underneath it. I hung my pajamas in the closet and got in bed next to her.

Scorpio lay on her stomach, barely keeping her eyes open. It didn't take her long to fall asleep. Some of her hair covered her face, and I moved it over to the side so I could look at her. She was an amazingly beautiful woman, but I didn't know much about her. Was she really feeling me, or could I have finally met my match? I didn't see her as being gullible, but she didn't seem bothered by me mentioning other women. I hoped like hell that she wasn't a gold-digger, but if she was, she was definitely wasting her time.

I hadn't decided if I wanted to keep her in my life; then, I lifted the cover and looked at her well-shaped naked body. After getting a good look, I decided she was a keeper. She needed some work, but that wouldn't be a problem for me. I'd just have to deal with her child and add a few enhancements to her so she could fit into my circle.

5

FELICIA

Jaylin didn't even call last night. I called his house all night but got no answer. I started to pay him a visit, but I was sure Miss Homebody was probably over there. But even if she was, he usually still answered the phone, so I didn't know what was up.

Today, I went to the Galleria at lunch to buy myself something nice. After all the bullshit I put up with from Jaylin, the least I could do was take good care of myself. As soon as I walked into Macy's, I saw Nokea on her way out with a shopping bag, which looked to be filled with men's clothing.

"I see Jaylin's got his mother going shopping for him again," I said.

"Felicia, give me a break. You know I'm not trying to be anything like Jaylin's mother. Just in case you didn't notice, he is my man, and I do take good care of him."

I could have choked. How could she be taking good care of him and wasn't even satisfying his needs? "Nokea, feel free to spend all of your little money on Jaylin. If you think buying him clothes is going to keep him, my dear, you got another thing coming."

"And Felicia, if you think screwing his brains out is going to keep him, then you got another thing coming."

"Bitch, when are you going to wake up and smell the coffee? All Jaylin wants is a good woman who can fuck him like I can. You're sadly mistaken if you think he's going to settle down with you and you ain't upping nothing. In this day and age, that just doesn't keep a man."

"In case you want to know, I'm meeting with Jaylin about our little problem tonight. Whenever I decide to give myself to him, you are done. So, please, enjoy his strokes while they last because your last stroke is almost over."

"If that's the case, you should've talked to him about that last night when you were there. If your decision to give it up all of a sudden didn't change anything last night, then today definitely ain't going to make a difference."

"I wasn't at his place last night. When I spoke to him, he was tired. Tired of your mess, and all these other females' mess. So, as I said before, after tonight, you're history." She turned and walked away.

I hated that little preppy bitch—maybe because deep down I knew Jaylin cared about her a little more than he did me. I overheard him speaking to Stephon one day about how she meant so much to him. He even referred to her as his soul-mate. He said that if it wasn't for *her* being there for him, he would be lost. I couldn't ignore his strong feelings for her.

Maybe it was time to face reality. What if Jaylin decided to settle down with Nokea? Where would that leave me? I knew I was too good for this kind of bullshit, but I just couldn't help myself. His sex was too good for me to let go, and until I found better, I was staying put. Yes, there were more men who had it going on like Jaylin and who were interested in me. Especially where I worked. I just didn't want to go there because relation-ships in the workplace never seemed to work out.

I flew down Brentwood Boulevard in my Lexus thinking about what Nokea had said about giving it up to Jaylin. Now, as far as I knew, it had been me and only me for a while. Would he really be willing to end this for a virgin who obviously didn't know how to show him the ropes? The thought frustrated me.

When I got back to work, I asked my secretary to get Jaylin on the phone. She called his office, but then told me he didn't go to work today. I tried him at home and got his voicemail. *Damn, where is he?* I thought. I hadn't talked to him since Saturday morning. Normally, by now, he would've called to say hello.

Then it hit me. Nokea said she wasn't at his place last night, so that probably meant somebody else was. He wasn't calling because he had a new bitch. Every time somebody new came along, he distanced himself. Then when he realized nobody could give it to him like I could, he would dismiss the new bitch. *So, here we go again.* I was gonna have to go over there and fuck his brains out so he could get his mind back on the right track.

As a matter of fact, since Nokea would be there, we'd have a good ole time. We hadn't had one of our deep arguments in a long time, and it was well overdue. The last time I confronted Nokea was a few months ago, but she backed down easy. I'd paid Jaylin an unexpected visit, and she was there. Jaylin asked me to leave, but I wasn't doing that before I made it clear to her where things stood between him and me.

Nokea didn't even put up a fuss, but as usual, Jaylin always sided with her and chewed me out the following day. He flat out told me that if I ever made him choose, he'd choose her. His words stung, but since I was in this for one thing and one thing only, I didn't trip.

Tonight, though, I needed to know where things stood between us. I think I felt more for Jaylin than I wanted to admit. If he all of a sudden had plans to end this, then I didn't know what I was going to do. Knowing him, he was gonna stick to the same words he'd been saying for years: "Y'all know my situation. I can't be with one woman. If you don't like it, then you know what you can do." Realistically, adding Nokea to our sexual mix wasn't going to fly, and another new woman would only make it worse.

6

NOKEA

Jaylin was ending it with Felicia tonight. This was the last straw.

After seeing her at the Galleria, I stopped at the Saint Louis Bread Company on Carondelet Avenue and saw Mona, an old girlfriend of mine from college. She sat down to have a cup of coffee and Danish with me.

"So, how's everything going, Nokea? I haven't seen you in a long time."

"It's going fine, Mona. I just got a promotion and things are going well. How about you? I heard you and Carlos tied the knot."

"Yeah, we finally got married a little over a year ago. I have a little girl. Her name is Tory Marie, and she's a beauty." Mona reached in her wallet to show me a picture of her baby.

"Mona, she's beautiful. You are so lucky." I gave the picture back to her.

"So, Nokea, you haven't tied the knot yet? I know the last time we talked, you were dating that fine investment broker. Whatever happened to him?"

"He's still around. We haven't decided to walk down the aisle yet, but it's coming. Probably sooner than I think."

"Well, don't wait too long. You know we aren't getting any younger. I had to lay it on the line for Carlos. We'd been together since college, and he still wanted to play the field. I took him to dinner one night and said 'Look, brotha, it's either the streets or me.' I made it perfectly clear that when I was gone, I wasn't coming back. Two weeks later, he proposed. Sometimes a man needs a little help. He doesn't realize a good thing until it's gone. And even though he was somewhat pressured, we have a good life together. Every day he thanks me for getting him on the right track."

"I'm sure everything will work out for Jaylin and me. We've known each other a long time—and you're right, we're not getting any younger. I can't wait to have beautiful babies with him like you have with Carlos. Are you planning to have any more?"

"I sure am. Carlos wants to wait, but he doesn't know I stopped taking my birth control pills. So, I'll have another surprise for him very soon, I hope."

"Girl, you crazy. But it's good to see things are going well for you."

"Same here, Nokea. But you get that handsome man to marry you so y'all can start making those beautiful babies." She looked down at her watch. "Look, I gotta go. I have a hair appointment at three, and since I know I probably won't get out until late, I'd better get on my way. It was good seeing you, Nokea. Call me some time." She gave me a piece of paper with her number on it.

I watched Mona get into a brand new Jaguar. She appeared to have it going on. Carlos had a good job and she didn't even have to work unless she wanted to. If she did, she had her marketing degree to fall back on.

I knew what she said was right. I couldn't put this off with

Jaylin any longer. My birthday was just two weeks away and I'd be thirty years old. I was ready to give myself to the man I loved. I'd had thoughts of doing so for a very long time. Bottom line was I'd given Jaylin nine years of my life and things hadn't changed since day one. He'd been with plenty of other women, and I'd put up with it simply because he promised that some day all of it would end. How stupid could I be? I must be out of my mind to put all of this into a relationship and not expect a marriage proposal by now. Our quality time together had to be on specific days because he had to make time for his other women. That was ridiculous and I knew it.

I sighed deeply and thought about my stupidity. I shouldn't have been letting him treat me that way. But then again, maybe it was my fault for not giving myself to him sooner. Maybe if I just did it, then we could finally take our relationship to the next level.

That prompted me to call him to make sure we were still on for tonight. His secretary, Angela, said that he had worked from home that day, but when I called, he didn't answer. I supposed he had to run an errand or something, so I headed for home to change into something more enticing to wear that night. I had a feeling that this would be a turning point in our relationship. I couldn't wait to give Jaylin exactly what he'd been waiting for.

7

JAYLIN

"Mmm-mm-mm, Scorpio, you sure know how to fuck up a brotha's mind," I said, lying next to her in bed.

"I told you I can go forever, as long as I'm with someone like you."

"Well, Ms. Energizer Bunny, you just keep on going." I rolled on top of her and kissed her again.

We had been at it all day long—on the floor, in the tub, on the chaise in my room, and of course, in my bed. Time flew by. I didn't even have enough strength to get my ass up and go to work. I called Angela and told her to take messages for me today, and if anybody important called, to hit me on my private line at home. The only people who had that number were her and Stephon. Since that phone didn't ring, I spent the entire day fucking Scorpio. She just couldn't get enough of me and I couldn't get enough of her. This woman was mine, and I didn't care what anybody thought. She wasn't leaving my life anytime soon.

Scorpio got up and took a shower. I watched her through the glass door, standing with soap and water dripping down her naked body. My dick got hard again, but I was too tired to go at it. I picked up the phone and called Angela to see if anybody had called.

"Jaylin, where have you been? Are you coming in at all today?" she asked anxiously.

"Hold on, what's the problem? I told you earlier I wasn't coming in. I also told you if it was important to call me on my private line."

"It's nothing important, but your friends—I mean your girl-friends, or whoever the hell they are—been calling here like crazy looking for you. I can't get anything done if I'm interrupted by personal calls for you."

"Sorry, Angela. I'll call them in a minute. How's the market doing today?"

"Actually, it's up. Everything is looking pretty good, but you know how the market can be."

"Trust me, I know. I had a feeling that today would be a good day. That's why I stayed my ass at home."

"Negro, please. You know you stayed at home because you got some female over there. But that's your business, not mine."

"That's right, Angela, it is my business. When I was at home smacking bellies with you, you didn't seem to have a problem with it."

She laughed. "You know I'm just messing with you. But it would be nice to get things going again."

"Not a chance in hell. You're married now—to my boss' son—and we can never go there again."

"Darn. I had hoped there was something I could do to change your mind about that."

"Nothing. Now, transfer me to my voicemail so I can check my messages."

Angela transferred me to voicemail and I heard messages from both Felicia and Nokea. One of my most important clients had also called and said he wanted to buy some more shares of this company that was booming on the West Coast. That meant more money for me, so I went downstairs to my office to call him.

"Mr. Higgins, how are you, sir? I just got your message. What deed can I do for you today?"

"Jaylin, I think this fucking company is going to explode. I want to buy more shares now because when it does, buddy, I'm going to take my family and move my ass to a different country. Maybe even Africa," he said, laughing.

Ha, ha, ha. Africa my ass.

"Sounds like a plan, Mr. Higgins," I said, laughing right along with him. "I'll take care of that for you immediately. How many additional shares would you like to purchase?" Higgins gave me a figure that could help set me up even more.

I continued sucking up to him and laughed at his corny jokes. Fifteen minutes into our conversation, the door to my office squeaked open and Scorpio appeared, with only a towel wrapped around her. I put my finger on my lips, gesturing for her to be quiet. She smiled and walked over to my desk, pushing my papers aside so she could sit on it. I leaned back in my leather chair and watched as she removed the towel. I closed my eyes and tried to focus on my conversation with Higgins.

She took my hand and made me feel her insides. Getting excited, I tried to end my conversation with Higgins, but he just kept on talking. I stood up and slid my boxers down with the phone rested on my shoulder. I hurriedly inserted myself, and we rocked back and forth for a while; then Scorpio loudly added her famous words, "Fuck me, Jaylin."

Higgins cleared his throat and asked, "Jaylin, buddy, am I interrupting something?"

"No, not at all." I placed my hand over Scorpio's mouth. "That was just a friend of mine joking around with me, that's all."

"Sounds like she's doing more than just playing around with you, buddy. Sounds like she's fucking the shit out of you, or you her," he laughed.

"Well, you know how it is," I shot back.

"Why don't I just call you tomorrow? Hey, I got a better idea. Why don't we get together for a game of golf on Friday? The last time, you beat me and I owe you one."

"That's fine, Mr. Higgins. I'll see you Friday."

"Hey, Jaylin, suck on those tits for me," he said, laughing and finally hanging up.

I let the phone drop to the floor and Scorpio and I continued our midday session on my desk. It took a while for me to come because she had nearly drained me. Then, when she gave me some love and tender care with her mouth, I was forced to release myself.

I fell back in my chair and she took a seat on my lap. "Baby, that's it for the day," I said. "Don't you ever get tired?"

"Not really. I thought you were going to join me in the shower, but when you didn't, I came looking for you."

"That's cool and all, but you can't be messing with me like that when I'm talking to my clients. Luckily, he's cool like that. Some of them be tripping when it comes to their money. They want a broker who sits in front of the monitor all day long and does nothing but watch the market go up and down."

"Sorry, but I couldn't help myself. You make me feel so good that when I want to feel you, I just got to feel you, no matter where you are."

My private line rang, so I patted Scorpio on her ass and made her get up.

"Man, why haven't you been answering your phone?" It was Stephon. "I called you at work and Angela's crazy ass told me to hit you on your private line."

"I was too tired to go in today, bro. Just wanted to lay my head down for an extra day. You know how that is."

"So, I guess that means Scorpio wore that ass out last night, huh?"

Scorpio was listening in on my conversation, so I put Stephon on hold.

"Say, baby, do you mind? I need to take this call. Why don't you go to the kitchen and find us something to eat? I'm hungry, aren't you?"

"All right. I'll try and find something," she said, walking out.

"And baby," I yelled, "don't cook nothing! Put together a salad or something."

She put her hand on her hip and rolled her eyes at me then gave me the finger.

"Now, I'll stick something up your ass if you want me to," I said, laughing.

"We might have to try that later."

She winked and walked out.

"Damn," I said, shaking my head and putting the phone back on my ear. "Yeah, man, I'm back."

"What the hell's going on over there? What's all this 'stick it here and there' stuff I hear you talking?"

"Stephon, this woman is bad! She's been over here since y'all left, wearing my ass out. I ain't never, and I mean never . . . Did I say never?"

"Yeah, you did, man."

"Never has a sista put it on me like that. She done set that shit out!"

"Damn, I knew she would be good. She had that seductive look about her that said she was capable of putting it on your ass. As soon as she walked in the door, her pussy screamed your name."

"Yeah, and it's been calling me ever since."

"My question is, what you gon' do with it? You know Nokea and Felicia ain't having it this time. They start acting funny every time you bring somebody new to the circle. And if I can recall, the last time you tried that shit, they were both about ready to kill you."

"Bro, how many times I gotta tell you I got this under control over here? I know I'm playing with fire, and you're right, the last time brought about much chaos. But it also showed me that no matter what, Nokea and Felicia ain't going nowhere. I've been with Nokea for nine years and Felicia for four. If they ain't stepped by now, they're here to stay."

"You g'on with your bad self. But, uh, I thought today you were going to be passing Scorpio to me."

"Now, I know what I said last night, but this a different day. Let me enjoy things while they last. If I get tired by next week, next month, or next year, I'll send her your way then."

"Sounds like you're gonna buy that car sooner than you thought?"

I laughed. "Yeah, I guess she would look pretty damn good in a Navigator or an Escalade, but, uh, she gotta do a little more work on me before I consider that."

"Seems like she's already moving in the right direction. She done stepped up since last night. She wasn't getting a damn thing then."

"And she still might not, but maaaan, the way she be popping that thang . . . whew! It's enough to make any man go crazy."

"You got my shit over here on the rise just thinking about it. Let me call one of my ladies so they can shake a brotha down tonight."

"You do that. I'll call you later."

When I hung up, I called Nokea. She answered on the first ring.

"Jaylin, where have you been? I was coming over to talk to you in about an hour."

"Talk to me about what?"

"About what I mentioned last night, silly. You said we could continue our conversation today."

Damn, I had completely forgotten about Nokea coming over today. Scorpio had my mind twisted. All I'd been thinking about was being in between her legs. Her sex was the best. I didn't think any woman was capable of taking in my nine-plus inches without a fight, but Scorpio had done it.

I rubbed my goatee and sucked in my bottom lip. "Nokea, baby, I'm sorry. I forgot you wanted to talk. Look, my decision still stands. I don't want you to give yourself to me right now. So, really, there's nothing for us to discuss."

"I don't care what you say. We have a lot to discuss, and I'll be over there within the hour. Tired or not, you're going to hear me out." She hung up.

I didn't call back because I heard something fall in the kitchen. I ran to see what it was. Scorpio had dropped a glass bowl on the floor.

"What are you doing?" I asked, irritated.

"It just fell, Jaylin. When I turned around, my elbow must've knocked into it and it fell."

Since she was in the kitchen with no clothes on, I helped her bend down and pick up the glass and eventually forgave her. We sat on the stools and ate the salad she'd made. I'd had better, but since I didn't have any cooked ham to jazz it up, the vegetables had to do.

I knew Nokea said she was on her way, but I wasn't going to make Scorpio leave just because Nokea insisted she wanted to talk. If anything, she knew better than to pressure me into doing something I didn't feel like doing. Out of respect, though, I explained the situation to Scorpio as she lay across my bed.

"If you don't mind, I have some company on the way. She wants to discuss some things with me, and it shouldn't take long at all. If you wouldn't mind staying in my bedroom, that would prevent me from answering any questions about us."

Scorpio sat up and placed her long hair behind her ears. She avoided eye contact with me and rubbed the tips of her manicured nails. "Is she your girlfriend?"

"Well . . ." I hesitated. "We're very close friends."

"Intimate friends?" she asked, finally making eye contact.

"No, but a friend who would trip if she knew about our actions for the past two days."

"I thought you had an understanding with your women. If she's coming over here to start any trouble, I can just leave. I don't believe in fighting over a man. No offense, but there are plenty of men to go around."

"I agree, but there's only one of me." I stood up and stretched. "Nokea ain't the kind of woman who would pick a fight either, so can I count on you to stay in my room? I'd really like for you to stay. We still have plenty of unfinished business to take care of."

"I'll stay, Jaylin, but you'd better hope things don't get out of hand. If so, you'll see a side of me that you may not like."

"I didn't know that side of you existed. Thus far, I'm digging you from every angle."

When the doorbell rang, Nokea wasn't bullshitting. She was right on time. Her face did not display a smile.

"Baby, what's up?" I said, knowing that I didn't want to be bothered.

"What's up is whose darn car is that in your driveway?" she yelled.

"Come in, have a seat, and lower your voice. I don't like you yelling at me like that. It definitely ain't your style."

Nokea folded her arms and went over to the couch. As usual, my baby looked and smelled good. She had her hair neatly layered on the sides and spiked in the front. Her sexy little blue dress showed every curve on her petite frame, and her hips swayed as she sauntered into the living room. She turned and pointed her finger at me.

"I'm not sitting down, Jaylin. I'm interested in knowing whose car that is outside!"

"For the last time, don't be yelling in my house like that. My neighbors don't need any reason to call the police. You know these folks in Chesterfield don't play. Sit down so we can talk."

She finally sat down and I sat next to her. I took her hand.

"The car outside belongs to a nice young lady that I met not too long ago. She's upstairs in my room watching TV, and she's leaving tonight."

Nokea snatched her hand away from mine. "Was she here last night when I called you? Is that why you didn't want me to come over, and why you haven't been answering your phone?"

"Because I've been busy. I had some work to do, and when I spoke to you last night, I was in my office trying to catch up."

She rolled her eyes. I could practically see the smoke coming from her ears.

"You still haven't answered my question. Was she here last night?"

I dropped my head back and looked up. "Yes, she was, but—"

Nokea pushed my face, and when I sat up straight, she smacked me. I closed my eyes and turned my head to prevent myself from fucking her up. I realized I deserved it for lying to her, so I couldn't do anything but shake it off.

She covered her face with her hands and started to cry. I felt worse than I'd ever felt before because I'd never seen her cry like that. I leaned over and wrapped my arms around her.

"Look, I'm sorry. The last thing I want to do is hurt you, but it ain't like you don't know my situation. I don't know what you want from me. For years, you've been telling me you don't want to have sex with me, and now you've changed your mind. You've been on and off, Nokea, and how do you think that makes me feel?"

She shook her head from side to side and slapped me again. "You are so full of it. You know darn well what I want, but you've refused to give it to me. This sex thing wouldn't even be an issue if you would've focused your time and energy on our relationship only. But that's asking too much of you, Jaylin, isn't it?"

I rubbed my goatee and pressed my lips together. Nokea had definitely touched a nerve by slapping me and by not understanding what I was saying.

"Look, if you say you love me like you do, then there shouldn't have been no problem with you wanting to give yourself to me. Now you expect me to drop everything and be done with it. It doesn't work like that, Nokea. This process takes time."

Nokea dropped her head on my shoulder to cry, and I felt terrible. I hated to see her like this, but nothing I said seemed to soothe her pain. "Baby, do you hear what I'm saying to you? What do you want from me? I can't change things overnight, and I'd be lying to you if I told you I would." Besides, I had no intention of dropping Scorpio any time soon now that I knew what a freak she could be.

She lifted her head and wiped her tears. "Jaylin, I love you. I've always loved you, but you have been too blind to see that all along you've had everything you've needed. Did it ever occur to you that if you gave our relationship a chance, I would eventually come around and give myself to you? Not once did you give up your women for me. I've always been in this with somebody else.

"I refuse to go on like this anymore. Some things need to change. All of my girlfriends are getting married, making commitments, and I'm still hoping for things to work out for us. I'm not getting any younger, and neither are you."

I couldn't say anything. I knew what I had put her through, but I thought she understood what a man like me needed. I got up to pour myself a shot of Martel. When the doorbell rang, I poured a double shot because I felt something heavy about to go down.

When I opened the door, Felicia walked in, Scorpio stepped out of my bedroom, and Nokea stood up next to the couch. *Damn*, I thought. *What in the hell am I going to do now?*

Since Scorpio was my new lover, all eyes were on her. She had on my black silk robe, tied so low that we could see part of her left breast.

"Who in the fuck is that?" Felicia asked.

"You know, for a woman who's supposed to be classy, your mouth is extremely foul. Chill out with that, all right?" I tried to play it cool; after all, this was my house and I was in control.

I looked up at Scorpio. "Hey, why don't you come down-stairs? I want to introduce you to some friends."

As Scorpio walked down the steps, her pretty, tanned legs and private parts peeked through my robe. I know damn well Felicia and Nokea got a peek because they looked as if their in-sides burned with fire. Scorpio stepped into the living room with Felicia and Nokea, who were already moments away from killing each other.

"Ladies, first let me say that I don't want no shit up in here tonight. We're going to settle this like adults, and everybody's gonna go home happy, all right?"

Scorpio had a smirk on her face. She appeared to be getting a kick out of the drama. "I heard all the yelling, so I stepped out of the bedroom to make sure everything was okay. I really don't want to be a part of this, and if you don't mind, I can just go. You've already made it clear to me where things stand with us, so there's no need for me to stay and battle it out with these two women."

Now, that was my kind of woman. She was thrilled by the drama, but she wasn't going to put me on blast in front of everyone. "Thanks, Scorpio. I appreciate you not stressing a brotha. Just leave the robe on my bed when you change."

"Of course," she said, making her way back up the steps.

Felicia cleared her throat and started working her neck. "Sorry, Mr. Rogers, but it's not that easy for me. I need to know what's up with us right now. I'm not going to play second to neither one of these bitches because I've done it long enough. When I saw Miss Homebody over there today, she said you were closing some doors in your life. I want to know if that door is supposed to slam on me. If so, I came to hear it straight from the horse's mouth."

I looked at Nokea. She didn't say a word, but a lock of disgust was written all over her face. But tonight, I was standing my ground. If neither of them liked it, too bad. The world was mine, and I determined who stayed in it. At this point, I didn't think either of them were capable of stepping.

"Felicia, I'm gonna say this to you and Nokea—if she's listening. I am not going to limit myself to just one woman right now. Maybe in the future, but that is something I can not predict. I enjoy being with the both of you, and I refuse to choose one over the other. If you can't roll with that, then roll out. If you don't appreciate a brotha's honesty, then I don't know what else to say. I'm tired of repeating myself over and over again. It's starting to get very frustrating for me. So, tonight, I'll let the both of you decide. Either you're gonna roll with me or you're not. I'm not going to lose any sleep either way it goes."

There was silence. Scorpio walked downstairs with her white jumpsuit on, looking just as spectacular as she did when she came in last night. Nokea and Felicia looked at her with jealousy in their eyes as she walked over and kissed me on the lips.

"I'll call you tomorrow," she whispered then made her way to the door.

I hated to see her go, but I was sure she'd be making her way back to me soon. I turned my attention back to Felicia and Nokea.

"So, ladies, what's it going to be?" I rubbed my hands together, waiting for an answer.

Nokea didn't say anything, but as usual, Felicia was the first to open her big mouth.

"All I wanted to know is if you were ending it tonight to be with Nokea. Since you've made it perfectly clear that you're not," she said, looking at Nokea, "we might have been able to work out something. But I have a problem with this Scorpio chick. Sex has only been between you and me for some time. I don't know if I can get with you screwing around with someone else. So, what the hell is up with that?"

"What's up is that I like her. I'd like to kick it with her like I do y'all, but it seems to be a problem all of a sudden."

"You damn right it is! It's a problem because I don't want no diseases from that bitch. If you ask me, she looks nasty, so I'm calling the shots on this one. When you're done with her, call me. Maybe I'll be there or maybe I won't. Who knows? But I don't want to hear from you as long as you're still with her. This one here," she said pointing at Nokea, "I can deal with. But that tramp who just left, I can't."

"So, in other words, the competition is getting too steep for you, huh? See ya later, Felicia, and don't let the door hit you on the way out."

Felicia tucked her purse underneath her arm and stamped her way to the door.

"Hey!" I yelled. "Don't have a change of heart tomorrow, because you know I don't play these back and forth games."

She ignored my comment and slammed the door. I wasn't bothered one bit by her departure. I knew Felicia would come running back. This time, though, I'd found a replacement for her, so it wouldn't be as easy for her to get back in.

Nokea sat on the couch with her fingernail in her mouth, staring at the wall in front of her.

"So, Miss Lady, are you a goner too?" I wasn't in the mood for any more bullshit.

"I'm not going anywhere, Jaylin. I refuse to lose you to women like them, and with our history, I know that one day you'll come around. I just hope I can deal with—"

I sat beside her and rubbed her hand. "Nokea, you understand me better than any woman I've been with. And deep down, you know how I feel. So, trust me this time. It'll all work out for the best."

She laid her head on my shoulder and closed her eyes. "I hope so, Jaylin. I truly hope it does."

My hopes weren't as high as Nokea's. There was no doubt that Scorpio would interfere, but I just wasn't ready to part ways with her yet. Her good-ass loving had me hooked. Maybe even more hooked than I was willing to admit. I hoped that tonight's events didn't compromise my arrangements in any way. Nokea seemed to be consistent with the new program, and I would bet a million dollars that, by the end of the week, Felicia would jump back on the bandwagon too.

8

NOKEA

Today would change my life forever. It was my birthday, and Jaylin had made plans to take me to Cardwell's at the Plaza for dinner. Afterward, we arranged to get a room at the Sheraton Clayton Plaza Hotel so I could finally show him how much I really loved him. It was time. And just maybe, things between us would be different now.

When I talked to him last night, he said he hadn't talked to Scorpio or Felicia. So, it was time to make my man as happy as I could, since his other women were out of the picture. He apologized for the other night and told me that he regretted the confrontation, that he never intended to hurt my feeling, and that he'd used a bad choice of words, referring to settling down with one woman. I still didn't know whether to believe him, but it was partially my own fault. After all, the choices in this relationship were really mine. I couldn't get mad at him for sleeping with other women if I allowed him to do it. If I could just hang on for a while, this drama would soon be over. Being with Jaylin was what I truly wanted.

Besides, Daddy loved Jaylin, and so did Mama. They always wanted us to be together. When I called Mama the other night and told her about what happened, she told me Jaylin was just going through a phase every man goes through. She said Daddy had done the same thing to her before he decided to settle down. And even though she insisted she was ready for some grandbabies, she wanted me to be sure about committing myself to Jaylin, and encouraged me not to be a fool.

After work, I drove to Macy's and bought a beautiful powder-blue negligee that accented my light brown skin. The front was lace and had a V-dip all the way down to the tip of my coochie hairs. The back was a thong and showed my butt that Jaylin admired so much. I bought some strawberries and cream body lotion to make sure I smelled extra fresh for him tonight. Then, I called him at work to make sure we were still on, and to thank him for the roses he had delivered to my office today. Angela answered with her usual attitude, and then she asked me to hold.

"Jaylin Rogers." It sounded like he was busy.

"Would you like for me to call you back?" I asked, knowing that I would be disappointed if he did.

"Naw, I got a minute. What's up?"

"Nothing much. I just wanted to thank you for the roses, and I wanted to find out what time you're picking me up tonight."

"You're welcome—nothing but the best for my lady. I'll see you around . . . sevenish?"

"Jaylin, are you sure you want to do this tonight? I mean, I'm ready, but I know you had your doubts before."

"I'm as ready as I'm ever going to be. I want to make sure you're ready. If not, baby, then now is the time to tell me. I've been thinking about your sexy little self all damn day."

"I'll see you tonight." I blew him a kiss before I hung up. It was good to know his thoughts were about me. I just hoped I didn't disappoint him. I'd dreamed of our moment together, and everything felt so right.

When I got home, I called the Sheraton to make sure everything was set for tonight. Jaylin had already taken care of things, but I didn't want anything to go wrong. So, I called reservations just to confirm.

I pranced around in front of the mirror in my blue negligee, hoping it was more than satisfying for Jaylin. I even called my best friend, Patricia, to get her opinion about the negligee and to get sex advice.

"Girl, whatever you wear, Jaylin will be pleased. Personally, I think he don't deserve you, but anyway—"

"I didn't ask for your negative opinion about Jaylin, Pat. I just wanted to know what you would wear to turn Chad on."

"Nothing. Chad doesn't give a shit what I put on. As long as I'm naked, he's good to go. And if I know Jaylin, he's the same way. He only cares about what's underneath."

"I know, but I want to kind of tease him a little bit . . . you know? He's been with all these women and has so much experience. I just hope I can please him. I wondered if you could share some tips with me."

"The only tip I'm going to give you is don't have sex with him yet. I ain't trying to be hard on you, but if you're having doubts about it, then why do it? All of these years, I've been so proud of you for not giving in to him. I wish there were more women like you who would wait until they get married. At the rate these men are going, nobody should be fucking."

"Well, you got that right, but I need to do this for me. If I really love Jaylin, and know deep in my heart we're going to be together, then why not?"

"I just want you to be sure, that's all. I don't know if giving yourself to him is going to change anything about him. He's got some personal issues he needs to work on, and it ain't got a damn thing to do with you."

I disagreed, but Pat was more than welcome to offer her opinion. After tonight, things would be different between Jaylin and me. After all, it seemed like he'd almost waited a lifetime for this moment to come, and nothing was going to stop it from happening.

9

JAYLIN

It was good to be off work. I rushed home and changed so I wouldn't be late for dinner with Nokea. She was so sweet. I had put all my issues with other women aside for the week just to make her happy. Felicia called and left me several messages, but I didn't call her back. I guess she finally realized that when I say something, I mean it. She walked out on me, and for now, she was staying out until I was ready.

My mind, though, had been kind of messed up. The thought of fucking Scorpio again stuck with me twenty-four/seven. I thought about her ass at work, at home, and even looked for her at the gym. She called and said she would be out of town for a few days and would call when she got back. And even though I wanted to hear from her, maybe a relationship between us wasn't going to work out. I couldn't stop thinking about her lack of cooking skills and her child, not to mention the fact that her fucked up car didn't look too good in my driveway. I wasn't looking for a perfect woman, but I at least wanted a woman who could cook.

I dropped the keys on the kitchen table and hurried to my

room to change. I put on the gray suit Nokea had picked out for me at Saks Fifth Avenue and put on a crisp white shirt underneath. I left a few buttons undone so she could see my chest that she admired so much.

As soon as I put on my Rolex, the doorbell rang. I'd told Nokea I would pick her up tonight, but knowing her, she was anxious to see me and couldn't wait. I jogged down the steps with one black sock in my hand and the other on my foot.

Looking through the glass doors, I could clearly see it was Scorpio. I was pressed for time, but she was a sight for tired eyes, so I opened the door. I couldn't help but display a tiny smile.

"What brings you by?" I asked, closing the door behind her.

"I just got back in town. My daughter and I took a short vacation, and when we got back, she wanted to spend some time with my sister. I've been thinking about you, so I took this opportunity to come see you." She looked me up and down. "Are you about to go somewhere?"

"Yeah, I was. I have a dinner engagement tonight that I'm running a little late for."

"Do you mind if I stay here until you come home? I promise I'll have something sweet for you when you get back." She walked up to me and buttoned my shirt. I placed my hand over hers to stop her.

"Look, why don't I just call you tomorrow. I'd hate to keep you waiting all night long."

"So, your dinner engagement is going to take all night?" She pressed herself against me and my dick throbbed for her. I had to get to Nokea, but I was starting to think I could possibly cut our evening short and come home.

"No, my dinner engagement shouldn't take all night. I'll try to get back here as soon as I can."

Scorpio turned and walked up the stairs. She wore a shiny black leather skirt and a halter top with a string that crossed in the back and wrapped around to the front. Her black heels made her damn near as tall as me.

When we entered my bedroom, she sat on the edge of my bed, and I sat on the other side to slide on my sock. I knew time was getting away from me, so I went to the closet and stepped into my shoes. I looked for my black belt that was hidden away in the back of my closet. When I stepped out of the closet, Scorpio was already naked underneath the covers.

"You look awesome," she said. "I'm jealous because I'd love to be by your side tonight."

I would've loved that as well, but I knew it would be wrong to play Nokea on her birthday.

"I'll be back," was all I could say. I took my wallet off my nightstand and headed toward the door.

"Oh, Jaylin," Scorpio said softly. I turned, and she pulled back the covers and opened her legs so I could get a peek. "Try not to be too long. I'm anxious to feel you, and returning home early will bring you great rewards."

I walked over to the bed and leaned down to kiss Scorpio's lips. She aggressively pulled me down, and I eased my body on top of hers. Her body was so soft like Charmin. My hands wandered all over her, but when my dick got hard, I quickly hopped up.

"I'll be back as soon as I can, all right?"

She nodded and I left.

Nokea opened the door, looking amazing. I had stopped thinking about Scorpio at home in my bed so that I could give Nokea the attention I thought she truly deserved. She always presented herself as a classy woman. Tonight, she wore a peach stretch dress that hung off her shoulders. Her short cut was neatly lined, and her make-up had been perfectly done. Her beautiful round eyes shone when she saw me come through the door.

"Hello," she said, wrapping her arms around my waist. "You look handsome."

"You look beautiful too. Turn around so I can get a good look at you." All I could think about was taking off her dress tonight.

"So, are you still taking me to Cardwells?"

"Yes, but I want a kiss before we go."

Nokea smiled and gave me a few short pecks on the lips. She redid her MAC lip gloss, and then we left.

While driving down Interstate 70, my mind wandered back to Scorpio. She had it going on. When I visualized the prettiness between her legs, I licked my lips. I wanted to fuck her so badly, and thoughts of it made my dick hard.

Nokea reached for my hand. "Did you hear me?" she asked.

"No, I . . . I didn't. What did you say?"

"I said you're driving awfully fast. We're going to get there, okay?"

I chuckled, but no matter how hard I tried to focus on my conversation with Nokea, I couldn't. I drove to the lake, and after realizing I was an hour away from St. Louis, I knew there was no way in hell I would make it back to Scorpio before the night was over. I parked my car by the dock and we got out.

"Jaylin, what is this?" she said, looking at the double-deck party boat surrounded with lights and a sign that read HAPPY BIRTHDAY.

"Come on." I took Nokea's hand. "Let me show you."

Nokea and I stepped on the boat. The top deck had a table set with fine china, wineglasses, and a vase of flowers in the middle. I had even gone to the extreme of hiring some musicians from Freddy's Jazz Club in town to play some soothing music while we ate dinner. Nokea looked like a kid in a candy store. When I escorted her to the bottom deck, she opened her mouth wide. The room was lit with scented candles, giving it the smell of a flower garden; the bed had rose petals spread all over the gold satin sheets. There was a teddy bear on the bed with a T-shirt that read: *Happy Birthday! Yours forever, Jaylin.* She picked up the bear and held it close to her chest.

"Jaylin, I don't know what to say. I thought you made reservations at the Sheraton."

"I did. But at the last minute, I changed my mind. I wanted to do something special for you. I told you before how much I appreciate you being there for me, didn't I?"

"Yes, but I didn't expect this. This is way too much."

"Not for you, baby. You mean a lot to me, and this is nothing. Now, put that bear down so we can eat. I'm starving."

We both knew what the night had in store for us, so dinner was rushed. We slow danced through a couple of songs, and as I held Nokea's sexy little body in my arms, I told her how much she meant to me and apologized for any headaches I'd caused.

Moments later, I dismissed the jazz players and the waiters because it was time to get down to business. I hadn't had no loving in a little over a week, and I was ready to release this tension I had built up inside me.

Nokea took my hand and led the way to the lower level.

When we got there, she didn't waste any time. She laid me back on the bed and stuck her tongue deeply into my mouth. She unbuttoned my shirt and reached down to remove my belt.

"I'll be back," she whispered, and then walked to the bathroom in the far corner.

I took off my clothes then got underneath the gold sheets and waited for her. My dick climbed, and when Scorpio crossed my mind again, it was on full rise. I fantasized again about being between her legs, and wondered how long she'd wait at my house for me.

When Nokea stepped out of the bathroom, I turned my head and my thoughts quickly changed to her. She was one

sexy woman, and through the lace in her negligee, I could see
her hard nipples and trimmed coochie hairs.

"Do you like?" she said, easing her strawberry-fragranced
body on top of me. "I bought this just for you. I hope you enjoy
taking it off me."

A satisfied smile covered my face. I laid her back so I could
get on top and take control. I'd been with many virgins before,
so I knew how to handle things in order to keep the rhythm
flowing. I eased down her negligee and drew her breasts into
my mouth. As I sucked those, she could barely keep still, so I
knew when it came time for me to lick her insides, she would
have a fit. And that she did. Her legs squeezed my head so
tight that I could barely hear. I held her down to keep her still.
My purpose was to soak her insides so it would be easier for me
to enter. But as I gently went in, she got tense and backed up.

"Jaylin, I'm sorry. It . . . it doesn't feel right." Her words
sounded painfully strained.

"Baby, just relax," I whispered. "I know it hurts but you
gotta help me do this."

Nokea took a deep breath and I teased her walls with the
head of my dick. I inched my way in, but the warmth of
Nokea's insides made me think of Scorpio. I squeezed my eyes
together and tried to stay focused. Nokea, however, stopped
me again.

"Jaylin, you're hurting me." She pushed me back. "Please
stop. I can't take this."

This time I was upset. I couldn't get my shit off like I wanted
to, or for that matter, how I had planned to. Only half of my
nine remained inside, and I tried to reason with her.

"Baby, I've waited so long to feel you like this, and you've
got to let me finish."

Nokea gave me a blank stare and slowly nodded. I wrapped
her legs around my back, and as I started to stroke her, she
grabbed my hips. I couldn't go any easier than I already was.

"If you could just stand the pain after a few more strokes, everything will be cool," I whispered.

I gave Nokea a couple more inches of me, and her fingernails pinched my skin. She wiggled her legs from my shoulders and dropped them on the bed.

"Baby, I can't," she said tearfully. "Take it out, all right?"

I stopped my motion and stared down at Nokea.

"I'm almost there. It's opening up for me, and the pain will go away."

Nokea moved her head from side to side. "You're way too big for me, Jaylin. I just can't take that kind of pain right now."

I let out a deep sigh and felt my dick deflate inside of her. Nokea apologized and backed away from me. She rushed off to the bathroom and closed the door. Fuck it! If I had gotten my shit off with Scorpio before I came, I would've been all right. This was bullshit and Nokea knew I was pissed. I couldn't believe that I'd waited years and years for this. Wasn't shit I could do but try again later.

Nokea came out of the bathroom with an embarrassed look on her face. I didn't want her to feel embarrassed about not being able to hang with me, because little did she know, there weren't too many women who could handle my length and thickness.

I patted the spot next to me. "Come here, baby. Come lay down with me. At least let me hold you."

Nokea lay next to me and rested her head on my chest. "Please forgive me," she said. "I had no idea it would be so painful. I know you're disappointed, but I—"

"Shhh . . . no need to apologize. We have to start somewhere, and I really didn't expect to get that far. But at least I got to taste you."

"Yeah, that was wild. Kind of felt good too."

"Shit, the way you squirmed around, it was better than good."

She laughed and leaned in for a kiss. I scrolled my fingertips on her back and we lay silent for a while.

"I love you, Jaylin. I love you so much."

Unable to say those words, I responded, "And you know how I feel."

Nokea had crashed out, but I couldn't sleep. My thang wouldn't go down as I thought about Scorpio at my house. It was two o'clock in the morning. I hoped she was still there waiting for me. I quietly went into the bathroom, took a shower, and tried not to wake Nokea. When I came out, I tripped over an ice bucket on the floor and awakened her. She sat up and yawned.

"Are you okay?" she asked. "Why are you dressed?"

"Baby, Stephon called and said he had car trouble. He's several miles down the highway on Interstate 70 and Lindbergh, so . . . I'm gonna go help him out. I'll be right back."

"Do you need me to go with you?"

"No, no. Go ahead and go back to sleep. I'll be back before you know it."

"Be careful."

"I will."

I flew down Highway K and took the quickest route to Chesterfield. I unlocked the door and ran upstairs to my bedroom. When I opened the door, I was happy to see that Scorpio was still there. She lay on her stomach in a deep sleep. I yanked off the covers and gazed at her naked body. Then I took off my clothes to do what I'd been thinking about all night. I eased myself into her from behind and felt instant relief. She flinched a bit and woke up.

"It's about time," she said, getting into position on her hands and knees. "I thought you forgot about me."

"Not a chance in hell, baby," I whispered. "Not a chance in hell."

10

FELICIA

I tossed and turned all night. It was damn near six o'clock in the morning and I was up thinking about that son of a bitch, Jaylin. I was furious he hadn't returned my phone calls. I tried to forget about him, but when I invited this brotha over from the past, I realized how much Jaylin really meant to me. Sex was horrible. Only lasted for about three minutes and wasn't even worth my time.

I had even given this brotha at work my phone number. Our conversation was cool, but when he told me he was married, I cut him short.

I missed the hell out of Jaylin. Friday nights were supposed to be our night, and when I didn't hear from him last night, I was really disappointed. I remembered it was Nokea's birthday, so I figured he was probably with her. When I drove by his house last night, Scorpio's raggedy-ass car was in his driveway. The funny thing was, his car wasn't there. I thought maybe it was in the garage, but when I got out and peeped inside, the only thing I saw was his motorcycle and his red Porsche Boxster.

Throughout the night, I called his house severa. times but got no answer. Yes, it was Nokea's birthday, but I still expected to hear from him.

I called his house again and left a nasty message on his voicemail. I decided to call his cell phone again, and after a few rings, a female answered.

"Hello," she said in a sleepy voice.

"Is Jaylin there?" I snapped.

"Who is this?"

"Just put Jaylin on the phone."

"Is this Felicia?" Nokea asked.

"Yes, it is. But bitch, I didn't call to talk to you. Put Jaylin on the phone. I have to ask him something."

"Felicia, Jaylin doesn't want to talk to you. Besides, he isn't here. Why are you calling him anyway? I thought you didn't want to have anything else to do with him."

"Don't worry about why I'm calling him. That ain't your business. I know you thought he was all yours, but there's been another change in plans. You'll never have him to yourself. N-E-V-E-R."

Nokea snickered. "Felicia, you are so wrong. I don't know when you're going to wake up and smell the coffee. Jaylin and I spent a wonderful night together. Since you walked out the other night, we've done nothing but show each other love. As a matter of fact, we spent the entire night on a boat to celebrate my birthday. Just a few more weeks of this and I'll soon be Mrs. Rogers. So, my dear, it's really time to move on. Why don't you go find somebody else to lay you? Jaylin now has me for those intimate moments, so your services are no longer needed."

Nokea had me upset, but I wasn't going to let her know she had touched a nerve.

"Oh, you'd better enjoy your fame and fortune while it lasts. I'll be back. You can bet your life on that. And when I do see

Jaylin again, I'll be sure to call you and share the details. In the meantime, you need to be worried about that other bitch that's got his ass all wrapped up. If you claim he was with you last night, then what the hell was her car doing at his house? Don't flatter your fucking self thinking he doesn't have anyone in his life but you. I find it quite sickening that you're the one who he keeps stepping on like a piece of trash. Not me, and damn sure not that new bitch." Nokea was silent. "So, Miss Homebody, I've argued with you long enough. Give Jaylin the phone, would you?"

Nokea hung up. I called back to check her for hanging up on me, but she wouldn't answer. I couldn't believe I was up this early in the morning tripping with her. He was probably lying right there and had her doing his dirty work for him.

I also couldn't believe she had given herself to him. She was probably so desperate to keep him that she thought of it as a last resort. Even though I hated the bitch, I kind of felt sorry for her. She had no clue what she'd gotten herself into with Jaylin. As a matter of fact, I was discovering that I didn't either.

11

NOKEA

I was worried because Jaylin hadn't made it back yet, and what Felicia had said weighed heavy on my mind. Like always, I reached for the phone to call Stephon to see what was up. When a chick answered, I was about to hang up, as I thought I had the wrong number. Instead, I asked for him.

"Who's calling?" she asked with a slight attitude.

"This is Nokea. I'm Jaylin's girlfriend."

"Aw . . . okay. Hold on a second, Nokea, let me wake him up."

Several seconds later, Stephon got on the phone. "Yeah," he said in a raspy tone.

"Stephon, I'm sorry to bother you, but have you seen Jaylin? He left this morning and said he was on his way to get you because you had car trouble."

"Yeah, I saw him. He left, though."

"What time did he leave?"

"Shit, uh, I . . . I can't remember. Not too long ago I think."

"What's not too long ago? An hour ago, two hours ago? When did he leave?"

"He left about an hour ago."

"So, where did he meet you at?" I said, pressing some more.

"Nokea, look, I'm tired. You calling here with all these questions and I just got in the bed. He didn't meet me any-where. We worked on my car in my driveway, okay?"

"Okay, Stephon. Sorry to bother you. Thanks for your help."

"You're welcome. And I didn't mean to get upset with you, but it's early and I'm tired."

"I understand. Thanks again." I hung up.

I knew the moment Stephon opened his mouth that he was covering up for Jaylin. He tripped when he said they worked on his car at home. Jaylin told me his car stopped on him right down the highway.

I got out of bed and put on my clothes. I didn't have a car, but I did have money for a taxi. The dispatcher said they'd send one right over. I sat on the bed and racked my brain. What if Jaylin lied to me? There was no way he would disre-spect me like that just to be with someone else. It didn't make sense that he would go through all this trouble to get me in bed, then go home and be with somebody else. Just didn't seem like something he would do.

Before the taxi came, I called his house a couple of times, but there was no answer.

When the horn blew, I grabbed my purse and my teddy bear and left. The ride was long; the taxi driver drove extra slow down Highway 40, and the meter added up. I laid my head back on the seat and closed my eyes.

I thought about Jaylin trying to make love to me last night. His touch was so gentle, but his dick was just too much for me. I'd touched it before, and even made it grow with the stroke of my hand. Having it inside of me was so much different. I never thought it would be so painful. It had, however, made me ex-tremely wet. No wonder all these women were going crazy over him. The way he sucked my breasts and licked my insides made me want him even more. We'd just have to take our time, though. He said he'd be willing to give it another try, as long as I was. For now, I had to find out where he'd gone and why he'd left so abruptly.

The taxi was on Chesterfield Parkway, right around the corner from Jaylin's house. My stomach felt queasy. I had a feeling something wasn't right. When the driver pulled in front of his house and I saw Scorpio's car in the driveway next to Jaylin's Mercedes, I damn near died. I paid the driver and got out of the car.

I paced myself to the door. It was unlocked, so I went inside. I quietly closed the door behind me and stood in the spacious foyer. There was no sign of Jaylin downstairs. That probably meant he was upstairs—most likely in his bedroom.

I walked up the steps and heard laughter. I also heard water and loud, satisfied moans.

My heart raced as I stepped into the bedroom. His bed was empty, but when I looked into his bathroom, I couldn't believe my eyes. Jaylin and Scorpio were in the shower. He had her pinned against the marble tile and was taking deep strokes inside of her. They were so into each other that they didn't even notice me standing in the doorway. Scorpio had her legs wrapped around his waist, and ran her fingers through his coal black, curly hair. The hot water sprinkled down on their naked bodies, and steamed filled the room. I could only see Jaylin's backside, but from the sounds he made and the dirty talk between them, I could tell he was enjoying himself.

Scorpio faced the doorway with a pleased look on her face. She kissed him like she was out of her mind, and dropped her head back with a sigh of relief.

"Your dick feels damn good inside of me. I love this dick, Jaylin. Don't you love the way this pussy feels too?"

Filled with excitement, he could barely strain the word

"yes" from his mouth, but then added "hell yes." Scorpio lifted
her head, and her eyes connected with mine. She opened her
eyes wider and pushed Jaylin back.

"What's the matter, baby?" I heard him ask as she continued
to look in my direction. He snapped his head to the side and
got a glimpse of me standing tearfully in the doorway. He lowered Scorpio's legs, wiped the water off his face, and turned off
the water.

I turned my back and stepped away from the doorway. I felt
myself about to lose it, and covered my mouth with my hand.

Scorpio came out of the bathroom first, naked. She walked
right past me as if I weren't even there. Jaylin came out with a
towel wrapped around his waist and tossed Scorpio a towel to
cover up.

"Would you mind going downstairs so I can talk to Nokea
for a minute?"

She wrapped the towel around her body and grinned at me
on her way out. Jaylin stood in front of me and tried to explain. "Nokea, I know what you're thinking, but it ain't even
like that. I came here because—"

I stopped him. My chest heaved in and out. I felt like I
wanted to throw up.

"This is over," I blurted out. "How could you do this to me,
Jaylin? I did nothing—I mean nothing—to deserve this. What
did I ever do to you but love you?"

He looked down at the ground, and then stared deeply into
my eyes. "Nothing. I've always said this was my problem, not
yours. But I also said that times would get challenging for us,
didn't I? Please don't be upset with me. I just need time, baby,
that's all. Time to sort through some—"

"Time isn't what you need. I've given you nothing but time!
You have a serious problem with committing yourself to me,
and I will no longer be there for you. To hell with you, Jaylin.

I regret wasting all this time with you." I swiftly pushed by him and stormed out of his bedroom.

On my way out, I saw Scorpio in his bonus room, with her legs folded up on the couch like it was her darn house or something.

Jaylin came out of his bedroom and called my name, but I ignored him.

"All right then, Nokea! Have it your way, baby! Remember, though, if you walk out on me, you walk out for good!"

I slammed the door on my way out. I walked to the BP gas station on Olive Street Road and called Pat to come pick me up. She said she was on her way. I sat on the curb in front of the gas station and cried like a baby. I cried so hard that a man stopped and asked if I needed a doctor. I declined, but I held my stomach in pain. By the time Pat came, she had to get out of the car to help me get in. My body was numb and I shook like a leaf.

"What happened?" Pat asked anxiously. "Calm down and tell me what happened." She drove off.

"You were right," I sobbed. "But I just didn't want to listen."

"I know I was right, but calm down and tell me what happened."

"He left me early this morning." I wiped my tears. "He left me so he could go home and screw this new chick he's been seeing. I had just given myself to him and everything."

"Nokea, you're bullshitting, right? Are you telling me he had sex with you and then went home to have sex with her?"

"Yes. He wasn't able to perform like he wanted to with me, so he made up a lie about going to help Stephon with his car. In reality, he went home to be with her."

"Now, that's a dirty son of a bitch! You don't even need him in your life if he's going to treat you like that. I can't believe Jaylin. I could just take my ass around to his house and give him a piece of my mind." Pat made a quick U-turn.

"Pat, please. Don't go over there. I don't want him to see me like this. I just want to let it go and move on with my life. I don't have anyone to blame but me. I made him believe that for many years it was okay for him to dump on me like this. For God's sake, that's all he knew how to do. How can I get mad if I was the one in control of my own happiness?"

Pat shook her head. "Yeah, you're right, sweetie, but you deserve so much better. And if I can help in any way by hooking you up with some of Chad's friends, let me know. They ask about you all the time, and I'd love to hook you up with one of them."

I wiped my eyes and chuckled. My best friend always seemed to have the right answer, and I hated like hell that I hadn't listened to her advice before. Maybe it was time for me to meet someone else, and making myself available was the best thing I could do.

12

JAYLIN

Scorpio and I sat up on my bed, ate popcorn, and watched the Lifetime channel. Snacking in my room and watching a channel that was made for women was definitely not my style, but I went with the flow. I laid my head on her lap and she twirled her fingers around the curls in my hair.

"Jaylin, I think I'm falling in love with you already. I can't go a day without thinking about you, and when I'm with you, I forget about the outside world."

Now, she was really rushing things. How could you love somebody and know so little about them? This was strictly a fuck thing for me, and love could not, should not be entered into the equation.

"One day at a time, all right? I mean, I got some deep feelings for you too, but let's not go talking this love stuff yet. Besides, as you can see, I already got a full plate right now."

"I know, but you can't tell me that you don't think about me more than any other woman you've been with. We have a connection. It's not only the sex, either. Like now, I feel like I've been here with you before."

I sat up and looked at her. "I'm not saying I don't feel different about you, but this love talk got to stop. Can't we just enjoy ourselves without the hassles of a loving relationship? Hell, I don't know nothing about you. I don't know where you live, don't know what you do for a living, and don't even know how old you are. I do know that your sex be off the chain, but honestly, that's it. Women always talking about love, but give me a reason to love you, that's all I'm saying."

"Oh, I can give you several reasons to love me. But first, if you want to know more about me . . . I live in Olivette, I'm a playwright who's starving to write some new material, and I'm twenty-eight years old. When you do get to know me better, you'll eventually love me because I'm sweet, I'm very kind, and I definitely know how to please my man."

I wanted to get to know Scorpio better. At this point, giving her a chance to show that she was worthy of being more than just a sex partner wasn't going to hurt a thing. "All right, Miss Playwright, sit up here and tell me a story."

Scorpio straddled my lap with her beautifully curved, plump titties staring me right in the face.

"Well," she said with a smile, "there was this sexy, fine-ass brotha who just couldn't get enough of this woman who had come into his life and changed his whole world around. She made love to him over and over and over again, until one day, she got tired. He was afraid to love her back, and eventually she left him."

"Cut," I said, putting my hands on her waist. "It's not that I don't want to love you, Scorpio. It's just that I don't know much about love. Like I said, no woman has given me enough of a reason to love her. If you give me a reason, then maybe I'll figure this shit out. Right?"

Scorpio didn't respond. She leaned forward and gave me a peck on the lips. I knew she probably wanted more, but for now, it was strictly a fuck thing for me.

*   *   *

Scorpio left late Saturday night. Before I let her go, I went up in her about three more times that day. I was getting so accustomed to her, I hadn't really thought much about my situation with Nokea or Felicia. I guess it helped that Scorpio hadn't mentioned them either. I was so glad that she seemed to be a woman who didn't let my relationships with others intimidate her.

Sunday was my day. I wanted to be alone. I was tired—exhausted from all the female setbacks—so I took time for myself. I drove to C&K Barbecue on Jennings Station Road and gobbled down a tripe sandwich that I'd craved. Then I drove by North Oaks Bowling Lanes on the corner of Natural Bridge and Lucas and Hunt to see if Stephon and my boys from the barbershop were hanging out. Since I'd moved to Chesterfield, I missed hanging with the fellas, so every opportunity I got, I made my way back to the hood.

Since Stephon was nowhere to be found, I went back home and cleaned my house until it was spotless. Scorpio had left a towel here and there, which had me a little upset. I cleaned off the desk in my office and vacuumed the carpet throughout the house. My kitchen took up the most time. I mopped the floor and wiped down the stainless steel appliances. There were a few dishes in the sink, so I knocked those out too.

By early evening, I went into my bonus room and played a game of pool. The thought of calling Nokea to apologize crossed my mind, but I didn't feel like hearing her cry again. I felt kind of bad about what had happened, but I needed so much more than what Nokea was offering. I didn't want to settle, and I wasn't going to pretend that I was happy just to spare her feelings.

Felicia had been bugging the fuck out of me. I ignored her calls because I wasn't ready to patch up things with her yet. Scorpio left a message too, saying that she was thinking about me. As hard as I tried not to, I was thinking about her too. I was starting to catch some deep feelings for her—feelings that I hadn't had for any woman other than Nokea. I worried that my feelings were a bit premature, especially since I knew so little about her. I thought about the way she be putting it on me. Even thought about what she said about me. She said she would tear down my walls and make me love her. The only person who I thought might be a little deserving of my love was Nokea. But since she didn't want to hang around and find out, what the hell?

My private line rang in my office. It was Stephon. "Say, man, you busy?" he asked.

"Nope. Just sitting around chilling, that's all."

"You don't sound too good, my brotha. What's ailing you?"

"Shit . . . nothing. Just beat. Ready to get back to business tomorrow. The Stock Market been tripping, and it got some of my clients worried."

"I know how that is because I'm losing money in that motherfucker too. But the purpose for my call is to tell you I had a visitor today."

"Who?"

"Nokea. She stopped by and apologized for calling me early yesterday morning."

"Calling you for what?"

"She called looking for you, and I didn't know what to tell her. She said you told her you were coming to help me fix my car, and I didn't know what the fuck she was talking about. I covered for you, but I really didn't know what to say."

"Man, I'm sorry. I forgot to call and tell you what to say just in case she did call. My mind was so fucked up, I didn't know whether I was coming or going."

"Well, all I wanna know is, did you really play her like that? She was in tears over here telling me about what happened. I kind of felt sorry for her."

"Negro, please. I didn't play nobody. Nokea knew what time it was. She fucked around that night, so I left. Came home and got some from a for-real woman. Now she's running over there telling you about it. Man, I tell you, women be doing some fucked up shit."

"Yeah, they do, but I ain't never seen you diss her to that level. This Scorpio chick must be a bad motherfucker."

I laughed. "As a matter of fact, she is. I kind of like her ass too."

"You like that pu-tain she be whippin' on you. I had a chick set me out like that before, and at times, I still think about her. But it was over before it started. She got all demanding and shit. Wanted me to fuck her all the time and I couldn't. You remember that chick named Claire, don't you?"

"Yeah, I remember, but I thought the reason you stopped seeing her was because she got married."

"Yeah, that's right. And I got my feelings hurt too. All I'm saying is take it easy with this chick. I have one other question for you too."

"What's that?"

"Is she worth losing Nokea over? That gal's been in your corner for a long time."

"Stephon, you know better than I do how tight Nokea and me are. She's playing that role right now, but she'll have a change of heart in a couple of days."

"For your sake, I hope so, because today when we talked, she seemed pretty confident that it was over."

"Confident, huh? Did she tell you I tried to make love to her on her birthday?"

"Naw, man, you lying. She finally let you tackle those panties?"

"Yep, that's how I know she ain't going nowhere."

"How was it, dog? Was it everything you expected it to be?"

"It was all right, man. You know how it is when you dealing with a virgin. I'm too old for that 'let me train you how to fuck me' shit, but I was willing to do it for her, so it was cool."

"Cool, huh? I don't know what you're going to do, but I got your back if you need me."

"Thanks, cuz, I'll call you later."

"Holla back," Stephon said and hung up.

I sat in my office for a while and played solitaire on my computer. I couldn't concentrate, as I thought about what Stephon said about Nokea.

I picked up the phone to call her, wanting to see why she had gone to Stephon's house to dump on me. Who was I fooling? I was actually calling because I hadn't heard her squeaky little voice today. When I dialed her number, a recorded voice answered.

"We're sorry, the number you have dialed has been changed. At the customer's request, the new number is not listed." I hung up and tried again. I thought I'd dialed the wrong number.

Again, "We're sorry, the number . . ."

Damn, she'd gotten her number changed already? Was she that upset with me that she didn't even want to talk? I thought about going to see her so we could discuss our unfortunate situation, but not today. I'd give her time to cool off and then see if I could persuade her to forgive me. Hopefully, that wouldn't be too hard.

13

FELICIA

Now, Jaylin was really pissing me off. My phone calls weren't working, so I decided to make my way to his office today. Clowning or not, I needed to know where things stood between us. I knew what I said the other night, but I missed the hell out of him. Missed his touch, his kiss, and of course, his loving. I put my braids into a bun, threw on my gray DKNY jogging suit, and my white DKNY tennis shoes. I left my jacket open so he could see my bare midriff and my orange sports bra underneath. I wanted to pretend like I'd been to the gym working out because Jaylin loved a woman who kept herself fit and trim.

I got off the elevator on the ninth floor of the Berkshire's Building, and went to the water fountain to splash water on me like I'd been working hard. I walked through the lobby and found myself standing in front of that bitch Angela.

"May I help you?" she said, knowing damn well who I was, and who I was there to see.

"Don't play with me, bitch. You know who I'm here to see."

"Do you have an appointment?" She tried to sound professional, but she wasn't nothing but a two-dollar ho.

"Angela, I'm going to say this as nicely as I can. . . . Bitch, call Jaylin and tell him I'm here to see him."

She rolled her eyes and called him.

"He said have a seat; he'll be out shortly."

"Thank you," I said sharply then walked over to one of the leather chairs to wait.

Jaylin came out with one of his clients, smiling as he shook the man's hand. He looked scrumptious in a dark blue Brooks Brothers suit with a cream-colored shirt underneath and some dark-blue-and-cream, square-toed shoes to match. His hair looked like it had just been freshly cut, his thin beard was trimmed to perfection, and the goatee he wore fit his chin well.

I stood up as he looked at me with his catlike gray eyes, and he motioned for me to come back to his office. He stopped and told Angela to hold his calls. She nodded and cut her eyes at me.

Jaylin closed the door behind us and walked around his desk to sit in his chair. The first thing I did was look around to see if the gold pen set I'd purchased for him from Things Remembered was still on his desk. He'd always kept it on display, but now I didn't see it.

"So, what's up, Felicia? Why you bugging, baby? If my memory serves me correctly, you said you were finished with my black ass, didn't you?"

"Where are my pens at, Jaylin?"

"Cut with the bullshit, Felicia. You didn't come all the way over here to talk about no damn pens. What do you want?"

"Jaylin, calm down. I know you ain't trying to act a fool up in here, are you?"

"You got one minute to state your business. After that, I'm calling security. So, go," he said, looking at his diamond Rolex.

"All right, look. I'm sorry about the other night. I was

wrong for trying to give you an ultimatum like that, but I was upset. From now on, who you see is your business. I don't care to know about your other women; just keep them far away from me.

"All I'm saying is I miss you. I miss what we shared on Friday nights, and I want to know if you wouldn't mind having me back in your so-called world."

Jaylin glared at me from across his desk and remained silent. Of course I wasn't going to put up with another woman being in the picture, and if Scorpio was going to remain in his life, Jaylin and her both were going to catch hell from me. For now, though, I had to say whatever to get my man back.

He rubbed his fingers across his lips and slowly stroked his goatee. "Felicia, you don't miss me. You don't miss a damn thing about me. That is, of course, with the exception of my big dick. Go ahead, tell me . . . and be honest. That's what it is. You miss my dick, don't you?"

"No, Jaylin, that's not it. I really miss what we had. We shared something special, just in case you can't remember."

"Something special? Yeah, I've been hearing that shit a lot lately. We ain't got nothing special, Felicia. All we've ever had was a fuck thang, baby. I like to take good care of my fuck thangs, so that's why every once in a while we go do something special. You see, there are those famous words again: *something special*. Don't get confused. There really ain't a damn thing special about it."

"So, what are you saying? I've wasted my time coming here? Listen, do you want to do this or not?"

"You wanna do this, Felicia?" He pulled a condom from his drawer and got out of his chair. "You really want to do this? Come on, baby. Let me fuck you. That's what you came here for, so let's just get it over with." He removed his belt and unzipped his pants.

"Jaylin, no, stop!" I pulled myself away from him as he tried to lower my sweatpants. He grabbed my face and kissed me hard on the lips. I smacked his face, but he didn't flinch. He must've known that I was turned on by his aggressiveness. When he reached over and turned off the lights, I was turned on even more. He lifted me on his desk.

"Felicia, don't you ever walk out on me again. If you do, you will never, and I mean never, be able to come back to me." He forced himself inside me.

The feel of him was too good to turn away, and the only reply that I could offer was, "I will never be that foolish again. I promise you I won't."

I felt like a million dollars leaving Jaylin's office. There was no way in hell for me to allow another woman to come in and take what was mine. Scorpio had a good fight awaiting her. I wasn't about to give up Jaylin so easily.

When I passed Angela on my way out, she tooted her lips and rolled her eyes again. I'm sure she knew sex was on the agenda, because when she knocked on the door, Jaylin hadn't answered.

"See you later, bitch," I said as I exited with my leather Coach purse clutched to my side. I went home, took a shower, and drove to the office to get something else accomplished for the day. First order of business was to figure out how I could make Scorpio and Nokea disappear.

14

NOKEA

I was miserable not talking to Jaylin, but I knew there was no way I would go back to him. My girl Pat would kill me, and so would Mama. I told Mama about seeing Jaylin with another woman and for the first time, she was disappointed. What I didn't tell her was that I gave myself to Jaylin that night. Had she known, she would have died.

She basically advised me to get on with my life and encouraged me to meet somebody new, and that's what I intended to do. I had changed my number so Jaylin wouldn't be able to reach me with another one of his lies. In fact, I even thought about moving, but I knew that would be taking things to the extreme. Since I had just gotten a promotion, I dedicated my time to my new career.

I was the new sales director for Atlas Computer Company and had to show my colleagues they had chosen the right person. It wasn't easy to do. During my first presentation, thoughts of Jaylin and Scorpio kept coming to my mind. I didn't know how I could compete with a woman who gave him so much sexual pleasure. She seemed to have the right moves, and it was just a matter of time before she worked her way into Jaylin's heart. I thought his heart belonged to me, but boy, was I wrong. I'd never seen him so anxious for a woman. For her to be around for such a short period, she was already causing a major impact.

I was so glad when my presentation was finished so I could go somewhere and get a grip on myself. No matter how hard I tried to stop the tears, they kept on coming; late at night, early in the morning. I even cried at lunch with a few of my co-workers today. They asked me what was wrong and I told them my grandfather had passed away in Mississippi. Since he'd died years ago, I felt like I hadn't burned any bread on him by not telling the truth.

After breaking down again in the bathroom stall at work, I asked my boss if I could take off the rest of the week. I told him I needed to go to my grandfather's funeral in Mississippi, and he allowed me to leave.

On my way home, I stopped to pick up some groceries at Schnucks on West Florissant Avenue. Whenever I'm stressed, I always pig out. My cart was full of junk: potato chips, cookies, ice cream, and pizza rolls. You name it, it was there. I stood in the long line and picked up a magazine to keep myself occupied.

"Shorty?" I heard a voice from behind. It was Stephon.

"Hey, Stephon," I said, giving him a hug. "How are you?"

"Naw, the question is how you are? I hope you're feeling better since your visit the other day. You had me kind of worried."

"Worried for what? I know you didn't think I would kill myself or anything like that, did you?"

Stephon chuckled. "Nah, nothing like that. I was just worried. You've been with my cousin for a long time and you kind of like family."

"Yeah, well, even family can snake you sometimes." I reached in my cart and laid my groceries on the conveyor belt.

Stephon reached in and helped me—until he came across a bag of maxi pads. He dropped them back in the cart like they were on fire or something.

"Now, if you're going to help, those need to be put up there too," I said, smiling. He laughed.

"I'll let you handle those."

As the cashier rang up my groceries and provided me with a total, I looked at her like she was crazy. I didn't think I'd put that many things into my cart. I reached into my purse to pay her.

"I got it." Stephon gave the cashier his credit card.

"Stephon, thanks, but I think I can handle my grocery bill."

"No problem. Besides, I owe you one anyway."

"For what?"

Stephon didn't say anything. He put my bags into the cart and pushed it out the door. When we got to my car, he loaded everything into my trunk.

"There you go, Shorty. Don't say I ain't never done nothing for you."

"I never did, but why do you owe me one? That's what I want to know."

"Because I really felt bad about the lie I told you the other day. I love my cuz and everything, but I seriously think y'all need to work it out. When I talked to him Sunday, he sounded pretty down. Why don't you call him?"

"Stephon, please stay out of this. You of all people know Jaylin has done nothing but manipulate me over the years. Why would you even want me to continue to be with him?"

"Because you're miserable; he's miserable. Don't make sense for two people who love each other to be miserable."

"You know better than I do Jaylin isn't miserable. He's got

that . . . that thing over there with him and he's enjoying every minute of the day being with her. You didn't see the way he was all into her; I did. Just standing here thinking about it hurts so badly—" I got teary-eyed again.

"Nokea, I didn't mean to upset you. But you know how Jaylin is. After he gets what he wants from her, he'll be knocking at your door."

"Well, he can knock all he wants to. I will no longer be there for him."

Stephon tried to persuade me to give Jaylin another chance, but I got in my car and waved goodbye. I hated conversing with Stephon about Jaylin; all he was going to do was go back and tell him.

When I got home, I put away my groceries and slipped into my nightgown. I lay in bed and watched Mandy Murphey on Fox 2 News while eating chocolates. This was the life. I wished I could lay there and eat chocolates forever.

After a while, the news depressed me with black folks killing each other, so I turned off the TV and grabbed a book to read. I quickly got bored with that and picked up the phone next to me. My conversation with Stephon made me want to speak to Jaylin, so I dialed his number. But when I got to the sixth digit, I hung up. He was the one who wronged me, so why should I pick up the phone to call him? Besides, I knew he probably wasn't home from work yet. The thought of leaving him a message crossed my mind. I could say I forgot something or I needed him to pick up something he'd left at my place. I struggled with the idea for a moment then I dropped the thought.

I turned the radio on Foxy 95.5 and listened to my girl Niecy Davis. The music helped relax me, and before I knew it, I had dozed off.

I was awakened by a knock at the door. My house was pitch black, so I knew it had to be pretty late. I glanced out the peephole to see who it was. It was Jaylin, standing on my porch with his hands in his pockets and his head down. I backed away from the door because the look of him always made my heart melt. I didn't want my hormones answering the door for me. When I didn't answer, he banged harder.

"Nokea, I know you're in there. I saw the light come on. Open the door, baby."

Wasn't any sense in me trying to pretend I wasn't home, so I cracked the door enough to tell him I didn't want to talk.

"What do you mean you don't want to talk? You've always been able to talk to me. Open the door."

"This time is different, Jaylin. I don't want to talk. That's why I got my number changed. Please, just go away."

"No, Nokea. I'm not leaving, so you might as well open the door."

I hesitated, but then admitted to myself how badly I wanted to see him. I needed him to say that he was sorry. I wanted him to know how much his actions had hurt me. I took the chain off the door and opened it.

"Now, that wasn't so hard, was it?" he said. He walked in and took off his cap and jacket. He obviously intended to stay a while.

"Why are you here?" I said softly. "Let's just move on, okay?"

"Are you crazy? Move on my ass. You know damn well we were meant to be together, so why you tripping?" He moved closer to me, but I pushed him back.

"Would you please just go? I don't need this right now."

"I told you once, I'm not leaving until you forgive me. Just a couple of weeks ago you made me a promise. You said that when things got rough between us, you wouldn't leave. As long as I've known you, you've always been a woman of your word. What's the sudden change?"

I raised my voice and pointed my finger at him. "I handled you being with other women for nine years, but I can't do it anymore. Especially after I saw you making love to Scorpio in the shower. That just did something to me, Jaylin, and no matter how hard I try to erase that day from my memory, I can't. The thought of it sticks with me twenty-four/seven, and—"

Jaylin saw me getting emotional and stepped up to put his arms around me. He rubbed my back and kissed my forehead. I wanted to push him away, but his touch was what I needed.

"Baby, I don't know what to say. I was wrong. If that's what you need to hear me say, then yes, I was wrong. But please don't hold it against me for the rest of our lives. Without you, life has been very lonely for me."

The pressure was on. I couldn't even respond to him. Jaylin had me in the palms of his hands and my emotions were all over the place. He lifted my chin to kiss me, and I felt myself getting weaker by the minute.

"Let me make love to you," he whispered in my ear. "I want to hold you tonight, and if you still feel the same way tomorrow, then I promise I will never come here again."

I stood in silence, and he took my hand and led me to my bedroom. He removed my nightgown, and even though I knew better than to give myself to him, I couldn't ignore how much I wanted to feel him again. I couldn't deny how much I still loved him, and now was another opportunity to show him just that.

He rubbed his hands over my naked body and felt my moist insides. The thought of him making love to Scorpio was still fresh in my mind, but when he opened my legs and did what he knew best, I squirmed like a slithering snake.

I gave him a good taste of me, and then he inserted himself. Tears rolled down my face in the dark, but I was willing to bear the pain this time. I wanted this man so much it was almost frightening. Yes, I was vulnerable, and I wasn't sure if Jaylin had taken advantage of that. It was too late for me to think about his motives. I had made a promise to myself to never let this happen again, but there I was enjoying every deep stroke he gave me. His loving was so satisfying to me, and after a while, the pain seemed to ease up a bit. I allowed him to proceed without any interruptions.

Jaylin got tense, and when I felt the muscles in his butt tighten, I squeezed it. We both took several deep breaths, and as they slowed, he rolled on his back. The shameful guilt I had for allowing this to happen immediately kicked in. I felt like such a fool for the choice I'd made. Jaylin almost looked like he was smirking. Why in the heck was I continuing to make things easy for him?

I turned to my side. "Jaylin, if you don't mind, I'd like to be alone."

He turned face-to-face with me and rubbed my hip. "Come on baby. I thought you wanted me to stay the night."

"No. I really need to be alone right now. What we shared was nice, but I need time to get my head straight."

Jaylin sat up and shook his head. "I'm not going to pressure you, Nokea. I told you, if you're not feeling this relationship anymore then let me know."

"Oh, I am definitely feeling us, but I can't be with you under these conditions. There's just no way I can do it."

"Hey, whatever you say. I hope you find a place in your heart to forgive me. That way, we can get on with our relationship."

"Is this what we're calling relationships these days? You screw whoever you want to and I'm there for you no matter what? That doesn't seem quite fair to me." I turned and pulled the cover over me. Jaylin bent down and gave me a tiny peck on the tip of my nose.

"It is what it is, Nokea. The ball is in your court, and it's up to you to shoot it. Get some rest. I hope to hear from you tomorrow," he said before leaving.

I realized how tough it was going to be for me to distance

myself from him. All I had to do was not open the door, but when I saw him, I got weak. There had to be somewhere I could go for help. I was losing respect for myself, slowly but surely. But, my word as my bond, I promised to never open up my legs to him again, unless he made a commitment to me.

15

JAYLIN

"**D**idn't I tell you I'm the man?" I yelled while talking to Stephon at work with my feet propped up on the desk.

"Man, I just can't believe she gave in like that. When I saw her at the grocery store, she seemed so confident it was over."

"Yeah, she was confident all right. Confident that she wanted some of this good loving I be dishing out."

"Jay, you know you crazy. That woman just loves your black ass, that's all. If she could get past that, she'd be okay. As for Felicia—damn, she just trying to get laid."

"And so am I. That's why when she came here yesterday, I waxed that ass all on my desk and had her begging for more."

"You wild dog. Straight up fucking wild. How much pussy can a nigga get? After one time a day my ass be wore out! If I had to go two or three times, that would kill me. And then with different women . . . shit, I hope you're strapped up good."

"Well, you know how it is. Sometimes I do, sometimes I don't. Depending on who it is. With Felicia I most definitely break one out because ain't no telling who been up in that. But Nokea, that's all good. I'm the only brotha who will ever have a mark on her stuff. As for Scorpio, it depends. Her shit be so good, I just like to get the real deal. You know what I mean?"

"Yeah, sure in the hell do. Been there and done that, so I ain't knocking you at all, my brotha. Hey, listen, while I have you on the phone, Ray-Ray proposed to that skinny dark chick he's been dating for six months. They haven't set a date yet, but he told me to tell you to hook a brotha up with some nice females at his bachelor party. He's looking for something a little extravagant—none of that strip club action, please. We've been there, done that."

"I agree, and tell the brotha I said congrats. I'll see what I can do." Angela walked in and told me one of my clients was there to see me. "Say, man, I'll call you later." Stephon hung up and Angela let Higgins into my office.

"Jaylin, what's up, bro?" he said, shaking my hand.

"Hey, how you doing, Mr. Higgins? Have a seat, sir." He sat down and lit up a Cuban cigar. The smell of it drove me crazy, but since he was one of my major clients, what the hell?

"Jaylin, I never received confirmation on those additional shares I talked to you about. I checked the market today and this company is moving. How are we looking?"

Damn. I'd forgotten to take care of those shares for Higgins. Focusing so much time on Scorpio's good loving and rekindling my relationship with Nokea, it totally slipped my mind.

"Let me see . . ." I said, turning around to my monitor. I hit the keyboard and took a quick glance at my own stocks. "Looks like everything is moving right along. You were right about this company. It's moving at a fast pace."

"That's good to know."

I checked Higgins' mutual funds and gave him an accurate number as to how much they'd gone up. I also shared with him how much money he'd made in the past week. He was pleased.

"Any extra money I make, Jaylin, is good news. What I would like for you to do is call up some of my friends who are clients of yours and let them know what it would cost to buy into Mason Technologies immediately. That way, hopefully, we'll all be rich like you." He laughed and looked for an ashtray to dump his ashes.

"Here you go." I handed him a coaster. "I don't have ashtrays in here because the smell of smoke sometimes irritates me. And I'll be happy to call everyone to let them know about Mason Technologies."

"Thanks, Jaylin. I'm not going to take up much more of your time. Just keep in touch; you've been a hard man to catch up with lately. I guess that lady who was screwing your brains out the other day is keeping you busy, huh?"

"Nah, nothing like that. Anyway, sorry for the interruption. She just couldn't get enough of me that day," I said, laughing. He laughed too, reached into his pocket and gave me an envelope.

"Here's a little something extra my wife and I put together for all your hard work and dedication to making us very wealthy people. I trust you with my life and hope you'll continue to make good decisions so we can have everything we've always dreamed of."

"Thanks, Mr. Higgins." I reached for the envelope. "And as always, you can count on me."

I could hear Higgins outside my office as he flirted with Angela. If I didn't know any better, I'd think they had slept together before. Angela was a gold digger and looked for anybody who had money. She tried to work that thang on me, but I wasn't having it. As soon as she married my boss' son, I ended it. He treated her like a queen, but for her, that still wasn't enough. He even told her she didn't have to work, but she insisted on being out of the house. That's what I have a beef with some men about; always wanting their women to stay at home and shit. Two salaries are always better than one. I don't care what anybody says.

Shortly after I heard Higgins leave, I opened the envelope he'd given me. Enclosed was a check for $25,000 and two tickets for a cruise to the Bahamas. Seven days and six nights. Already paid for. I'd been to the Bahamas before with Felicia, but we argued so much it was ridiculous. So, taking her again was definitely out of the question. Nokea hadn't called all day, so it was obvious she needed more time to get herself together. I'd take Scorpio. She would be perfect to kick it with in the Bahamas. Besides, with her I knew I'd be getting my fuck on every single day.

Before I called her, I called Higgins and left him a thank you message addressed to him and his wife. I then sat back and tried to fix the problem I had with not buying his shares when he asked me to. The only solution was for me to make up the loss of profit with my own money. I wasn't happy about doing so, but I had no one to blame but myself.

I called Angela in my office to see if she would stay late and help me make some calls to get Higgins' buddies invested as well. They had been nothing but good to me, so the more money I made them, the better off I would be.

Angela and I were in the office until 9:00 that night trying to cut deals over the phone for Higgins' buddies. Since they made up at least sixty percent of my salary, I didn't care how long it took. Exhausted, I took off my jacket and sat back on the small hunter green sofa in my office.

Angela came in with a glass of wine for each of us; she knew how well wine relaxed me. She sat on the plush carpeted floor in front of me with her legs folded. I could see right up her short skirt, and I'm sure her intention was to let me see.

She came over to me on her knees. "Jaylin, let's give a toast."

"Toast to what? To how tired I am?"

"Well, if that's what you want to toast to, then go right ahead. But I was thinking more like a toast to mo' money, mo' money, and mo' money."

"Now, I'll drink to that." We both laughed and clinked our glasses together. She tapped my glass so hard the wine splashed on my expensive pants. I jumped so the wine wouldn't seep through them. "Damn, Angela, what are you doing?"

"Sorry. I didn't mean for that much to spill on you."

"What do you mean, you didn't mean for that much to spill on me? Did you do that shit purposely?"

She looked at me and smiled. "You know I did. I was hoping you'd take them off and send a sista home with a smile on her face like you did for Felicia the other day."

I walked over to my desk and dabbed my pants with a hand-kerchief.

"Angela, I ain't trying to go there with you. Old man Schmidt would kill me if he knew what we used to be doing up in here, and you know he works late every single night. Sorry, baby, but I can't take the risk anymore. Besides, ain't your husband satisfying your needs?"

"No, he's really not. I mean, he's satisfying my financial needs, but I'm always up to having sex with you."

"Um . . . sorry to hear that your needs aren't being met. I can't help you though. Once again, there's too much risk involved."

While I continued to dab my pants, Angela closed the door then came over and kneeled down in front of me again.

"Let me at least have these pants cleaned for you." She started to unbuckle my belt. I grabbed her hand, unable to believe I was turning down some pussy.

"Look, I can't go out like that, Angela. Sorry."

"All I want to do is taste it, Jaylin. You don't have a problem with me doing that, do you?"

My thang was already on the rise, and taking a risk might be worth it. At this point, there wasn't no sense in trying to reject her. A little blowjob never hurt anyone.

I closed my eyes and allowed her to go to work. She must have really been practicing on her husband because her slurps and deep throat had me on cloud nine. She wasn't good at this before, but had earned herself a B+ tonight. I was in a trance, leaned back in my chair, until I heard two people talking. Angela hopped up and I quickly buttoned my pants.

No sooner had I zipped them and sat at my desk than Schmidt knocked and stuck his head in my office. He introduced Angela to one of his friends, and I scooted my chair close to my desk so he wouldn't notice my wet pants.

"How do you do, Roy? It's nice to finally meet you," she said, nervously shaking his hand.

"Doug wasn't kidding. He does have a beautiful wife. It's good to finally meet you too."

"And this here is my top investment broker, Jaylin 'Millionaire' Rogers. Jaylin, this is Roy Johnson. He's going to be our new sales and marketing manager."

I reached out and shook Roy's hand. "Nice to meet you. Good luck on your new position."

"Thanks," he said.

"Jaylin, Angela, we'll let you two get back to work. Angela, Doug said he's been trying to reach you. Give him a call to let him know when you'll be leaving."

"I sure will, Pops. I'll call him right now." She gave him a kiss on the cheek.

Now he had the fragrance of my goods on his face. Never—and I mean never—again.

I made that clear to Angela, and she left my office with an attitude. Afterward, I closed my door and picked up the phone to call Scorpio. Angela had gotten me pretty worked up, so I figured I'd finish off the night with some workable pussy. The sound of Scorpio's sexy voice caused me to display my pearly whites.

"Say, baby, it's Jaylin."

"I know who this is. Not only that, but I know what you want."

"Oh yeah? And what might that be?"

"You want me to meet you at your place and make love to you all night long."

"You're partially correct. First, I want to invite you to go on a cruise with me to the Bahamas in a couple of weeks, and then I want you to meet me at my place tonight so we can exchange some juices."

"What if I tell you I'm busy or I can't find a sitter? Will you call someone else to exchange some juices with tonight?"

"Good question, baby, but nobody can make my juices flow the way you do. So, what time should I expect you?"

"Your juice sounds delicious. Give me an hour and I'll be there. Don't have me waiting, because I don't like to wait when I'm anxious."

"You, wait on me? Shit . . . never. I'm leaving the office now."

"And, Jaylin, I like swimming pools too. Why don't I meet you in the pool area? Let's say the Jacuzzi?"

"I'll go home and get it warm for you."

I hung up and got my ass out of the office as quickly as I could. Angela and I took the elevator down to the parking garage, and when I rushed her to her car, she started in with the questions.

"Jaylin, who were you talking to? I heard you tell somebody you were on your way," she said with one leg hanging out of her car.

"Angela, don't go questioning me. We don't have that type of relationship, so please don't start. And as for what happened in my office today, it will never happen again. If those two had been just a minute earlier, we could've lost our jobs."

"Now, you know that isn't going to happen. Pops trusts me and so does Doug. They have no idea what went on with us in the past, and they surely don't know what's up with us now."

"Well, good, because there's nothing going on with us now and I'd like to keep it that way. So, goodnight and be careful." I closed her door.

She rolled her big bubble eyes and started her car. I didn't care how mad she was, I just couldn't continue to do shit like that. My career meant more to me than anything.

Somehow, I managed to get stuck in traffic on Manchester Road, since I tried to take a shortcut. But by the time I got home, Scorpio's car wasn't there, so I figured I had time to warm up the Jacuzzi and put on some relaxing music. I got out of my work clothes, showered, and went into the kitchen to get some chocolate-covered strawberries I had in the refrigerator just in case I wanted to set the mood.

I went to the pool area and turned on the Jacuzzi so it would be nice and warm before Scorpio came. Then I put on some soft music and stepped my naked body into the Jacuzzi and waited for her. I poured myself a glass of wine and set her glass next to the tray of strawberries. I left the front door slightly cracked so she wouldn't have to knock when she came.

As the water bubbled and steamed, I closed my eyes and dozed off. Shortly after, I was awakened by the touch of her soft, wet lips. But when I opened my eyes, I saw that is was Felicia standing over me.

"Are you expecting someone, Jaylin? I know you ain't sitting out here butt naked in the Jacuzzi by yourself."

"Yes, I am expecting someone, Felicia. Why don't you go home and I'll give you a call tomorrow."

"Nope, can't do that. I've been leaving you messages all day long and you haven't returned any of them. I thought we had an understanding."

"Look, I've been busy! That's why I haven't returned your phone calls. I planned on doing so, but I just hadn't gotten around to it."

"But you've gotten around to calling some other bitch over here. Who is it? I hope it ain't who I think it is."

"Felicia, it ain't none of your business. I told you before, don't be coming over here unannounced. It used to be cool, but since you tripped like you did the other day, the rules have changed."

"So, you got rules now, huh? I'm scared of you. Look, I'll let you have your little shindig over here tonight, but when I call you, you need to return my phone calls."

"And you need to go before my company gets here."

Felicia put her hand in the water and tried to grab my goods. I grabbed her hand and asked her again to leave.

As soon as Felicia stood up, Scorpio stepped into the pool area and closed the sliding glass doors behind her. She looked delicious in a red fishnet bikini that revealed everything. She dropped her flowered wrap at the door and strutted over to me like Felicia didn't exist. Her long, shiny hair was slicked back, and her curls dangled on the left side of her shoulder.

Felicia's eyes looked like they were shooting ammunition. She couldn't keep them off Scorpio's stunning beauty.

When Scorpio picked up her wineglass and sat in the Jacuzzi beside me, it was time for me to escort Felicia out. I stepped out of the water, bare-bodied and all, and told Felicia it was time to go.

"I'm leaving, Jaylin, but would you at least have the decency to walk me to the door?"

I bent down and gave Scorpio a kiss. As expected, she made it juicy and teased my lips with her tongue. "I'll be right back. Don't you go nowhere," I said.

"Hurry. I can't wait much longer," she said, starting to remove her bikini top.

Felicia rolled her eyes and shook her head. I pulled the sliding door over and motioned for Felicia to follow. When we got to the living room, she paused and poked her finger at my chest.

"This is ridiculous and you know it. This bitch ain't nothing but a freak! The both of you walking around here with no damn clothes on like it's a freak fest or something." She gazed at my stuff. I knew damn well she wished it was her in that Jacuzzi instead of Scorpio.

"Look, Felicia, get your fucking finger off my chest. This is what's going to happen when you come over here without an invitation. I'm not doing this to hurt you, but when you go searching for shit, you're definitely going to find it. So stop searching. I'll call you tomorrow. Just maybe, I'll see you on Friday."

"To hell with Friday, Jaylin. One day, you're going to regret everything you're doing to me."

"You're doing it to yourself, Felicia. You for damn sure can't blame me for nothing."

She slammed the door and Mama's picture fell off the mantle. I walked over and picked it up. I stood for a moment and thought about Mama. I wondered if she was proud of me. Wondered if she knew what I'd been through after she died. And I wondered if she was upset with me for not being with Nokea.

I placed my lips on her picture and put it back on the mantle.

When I went back outside, Scorpio was still in the Jacuzzi, enjoying the chocolate-covered strawberries. I got back in, and after she straddled my lap, I wrapped my arms around her. She put a strawberry in my mouth then poured wine on her breasts for me to suck them. Her nipples were at full attention when she intervened during my performance.

"Jaylin?"

"Yeah, baby."

"I don't ever want to see Felicia over here again. She's becoming a pain, and I don't like to be hurt."

"I'll take care of her. Don't you worry your pretty little self about Felicia because she won't be coming back any time soon."

I put Scorpio into position and prepared myself for a long and enjoyable night. As for Felicia, she had to go. Not only because Scorpio wanted me to let her go, but because she was becoming a pain in the ass. I didn't know how I would break it to her, but I knew ending it with her had to be done soon.

16

FELICIA

Friday came before I knew it, and Jaylin was a no show. I didn't know how to handle his rejection. It sure as hell didn't feel good. This Scorpio bitch took up too much of his time, even time away from Nokea, I suspected. I had no clue when he saw her. It appeared that she was put on the back burner like I was. If that was true, then maybe it was time for us to pull together and try to get Jaylin to come back to reality. He was somewhere in la-la land thinking that all he needed to satisfy him was Scorpio.

She was nasty-looking to me. I didn't care what he said. I mean, she had a nice body, but did she have to flaunt that motherfucker in front of females? I wasn't interested in looking at the ho, but any time a woman got a red rose tattooed on the back of her ass, you can't help but notice. She might as well have shown up naked. Tiny-ass red bikini wasn't hiding an inch.

Jaylin didn't think I noticed, but he was full of lust as he watched her. I was afraid he'd fuck her right there in front of me. He never looked at me like that, and I can't even recall if

I'd seen him look at Nokea like that. He'd definitely fallen for this hoochie, and the only one who could come between them was Nokea.

When I got home from work, I called Nokea's house. Her number had been changed, and when I tried her cell phone, I found out that had been changed too. What was up? Something wasn't right, and I was anxious to find out what it was.

I called my ex-boyfriend, Damion, and told him to meet me at my house later on tonight. I refused to be alone on another Friday night, and since Jaylin was full of games, Damion would just have to do.

I changed clothes and decided to pay Miss Homebody a visit at her house off New Halls Ferry Road. I knew she would be stupid enough to let me in, especially if I pretended I was looking out for what was in Jaylin's best interests.

Her black Acura Legend was parked in front of her house. I could see a light on in her bedroom and that was it. The rest of the house was dark. I rang the doorbell repeatedly, not caring if she was asleep or not. I could see her through the glass door.

"Who is it?" she asked, as if she really couldn't tell it was me.

"Nokea, it's me, Felicia. I just want to talk to you for a minute, if you don't mind."

"About what, Felicia? You and I have nothing to talk about."

"Yes we do, so please open the door. This is about Jaylin and his new woman. He and I got into a confrontation, and I wondered if you could help me with something. Please."

I couldn't believe I begged her to talk, but I was desperate. She opened the door looking terrible. I'd never seen her look so bad. The bags underneath her eyes showed stress. She looked as if she hadn't slept in days; her hair was in tiny pink rollers, and her pink bathrobe was a wrinkled mess.

"Come in, but make it quick. I'm tired and need to get some rest." She put her hands in her pockets and stood by the door.

"Do you mind if I at least have a seat? It won't take long, but I really need to talk to you about something."

We walked over to her sofa in the living room. She had really jazzed up the place since I'd last seen it. I'd come to her house three months after I met Jaylin and confronted her. He told me about their relationship, but I wanted to find out just how serious it was. I followed him to her place, and after he left, I went to door. At the time, Nokea seemed confident that Jaylin would dump me right away. She said it was something he routinely did, but I assured her that I wasn't going anywhere anytime soon. Four years later, I was still here.

From what I could see, her place wasn't that spectacular then, but now she had it fixed up like an African exhibit. All kinds of black art covered the walls, and she had a black statue in one corner that damn near reached the twelve-foot ceiling in her living room. She had a plush loveseat and sofa covered in Nefertiti cloth, and an old black baby grand piano jazzed up the room. A huge honey-mustard, green, and burgundy rug with swirls covered the shiny hardwood floors, and the burning candles gave the room a nice subtle fragrance.

"So, Felicia, what trouble are you here to cause today?"

"I'm not here to cause any trouble. I just want to find out where things stand with you and Jaylin. I know he's been spending a lot of time with Scorpio and I wondered if you've seen him lately."

"What do you mean, he's been spending a lot of time with Scorpio? How do you know how much time he spends with her?"

"I know because every time I call him she's over there. The other night, I stopped by his place and they were in his Jacuzzi having sex," I said, spicing things up like I had seen it for myself.

"So, you had the pleasure of seeing them in action too, huh?

I walked in on them in the shower, and after that, I ended it. Well, I tried to end it."

"What? You saw them together in his shower? What did he say?"

"He didn't say much. You know the usual excuses he makes for his behavior. He came over Monday night and apologized. And, stupid me, I was so vulnerable that I forgave him."

"Monday night, huh? I had just seen him Monday afternoon. I went to his office and he couldn't keep his hands off me. Tried to have sex with me right then and there. I went ahead and gave in, but I told him if he wanted to make love to me again, it would have to be in a better place."

Nokea was quiet. She turned her head, and I could see her throat move in and out as she took a hard swallow.

"Felicia, after work, Jaylin came over here Monday night and made love to me. I felt something wasn't right, but I let him do it anyway. How could I be so stupid?" She yelled and tightened her fist as she took a seat on the piano bench.

Her confirmation that she and Jaylin had already been intimate rubbed me the wrong way. Now I felt as if she was a bigger competition for me, and getting rid of Scorpio wasn't going to be enough. I had to get rid of her too, but I didn't want to let her know that her words had gotten underneath my skin.

"How could we both be so stupid, Nokea? I'm just as guilty, so don't feel bad. The question is what are we going to do about it? If you want things to change, then we got to figure out what we can do to change them."

"I'm not doing anything. I don't want Jaylin anymore. I haven't talked to him since Monday, and for me, that's only the first step. If you want to fight for him, you go right ahead. But you won't be battling with me."

"Nokea, you know you've said that a million times before. What makes you think this time it's a for sure thing?"

"Because I know. I feel it in my heart and in my soul. The only thing I need to do is figure out a way to get my energy back. I feel beat. I'm exhausted from all this crying, and it's wearing me down."

"I don't mean any harm, Nokea, but I can tell. I ain't never seen you look like this. The difference between you and me is Jaylin will never bring me down no matter how hard he may try."

"No, Felicia. The difference between you and me is I love him and you don't. That's why it's harder for me than it is for you. I'm not saying you don't care for him, but that's all it is. You will be able to walk away whenever you eventually get tired. Me, it's going to take time. More time than I anticipated. But for now, as long as I don't see him, I'm doing okay."

Even though I hated to admit it, Nokea was right. I didn't love Jaylin as much as she did—but if I couldn't have him, no one would.

I left Nokea's house on a good note. I didn't tell her what I intended to do, but she made it perfectly clear that she was out of it. I couldn't blame her; she had to be the one who suffered the most pain from Jaylin. I had only stepped into this mess four years ago and was already exhausted from the female bullshit.

When I got back home, I called Jaylin and left him another nasty message for dissing me again on Friday night. I changed clothes and waited for Damion to come over so I could get some type of satisfaction for the night. I was sure he'd be lacking somewhere, someway, or somehow, and that's why I had to make sure Jaylin's and my relationship got back on track. Soon.

17

NOKEA

It had been three whole weeks since I last talked to or saw Jaylin. I went to Infiniti Styles on the corner of Chambers and West Florissant Avenue to get my hair done, and then I shopped at the Galleria to find some outfits for the fall. As far as I was concerned, I was back in action. Not only did I look good again, but I felt good as well.

That was until late Sunday night. I'd eaten some greasy fried chicken at Pat's place, and it had my stomach upset. I went to the bathroom and threw up. I thought it would make me feel better, but it didn't; I felt nauseated and faint.

I went home, lay down in my bed with a cold rag across my forehead, and tried to figure out what was wrong with me. By morning, I had thrown up again. I called my doctor to make an appointment, and then called my boss and told him I would be late. The thought of food poisoning crossed my mind because for some reason, the chicken didn't taste right to me.

I arrived at Dr. Beckwith's office in the Central West End about nine-thirty in the morning. Immediately, the nurse called my name, so I didn't have to wait long. When Dr. Beckwith came in, he asked me all kinds of questions. When I told him what my symptoms were, he said it didn't sound like I had food poisoning and told me he wanted to give me a pregnancy test. Since I hadn't missed my period, I knew it wasn't possible. Besides, Jaylin and I only had sex one and a half times. Still, I knew one time is all it takes, so I anxiously waited for the results.

Dr. Beckwith came back into the room and pulled a chair next to me. He had a smile on his face as he slid his pen along the side of his ear.

"Nokea, I have good news and more good news. Which one would you like to hear first?" I'd been with Dr. Beckwith since I was a little girl, and he always joked around with me when something was wrong.

"Well, Dr. Beckwith, if it's double good news, then let's hear it."

"First, you don't have food poisoning, and second, you're going to have a baby."

The grin on my face vanished.

"Wha . . . what did you say?"

"Yes, Nokea, you're pregnant. And we're going to do everything possible to make sure you have a healthy baby."

I was speechless. When Dr. Beckwith left the room, I dropped my head and burst into tears. I never thought I would have a baby out of wedlock. Mama and Daddy wouldn't be happy about the news. I knew they'd be disappointed in me and Jaylin.

For the last few months, I had really been a disappointment to myself. Why did I have to make so many messed-up decisions? Decisions that cost me big-time.

Dr. Beckwith's nurse came in and congratulated me. She gave me a hug and immediately noticed that I'd been crying.

"Are those tears of joy?" she asked, helping me off the examination table.

"No . . . I don't know. I'm confused right now. Really, I don't know how I feel."

"I know it comes as a shock today, but once you get home and think about how much happiness this baby is going to bring to your life, you'll feel a whole lot better. It's normal for you to feel the way you are. Just don't go making any decisions until you've had time to think about it."

"Thank you," I said, giving her another hug.

I called my boss and asked for some personal time off. Hearing how anxious I sounded, he didn't seem to have a problem with it.

I drove down Euclid Avenue and thought about how Jaylin would feel about this. I knew how much he loved his daughter, who disappeared with her mother years ago, so I was positive he wouldn't have a problem loving the baby I carried. Would this baby finally change our lives? Was this a sign from God we needed to be together as a family? The big question was, when would I break the news to him—or would I do it at all?

I needed advice, so I went to Barnes Jewish Hospital on Kingshighway, where Pat worked, to see if she would take an early lunch with me. She told her boss it was urgent, grabbed her purse, and we headed to the Pasta House.

"So, why are you dragging my butt out of the office like this couldn't wait until I got home?" Pat asked. The waiter poured our water and handed us menus. I wanted to wait until he was gone to answer Pat's question.

"If you don't mind," I said, "give us about ten minutes and we'll be ready to order." The waiter nodded and walked away.

"Okay, Nokea, out with it. He's gone, so what's on your mind?"

I reached my hands across the table and held hers. "Pat, I'm having a baby. The doctor confirmed it this morning, and I'm confused about what I need to do."

She squeezed my hands tighter and yelled. "Girl, I'm so happy for you!" Her voice lowered. "But please don't tell me it's Jaylin's baby. I know he's the only one you've been with, but just make up somebody, please."

I laughed with her.

"Girl, you know I can't lie like that. You know its Jaylin's. The question is, what am I going to do? I haven't called him in weeks, and I've been working hard trying to get him out of my system. And just when I thought things were going well, bam—I'm pregnant."

"I know I'm your best friend, but when it comes to Jaylin, I'm not one to give you advice."

"Yes, you are, Pat. You've always given me good advice. I just never do what you tell me."

"Well, I'm going to tell you how I see it. If you decide to listen to me, then fine. If you don't, I won't be mad."

"Okay, that's fair enough. I just need to hear your input. Then you can tell me how disappointed you think my very religious parents will be."

"I don't think your parents will be disappointed at all, especially since they like Jaylin."

"You mean as much as they used to like Jaylin. I told Mama about what happened and she told me to move on with my life. Daddy came by to see me the other day, and when I cried on his shoulder about our ups and downs, he wasn't too happy. Actually, he said he was going by Jaylin's place to have a few words with him about how he's been treating me lately. Of course, I stopped him."

"Your parents love you. They'll understand. You're a grown woman, and I don't think they're going to be disappointed in their thirty-year-old daughter for having a baby out of wedlock. You have a good job, and you'll definitely be able to provide for this baby. As for you and Jaylin, don't tell him."

"Why not?"

"I mean don't tell him right now. Wait a while. And if he starts showing you some love without knowing you're pregnant, then work things out with him. If he doesn't call or come around, then raise this baby by yourself and do the best you can. The worst thing you can do is let him think you had this baby just to trap him. If he thinks that, you're going to hear about it for the rest of your life."

"But, Pat, you know I didn't get pregnant on purpose. When he finds out, Jaylin is going to be excited."

"I'm not saying he wouldn't be. But you know how some men are. Always thinking somebody's trying to trap their ass when they're right there making that baby with you."

"I really don't care what Jaylin or anybody else thinks. I didn't get pregnant on purpose to trap him."

"Okay, Nokea, do what you want to. If you want to tell him, by all means, do. If it's meant to be, then things will work out." That was the best thing Pat said to me all day. Her advice wasn't what I wanted to hear, but I always appreciated her input.

After lunch, I decided to stop by the barbershop to see Stephon. Since he knew Jaylin better than anybody, I thought he might be able to offer me better advice than Pat did.

When I walked in, he was on the phone while working on somebody's hair. He looked at me and smiled, then hurried to end his call.

"What's up, Shorty? I know you didn't come in here to get your hair cut."

"No, I didn't. I wondered if you had a minute to talk."

"Yeah, let me finish this young man's hair and I'll step outside with you to chat. In the meantime, get a soda out of the machine," he said, handing me a dollar bill. "While you're at it, get me one too."

I went to the machine, got us some sodas, and then put his drink on the counter of his workstation. I looked at the pictures lined on his mirror; it was all about him and Jaylin. He had a few pictures of some females, but you'd have thought Jaylin was his girlfriend.

I looked at one picture where Jaylin had on a black gangster hat with a toothpick in his mouth. He looked ghetto, kneeling down with a peace sign held up. It was a good picture, but trying to put on the ghetto look wasn't working for him.

As the fellows in the shop rambled on about women, I found myself a chair and took a seat. They didn't care if I was around; they dissed women so badly that I was almost forced to say something. Just when I was about to intervene, Stephon finished his customer's hair.

"Come on, Shorty. Let's go to my car," he said, opening the door to his BMW so I could get in.

"So, what's so important that you came to see little ole me on the job?"

"First, I want to know if you've talked to Jaylin."

"Yes, that was him I was talking to when you walked through the door. He's in the Ba—" He shut his mouth before finishing.

"Don't stop now. Where is he?"

"Nokea, why you always making me tell you shit about Jaylin? You know how tight we are. I don't want to be caught in the middle of this chaos between the both of you."

"I don't want you caught in the middle either, but I have a serious problem I'm trying to work through right now. So, the more I know what's going on with him, the easier my decision is going to be."

"What kind of serious problem do you have?"

"Where is he? Once I know, I'll be happy to tell you about my problem."

Stephon hesitated to tell me, but I begged and pleaded with him. I expressed how it was in my best interests to find out as much as I could about Jaylin and his new woman. I knew that he and Jaylin were close, but I also knew he thought of me as a friend. Stephon had always shown me that he had a good heart. That made it much easier for me to trust him with my secret. I believed that no matter how close he was to Jaylin, he wouldn't betray me by telling Jaylin the news that was mine to tell or not tell.

He scratched his head then put his hands in his pockets. "He . . . he's in the Bahamas. He'll be back on Monday night. So, what's your problem?"

"Who is he with? I know it isn't Felicia because she came to see me the other day and said she was out of the picture. And I also know he isn't there alone."

"Then I guess you answered your own question."

"Tell me, what is it with him and Scorpio? Is he in love with her?"

"Nope, don't think so. I just think she got a hold on him right now. If you know Jaylin, this phase will be over soon."

"I don't know, Stephon. I see more to it than just that. He's different. He's had this I-don't-give-a-shit attitude about everything lately, and that's a side of him I've never seen before."

"Yeah, he has changed a little bit, but men always get excited about something new in their lives."

"Well, I hope he gets excited about this baby I'm carrying."

Stephon's eyes bucked and his mouth opened wide. "What? Nokea, are you pregnant?"

"Yes, and . . . and I don't quite know how I'm feeling about it. I just found out this morning, and since then I've laughed and I've cried—don't know if I'm happy or sad."

"I . . . I'm very happy for you and Jaylin," he said, reaching over and giving me a hug. "And if you came to ask me if Jaylin is going to be excited about the news, hell yes! He's going to be ecstatic. He misses the hell out of his daughter, and your news will be like music to his ears."

"Yeah, but since things haven't worked out between us, do you think he'll feel differently about having a baby with me?"

"No. And things are going to work out for you two. There's no way you can let another woman stand in your way. When he gets back on Monday, you go right over there and tell him."

"I'll make a nice dinner for him and then tell him. Thanks so much, Stephon. You don't know how much you've put me at ease."

Stephon kissed my forehead and said he had to get back to work. His advice was definitely the kind I needed to hear. He lifted my spirits up so high that I stopped by the mall and bought two outfits for my son. I had a deep feeling it was going to be a boy. I also threw in a bib that said I LOVE MY DADDY and some pacifiers. I couldn't wait to tell Jaylin about the baby. Monday couldn't get here fast enough for me.

18

JAYLIN

Scorpio and I had the time of our lives in the Bahamas. She was good, relaxing company for me; exactly what I needed to get my head on straight. The moment we arrived on the ship, it was on. Men checked her out like she was some kind of beauty queen or something. I had the women all checking me out, too, but not like the men rode Scorpio. And it seemed like the harder they looked, the closer she clung to me. She didn't leave my side. She didn't complain about anything, and she definitely had enough sense not to bring up Nokea or Felicia on our vacation.

Before we left St. Louis, I'd gone to Saks Fifth Avenue and bought her two beautiful evening gowns to wear for dinner. One of them was black with pearls that gathered around the neckline. The back was open and the bottom had a tail-like flare. The other was short and red with a sheer scarf that draped on her side as she walked. The edges were trimmed with rhinestones and perfectly matched the sexy red shoes I bought. The dresses and shoes cost a fortune, but when I saw her in them, she was definitely fit to be in Jaylin Rogers' world.

At our first dinner, we got so many compliments as a couple that she lied to people and told them we were on our honeymoon. For me, that took shit a bit far. When Scorpio said it, I didn't correct her right then and there, but while we were in our cabin, I did.

Other than that incident, she really knew how to keep a brotha happy. Rubbed my feet at night, massaged my body with oil, and washed me up in the shower. Of course, I returned the favor and rubbed her body too, but she did it to the extreme. And the sex—whew—it was on. Every time we stepped foot in our room, we were at it. Could barely get the door open before we ripped each other's clothes off. I had even gotten some at four o'clock in the morning on the upper deck of the ship while mostly everybody else was sleep. Scorpio didn't mind being creative, and that was a positive thing.

I enjoyed being with this woman, and frankly, I hadn't thought about kicking her to the curb anytime soon. She'd been taking damn good care of me, and I had no problem splurging my money on her.

Our second to last night in the Bahamas, I went to a jewelry store and bought her a diamond Rolex she seemed to be infatuated with when we browsed earlier. She didn't know I'd purchased it until we got back to our cabin. After I showed it to her, her eyes filled with tears. She made love to me that night like sex was going out of style. Fucked me so good, I damn near cried myself.

But after tonight, our last night of vacation, it would be time to get back to reality. I had to decide where I was headed from here. I was tired of my situation with Felicia and Nokea, and was ready to try something different. Maybe settling down with one woman wasn't a bad idea. For now, Scorpio was giving me all the things I needed, with the exception of cooking for me. But with sex as good as it was, I could hire a chef to cook for me, or very well do it myself. I had some serious thinking to do, and this vacation allowed me time to think about my future.

Scorpio and I put on our swimming gear and went for a late night swim on the upper deck with some of the other couples. She laid her pretty self between my legs as we looked up at the sky and tried to count the stars.

"I counted six hundred twenty, Jaylin. How many did you count?" she asked.

"I only counted ten. Ten over here, ten over there. I don't know. . . . Why don't you help me count?" I picked up her hand and we reached for the sky. We counted together and when we got to twenty, I took her hand and kissed it.

"Jaylin, what's on your mind? You've been awfully quiet today."

"Nothing much. Just thinking about how much I've enjoyed these past several days with you. Thinking about how good it's been to get away from all the bullshit at home. That's all."

"Well, I'm glad you asked me to come along. I never imagined the Bahamas being so beautiful. And Paradise Island, it's to die for. Just amazing." She leaned back and I put my arms around her waist.

"I'm glad you had a good time too. Next time, though, I'm going to take you somewhere even better."

"Jaylin, please, it doesn't get any better than this. I don't care where I am, as long as I'm with you."

"Aw, trust me, it gets a whole lot better than this. There are places we can go that are more beautiful than you've ever imagined."

"And I'll still say anywhere is great as long as I'm with you. It's just so funny how well I've taken to you. I thought I was in love with you before, but now I definitely know I am."

I looked away, wanting to change the subject. I was feeling Scorpio too, but it was too early for us to be talking about falling in love. I had no control over her feelings, but they were making me a bit uncomfortable.

Scorpio noticed that I hadn't responded so she continued. "I know you didn't want to hear that, but what else am I supposed to say? If I feel a certain way in my heart, why should I have to hide it because those words frighten you?"

"Scorpio, I didn't say that I didn't want to hear it. All I'm saying, as I said before, is love complicates things. I'm just not ready for that kind of relationship, baby."

"You also said you haven't had a woman in your life that has made you love her. If I'm not making you love me, then you tell me what else I need to do. I'm trying, but eventually, my energy is going to run out."

She had touched a nerve. This was one subject I didn't want to delve into on our vacation. "Baby, please. We're having such a good time. Don't spoil it talking this nonsense that don't really matter right now. Can I please just enjoy my last day here with you?"

"Sure. But since you don't want to talk about that, can we talk about what happens when we get back to St. Louis? I really would like to know where things stand between us."

"What do you mean, where things stand? I thought things were cool just the way they are."

"They are, but . . . but I want to be in your life at all times. In fact, I'd like to move in with you. Be with you around the clock to take care of all your needs."

I fell silent again. I hadn't given much thought to allowing any woman to move in with me. Scorpio was really pushing it, and I was concerned about her urgency. I tried not to ruin our vacation, so I remained calm and spoke truthfully. "I don't know if I'm ready for that. When we get back, we'll talk about it then, okay?"

Scorpio laid her head back on me and closed her eyes.

When we got back to the room, I guess she was a bit upset because she went right to sleep without upping no booty. I couldn't sleep, so I slid on my sandals and some shorts and went for a walk on the deck to clear my head. The wind blew a strong breeze, and the high waves splashed against the boat, making it rock.

I rested my arms on the rail and thought about what I planned to do about my situation. I loved being with Scorpio better than anybody, and I knew that giving up my relationships with Nokea and Felicia would give me a fresh start. Still, I had to be careful about my approach because they had always been there for a brotha—up until lately.

Nokea talked about all this time she needed to get herself together, and as far as I was concerned, time wasn't on her side. I was the one who called the shots, so by now, if she hadn't figured out what she wanted to do, then fuck her.

And Felicia? I just wanted to make sure I had some back-up booty if things weren't going cool with Scorpio and me. They were, and even though she was currently upset with me, I knew our problem could be resolved.

I had to seriously think about Scorpio moving in, and not just her, but her child as well. How would I be able to deal with a woman and her child in my home? The downsides would be not having my privacy, not having female company when I wanted to, having a junky house, more mouths to feed . . . my list went on and on. On a positive note, she wasn't a nag, she cared about my needs, and she hadn't forced me to be with only her. Her daughter could possibly help ease some of the pain I still had about not being with my own daughter, but I wasn't sure how well she'd take to me.

Was a man like me ready for this kind of change? This . . . this was too premature, I thought. But then I asked myself, *If not now, when?*

If I didn't like how things were going, I could always just ask her to leave. We could part ways and I could at least say I gave it a try. She couldn't be mad about that.

So . . . I'd let her move in with me. I hoped like hell that I wouldn't regret my decision.

As I stood and watched the water rock the ship, Scorpio came up from behind, wrapped her arms around me, and rubbed my chest in a circular motion.

"I guess I know what you're thinking about," she said.

I turned around and held her in my arms.

"I'm sure you do know. First, I want to apologize for snapping at you earlier. You didn't deserve that, and I know exactly where you're coming from." I kissed her nose. "Second, when we get back to St. Louis, I want you to move in with me. I know I still have some unfinished business to take care of, but I'll work that out when I get back."

"Jaylin, are you sure? I mean, I do have a daughter, too, you know. She'd have to move in with us as well."

"Yeah, I know. I thought about that too, but it's okay. I can hire a nanny to come in and take care of her during the week. She can have the room I fixed up for my little girl before she moved away with her mother."

"Again, are you sure you want to do this? It's going to be a big change for you, and I don't want you to do this unless you're ready."

"Scorpio, it's time for me to make some changes. I can't make you any promises about being faithful, but at least I'll try."

"I'm not worried about you being faithful to me. I'm going to make you so happy that you're not going to have enough time to think about another woman."

I picked her up and laid her on one of the recliners behind us on the deck. I covered my ass with a towel and gave her insides a tickle, not even caring if other people were around.

There were only a few other couples on the deck, but they seemed to have the same idea as we did at four o'clock in the morning.

I hoped I hadn't made a bad decision by telling Scorpio she could move in with me. The worst thing that could happen was I'd fall in love with her—but I had my guards up, and there was no way for a brotha like me to slip.

19

FELICIA

After not hearing from Jaylin, I tried to move on and put my plans on hold to get him back. I left him a few messages just in case he decided to return my phone call, but then decided to stop. I'd become banging buddies with Damion and was making the best of it. After all, he wasn't that bad. I pretended he was Jaylin, and everything was cool.

Because Damion didn't completely fill the void, I'd gotten so lonely that I also made a connection with this white man name Paul from work. He was fine and had entered my life at the right time. I invited him over to my place on Saturday night and he was good company. Our conversation was interesting and flowed like we'd known each other for years. He was such a gentleman and treated me with a lot of respect. Unlike the way Jaylin criticized me for every little thing, Paul paid me many compliments. He talked about how he'd had his eyes on me for a long time, but he wasn't sure if I was interested in dating white men. Told me many of the white men who I worked with wanted to get to know me, and I laughed because I never thought none of them would be interested in me.

After dinner, I thought Paul would try to lay me, but he didn't. He walked himself to the door, gave me a kiss, and said he'd call me the next day.

And that he did. I admired a man who kept his promises. He even had five dozen yellow, pink, and red roses delivered to my house the next day and thanked me for such a wonderful time. I was flabbergasted. The only thing I worried about was rushing things with him. I'd heard the rumors about white men not being as competent as black men in the bedroom, and I was a little afraid of taking our relationship to the next level.

One thing about me: a man must be able to display talent in the bedroom. If not, he'd eventually be history. That's what I liked so much about Jaylin. There was no way a woman would leave his bedroom unsatisfied. He went above and beyond the call of duty. Did whatever he had to do to make sure a woman's needs were met. And if you did go home feeling unfulfilled and he knew it, he'd be sure to make it up to you the next day.

I just couldn't understand why things had to change between us. Our sex life was off the chain until that bitch Scorpio came into the picture. If he hadn't met her, we'd probably be sexing each other up right now. Just the thought of him being with her upset me, but I knew for the time being, I had to keep myself occupied elsewhere.

For lunch, Paul and I went to Café Calimino not too far from work. We tried to keep things on the down-low so no one would find out about us. People always seemed to make a big fucking deal about mixed relationships, and I wasn't prepared to answer any questions. Seemed like everybody and their mama from work came in the café and spoke to either Paul or me. They didn't question us, but we could see and hear all the whispers going on.

I asked Paul if we could leave and invited him over to my place for dinner that night. He didn't seem the least bit bothered by all the attention we got and asked me to stay.

I stood up and left my tray of food on the table. "No, I'm ready to go. I don't like to be watched when I'm eating."

"Felicia, would you please take a seat. Who cares what other people think? I'm enjoying our lunch together, and wish you were too."

"I am too, but would you mind if we take it with us? Maybe be can go to a park or something, but I don't feel comfortable being here."

Paul didn't seem pleased by my actions, but instead of putting up a fuss, he got our to-go boxes and we left.

I left work early so I could go home to prepare a scrumptious dinner for us that night. I stopped by Saveway on Broadway and picked up some coleslaw and catfish nuggets. Everything was perfect. I set the table and put on some reggae music to set the mood. I changed into a red silk thigh-high dress and left off my panties just in case Paul decided he wanted some action.

As I lit the peach-scented candles on the table, the phone rang. I knew it was probably Paul calling to tell me he was on his way, but when I answered, I heard Jaylin's voice.

"Surprise, surprise," I said, filled with excitement just to hear his voice.

"Hey, Felicia, I need to see you tonight. Do you mind if I come over?" He sounded like it was important.

"Uh . . . sure, why not? What time should I expect you?"

"Give me about an hour and I'll be there."

"Okay, I'll see you in an hour."

I hung up and rushed to call Paul to cancel our dinner plans. Before I could, he rang the doorbell. I had to get rid of him. I missed Jaylin too much to turn him away. I'd make it up to Paul some other time, but tonight, my ass belonged to Jaylin.

"Pauuul," I said, smiling as I opened the door. He had a red rose in his hand and gave it to me as he entered.

"Hello, Felicia." He kissed me on the cheek. "You look wonderful."

"Thanks. You look nice too," I said, trying to think up a lie to tell him so he could leave.

"Dinner smells delicious. What are we having?" He took off his jacket and hung it up.

"Some fish and slaw, but I . . . I just got a call from one of my girlfriends. She had an argument with her husband and asked if I could come by and talk to her. She's one of those emotional-type women, and I'm afraid if I don't go, she might try to do something to herself."

"By all means, Felicia, go. Would you like for me to wait until you come back?"

"No. I'm not sure how long I'm going to be, and I'd hate to have you here waiting for me all night. Can we make plans another time?"

"Sure. No problem. I hope everything works out for your friend. She's very lucky to have a friend as caring as you are."

"Yes, she is. I tell her that every day," I said, handing him his jacket so he could hurry up and leave.

"I'll see you tomorrow at work."

"Okay, Paul. Thanks for being so understanding."

I waved goodbye, shut the door, and ran upstairs to change into something more sleazy for Jaylin. What I had on hid all my good body parts, and if I wanted to compete with Scorpio, I had to reveal something. I put on my purple see-through nightie with a purple silk bra and thong underneath. I sprayed myself with a dash of the Chanel No. 5 that Jaylin bought me a while back, and put the food on the table so we could talk over dinner.

When the doorbell rang, I grabbed the phone and pretended as if I were in deep conversation with somebody important. He walked in looking out of sight. Had a deep tan that made his gray eyes glitter even more. I could tell he was coming from work because he still wore his navy blue tailored suit and multi-colored silk tie.

As he waited in the hallway for me to end my call, I saw him check out the five dozen roses Paul bought me that were all over the living room. I turned and walked toward the kitchen so he could get a glimpse of my butt that he could see so well through my nightie. When I turned to face him, I could see the come-fuck-me look in his eyes. I gave a few more laughs on the phone and told no one on the other end that I'd have to call them back because I had company.

"Jaylin, don't just stand there. Come have a seat. I fixed you a little something because I figured you'd probably be hungry by the time you got here." He stepped into the dining room and took a seat.

"Felicia, how did you cook dinner that fast? It only took me an hour to get here."

"Please. It don't take me long to cook. When you called, my fish was almost finished. All I had to do was prepare the slaw."

He shrugged his shoulders. "If you insist. But look, I really didn't come over here to eat dinner—"

"I know you didn't. It was supposed to be a surprise. I've missed hearing from you. Not only that, I miss being with you. Do you ever think things will be the way they were before between us?"

"Felicia, that's what I came over here to talk to you about. I just got back from the Bahamas, and when I got home, I got all twenty-nine of your messages. Baby, this gotta stop. If a brotha don't return your phone calls, that means he doesn't want to be bothered."

"Ya see, I had no other choice. You kept telling me you were going to call but you didn't. I guess it was because you were in the Bahamas. And I guess I don't have to ask you with who, do I?"

"And I guess I don't have to feel any shame when I tell you I was with Scorpio."

"So, what is it with you and her? Don't I mean anything to you anymore?"

Jaylin looked sternly into my eyes. "It's over, Felicia. I can't continue to see you because it just ain't enough of me to go around. I'm tired of being pressured by you, and I need to start making some sense out of my life. More than that, I need a woman who understands me. You used to be that woman, but lately, you're starting to create too much drama. Drama I can't and won't deal with."

"You mean drama that you've brought on yourself? I can't believe that just like that it's over for you. Do you really think you can go without being with me, Jaylin? Every time you meet somebody else, I get set aside like a week-old piece of bread. Do you think I'm going to let you continue to do this to me?"

"This time is different. I'm with a woman who I have a good feeling about. I didn't feel that way about the other women, and I've never come to you before and asked you to end this either. So, if we end this tonight, then no, I won't continue to do this to you."

I shook my head from side to side. "I can't believe your sorry ass. This bitch got your mind all fucked up and you have the nerve to come over here and tell me it's over? Just tell me one thing: are you in love with her?"

"I ain't in love with anyone. I'm just trying to live decent for one time in my life, that's all. Scorpio gives me something you or Nokea have never given me, and that's a peace of mind. She don't nag, she don't bitch, and anything I ask her to do for me, she does it. She's been patient with my situation and has never forced me to choose. You, on the other hand, are the opposite. Your mouth . . . it's been good for some things, but it's foul. I don't like for my women to use the type of language that you do, and it irritates the hell out of me.

"For now, Scorpio's the kind of woman I need in my life. Will that change? I don't know. But if it does, I won't be coming back your way any time soon. We're done."

I was lost for words. Here I had spent four years of my life putting up with this son of a bitch and his bullshit, and he had the nerve to step up in here and brag about another bitch? And as for my mouth, how dare he complain when my mouth was responsible for making his eyes roll to the back of his head! I had been nothing but patient with Jaylin, and who in the hell was he to toss me aside like I wasn't nothing? I felt like getting a gun and killing his ass right then.

As I felt my emotions about to take over, I took a deep breath and tightly clinched my hands together. "So, I guess you'll be having this same conversation with Nokea? That's provided you haven't already."

"Yes, I will. I haven't seen or heard from her in a while, but I'll be sure to let her know as soon as possible where things stand between us."

Jaylin didn't seem to be bullshitting this time. I was desperate to somehow make things right between us. I knew that pussy was his weakness, so I stood up and removed my lingerie. I walked over to his side of the table.

"We can end this, but only after you make love to me. Just this last time, please. If you do, I promise you I won't interfere with your relationship with Scorpio. And whenever she fucks up—because she will—I'll be here for you." I placed my ass on his lap and leaned in to kiss him. He rubbed my ass, but avoided my kiss.

"Felicia, I said it's over. Don't make a fool of yourself, all right?"

"Please don't do this to us," I begged. "Don't leave me like this. We've been through too much."

I leaned in to kiss him again, but got the same response. I couldn't hold back any longer; tears started to trickle down my face. All the years I'd been with him, I'd never let him see me cry, but this time, I couldn't help myself because no matter how bad things had gotten between us, he'd never turned down making love to me.

He ignored my tears and forced me away. "Save the tears, Felicia. It ain't like our relationship was all that anyway. You know you played second best to Nokea for a long time, so cut the act and let me get out of here."

He stood, but I grabbed at his jacket so he wouldn't go. By the time he made it to the door, I managed to pull it off and ripped his shirt.

"Damn, Felicia! What did I tell you?" He ripped the rest of his shirt from his chest and threw it on the floor. "Come on! Let me fuck you! Even though things aren't going to be different tomorrow, let me just give you what you want so you can get the fuck off my back!" he yelled, and pushed me against the wall.

He pulled my braids back and gave me a wet kiss on the cheek. I knew he didn't really want to be here, but his angry aggression excited me. He pulled the string on my thong so tight that it tore and hit the floor. Then he unzipped his pants, and as they fell to his ankles, he lifted me and forced himself inside of me. I held his neck tight as he pounded my back against the wall.

"Are you happy now, Felicia? Is this what you wanted? Is this all the fuck you wanted?" he said, pounding me harder.

"I want you, baby! That's all I want is you." I continued to cry as the feel of him sliding against my slippery walls excited me.

He took charge, and after I came, he slowed down his pace. He rested his sweaty forehead on my shoulder while he held my legs apart in his arms. He then gave me a quick peck on the cheek.

"I know how badly you want me, but you can't have me anymore." He dropped my legs and I eased to the floor and watched as he slid back into his pants. He stood proudly with a smirk on his face. He had no sympathy for me.

"Get out, Jaylin!" I yelled as I helped myself off the floor. "Get the fuck out!"

He nonchalantly gazed at me and then continued to straighten his clothes while looking in the mirror. I rushed to the dining room, picked up the plates on the table, and threw them at him. I wanted to cut his motherfucking face up.

"I hate you!" I yelled as I continued to throw damn near every piece of china that was on my table. My aim wasn't worth a damn, but he ducked a few times as he tried to unlock the front door.

By the time he slammed it, food was everywhere. I'd made a complete mess, but it was certainly a good way to let go of my frustrations. I dropped to a chair behind me and pressed my knees closely to my chest. I cried like I'd just lost my best friend, and deep down, I really thought I had. I knew Jaylin wasn't coming back my way anytime soon. All I was left with were memories.

20

NOKEA

I probably jumped the gun, but I'd been to the mall about five more times looking at clothes and furniture for the baby. According to Stephon, Jaylin was back from the Bahamas, but I got nervous and didn't go talk to him right away. I decided to wait until the weekend to surprise him with the news. He was probably exhausted after leaving the Bahamas then going straight to work on Monday. I knew that the more rest he had, the better my news would be for him. I still contemplated when I would break the news to Mama and Daddy, but Jaylin had to be the first to know. If I didn't get it out of my system soon, I'd probably listen to Pat and never tell him.

Either way, when Saturday morning rolled around, I didn't hesitate. I got up, showered, and cooked a fulfilling breakfast so I wouldn't feel lightheaded when I talked to him. Then I hugged the teddy bear he'd given me and put it in the room that would soon have our new baby in it. I drove slowly down Wild Horse Creek Road to his house, thinking about what he would say. We'd probably sit around all day thinking about what to name the baby or discuss who it would look like.

There was no doubt in my mind that Jaylin would be happy—until I turned the corner and saw Scorpio's car in his driveway. My heart raced. It was nine o'clock in the morning, so she must have spent the night with him.

I started to call him on my cell phone, but I was there to tell him about his baby, and so that's what I intended to do. I rang the doorbell because I didn't want to use my key and walk into what I did the last time.

It took a minute for someone to come to the door, and it was Scorpio. She had on Jaylin's burgundy silk robe and looked at me with a blank stare on her face.

"Hi, Scorpio, is Jaylin here?" Since I was uninvited, I tried to show her a little respect.

She didn't say anything; she just opened the door and let me walk in. I went into the living room and sat down on the couch. I immediately noticed toys all over the floor. Moments later, Jaylin came from the swinging kitchen door with what looked to be a four or five-year-old beautiful little girl on his shoulders. I was shocked.

"She's here to see you," Scorpio said as she walked back into the kitchen. Jaylin put the little girl down, and after she kissed his cheek, she ran back into the kitchen after Scorpio.

"So, what's up, Miss Lady?" he said, picking up the toys on the floor.

"No. You tell me. Seems like you got yourself a new family over here."

"Something like that. So, what brings you by?"

I wasn't about to tell him about the baby until I found out what was up with him, this little girl, and Scorpio. Maybe he wouldn't be as happy about my news as I'd thought he'd be.

"Is that her daughter?" I asked.

"Yes. Her name is Mackenzie."

"So, what is she doing over here? And why are all these toys here?"

"Because, Nokea, she lives with me. After we came back from the Bahamas, both of them moved in with me. Is there anything else you'd like to know?"

"What's going on with the two of you? I mean, I see you've made a commitment to her, but you were so unwilling to commit to me."

"Put it like this: it's a commitment I'm making to myself. See, when you were busy trying to decide if you were going to give yourself to me or not, I decided for you. I'm moving on, Nokea, moving on to bigger and better things. Leaving all bullshit behind me, baby."

"In other words, you're ending our nine-year relationship to be with this woman and her daughter?"

"If that's how you want to look at it, feel free. You didn't make my decision any harder. You were the one playing games like you didn't want this, and holding back on the sex didn't help us much either. So like I said, it's time to move on. Now, if you don't mind, I was in the middle of eating breakfast. Do I need to show you the way out or can you find it yourself?"

I couldn't believe Jaylin's tone. He'd never talked to me like that. He had an attitude like he just didn't give a damn. There was no way I would tell him about the baby now. He'd definitely think it was a trap right about now, and I didn't want my baby being raised with a father who had such a horrible attitude. I got off the couch, unable to even look at him.

"Hey, Nokea?" he said as I walked to the door. "Do you still have the key to my house?"

"Yes." I turned and swallowed the huge lump in my throat.

"On your way out, leave it on the table." He walked back into the kitchen.

My eyes filled with tears as I dug in my purse and removed his key from my key ring. I laid it on the table and shut the door behind me.

I barely made it to my car before I gagged and threw up all

over myself. I started my car, jetted down the street, and thought about my only other option: abortion. There was no way I would raise this baby alone. How could I have been so foolish to think he'd be happy about me having his baby? He already had his homemade family and seemed to be just fine with it.

I was so miserable and needed someone to talk to. I didn't feel like talking to Pat; I wasn't in the mood to hear "I told you so." I decided to stop by the barbershop and give Stephon a piece of my mind, since he was the one who assured me Jaylin would be happy.

I went home first and cleaned myself up, and then headed to the shop to see him. By the time I got there, my eyes were so puffy from crying that he stopped cutting his customer's hair to come outside and calm me.

As soon as he walked out, I grabbed him by his shirt.

"Why did you tell me to go see him, Stephon? You knew how he would react, didn't you!" I said hysterically.

"Hold on, Shorty." He grabbed my arms. "What are you talking about? Calm down and tell me what happened!"

"He doesn't want me anymore! He doesn't want this baby! He asked me to leave and told me to give him his key back!"

"Did you tell him about the baby? I know he wouldn't have told you to leave if you told him."

"After he told me he was moving on, I couldn't tell him about the baby." I wiped the salty tears from my face. "He basically said he was with who he wanted to be with, so there was no sense in me hanging around."

"You should've told him about the baby, Nokea. I knew Scorpio had moved in with him, but I thought once you told him the news, things would be different. If you don't tell him, I'm going inside right now and call him."

"No, Stephon! Please don't call him. Please! I wish like hell you would've told me about her moving in with him. I never would've gone to his house and embarrassed myself like that. Now," I begged, "I don't want him to know anything. You can't tell him, Stephon, please!"

"Then when are you going to tell him?" he asked. "He needs to know that he's got a baby on the way. And I can't make you any promises that I won't tell him."

I looked at Stephon with serious hurt in my eyes. "Stephon, please. Let me decide how to handle this. I don't even know if I'm going to keep this baby."

"Now, that ain't even an option. You're definitely going to keep it. If I'm going to keep my mouth shut, you gotta promise me you won't have an abortion. If Jaylin finds out you did, he's really going to be upset. Not only at you for doing it, but at me for not telling him. So, go home and think about being a good mother to the baby you're carrying. I'm kind of looking forward to having a little Jaylin around."

"Jaylin could care less if I had an abortion, Stephon. He doesn't even care about me, and I don't care what you say, his actions show it."

"He cares, and deep in your heart, you know he cares. I care too, and I want you to relax and think about this before you make any drastic decisions. If you need me, Shorty, I'm here."

Stephon wrapped his arms around me. Whenever I had problems with Jaylin, Stephon always seemed to be there for me. He was the only one who could turn a bad situation into a good one.

I thanked him for lifting my spirits and headed for home with a better attitude. An abortion was out of the question. If Jaylin didn't want anything to do with me, then maybe it was time to move on. I had a bigger thing in my life to worry about now than trying to get him to be with me. This baby was going to need all the love and support a mother could give. If I continued to stress myself with his mess, I'd probably have a miscarriage or something. From what I heard, those ain't no picnic.

I felt so confident about continuing my pregnancy that I stopped by my parents' house to tell them about the baby. I stood on the porch, as they'd just come home from a prayer meeting at church. Seemed like they lived in church. I didn't mind going, but my Saturdays always kept me occupied.

Mama got out of the car and put her arms around me; she'd said no matter what, she could always tell when something was wrong with me.

"Nokea, are you all right?" she asked as Daddy opened the door.

"Yeah, Mama, I'm fine. I just came over to see how you and Daddy were doing."

"Well, you could've called to see how we were doing," Daddy said.

Daddy and I sat at the kitchen table while Mama poured us each a glass of orange juice. I took a few sips.

"So, how was church? Did Reverend James preach today?"

"Church was good, Nokea. And Reverend James always preaches a good sermon. Even on Saturday. Now, you know that.

"Everybody's been asking about you. Asking when you're going to come back to church. You haven't been there in a while. Why don't you make plans to go with us tomorrow morning?" Mama said.

"I don't know, Mama. I've been going to Pat's church with her. Kind of like hers a little better, that's all."

"Okay, well, when you're ready to visit, let us know."

"I will. I promise you I will." I finished up the orange juice and got up to pour another glass. Mama and Daddy looked at each other.

"Nokea, what's on your mind, girl? You've always been able

to talk to us about things, so come on, out with it," Mama said, seeming tired of all my fidgeting.

I stood in front of the sink and took another sip of orange juice. I put the glass on the counter and looked directly at Mama first, then Daddy.

"Mama, Daddy," I said, swallowing. "You're going to be grandparents."

Immediately, Mama smiled and I was relieved. Her reaction was a lot better than I thought it would be. She stood up and ran over to embrace me. Daddy, however, didn't say a word.

"Oh, Nokea, I'm so happy for you," Mama said. "I thought you'd never say those words to me. How far along are you? Do you know what you're having yet?" She leaned back and looked at my stomach. She didn't notice Daddy's demeanor like I did.

"Daddy, is everything okay?" I asked.

"Where's Jaylin?" he asked in a deep, strong voice.

"He's at home, I guess."

"Are the two of you planning on getting married?"

"No. As a matter of fact, we're not. Sorry to tell you this, Daddy, but Jaylin and me never got back together. Because I'm pregnant, I'm not going to force him to be with me."

"No, Nokea, that's nonsense. You're not going to raise this baby alone. If Jaylin helped you make it, then it's his responsibility to take care of it too," Daddy said, raising his voice.

"I'm gonna have to agree with your father on this one, Nokea. You and Jaylin need to try and work things out so you two can raise this child together," Mama said.

"Mama, you and Daddy both know women raise children by themselves all the time. I've already talked to Jaylin, and he doesn't want to have anything to do with me. He's with somebody else, and I can't make him be a father if he doesn't want to."

"Well, whether he likes it or not, I'm going over there to talk to him tomorrow—"

"Daddy, don't. Let me handle my own business. I'm a grown woman and I'm quite capable of making the right decisions."

"Nokea, I thought you and Jaylin always talked about waiting until you were married to have sex. Not too long ago, he promised me that he would wait until you all were married. What happened? Was it all just a bunch of lies?"

"Daddy, believe me when I say we tried to wait. We waited a little over nine years, and one day, things just happened. I don't regret giving myself to him because I'm going to have a beautiful baby. And the two of you are going to be wonderful grandparents. Just please be happy for me, okay?" I gave him a hug.

Daddy smiled and when Mama saw he wasn't tripping, she smiled at me too. By the time I left, they were planning for everything, even for the baby's education. I just threw my hands up in the air, thanked them, and told them goodbye. I thanked God for giving me understanding parents. I wished that my attempt to tell Jaylin about the baby had been this simple.

21

JAYLIN

The nanny didn't show up, and since Scorpio was still asleep from coming in late last night, I worked from my home office. Last night, Scorpio had left to go spend some time with her sister, saying that I could probably use some quiet time. They'd stayed up late playing cards and watching movies with the kids, and I did enjoy a little time by myself. I liked having them around, but I was still adjusting to having a woman and a child in my house.

I couldn't get much done in my office because Mackenzie drove her Barbie around in a toy car on my desk. My papers dropped on the floor, and as I talked to one of my clients on the phone, she disconnected it.

"Mackenzie! What are you doing, sweetie?" I tried to calm down as I looked at her cute little face that looked exactly like her mother's. I sat her on my lap and she reached out her arms for me.

"Nothing, Uncle Jaylin. I just want somebody to help me play with my dolls."

"Well, as soon I get off the phone, I'll play with you, okay?"

"You said that the last time, but you didn't. Do you promise this time you'll play with me?"

I felt so bad about lying to her that I decided to play with her dolls in the middle of my office floor. I felt like such a damn fool as I put on different outfits for the dolls to look like they had some real money.

When the doorbell rang, it saved me. Mackenzie asked me to drive her Barbies to the mall to buy some more clothes.

"I'll be right back, Mackenzie. When I get back I'll take them."

"Okay," she said. "I'll get their purses so we can go."

I smiled at her and went to the door. When I looked out, I saw that it was Stephon. I hadn't seen him since I returned from the Bahamas.

"What's up, my nigga?" he said as I opened the door.

"You got the best go. What brings you by?" I said.

"I had a few things on my mind that I want to holla at you about. You got a minute?"

"For you, always, my brotha." I walked back into my office. Mackenzie was still on the floor playing with her dolls. I sat in the chair behind my desk and Stephon sat on the sofa. Mackenzie looked at Stephon and climbed on my lap. She put her arm around my neck.

"Uncle Jaylin, who is that? Is that your brother?"

"Naw, sweetie. That's my cousin. We like brothers, but he's my favorite cousin." She looked at Stephon and looked at me again.

"He looks like your brother. But you're a lot cuter than he is."

Stephon and I laughed.

"Fool, what you laughing at? The girl got good sense. She knows a fine brotha when she sees one," I said.

Stephon chuckled. "Only in the eye of the beholder. You know damn well you ain't got nothing on me." I threw one of Mackenzie's Barbie dolls at Stephon and he ducked. Mackenzie even tried to help, but she aimed at my expensive lamps and damn near broke one.

"Thanks, Mackenzie. Why don't you go upstairs and try to wake up Mommy," I said, taking her off my lap.

"Okay, but will you still play with my dolls when your cousin leaves?" I looked at Stephon and I could tell he was cracking up inside.

"Sure, Mackenzie. I'll play with your dolls." She ran out of the office, excited about my answer.

"Man, I thought I would never see the day when you played with dolls. I knew you had a thing for them when you were lit- ut ain't you a tad too old for that shit?"

ah, right. Don't be over here talking that bullshit. You mn well I don't like playing with dolls. I'm just trying little girl happy."

ooks of things, you seem to be doing a pretty good She's crazy about you already. But what's up with lking and Uncle Jaylin stuff?"

ar-old, she speaks very well. And the Uncle ed her not to call me that. I told her to call vant her thinking we're family. She's the dding the uncle. It bothers me a bit, but to call me by my name only."

eally changed. I haven't figured out if you're doing for that little girl, but I

m too, but so far,

ceful.

going to take Mackenzie and you'll be right back where you started. Personally, I think it's a bad idea that you're getting so attached to her."

"Who says Scorpio and I aren't going to work out? Man, believe it or not, that's a good woman up there. I mean, she might not have all the glamorous material shit like the other women I've messed with, but her personality counts for everything."

"So, honestly—and I mean honestly, Jay—are you falling in love with this woman?"

I hesitated to respond and got up and shut the door. Then I sat on the edge of my desk and looked Stephon directly i eyes.

"Honestly, my brotha, I can't say that I am. I mean, I shit out of her, but I . . . I don't understand why I ca woman like I should. You of all people know I had of love for Nokea, but lately, I'm not sure what it

"So, what about Nokea? Are you ever going to things out with her?"

"Nope, not right now. I'm going to play t and see where it leads me. If things don' sweat it. Maybe I'll see if she's availab needed a break anyway. I need this time or what I really need in my life. And going wherever my heart and my di that's with Scorpio."

"If you say so with N

going to take Mackenzie and you'll be right back where you started. Personally, I think it's a bad idea that you're getting so attached to her."

"Who says Scorpio and I aren't going to work out? Man, believe it or not, that's a good woman up there. I mean, she might not have all the glamorous material shit like the other women I've messed with, but her personality counts for everything."

"So, honestly—and I mean honestly, Jay—are you falling in love with this woman?"

I hesitated to respond and got up and shut the door. Then I sat on the edge of my desk and looked Stephon directly in his eyes.

"Honestly, my brotha, I can't say that I am. I mean, dig the shit out of her, but I . . . I don't understand why I can't love a woman like I should. You of all people know I had some type of love for Nokea, but lately, I'm not sure what it was."

"So, what about Nokea? Are you ever going to try and work things out with her?"

"Nope, not right now. I'm going to play this out for a while and see where it leads me. If things don't work out, I won't sweat it. Maybe I'll see if she's available then. I think we needed a break anyway. I need this time away to figure out who or what I really need in my life. And in the meantime, I'm going wherever my heart and my dick lead me. Right now, that's with Scorpio."

"If you say so. I really wish you'd reconsider your position with Nokea, but whatever you decide to do, you know I support you all the way."

"Thanks. You know I appreciate it. It's good to know I at least got some kind of family who supports me in my decisions."

*　*　*

zie even tried to help, but she aimed at my expensive lamps and damn near broke one.

"Thanks, Mackenzie. Why don't you go upstairs and try to wake up Mommy," I said, taking her off my lap.

"Okay, but will you still play with my dolls when your cousin leaves?" I looked at Stephon and I could tell he was cracking up inside.

"Sure, Mackenzie. I'll play with your dolls." She ran out of the office, excited about my answer.

"Man, I thought I would never see the day when you played with dolls. I knew you had a thing for them when you were little, ut ain't you a tad too old for that shit?"

"Yah, right. Don't be over here talking that bullshit. You know amn well I don't like playing with dolls. I'm just trying to make little girl happy."

"By the ooks of things, you seem to be doing a pretty good job at that. She's crazy about you already. But what's up with the proper talking and Uncle Jaylin stuff?"

"For a five-year-old, she speaks very well. And the Uncle Jaylin thing, I ased her not to call me that. I told her to call me Jaylin. I don't vant her thinking we're family. She's the one who insists on alding the uncle. It bothers me a bit, but eventually she'll learn to call me by my name only."

"You know, you've eally changed. I haven't figured out if it's good or bad. I dig what you're doing for that little girl, but I think you're rushing things a bit."

"I know you do. And sometimes I think I am too, but so far, I have no regrets. My house ain't been nothing but peaceful. The things Mackenzie says and does remind me of my little girl. Remind me how much I could kick Simone's ass for taking her away from me. So, if she can fill that void for right now, I'm okay with it."

"What if things don't work out with you and Scorpio? She's

Scorpio woke up and cooked Stephon and me some hamburgers and fries. She had my kitchen in a mess, but she was learning slowly but surely how to be a better housekeeper. She and Stephon got along well. She laughed when he told her about a few good times that we had growing up. Everything from the ass-whippings he gave me to the girls we tried to sneak in the basement. I was embarrassed. And since Stephon exaggerated some shit, he made the stories sound even more dramatic than what they really were.

When Stephon was ready to go, he pulled me aside in the bonus room where we had just finished up a game of pool. Scorpio was in the kitchen washing dishes, while Mackenzie helped her.

"Man, you know what I said to you earlier about how I didn't know if this was a good thing or a bad thing?" he said.

"Yeah, I remember. Why?"

"Let me just say that I like this change in you. Scorpio's a lot better than I thought she was, and if that little girl can bring joy to you like she has, then it's got to be all good. There is one thing I want you to do for me, though."

"What's that?"

Stephon had a serious look on his face. "Go see Nokea. Just tell her how happy you are and why. I think she deserves to know a little more than what you told her the other day—and let her know, just maybe, there's still a chance for you and her."

I wasn't sure why he seemed so concerned about my relationship with Nokea, though I knew he always had both of our best interests at heart. This time, though, I couldn't live up to his request.

"I'm sorry, my brotha, I can't do that. I already told Nokea what was up, and I'm afraid if I go see her, I'm going to wind up sleeping with her like I did Felicia when I tried to end it. Right now, I'm leaving well enough alone."

"Not even for me?"

"Not this time, not even for you. You know better than any-body when I stand my ground, it's hard to make me change my mind."

"All right," he said, giving me a hard handshake. "I'm going to let you get back to your beautiful woman and her daughter. I've taken up enough of y'all time today already."

I walked Stephon to the door, and then went into the kitchen to check on my sweet ladies. Mackenzie had water all over the floor and was trying to mop it up. Scorpio was wiping down the counter with a wet rag and didn't hear me come into the kitchen. I picked up a jug of cold water that was on the table and whispered for Mackenzie to be quiet. She smiled be-cause she knew I was getting ready to pour the water on Scor-pio.

"Mommy!" she yelled. "Watch out!"

Scorpio turned around so fast that she knocked the jug out of my hand and the water splashed on me.

"See, that's what you get for playing so much," she said as she and Mackenzie laughed. "Now, go upstairs and take off those wet clothes."

I held her waist and kissed her. "Only if you come and help me out of them. After all, you're the one who wet me up."

Scorpio looked down at Mackenzie still trying to mop up the water on the floor.

"Now, you know she's not going to let us be alone," she whispered. "Since I was so tired last night, I'll make it up to you later."

"You, tired? When did you start getting tired?"

"Ever since you've been making love to me two and three times a day. You know a sista gotta have some down time, Jaylin."

"I guess I'll let it slide this time, but only this time, beauti-ful. As a matter of fact, why don't you slide some clean clothes on you and Mackenzie so we can go shopping? I saw this cute little pink toy car for her to drive. It was in the paper today and I want to go get it."

"Really? Her mother needs a cute little car too, you know," she said, running her fingers through my hair.

"I know. So, like I said, why don't you go change clothes and maybe I can help you out in that department too." I hit Scorpio on the ass and then she and Mackenzie left the kitchen.

No woman of mine should be driving around in an old beat-up car, and I wanted my lady to have the best. Besides, her jacked-up car didn't look good in my driveway, and the appearance was a no-no in my neighborhood.

I cleaned up the kitchen to my satisfaction and went upstairs to get out of my wet clothes.

By ten o'clock that night, Mackenzie had her pink 4X4 Jeep wagon and Scorpio's old car was hauled away by J's Towing Service to make room for her new convertible red Corvette. She was in tears most of the night. And Mackenzie was right in bed with us as we watched TV and talked.

"Jaylin, I don't know what I would do without you. Why are you so good to me?"

"Scorpio, I ain't no stingy brotha. I take care of those who take care of me. You and Mackenzie do a damn good job of that, so like I said, when you take care of Jaylin, Jaylin takes care of you. It's as simple as that."

"But this is too much. First the cruise, then the dresses, and then the watch. The watch must have cost you a fortune. Now, a car? And not just any old car—an expensive car. I don't know how I'm ever going to be able to repay you."

"Woman, please. You don't have to repay me anything. All you have to do is keep making me happy, that's all. Now, it doesn't get any easier than that."

"I'd like to buy you some nice things too, but how do I compete? The only time I make decent money is when I get a call from Jackson. He looks over my scripts, and if he likes them, he pays me. If he doesn't, then I don't get a dime. I love to write, but it's not getting me the money I need to buy nice things for us. I don't want this relationship to be all on you.

"Maybe I need to give up writing and go back to school to study business. I've been thinking about it for a long time, and since you've hired a nanny to take care of Mackenzie, this might be the perfect opportunity for me."

"Sounds like a plan to me, Scorpio. An education never hurt anybody. If you're sure that's what you want to do, I'll even front you the money."

"I'm sure, but you don't have to pay for it. I will. Not that I don't appreciate the offer, but I want to do this on my own."

I truly felt as if Scorpio was sincere. She wasn't coming off as a gold digger. I did question how she intended to get the money, since she didn't have a full-time job.

"Jackson pays me pretty good money for my scripts. I'll use that money to pay for school."

"All right, Miss Lady. I'm not going to force you to take me up on my offer, but if there's anything I can do, let me know."

Mackenzie had fallen asleep in my bed. I picked her up and carried her into her bedroom. Just when I got ready to close the door, she stopped me.

"Uncle Jaylin, are you and Mommy going to get married?" I smiled and walked back into the room.

"It's Jaylin, Mackenzie, not Uncle Jaylin. And no, right now we're not. If we do, you'll be the first one to know. Okay?" I tucked her into bed.

"Would you read me a bedtime story?" Her eyes searched the room for a book.

I opened the closet and pulled out Cinderella. I sat on the bed next to her and started to read. I tried to hurry so I could go make love to Scorpio, but Mackenzie held me up, asking questions as I tried to finish the book. After I read it four times, she was finally sound asleep.

When I got back into the bedroom, Scorpio was already in the tub waiting patiently for me. I slid in behind her, but the water was slightly cold.

"I'll warm you up, so don't worry about how cold it is," she said, pecking my lips.

"Then stop talking and start warming."

"Jaylin, I . . . I love you," she whispered in my ear as I rubbed her silky smooth body.

"And you know how I feel."

22

FELICIA

I thought Paul was all I needed to get my mind off Jaylin, but when he tried to make love to me the other night, I didn't feel a thing inside of me. I was so disappointed, but after how kind he'd been to me, I couldn't find it in my heart to dismiss him.

He was constantly all over a sista at work and at home. Once I told him we had to cut the chatting at work, he backed off a little. I didn't mind him coming over to my house to see me, but when he showed up without calling, I had to bring it to his attention.

Damion was still coming over from time to time and I didn't want the two of them meeting up at once. It was okay for a brotha to get caught in his game, but a sista—we had to play it cool, pretend like we were only with one brotha at a time, knowing damn well some of us be knocking two or three behind closed doors.

I had learned a lot from Jaylin. Like him, I had specific days I asked Paul to come over and specific days I asked Damion to come over. Everything was right on schedule. I had Damion over when I needed some good loving, and Paul over when I needed a good friend to chill with.

The only problem was that Paul was falling in love with me. During dinner last night at the Macaroni Grill, it was his second time telling me since we'd met. I know I put it on him the other night, but this love shit was too soon for me.

Hell, I still hadn't gotten over Jaylin. I knew it would be a matter of time before he came back to me, but the question was when? I called his house a few times, but when his bitch answered, I hung up on her. She had to be living with him, because every time I called, she answered.

When I called him at work, Angela made up excuses for him, Saying he had just gone to lunch or he was in a meeting. I wanted to pay him another visit on his job, but I decided to just sit back and let this mess play itself out. Anyway, it wasn't like I didn't have two other men occupying my time.

I even thought about Nokea. The other day, I saw her at the Quik Trip pumping gas on New Halls Ferry Road. She looked a mess. Looked like she had put on a few pounds and her clothes didn't even match. I really felt bad for her. If she'd had another man on the side, she might not be in the situation she's in now. I know she didn't expect Jaylin to settle down and marry her. Then again, shit . . . I thought some day he would marry me.

Either way, I wasn't writing him off just yet. Whenever he was able to be alone with me and not make love to me, then I'd write him off completely. Until then, the door was always open.

Paul picked me up at 7:00 p.m. so we could go to the movies. His dark brown hair was slicked back and he had on some loose-fitting Levi's with a black button-down shirt. His dark tan almost had him looking like a brotha. His black shades covered his pretty green eyes.

He opened the door to his SLK 230 Mercedes Benz and I

felt like royalty riding with him. At every stop, people checked us out. I didn't know if they noticed us because we looked good together or because he was white and I was black. And when we got to the movie theater, the stares continued.

Paul always liked to hold hands and kiss in public, but I was uncomfortable with everybody checking us out. I loosened my fingers from his hand and pretended I had to sneeze. When nothing came out, I dropped my hand by my side.

As we stood in line waiting to get some popcorn, Paul looked at me.

"Felicia, why are you so uncomfortable with me?"

"I'm not uncomfortable with you; I'm just uncomfortable with all these people looking at us like they ain't never seen a mixed couple before."

"All you have to do is pretend they're not there. Just focus on me. If you do, you won't even know they exist."

"So, really, why don't all the stares bother you? One thing about black folks, we can't stand to be stared down. It's harder for me to ignore them than it is for you."

"No, it's not. I refuse to give them the attention they want. Besides, I'm here with a beautiful woman, and if I'm happy, who cares what other people think?"

I smiled because I knew Paul was right. I even reached over and gave him a kiss. Some girls behind us in line looked at each other and rolled their eyes. Paul saw it, and then he embarrassed the hell out of me.

"Excuse me, everyone," he said, with an English accent. "As you can see, I'm white and my stunning woman here is black. We've been noticing all the frightful stares we've been getting and would like to say thank you. You've made us feel like celebrities. So, my name is Paul and this is Felicia. We just got married yesterday, so would you all be so kind and give the gorgeous bride a big round of applause?"

Paul clapped and so did everybody else. When he kissed me,

the applause got louder. I couldn't believe how he embarrassed us, but it was quite funny. As we walked through the theater to our seats, some people smiled and told us congrats. Even though it was a stupid thing to do, it worked. I felt more at ease with him, and the stares had turned into smiles.

During the movie, I gripped Paul's muscles every time a scary moment came on the screen. He laughed but held me tightly in his arms.

"Felicia, are you really that scared? If so, we can watch something else."

"No, Paul, this is cool," I said, chewing on some gummy bears. "If you don't mind, I just like snuggling up with you."

"Of course I don't mind. Whatever you want, my dear." He held me tighter.

After the movie, we headed back to my place. The first thing I did was check my messages to see if Jaylin had called. He hadn't, so I went into the living room and entertained Paul. When it came to sex, if he was a bit more aggressive, maybe I would like him more. I always had to be the one to initiate it. It was like he was scared to touch me.

But when I changed into my black teddy and straddled his lap, he couldn't keep his hands off me. He laid me back on the couch and laid my coochie out with his tongue. Now, in my opinion, this was one thing white men sure knew how to do better than black men. For the first time, Jaylin had nothing on him. I could barely keep still. Damn near broke his neck as I squeezed it tightly with my thighs.

Once he finished, he slid himself inside me and the excitement faded. Damn, I thought, why couldn't he just keep licking? I moaned and groaned like it was the best thing ever.

When he left, I called Damion over to finish the job. In the meantime, I'd have to work on Paul until he got better. Eventually, I hoped, he would, but only time would tell.

23

NOKEA

I ate everything in the house, from the rooter to the tooter. I had been pigging out even when I wasn't hungry. The stress from not talking to Jaylin added to my bad eating habits. I was only a few months pregnant and already had picked up fourteen pounds. Dr. Beckwith said if I didn't slow down, I was headed for a difficult pregnancy.

When I left his office, I stopped by Burger King on West Florissant Avenue to get my last taste of a double Whopper with extra cheese and some French fries. Then I had the nerve to stop at Krispy Kreme and get three glazed donuts. By the time I got to the office, I felt like a pig. I had to struggle just to make it up the stairs. I went to the bathroom and looked at myself in the mirror. I could still see my curves, but if I kept at it, I knew they would soon disappear. I decided to take my doctor's advice and cut back on the fattening foods. From now on, it would be just salads and Jell-O. If I splurged, it would only be on the weekend, or if I felt like going out to dinner with Pat and her husband.

She was a charm. Since she was the closest friend I had, I confided in her a lot. She even started to pick up weight with me, forever bringing me ice cream and a bunch of other fattening foods. Every Saturday she took time away from Chad to come by my place and keep me company. She knew I missed Jaylin and tried to do everything in her power to make me forget him. But no matter how hard she and I both tried, he could never leave my memory. We had too much history together, and since we had a baby on the way, it would be even more difficult to get him out of my system.

On Saturday, Pat was right on time with some salads she made and movies she brought from Blockbuster. She rented *The Best Man* and *Training Day*, movies we had seen time and time again. She knew that Morris Chestnut and Denzel Washington were definitely a way to snap me out of my misery. We sat in my den mesmerized by the fineness in both of them and munched on our salads.

"Girl, I'm so hungry that I'm going to imagine this is the hamburger and fries I ate earlier this week," I said, picking all the meat out of the salad first.

"Nokea! I thought you said you weren't going to eat any more fast food."

"That was after I stopped at Burger King. Since then, I've been doing pretty good. And since it's Saturday, and I can splurge on the weekend, can we please order a pizza with everything on it?"

"No, Nokea. You know you need to eat a little healthier. If not for you, then for the baby."

"I didn't think it would be this hard for me to watch my weight, but this salad stuff is driving me crazy."

"Look, if you want to order a pizza, you go right ahead," Pat said, chewing slowly and picking at the salad like she really wanted me to order a pizza.

I reached over to the coffee table, picked up the phone, and ordered a supreme pizza with extra mushrooms and olives from Pizza Hut.

"Okay, don't blame me when your ass gets all fat. Then I'm going to have to listen to you gripe about that. In the meantime, what I don't understand is . . . why didn't you tell them to put extra cheese on the damn thing? Girl, call them back and tell them to add more cheese," she said.

We laughed as I picked up the phone and called Pizza Hut back. The man gave me a new total and I hung up.

"I'm sorry, but that salad was just not cutting it. And I made it. Shame on me for bringing that bullshit over here," Pat said.

"Well, at least you tried. And as hard as I tried to make it taste like a hamburger, it wouldn't."

"At least we got a good laugh out of it. I haven't seen you laugh like that in a long time. So, seriously, how have you been? And don't tell me what I want to hear, tell me the truth," Pat said, putting *Training Day* on pause.

"It's been tough, Pat. Really tough. Sometimes I want to pick up the phone and curse Jaylin out for doing this to me. And other times, I thank God he's out of my life. Then there's a part of me that thinks this is some day going to work itself out. How? I don't know, but I really wish that it would. I cry myself to sleep almost every night, torturing myself over seeing him with Scorpio. Wondering why it couldn't be me living there with him. With our son.

"He seemed so excited about her little girl, and I don't even know if he's going to be excited about his baby when he finds out—"

"What do you mean when he finds out? Are you planning on telling him?"

"No, but what if he does find out? I can't keep this from him forever. It would be impossible."

"Look, Nokea, nothing's impossible. You tried to tell him

and he didn't want to hear it. So, fuck him. Raise this child by yourself. You never know; somebody decent might come along and be a good father to him. He doesn't need a father like Jaylin setting bad examples for him, especially when it comes to how to treat women."

"You're talking like you know it's a boy too. I hope it is. And I hope he looks just like Jaylin. If I can't love the big one like I want to, then the little one will just have to do," I said, rubbing my belly.

"You are out of your mind. All I can say is go with your heart. It'll take you places no one else can."

'But my heart is with Jaylin, Pat."

'For now it might be, but you'll find somewhere else to place it. Just give it time." She took the movie off pause. "Who knows? Maybe somebody like Denzel Washington will come your way. And if he does, will you be so kind to a friend and share him with me?"

We laughed. "Now, I'll share Jaylin, but Denzel, or any man like him, I will not. Denzel is the kind of man you want to keep all to yourself."

"Okay, fine, keep Denzel. But when I show up at your door next week with Morris Chestnut, don't be mad at me."

"Only in your dreams, Pat. Only in your dreams."

The Pizza Hut driver came and we ate the pizza so fast that we ordered another one. When he came back, he laughed because I had pizza sauce all over my white T-shirt from the first one. Pat only had two slices of the second pizza, and I nearly ate five slices all by myself. I hated the thick edges, so when I pulled them off, it actually only accounted for four slices. No matter how many it actually was, I paid for it, and so did Pat. We lay on the floor in the den with cold rags on our bellies to cool them.

' You are a mess. Look at you, Nokea. I told you this was a bad idea." Pat rolled over on her side.

"No, you didn't, Pat. You told me to call them back and add more cheese. And in case you forgot, you were the one who suggested a second pizza."

"Damn, I was, wasn't I? And I have to drive home and face Chad looking like a big fat pig. You know, he's noticed this sudden weight gain I've had since you've been pregnant. He told me if I gained one more pound, he would leave me."

"Girl, please. That man loves you. I don't care how fat you get, he isn't going anywhere."

"I know, but girl, we've got to slow down. We got six more months to go and if we're eating like this now, we gon' be some fat chicks by the time you deliver."

"Okay, starting Monday. No more of this pigging out after Monday. I promise."

After *Training Day* was over, Pat helped me clean up the den and headed home. She called Chad to tell him she was on her way and gave me a sista-hug before she left. I didn't know what I would do without her in my life. Mama and Daddy tried to be there for me, but I couldn't talk to them about everything like I could Pat—even though she would never be accepting of Jaylin the way I'd wanted her to be.

I went to the kitchen and poured a soothing cup of the hot Chinese tea Mama had given me to relax. It didn't have any caffeine, so I had no problem going to sleep.

The phone woke me at one o'clock in the morning. When I heard Stephon's voice on the other end, it scared me.

"Stephon, is everything okay?" I asked, holding my chest.

"No. Not really. I just wanted to call and let you know that my mother passed away last night. You know she's been battling this drug addiction for years, and last night . . . she, uh . . . she decided to take her life."

I could hear the pain in his voice.

"Stephon, I'm so sorry. If there's anything I can do, please let me know. I know how you felt about your mother doing drugs, but at least you had the courage to make peace with her years ago. God will bless you for that, and you'll be able to go on knowing that you did all you could for her."

Stephon was quiet. "Yeah, but I guess it wasn't good enough. She called me last week and asked for some money, but I wouldn't give it to her. I knew what she wanted it for, but . . . but now I feel bad because I didn't give it to her."

"How could you feel bad about not contributing to her habit? Look at all the good things you did for her. Out of all her children, you were the one who stood by her. Please don't go dumping on yourself because you did the best you could."

He let out a deep sigh. "I'll call you in a couple of days and let you know about the arrangements. Sorry to call you so late. Go back to sleep, Shorty, and get some rest."

"Stephon, before you go . . . how's Jaylin taking the news? I mean, I know he's probably thinking about his mother at a time like this."

"He's doing okay. I think he's more hurt because I am. He never really cared too much for Mama anyway, but I think it bothers him knowing he wasn't there for her either."

"All right, Stephon. Thanks for calling, and call me as soon as you find out the arrangements."

I couldn't sleep a lick as I thought about Stephon's mother. The memory of her leaving them at home alone, night after night when they were kids, kept coming to mind. Several times, my mother even stepped in and fed them when Stephon's mother was out on one of her drug binges. And Jaylin, she treated him like crap. One time, one of her boyfriends badly beat him with an extension cord and he came to school with whip marks all over him. Some kids made fun of him, but I was always by his side. I couldn't blame him for not being hurt about her death, but I knew he would always be there when it came to Stephon. And so would I.

24

JAYLIN

The funeral was torture. I sat in the front pew with Stephon and his brothers, who I didn't get along with. We wore black suits and dark black shades. My glasses helped to hide the tears as I found myself thinking about Mama when she left me years ago to take her place in heaven.

Stephon took it the hardest. When he fell to his knees in front of his mother's casket, I damn near lost it myself. I walked up and put my arms around him. He grabbed my leg and asked the Lord, why? Why did He have to take her?

My other cousins sat there with a few tears here and there, but that was it. I wanted to kick all of them straight in the ass. One of the assholes was a crackhead his damn self and had the nerve to sit there like his shit didn't stink. And the other two were broke as hell, didn't have nothing going on but thug-ass women and a street corner. Basically, didn't have a pot to piss in or a window to throw it out of. Stephon was the only decent one. They couldn't stand either one of us because we didn't turn out like they did.

Stephon's girlfriend and I helped him back to his seat.

When I got back to mine, Scorpio was right there, waiting to comfort me. She held my hand and rubbed my back. I held back the tears because I definitely didn't want my woman to see me cry. I didn't care how bad things got.

When the funeral was over, there was a dinner in the lower level of the church, in remembrance of Aunt Betty. Stephon sat in a chair in the corner all by himself. It was obvious that he didn't want to be bothered. When I looked up, I saw Nokea talking to him. She looked beautiful in a knee-length, sky blue dress and some sexy high-heeled shoes. Her eyebrows were perfectly arched and her short hair had been freshly cut. She even looked as if she'd thickened up a bit. She wore the extra weight well, especially in the breast area.

Before my mind went into the gutter, I had to think about where I was. I couldn't be in church thinking about sexing up women, could I? But with all the fine women running around, it was hard not to. Since Scorpio watched my every move, I backed off. Especially on this nice li'l tender who mugged me from far across the room. She stared me down like she wanted to break a brotha down right then and there; however, now wasn't the time or the place.

After we chowed down, I walked to the water fountain and got a drink. When I lifted my head, I saw Nokea standing close by, waiting for me. Since I saw Scorpio looking at me I kept on walking like I didn't even see Nokea.

She grabbed my arm. "Listen, I'm not trying to come between you and your woman, but I wanted to tell you how sorry I am about your aunt. I know this has probably been a difficult time for you, and I wanted to tell you if you need anything, call me." She handed me a piece of paper.

"Thanks." I leaned forward to give her a hug just so I could feel her in my arms again. "I appreciate it. And . . . and take care."

I went back over to the table and sat next to Scorpio. She

smiled and encouraged me to go talk to Stephon because he seemed like he was out of it. I tried to give him some space because men don't like all that attention when they're feeling down. We like to get our thoughts together and deal with it whenever. But since Scorpio pressed the issue, I went over and pulled up a chair next to him.

"Man, are you going to be okay? I know it hurts; I've been there before. But it gets easier, my brotha. In due time, it gets easier," I said.

"I know, man, but why did she have to kill herself? If she was going to do that, she should've done it years ago. Just don't make sense. And then to make us suffer because she didn't want to anymore."

"Those suffering days were over a long time ago. For us anyway. Now, Aunt Betty had a choice. She could've cleaned up her act, and you gave her the opportunity to do so. I know when you asked me for that fifteen grand you gave it to her. I know every time that you borrowed from me you put it right into her hand. All I'm saying is you can't feel responsible for something she done to herself. And if you do, then that's too bad. But she knew out of everybody, you were the one who took care of her."

There was silence. Stephon closed his eyes and swallowed.

"Jay, I don't know what I'd do without you. After the way Mama abused you when you were growing up, you knew the money was for her all along, didn't you?"

"Yeah, but I also knew if I didn't give it to you, I'd lose the only family I had. I wasn't willing to lose you."

"Naw, you knew if you didn't give it to me, I would kick your ass like I did when we were little," he said, laughing.

"Whatever, nigga. I held back because I didn't want your brothers jumping in it, trying to help you kick my ass. But now I wish I would've fucked all y'all up." We both laughed again. Just to get one smile out of him made me feel good.

I looked over at Scorpio and blew her a kiss—only to see Nokea reach out her hand and catch it. I smiled and went back to conversing with Stephon.

"Say, man. Did you see Nokea? She's looking good, my brotha. Looking damn good," Stephon said, sounding like he wanted to hit that.

"She looks a'ight. I mean, if you ask me, she look like she's picked up some weight," I said, though there was no doubt in my mind that Nokea locked spectacular.

"Weight is good, bro, especially if you're wearing it like she is."

"So, what are you trying to say? You trying to get a piece of that action?"

"Naw, I'm just telling you like I see it. That woman got it going on. She's pretty, she's smart, got a good job, a good heart— she's the full package. Right about now, she'd give Scorpio a serious run for her money."

"Negro, please. She might be the full package, but when it comes to looks, Nokea don't even compare to Scorpio. They both fine, but Scorpio gets a ten-plus in my book. Nokea only gets a nine. With the exception of today; today I'll give her a ten."

"Well, I have that reversed. You're only thinking about the pu-tain but I'm strictly talking about appearance. And appearance-wise, Nokea looks much better than Scorpio."

"You are out of your mind! Look at them. Take a look at both of them now and tell me Nokea looks better than Scorpio."

We checked out both women. Stephon hesitated for a moment.

"All right. You got me convinced, but Nokea is still the bomb."

"Like I said, she's workable, but she ain't got my baby beat. Besides, why you riding Nokea so tough? Are you finding yourself a bit attracted to her?"

Stephon licked his lips and gave me a stern look.

"If I was, would you be mad?"

It didn't take me long to think about it. I gave him the most serious look he'd probably ever seen on my face.

"Man, we like brothers, but that's one woman we'll never share."

"So, are you saying she's only hands-off when it comes to me? Or to anybody?"

"All I'm saying is that's one woman we'll never share." My palms started to sweat. I could tell where this conversation was headed.

"But she deserves to have a good man in her life, don't she?"

"I'm saying that man won't be you, so let's drop it."

Stephon hopped up and grabbed my hand. We gave each other a pat on the back.

For the rest of the evening, I felt a tension between us— tension I had never felt before. When Nokea said goodbye to everyone, Stephon got up and offered to walk her to her car. Deep down, my insides burned, but I managed not to let it show.

Scorpio said she was ready to go, so I told her to wait in front of the church while I went to get the car. Outside, I noticed Stephon in the car, talking to Nokea. Looked like they were in a deep conversation, but once again, I kept my cool. When they saw me, Stephon got out and waved goodbye to her, then walked toward me.

"Man, what you looking all uptight for? I was just thanking her for coming," he said.

"Hey, that's cool. I ain't tripping. If you want my leftovers, that's all on you," I said, getting into Scorpio's Corvette.

I drove off, and then saw that sweet li'l tender that had her eyes on me all day. She flagged me down and I stopped the car.

"Hey, sexy. Can a sista get your phone number to call you

sometime?" she asked. I looked at her shiny, thick thighs that begged me to open them.

"Let me get yours and I'll call you when I get time."

She wrote down her number as I watched for Scorpio. I quickly took her number, put it in my pocket, and then drove around the corner to pick up Scorpio. I didn't know if I would ever call the girl, but it was always good to keep my options open in case things changed between me and Scorpio.

25

JAYLIN

The stock market was a serious blood bath. Everybody was calling like crazy trying to sell out. I'd even sold a few of my own stocks since they'd done so badly. If anything, losing money wasn't the name of my game.

A little after noon, Mr. Schmidt stepped in my office to talk. I thought it was about how badly the market was doing, but when he talked about my performance, he quickly got my attention.

"Jaylin, you're still my number-one producer, but lately you haven't been as dedicated to this company as you were before. And since you haven't, I've been losing money. If we could bring in some more business, it would make up for some of the losses when the market drops like it has today. So, I'm bringing in Roy to help you. I want you to train him to be like you, and then we can go from there."

"What!" I said angrily. "Train him to be like me? Mr. Schmidt, there's nobody on this planet like me. And there never will be. I don't care how well I train him, he's not going to be as productive as I am and you know it." It seriously sounded like this sucker was trying to replace me.

"You're right, Jaylin. That's why I need a second man. When you don't feel like giving one hundred percent of yourself, he can step in and fill the gap. Trust me; it'll all work out for the best. You'll see."

"Look, Mr. Schmidt, you're running the show around here. And whatever you say goes, so let's roll with it. But I hope you understand, if the situation gets sticky, I'm packing up and going elsewhere. Remember, I really don't have to be here," I said as matter-of-factly.

"I understand that, Jaylin, but at least give it a try. Will you do that for me?"

"It's whatever, Schmidt. Again, let's just roll with it."

For the rest of the day, I was in a shitty mood. I asked Angela to hold all my personal calls so I could finally get some things done. Besides, Roy watched my every move. He listened in on my conversations with my clients and followed me around, trying to learn "how to be like me."

I took a break and went downstairs to Barb's Coffee Shop to get a cherry Danish. Something about eating the filling out of the middle excited me. Roy came with me and tried to make conversation, but when I found myself thinking about how good Nokea looked at the funeral, I ignored him. I thought about calling to take her up on the offer she made: *if you need anything, call me.* But I didn't want to start complicating shit between Scorpio and me.

I was proud of myself for being with only one woman, and as much as I'd been thinking about Nokea, I knew I'd made the right decision. The only problem I had lately was that things between me and Scorpio had been a little less perfect than they were in the beginning.

Many nights, by the time she got home, Mackenzie and I

would already be asleep. Sometimes I was so tired, I didn't even hear her come in. If I rolled over and tried to get some sex, sometimes she would and sometimes she wouldn't.

Mackenzie kept me busy, though. She had me running around the house like a slave: "Jaylin, cook me this, read me this, write me this, comb my doll's hair, and play hide-and-go-seek with me." I did everything for her and I wasn't even her daddy! I had no clue where her biological father was, but he was a fool for not being a part of her life. Not only was she a beautiful little girl, but she was smart and funny as hell. The best thing about her was that she filled the void in me from when my own daughter was taken away from me.

As I sat in the coffee shop thinking about Mackenzie, I took my cell phone out and called to check on her. When Mackenzie answered, I pretended to be somebody else.

"Jaylin, I know it's you. When are you coming home?"

"Mackenzie, I'm going to be late tonight. It's kind of busy today, so I'll see you when I get home."

"Well, what if I fall asleep? When you come home, will you wake me up and read a story to me?"

"Yes, I will. And I have a surprise for you too."

"What! What! Tell me what it is."

"Now, it wouldn't be no surprise if I told you, would it?"

"No, so I'll see you later. Nanny B wants to talk to you."

Mackenzie put the nanny on the phone, and I told her I would be late, but she could leave if Scorpio came home. She was cool because we paid her a fortune to watch Mackenzie, and I kicked her out extra because she kept the place spotless, since it had gotten to be such a mess when Scorpio moved in.

I finished my Danish and my half-ass conversation with Roy. When we got back to my office, there were a dozen yellow roses on my desk.

"These came in for you while you were out," Angela said, standing with her hands on her hips. "So, who are they from?"

"None of your business, Miss Secretary. Roy you have to excuse my secretary; she tries to be my mother sometimes." I had to clear things up because Angela was tripping like we still had something going on. And since Roy was tight with her husband, I'd have to really watch it.

I opened the card. It read: *I know you thought these were from one of your lil' breezies, but I just wanted to say I'm sorry for reacting the way I did at the funeral. Love always, your only true brotha, Stephon.*

I chuckled. I figured Stephon had sent the flowers as a joke. Angela rolled her eyes and walked out the door. I wanted to call Stephon to thank him for trying to clear up our differences, but I didn't want Boy Roy all up in my business, so I decided to wait until later.

Roy and I didn't shut down until eleven o'clock. My eyelids were heavy and my bed was calling my name. Roy looked tired too. From what I could see, he seemed like a pretty cool person. Seemed to really know the business, and could possibly be what I needed to get things flowing again.

After he left, I called Stephon to thank him for the flowers. I had never gotten roses from anyone, and if I ever did, I was sure they'd come from one of my ladies. When Stephon answered the phone, he sounded like he was asleep. But when I heard a moan, I knew he was fucking.

"Damn, dog, if you were in it, why did you pick up the phone?" I said, wishing I was doing the same.

"Because I saw your number on the caller ID."

"I'll let you get back to business, but I wanted to say thanks for the bitch-ass flowers you sent today. I always knew you had a feminine side to you."

"Yeah, that feminine side of me working it right now. So, you're welcome, and I'll holla at you tomorrow." He rushed me off the phone.

"Hey, man?" I whispered.

"What?"

"That ain't Nokea over there, is it?" I said jokingly.

"I wish. Damn, I straight up wish."

He hung up on me.

I smiled, though I knew Stephon wasn't playing. We pretty much had the same taste in women, so I know if I was thinking about tagging that ass, he was too. As a matter of fact, when we were growing up, he was crazy about her. Since she always had her eyes on me, she never gave him a chance. But who was I to tell her who she could or couldn't date? I was doing my thing with Scorpio and doing it well.

I stopped at a twenty-four hour superstore and bought Mackenzie a Barbie that was bigger than her. My purpose was so she could have a friend to play and sleep with when I had to work late nights. I'd even thrown in a small CD player so they could listen to music together and Mackenzie could show her how to dance. And Scorpio, she liked books. I went through the book section and tried to find her one she didn't already have. I picked up Carl Weber's latest book and tossed it in the cart, planning to read it as well.

By the time I put the bags in the car and drove home, it was one o'clock in the morning. I didn't see Scorpio's car in the driveway, so I was a bit worried. She'd been spending a lot of time working at Jackson's place on her scripts, but her late nights were starting to bug me. According to her, either she was at her sister's house, or she was at Jackson's place. Still, one and two o'clock in the morning required me to start paying more attention.

Nanny B had fallen asleep on the couch in the bonus room while watching TV. I didn't even wake her. I went to the closet, got a blanket, and covered her. I took Mackenzie's doll and put it in my room. Since the house was freezing, I turned up the heat, and then I went to Mackenzie's room to check on her. When I opened the door, I found her sitting up in bed, crying.

I rushed in. "Mackenzie, are you okay?" I sat on the bed next to her. She continued to cry. I held her in my arms and moved her long, wavy hair away from her eyes. "Tell me, what's wrong?" I asked again.

"I didn't think you were going to be this late. I got up three times and went in your room to look for you." She hugged me back as the tears rolled over her cute little cheeks. I wiped them away.

"I'm sorry. I told you I had to work late. I promise you if I work this late again, I'll call and talk to you until I get home, okay?"

"Okay," she said, wiping her face. "Now, where's my surprise?"

"It's in my room. Come on." I took her hand.

We walked into my room. When I opened the door, she had a fit. She saw the big Barbie box, but when she looked at the doll, her smile vanished.

"What's wrong, Mackenzie? Don't you like her?"

She scratched her head and looked at me curiously. "She's too big, Jaylin. I wanted smaller ones. Lots of them."

"Oh, I see. But . . . but do you think you can give her a chance to be your friend? And if you don't like her, I'll take her back to the store in a couple of days."

"Okay." She frowned.

She didn't even play with the damn thing. For the rest of the night, it sat on the floor while she lay in bed next to me, sound asleep. I put my reading glasses on and started reading Carl Weber's book. I'd gotten so into it that I didn't even notice the time. When I heard the front door shut, I looked at my alarm clock on the nightstand. It was four-fifteen in the morning.

When Scorpio walked in, she looked surprised to see me up in bed. I tilted my reading glasses down and gave her a hard stare.

"So, you're reading now," she said, taking off her coat and laying it across the chaise.

"Hang it up!" I yelled and then calmed myself. "I mean, would you please hang it up instead of laying it there?"

"Excuse the heck out of me." She walked over to the closet to get a hanger.

"What's up with you strolling your ass in here at this time of the morning, Scorpio? You haven't called or anything. How's a brotha supposed to know where his woman at if you don't call?"

"Jaylin, you don't call me when you stay out late. Besides, I thought this was supposed to be an open relationship. You do your thing and I do mine. Right?"

"I can't recall saying all that, but if you're doing your thing with somebody else, why don't you pack your shit and go live with him?"

Her eyes shot daggers at me. "Are you putting me out?"

"No, I'm not putting you out. All I'm saying is show a brotha a little respect. Don't be strolling up in here at four in the morning like you don't owe me an explanation."

"Listen, I'm sorry. It's been a long and trying day. I had tests today in all of my classes, and from there I went straight to Jackson's place."

"Tell me more about Jackson?"

"You know, the one who reviews my scripts for me."

"Aw, that's right. So, what did he say?"

"Honestly, he said he didn't think I had what it took to be a full-time playwright. He went over my script several times and made a lot of changes to it. Finally, he gave up. Said he'd call me when he had some new ideas." She sounded disappointed.

"Sorry to hear that. Don't give up, though. Why don't you

take your work to somebody else to look at? Sort of like get a second opinion?"

"I don't know, Jaylin. I think it's time to give up on writing and focus on my education. I'm spending too much time away from Mackenzie and you. The last thing I want is to come in here every night arguing with you."

"That's the last thing I want too. And since it's our first real disagreement, let's make it our last," I said, getting out of bed. I wrapped my arms around her. "So, uh, are you tired?"

"Oh, I'm tired. But never too tired to make love to my man, especially since I've been thinking about his sexy ass all day. Let me take Mackenzie to her room, hop in the shower, and then give you this loving you've been waiting on."

"Now, you've been waiting just as much as I have."

"I concur. So, I'll hurry."

She kissed Mackenzie and carried her into her room. Then she took off her clothes and stepped into the shower.

My dick was so hard that I couldn't wait to feel her. I slid off my silk pajama pants and opened the shower door. We stood face-to-face, and I expressed once again how upset I was with her about her late nights.

"I'm sorry," she said. "It won't happen again. I never intended to upset you."

I pulled her hair back tightly and spoke with authority. "Don't make me be concerned about you again. If you're going to be late, you need to call and state your exact reason why. Better yet, coming in here after midnight might bring about confusion. Try your best to avoid it."

Scorpio nodded.

I grabbed her wet body from the shower and we made our way to the floor. I massaged her soaking wet breasts and held them together as I licked her nipples one by one. Then I positioned my curled tongue inside her pussy and rubbed her clitoris with the tip of my finger. When she seemed ready, I took my goodness and rubbed it up against her walls. She begged me to give it to her.

"Jaylin!" she said, grabbing my hand. "Stop teasing me, baby. Don't make me wait when I've waited all day to feel you."

I ignored her and continued my foreplay. And when I did give it to her, I waited until her body responded then I pulled out. She squeezed her fingernails in my ass and tried to force me back in, but I wouldn't let her.

"Why are you teasing me like this tonight?" she asked

With my hands holding me up on the floor, I lay over her. My eyes stared deeply into hers. "Because I don't want you to forget how good I am to you. And if you ever think about fucking this up, you'd better correct yourself."

She moved her head from side to side. "Never. Not in a million years."

I carried her to the edge of my bed, and when she bent over on her stomach, I separated her round, juicy ass and straddled it from behind. I stroked her insides so good, I could hear major juices flowing. The sound of her pussy excited me, but she was the one who hollered my name.

"Jaylin what, baby?" I said, continuing with my strokes. "What do you want from Jaylin? Whatever you want, Jaylin got it right here for you."

"I . . . I want you to love me," she strained as I kept the fast-paced rhythm going. "I want you to fuck me all day and all night, but I want you to love me too."

It wasn't that simple, I thought. I wanted to love her, but there was something about Scorpio I just didn't trust. I couldn't love a woman I didn't trust, and I couldn't stop thinking that our relationship was based purely on sex. No doubt, she had won my dick over, but my heart still wasn't in it like I expected it to be.

As we continued our sex session, I felt her body getting

tired. I didn't care. I turned her on her back, rested one of her legs on my shoulder, and pounded her insides with nine-plus hard inches of my loving. She couldn't hang as I rubbed, licked, and teased many of her hot spots all at once. She screamed as if she'd lost her mind, and professed that she'd never been to that level before.

I didn't finish my business with Scorpio until damn near eght o'clock in the morning. She lightly kissed the ridges of my six-pack and then rolled her pretty self over and went to sleep. I knew she was probably upset with me for sexing her up all night, but when I have to wait two days for some sex, it's a fucking crime and she knows it. I was glad it was Saturday because if I had to go to work, there was no way I would've made it.

At 11:00, I woke and paid Nanny B extra for staying overnight. She offered to cook us some breakfast before she left.

After Nanny B was gone, I sat on the kitchen stool with a piece of toast and read the *St. Louis American* newspaper. There was a picture of Felicia shaking the CEO's hand at her architectural firm as he handed her an award. It was probably for fucking him, knowing her, but the article said it was for the best creative design.

I wanted to call and congratulate her, but I didn't want to start up the bullshit with her again, especially since she'd chilled out. She still called every once in a while, but I hadn't returned any of her phone calls. When I say I'm done, I'm cone—until I get ready to come back.

Scorpio slept most of the day. Mackenzie and I went back to the store and exchanged her big Barbie doll for fifteen small ones. She had the nerve to throw in outfits and shoes for each one of them. Damn dolls were dressed better than I was. I couldn't believe I spent my money on this bullshit, but seeing the smile on her face made my day.

After we left the store, we went to Wehrenberg Theaters on

Manchester and watched a kiddie movie she was dying to see. The theatre was packed, and women were all over me, telling me how adorable me and my child were. Like me, Mackenzie enjoyed the compliments, but I think she enjoyed being at the movies with me more.

On the way home, she played with two of her Barbies in the car. When I turned up the music, she yelled, "Jaylin, that's too loud. My dolls are trying to sleep."

"They don't look like they trying to sleep to me. They actually look like they getting ready to go clubbing or something."

"No, they don't go out. They go to work like you and Mommy do."

"Well, that's good. Then I'll turn off the radio so they can get some sleep."

Mackenzie laid her dolls on her lap like they were asleep.

"Jaylin?"

"Yes, Mackenzie."

"Are you really my daddy? I heard you tell those women you were, but you told me you wasn't."

"Mackenzie, I'm not your biological father. I just told them that because they were being too nosy."

"If I be nosy, would you be my daddy then?"

I laughed. "It's not nice to be nosy, Mackenzie. Being nosy can sometimes get you in trouble."

"Okay, then I won't be nosy. But will you still be my daddy?"

I didn't want to confuse her, but I knew if I told her I wouldn't, it would probably hurt her feelings. I also knew if I tried to avoid the question, she'd find another time to ask me. For a little girl, she was smart, and had smoothed me over better than anybody had done before.

"Jaylin, you didn't answer my question," she said, looking up at me with her big, light brown eyes. "Are you going to be my daddy or not? If not, I'll find me another one," she said, pouting.

"Stop pouting, Mackenzie. I'll be your daddy only if you stop pouting when you don't get your way."

She cheesed and showed her pearly white teeth. "So, I can call you Daddy now instead of Jaylin?"

"No, Mackenzie. Continue to call me Jaylin. Daddies have names too, okay?"

I was so glad when we got home. Mackenzie helped me get the bags from the car and we carried them in the house. There was a note on the kitchen table from Scorpio that said she went to Jackson's house to pick up her script and she would call later. She even left his number for me to call, if I needed to reach her. I threw the number in the trash because I wasn't the type of brotha to check up on his woman.

Mackenzie ran to her room and played with her Barbies. When I heard the loud music from her CD player I went to her room to tell her to turn it down. I stood in the doorway and watched her dance like she was damn near twenty years old, twisting and turning her body like she was putting on a show.

"Mackenzie!" I yelled. "What are you doing? Little girls aren't supposed to dance like that. Who taught you how to dance like that?"

"My mommy. She dances like this all the time. She makes a lot of money when she dances like this," she said doing another one of her mother's moves.

I picked up Mackenzie and took her into my room. I sat her on the bed and put one of her Barbie dolls in her lap to keep her busy. Then I ran downstairs and searched the trashcan for Jackson's number. When I called, no one answered the phone just rang and rang. I tried three more times, only to get the same thing. *No, this bitch ain't a stripper,* I kept thinking. She couldn't be.

I jogged back up the stairs and went straight into my closet. Most of her clothes were neatly lined up on one side. I went through her clothes piece by piece, until I came to a gray garment bag that looked thick and full. It was in the far back of the closet, hidden away from all the rest of her clothes. I laid it on the bed next to Mackenzie and unzipped it. The evidence hit me right in the face: all kinds of slutty outfits, leather and lace two-piece sets, belts and whips. There were even a few pictures of her with next to nothing on. I guess she gave them to her fans, because her signature was on the bottom.

I crumbled the photo in my hand. The only thing I could think about was packing up her shit and kicking her ass out. But when I looked at Mackenzie, I didn't know what to do. I put Scorpio's belongings back in the garment bag and back into the closet.

As I searched for more evidence in the closet, the phone rang. Mackenzie answered and talked, so I knew it was Scorpio. When Mackenzie gave me the phone, I took a deep breath.

"Hey, baby, you miss me?" she asked, like shit was all good.

"Miss you so much. I need you, right here and right now," I said, trying to show Mackenzie a little respect by not dissing her mother.

"You know, I've been thinking about that good loving you gave me last night. I hope it's on again for tonight."

"Oh, you'd better believe it's on." I wanted to snatch her ass through the phone and beat the shit out of her. "How soon can you get here so I can give you some more?"

"I was calling to tell you I'm on my way. Jackson made some changes to my script and it looks pretty good. I'll tell you all about it when I get home."

"Sure, can't wait."

I hung up.

Mackenzie stood in front of me and dropped her head. "Daddy, are you mad at me for dancing like that?"

"No, Mackenzie, I'm not. But do you think you can do me a

huge favor?" I said, lifting her chin. She nodded. "Do you think you can take a bath and go in your room and play with your dolls?"

"Yes. I need a nap anyway. Can I borrow your pillow? Yours is thicker than mine is," she said, taking the pillow off my bed and heading toward the door. "Good night, Daddy. Thanks for the dolls and the movie today. I almost forgot to thank you."

"You're welcome, Mackenzie. Anytime." She ran back over and gave me a squeezing hug. I picked her up so she could kiss my cheek. She wiped the spit off my cheek with her hand and smiled.

"Daddy?"

"Yes, Mackenzie," I said, putting her down, trying to hurry her off.

"I love you, Daddy."

I was silent. She caught me completely off guard. She looked at me and waited for a response. And for the first time in my life, I felt good about saying, "I love you too."

She strolled out of my room with two of my pillows, as if her dolls needed one too. My heart ached; if I put Scorpio out, Mackenzie would leave too. I was in a no-win situation. I had no idea what I would do. Stephon warned me about getting too attached, but in no way did I see this shit coming.

No sooner had I tucked Mackenzie into bed than Scorpio was on her way up the steps. I met her at the top of the stairs right after I closed Mackenzie's bedroom door.

"Did I hurry enough for you?" She dropped her purse on the floor, put her arms around me, and puckered up to give me a kiss. I moved my head back to avoid her kiss and took her arms from around my waist.

"We need to talk," I said, walking into my bedroom.

"Jaylin, I hope you're not upset with me. I left Jackson's number so you could call me. And this time, I did call to check in."

She followed me into the bedroom. I sat on the chaise and slowly rubbed my hands together. Scorpio stood on the other side of the bed. I knew she could see the fire burning in my eyes.

"You got one chance to tell me the truth. If you fuck up, I'm gonna knock your ass straight to Egypt," I said sternly.

"Jaylin, you're scaring me. Are you that upset with me—"

"What in the fuck is your occupation?" I yelled.

"What? What do you mean by what's my occupation?"

I hopped up and stood right in front of her. "Please, don't make me do this," I gritted. "What in the hell do you do for a living?"

She looked down at the floor and removed her jacket. She laid it on the bed, and that's when I lost it.

"Hang the motherfucker up!" I grabbed her hair. "Stop leaving shit around the damn house and hang the motherfucker up!"

"Jaylin, what is wrong with you? Let my hair go!"

She tried to move my hand from her hair, but I grabbed it tighter and slung her ass on the bed. When she fell down, I hopped on top and pinned her hands down above her head so she couldn't move.

Soon, she started to cry. "Stop, Jaylin! Please stop! I'll tell you, if you just please get off of me!"

I continued to hold her hands down tightly, and the bitch tried to kick me in my motherfucking balls. I grabbed her ankles and pulled her off the bed as hard as I could. She went flying and her head hit the floor.

"Oh my God! Would you please stop and just listen for a minute?"

I sat on top of her again and held her hands because she tried to scratch me. We tussled for a while, and I couldn't believe it when my hand went up and smacked her face. She covered it and cried, but she had finally calmed down.

I saw my red handprint swelling on her face, and I got up

and went into the bathroom. I could see her in the mirror as she sat up beside my bed and continued to cry. I felt awful for what I had done. I'd never laid my hands on a woman. I took a towel from the closet and wet it.

"Here," I said, giving her the towel. She looked up and took it from my hand.

"Are you ready to listen to me now?" she said, looking at me with tears flowing down her face.

"No, I don't want to hear anything you have to say. All I want is for you to get your things and go." I calmly poured myself a drink.

"Jaylin, don't do this. Things have been going so well for us. The reason I didn't tell you about being a stripper is because I was ashamed, and I didn't think a man like you would be interested in someone like me. Since we've been together, I've slacked up on putting myself out there like that. I've been trying to better myself by going back to school, and I'm working hard at getting my script together."

I took a few sips of the Remy Martin and looked at her with disgust. "So, are you saying, all these late nights you've been coming in, you haven't been out doing your thing?"

"Twice, Jaylin, that's it. I did two parties just so I could pay for my tuition. I didn't want to ask you for the money, so I did what I had to do to get it myself. They were just parties, Jaylin. And after I made my money, I left."

I had firsthand experience with strip parties, so I couldn't do nothing but stand my ground. "Scorpio, just go. Listen, you don't owe me an explanation. Just get your shit and leave."

I left the room because I didn't want to hear any more of the bullshit. I went downstairs to my office and sat in my chair. She followed.

"Baby, I'm sorry. I never wanted to lie to you, but if I told you what I did for a living, there would be no way to earn your respect. You would've thought that sex was all I was good for."

"Am I missing something, Scorpio? Sex is the only thing you've shown me you're good for."

"You know that's not true. I . . . I hoped that maybe one day I would be able to look back at this and laugh. Laugh with you when I told you what I had to do to get my education paid for and make a better life for Mackenzie and me."

"Cut the fucking act, all right? You flat-out lied to me and that's all there is to it! One thing I can't stand is a lying, conniving-ass woman. You are not the type of woman I want to be with. When you get that education you're talking about, or when you become a real playwright, holla at me. Until then, let me go help you pack your shit."

Scorpio stood at the end of the stairs with tears streaming from her red eyes. I moved her ass aside and went back upstairs to my room. I pulled her things from the closet and laid them on my bed. She walked up and stood with her arms folded, as if she wasn't going anywhere.

When I put her last piece of clothing on my bed, she broke down and pleaded with me again. "Why do you have to be so stubborn? You know people make mistakes sometimes. All I'm asking for is another chance. I promise I will never take off my clothes for men again. All I care about is being here with you, and if I would've known you'd react this way, I never would've done it."

"And all I care about is you getting the fuck out of here. Now, if I have to tell you one more time, Scorpio, I'm gonna put you out of here my damn self."

I guess she got the picture because she started to make progress and got her clothes off the bed. "Jaylin, what about Mackenzie? If you want me to leave, you go wake her and tell her she's got to leave."

I stared at the wall. I had briefly forgotten about Mackenzie during our heated argument. She wasn't going anywhere, and that's all there was to it.

"Come pick her up tomorrow. Better yet, send somebody over here to get her. I don't want to see your face, so your cousin or sister will be just fine. Tell them to come late because I need time to tell her what happened."

"I need time too, but you won't allow me that. I'll wake her and take her with me tonight."

"No, you won't. I told you to send somebody over here tomorrow to pick her up, didn't I?"

"And I'm telling you she's my daughter and she's coming with me tonight."

Since Mackenzie liked me so much, I had to say something that would deeply hurt Scorpio's feelings. "If I wake Mackenzie and ask her if she wants to go with you or stay here with me, you know damn well what she'll say. She's well aware of your trifling-ass ways and doesn't take too well to you as it is."

"What did you say?" She walked over to me. "Trifling? Did you have the nerve to call me trifling?"

"I call it as I see it. Now get the fuck out of my face." I pushed her away.

She smacked my face. I felt a scratch and my face burned. I put my hand on the scratch, only to see a dab of blood on the tip of my finger. Before I knew it, I grabbed her hair again and slung her ass damn near across the room. I sat on top of her and smacked her around a few times, then tried to push her down the steps to get her the fuck out of my house. I threw bunches of her clothes and shoes over the handrail and they landed in the middle of the foyer. Then, I ran downstairs and forced her and her clothes out of the front door. I wanted the bitch to take a cab, but since I wanted her out so badly, I didn't even care that she took the damn Corvette.

When I threw the last piece of clothing on the front lawn, I went back into the house and slammed the door. I watched as she walked back and forth, loading up her car—no, my car—with her belongings. I wanted to go outside and kick her ass again. I had never stooped to this level with anybody, and if a bitch had made me go out like this, I didn't need her.

When I went upstairs to my room, I heard the Corvette speed off. I picked up my drink and stood at the bar cart, thinking about how this bitch had lied to me and then made me kick her ass. Flat-out tried to provoke me, when all she had to do was tell the truth. I felt like a fool for ending my relationships with Nokea and Felicia for a woman who was nothing but a liar. I picked up a wine bottle and threw it at my glass bedroom doors. They shattered, and the wine splashed on the walls and all over the carpet.

Seconds later, Mackenzie came down the hallway. "Mackenzie, watch out for the glass!" I yelled as she tried to step over the shards on the carpet. I picked her up to make sure she didn't cut her feet.

"Daddy, what happened?" She rubbed her eyes. "Is Mommy home yet?"

"Mackenzie, Mommy won't be home until tomorrow. Get in my bed and go back to sleep."

I was glad that she didn't ask any more questions because I wasn't prepared to answer her. I went into the bathroom and ran some bath water to relax me. I closed my eyes and thought about the drama with Mackenze that would surely arise soon. As far as I was concerned, she wasn't leaving my house with no one. If Scorpio sent her sister over to get Mackenzie, she'd be wasting her time.

26

NOKEA

My belly looked as if I'd swallowed a watermelon. I was busting out of everything in my closet. When Pat and I went the Galleria to buy some maternity clothes, I saw Stephon there with one of his boys in the food court. He told me Ray-Ray was getting married and said they were at the mall to get fitted for their tuxedos. When I asked about Jaylin, he didn't comment. He pretended as if he didn't hear me and quickly changed the subject. I knew something was up so after talking for a while, I invited him to my place for a friendly dinner.

What Jaylin and I shared was probably over, but I still thought about him a lot. I wondered how his new relationship was going, and I wondered if he was connecting with Mackenzie. The biggest thing I wondered about was if he was happy. Was there anything he'd told Stephon about missing me, and was Felicia still in the picture? I was sure that during our dinner, Stephon would entertain me by giving me the scoop on Jaylin.

Later that day, Stephon came in with what looked to be a bottle of wine. When I took the bottle from his hand, I saw that it was actually a bottle of Welch's sparkling white grape juice. I laughed as I carried it to the kitchen, where I was in the midst of finishing dinner.

Stephon looked remarkably well. He always kept his head clean-cut and shaven, and his goatee was trimmed and shaped perfectly. He had on a Sean Jean blue jean outfit and some clean white tennis shoes. When I asked for his jacket, I could see his thick muscles busting out of his oversized white T-shirt.

"So, Shorty, what you cooking?" he asked, standing over me and looking into the pot on the stove.

"I'm cooking some spaghetti with cheese and some garlic bread. I was going to fry some chicken, but I forgot to thaw it."

"Naw, this is cool. Actually, it smells pretty good."

"Here, would you like to taste it?" I put a dab of sauce on the tip of the spoon. "It's hot, though, so be careful."

Stephon blew on it and I put the spoon into his mouth. He moved the sauce around in his mouth and then nodded.

"Pretty good, Shorty. Jaylin told me you couldn't cook." He laughed.

"Oh, no, he didn't. If I put my mind to it, I can cook. Besides, we always used to go out. But whenever I cooked, he loved it."

"Before you go getting all upset, I'm just playing. Actually, he said you were a very good cook."

"You better had cleaned that up. Besides, don't go talking about a woman's cooking when she's in the midst of cooking for you."

Stephon set the table, and then he took the garlic bread out of the hot oven so I wouldn't burn myself. By the time the spaghetti was good and ready, I was tired from being on my feet. He pulled up a chair in front of the one I sat in, so I could elevate my feet. Then he served our dinners.

I had questions about Jaylin, but I didn't want to rush into it. Stephon went on and on about his job, how he was ready to do something different, and the women in his life. He and Jaylin had so much in common; only he seemed to treat his women with a little more respect than Jaylin did.

As I sat listening to him, I observed his muscles tighten every time he lifted his fork. I couldn't resist; I reached over and gave his arm a squeeze.

"You've been really working out, haven't you?" I said, sliding up his short sleeve so I could see the Q-Dog symbol on his arm.

"Yeah, Jaylin and me both. We've been meeting at the gym every morning trying to relieve some of this stress we've been under."

"Really? What kind of stress? I thought you all searched for women to relieve that."

Stephon chuckled. "Now, you know that ain't so, Nokea. A piece of ass doesn't relieve stress. If you ask me, it only adds to it. If you took me in your room right now and fucked my brains out, I'd still be stressed."

"See, if I wasn't pregnant with Jaylin's baby, I'd take you up on that offer," I flirted. "Stress is all in the mind. When sex takes your mind to a different level, you forget about it. Wouldn't you agree?"

"Depends on who you're having sex with. Maybe if it's somebody like you. But for the most part, I'm stressing no matter what."

"So, what are you trying to say? You sound like you got something on your mind."

Stephon was quiet. He stared at me while holding in his bottom lip. He got up and put his plate in the sink. I checked out his bulge as he walked back toward the table. Looked like he was hard to me, so I turned my head to look away. And if he wasn't hard, some sistas know they be in trouble.

He took my hand and led me into the living room. "Come here, Shorty. Sit. I have something I've wanted to tell you for a long time."

His tone made me a bit nervous. I took a seat on the couch and he sat next to me. He still hadn't cracked a smile. By the serious look on his face, I knew he wasn't joking.

He took my hands and closed them tightly with his. "Shorty, I think you're a beautiful woman and I'm finding myself attracted to you. I've always been crazy about you, but recently, my feelings have been beyond my control. Since you and Jaylin have been apart for a while, I think it's time you move on. You need to find happiness in your life; and not only that, you need a good father figure for this baby." He reached over and rubbed his hand on my stomach.

"I can give you both of those things and so much more. I've seen the way you've been checking me out too, and I say if you want to, then let's do this. Time is of essence. I don't want to sit around wasting any more time not being with the woman I've always cared deeply for."

I blinked my long eyelashes and pulled my hands away from him. When I reflected on it, I realized that the signs had always been there. Stephon would always console me during my troubled times with Jaylin, and now I knew what he meant by, "If you ever need me, just call." My mouth wouldn't even open, and my body was still.

He was right about me checking him out, but what was so wrong with a woman checking out a good looking brotha when she saw one? Maybe my interest in Stephon was due to the changes in my hormones during my pregnancy, I thought. I wasn't sure, but one thing I knew: Stephon made me feel wanted.

Before I could respond, he leaned forward and placed his lips on mine. I put my hand on the back of his head and pulled him closer to me. Our tongues explored each other's mouths, and then I backed up and softly touched my lips.

"Stephon, this isn't right. I can't do this with you."

Ignoring me, he stood up and removed his shirt. The sight of his dark brown skin, broad, thick shoulders, and tight six pack weakened me. His jeans hung low on his thick waist and fit him very, very well.

He sat back on the couch, and before I knew it, I eased my way back so he could lie on top of me.

"We can do this, Shorty," he whispered as he leaned in close to my ear. "Just between you and me, we can do this."

I rubbed his back and closed my eyes as he kissed down my neck. He lifted my shirt and pulled it over my head. I needed this so badly, and at this point, there was no turning back. He put his mouth between my breasts and unhooked my bra with his teeth. I smiled as he dangled it in his mouth like a tiger and growled. He stared at my breasts, and then slowly manipulated them with the tip of his tongue.

My insides steamed. I couldn't wait to see what else he had to offer, so I unbuttoned his jeans, just enough to reach my hands down his pants to massage his butt. It was solid as a rock, but smooth as a baby's bottom.

When he stood up and took off his pants, I damn near fainted. Body was cut in all the right places and dick hung longer than Jaylin's. I had no idea what I was about to get myself into, but I had some needs that had to be met.

Stephon pulled off my jeans but left my panties on. He sat up on the couch and put me on top of him. He massaged my breasts with his strong hands and held them like they were the most precious things he'd ever held before. I closed my eyes as he sucked them and rubbed one of his hands on my back. Then he reached his hands inside my panties and rubbed them across my hairs. I moaned to let him know how excited I was.

He took both sides of my panties and tore them. Then, with all of his strength, he lifted me and placed my goodness right on his face. I straddled his face and held on for dear life.

"Relax, Shorty. I got you." He soaked my walls. As I got more excited, it was hard for him to keep me balanced. He kissed my thighs and laid me back down on the couch.

"You taste good, Shorty. I wish you would keep still, though, until I'm finished with you."

"Stephon, I . . . I can't keep still. I'm just not used to all of this," I said, looking into his hazel eyes.

"Well, get used to it. I don't think this is going to be my last time here."

As he pressed himself up against me, I reached down and put his thickness inside me. I tightened my eyes and felt every bit of him. He worked from side to side and continued to hold my legs close to his chest. I figured he was trying not to lean on the baby, but when he opened my legs and leaned in forward, I knew the baby felt him because he was in my guts. He rubbed my hips with his hands and lowered his eyelids, as my body responded powerfully to his. He sucked in his bottom lip and quickly changed to another rhythm—one I kept up with very well.

"You feel good, Shorty. I knew it would feel like this. That's why I couldn't get you off my mind," he whispered.

"Stephon, what if Jay—"

"Shhh . . . I don't want to talk about Jaylin right now. We can talk about him later. Just for the record, I ain't stressing at all right now. My stress is a thing of the past."

I held Stephon's hips and stopped my motion.

"What's wrong?" he asked, and then gave me a kiss.

"Stephon, we don't ever have to talk about Jaylin again. Feeling as good as I do with you, you'll never hear his name come out of my mouth again."

Stephon smiled and the lovemaking went on. He was a gentle lover and definitely knew how to excite the heck out of me. By the end of the night, he'd taken me to my room and loved me all over again. I felt like a new woman. And by the time he left, which wasn't until Monday morning, I never wanted to see Jaylin again.

27

FELICIA

It had been months since I'd last slept with Jaylin, and I couldn't believe how well everything flowed without him. Paul and I made the best of our relationship. I had even kicked Damion to the curb. His baby's mama called here with some of that, "When's the last time you seen him?" bullshit. After I told the bitch what he had on, he had the nerve to call and curse me out. I told him, "Don't ever pick up the phone and call me again if you're going to put this out-of-shape, baby-having skeeza before me!" Since then, I hadn't talked to him.

Paul, though, had been a true gentleman. He had done anything I asked him to do and had gotten a little better in the bedroom.

There was no way to keep our relationship a secret at work. Since we spent so much time together, of course, people started asking questions. I wasn't ashamed of Paul's fine ass, so I didn't deny nothing. And since I was like some kind of prize for the white men, he was definitely treated like the winner.

For the weekend, we planned a fast trip to Chicago. Deep in

my heart, I thought he would ask me to marry him because he hinted about having beautiful children together and about us living together. I didn't know what my answer would be. I still had concerns about being with a white man, let alone marrying one. Plus, as much as I hated to admit it, Jaylin was still locked up in my system. Until I freed him, I wasn't marrying anyone.

When I was at home packing my things to go, I got a call. It was Jaylin, and it was definitely a setback for me.

"I was just sitting here thinking about you," he said softly. "I hadn't heard from you in a while and I was wondering how you were doing."

I was so shocked to hear his voice I could barely get any words to come out. "I . . . I'm doing fine. I'd be better if you'd invite me over."

"Nah, not today. Maybe some other time. It's good to know that you haven't given up on me, and I apologize for how things went down."

On that note, I figured things didn't work out for him and the Playboy bunny. This was the moment I'd been waiting for, so I jumped right on it. "Apology accepted. It's obvious that you want to talk, so I'm coming right over."

"No," he snapped. "Not today. I'll call you soon, but just be there for me, all right?"

"No problem."

He hung up, and when I tried to call him back, he didn't answer. When I called him at work, Angela said he hadn't come in that day.

I was confused, so I put on some clothes and drove to his house. When I got there, I rang the doorbell but got no answer. His cars were in the driveway, so I knew he had to be there. After banging for a few more minutes, I left.

I didn't know where else to go for answers but to Nokea's house. If anybody knew what the hell was going on, she would;

she didn't have the guts to stay away from Jaylin as long as I did. But if he really needed me, there was no way I would turn my back on him.

I rang Nokea's doorbell. She opened the door in her work clothes.

"Felicia, why do you keep coming over to my house like we're the best of friends?" She looked as if her face had swelled. When I looked down at her stomach, I could tell immediately what was going on.

"You're pregnant?" I asked, shocked.

"Why? What's it to you?"

"I just want to know. If you are, then maybe that's what's troubling your man."

She walked away from the door and I walked in and shut it behind me.

"Girl, look, I ain't here to start no trouble. I came over to find out if you've talked to Jaylin. And evidently you have. Looks like you've done more than talk to him."

"So, now what, Felicia? Yes, I'm pregnant, but it's not Jaylin's baby."

"Girl, shut your mouth! Since when did you become a little hoochie mama?"

"Since I learned from your trifling butt, that's when. So, if you don't have any more questions, would you please go?"

"Ouch. Now, that hurt coming from a self-righteous woman who pretended to love Jaylin so much. If you did, you wouldn't be knocked up by another man. I thought you had a little more class about yourself, but I should've known better. Once you lost your virginity, you just couldn't get enough, could you?"

"Felicia, why don't you take your butt home? If you came over here to find out anything about Jaylin, I don't have any answers for you. I haven't seen or heard from Jaylin in months. And frankly, I don't think I ever will. So, if information is what you're looking for, I suggest you find Scorpio. I'm sure she's got all the answers you want."

I shook my head as I walked toward the door and got ready to leave. "So, who's the lucky man, Nokea? Is it anybody I know?"

"No, Felicia, it's not anybody who you've had the pleasure of giving yourself to."

"I don't know, now, you never knew. I do get around, bitch, so watch your back." I slammed the door behind me.

I jumped in the car and backed out of Nokea's driveway. As I got ready to make a left onto New Halls Ferry Road, I saw Stephon in his white BMW. He looked directly at my face, but when he saw me, he turned his head like he didn't see me. I locked in my rearview mirror and watched as he drove by Nokea's house. I turned the corner like I was on my way out of her subdivision and drove around to another street.

I could see the front of Nokea's house, and I watched as Stephon pulled in her driveway. He got out with a box of Kentucky Fried Chicken in his hand. She opened the door, smiled and let him in. Instantly, he leaned forward and gave her a kiss.

My mouth opened wide and my eyes went buck. Where in the hell had I been? This bitch was pregnant by Stephon! No wonder Jaylin sounded upset; he probably just found out about the betrayal. Damn. Now would be the perfect time to get back with him. He would definitely need me now. My relationship with Paul would have to be put on hold.

I drove back to Jaylin's house. This time, I wasn't leaving until I got some answers from him. I knocked and banged until he finally cracked the door to talk to me.

"Jaylin, would you open the door so we can talk? I know something is wrong; I could tell by the sound of your voice. Please open the door. All I want to do is talk."

He cleared his throat. "Not right now, Felicia. I'm not in the mood for any company," he said softly.

"Then why did you call me? All you wanted to know is if I'd be there for you when you needed me, and yes, I'm here. So open the door."

I pleaded for a few more minutes before he finally let me in. I damn near melted when he gave me a hug. He had his shirt off and wore only some black Jockey boxer shorts that gripped his package. I could tell he'd just gotten out of the shower; he smelled delicious, his hair was wet, and so was his body.

When he walked up the steps, I followed, wishing like hell he'd put it on me tonight. But the sadness in his eyes told me wasn't nothing going on with us—tonight, anyway.

Outside his room, I noticed that the glass doors weren't tinted anymore. Looked like he had some new ones put in because they were clear, and I could see straight into his room. He held the door for me and I walked in. There was a cute little girl sitting on the floor with some dolls. She looked up at me and smiled.

"Daddy, who is she? Is this your new girlfriend?"

"No, Mackenzie. This is Felicia. Felicia, this is Mackenzie."

I said hello to Mackenzie, but I was busy thinking about how she'd called him Daddy. I'd definitely been away too long if this was his daughter.

"Mackenzie, would you go in your room and watch TV? I'll come in and read you a story in a minute," Jaylin said. She picked up her dolls and went into the other room. I looked at Jaylin with wrinkled lines on my forehead.

"What the fu—hell is going on?" I was careful to watch my foul mouth.

"Look, Felicia, I know you got questions, but right now, I'm not in the mood for them. I just called you because I hadn't heard from you in a while."

"Jaylin, don't bull—mess around with me. Tell me what's going on. And is that really your daughter? I mean, she's cute, but she doesn't look like you."

"She's not my daughter. She's Scorpio's daughter, and since we fell out the other night, she's been here with me.'

"So, what is she doing here with you? Did Scorpio just run off and leave her with you? I knew she was a trifling bitch." That time, I couldn't help myself.

"No. Her sister came to get Mackenzie, but I didn't open the door. I've really gotten attached to her, and I'm not ready to give her up yet."

"But you have to. That's kidnapping. You can be in a lot of trouble for that."

"Yeah, I know. But she's brought so much joy to my life these past few months. She reminds me of myself when I was little; how curious I used to be about shit. I can't let her go. Besides she doesn't want to leave me anyway. She told me she wanted me to be her daddy and she wanted to live with me forever.'

"But she's just a kid. Before this stuff gets out of hand, you need to take her back to her mother. Where's Scorpio at anyway? I thought she was here with you."

"She's gone, but I don't want to talk about her right now. I'm waiting to hear from my lawyer so he can tell me what I need to do. I know he's going to probably tell me nothing, but there's got to be something I can do to keep Mackenzie."

Jaylin sat on his bed looking pitiful. I couldn't believe how much love he had for this little girl. I was kind of jealous. Four years with him and the brotha still didn't have no love for me. I couldn't offer him any advice because what I said to him, he wasn't trying to hear. He was going to do things his way whether I liked it or not.

It seemed like he didn't know about Stephon and Nokea because if he did, he probably would've mentioned it. But maybe he was just trying not to talk about it. I had to dig for some answers.

"Hey, have you seen Nokea lately?" I asked.

"Ye—yes, why?"

I could tell he was lying.

"So, you know she's pregnant?"

Jaylin's thick brows went up. He looked as if he'd seen a ghost. "She's what?"

"Yes. I saw her today and she's pregnant. I asked her who the baby's father was, and she wouldn't tell me; however, she did tell me it wasn't yours."

"Really?" He paused and rubbed his goatee. "How many months is she? Or did she tell you?"

"Naw, she didn't say, but the moment I saw her, I could tell she was pregnant. You might want to ask Stephon," I said, spicing things up a bit. "Since he's been kicking it with her, I'm sure he knows something."

"What do you mean, kicking it with her?" This time, Jaylin's brows scrunched in and his forehead wrinkled. He was mad.

"I mean, I just left her place not too long ago and he was over there. Looked like they were a couple or something."

Jaylin jumped up and went into his closet. He put on his jeans and a white wife-beater. He grabbed his keys off his dresser and asked me to stay there until he got back. Mackenzie came running out after him, but he kissed her and begged her to stay with me. When she cried, he kissed her again and wiped her tears. Motherfucker didn't even give me a kiss, and I was the one who gave him the scoop.

I picked up Mackenzie and we went back in his room to watch cartoons.

28

JAYLIN

I was on a rampage. I was already upset about the shit that I went down with Scorpio, and now this. In my Mercedes, I drove about ninety miles per hour down Interstate 270. When I hit a bump, I almost lost control of the wheel.

Felicia had to be bullshitting. I knew damn well Nokea and Stephon weren't kicking it like that. I had just seen him Friday at the gym and he didn't say nothing about Nokea. And pregnant? That didn't sound right to me. If she was pregnant by Stephon, that would mean he'd been screwing her at the same time I was. But she was a virgin, so that couldn't be true.

I racked my brain, trying to figure out what the fuck was going on. I thought about Stephon's and my conversations about Nokea over the last few months. I made it perfectly clear that out of all my ladies, I didn't want him to ever involve himself with Nokea. He could've fucked with anybody he wanted to, but she was off limits.

I continued to speed, and when I flew past a police officer, it was too late to slow down. He pulled me over. He took nearly twenty minutes checking my license and registration, then hit me with a ticket for speeding. The motherfucker had the nerve to ask if I had any drugs in the car. As fired up as I was about Stephon and Nokea, I almost went to jail.

"Do *you* have any drugs in *your* car?" I asked disrespectfully.

"Sir, I just asked you a simple question. Do you or don't you?"

"And I just asked you a simple question too. If you don't, then I don't." I looked at my watch. "Look, this has been really fun, but I need to get going. If there's nothing else, have a good day and move on to the next black man. There are plenty of us to harass, and you seem to be awfully good at what you do."

"Very good," he said and tapped the hood of my car. "You have a swell day too."

"I will. And in the meantime, I'm gon' say a little prayer for you. Today wasn't your day, but you just never know . . . tomorrow may be. Be careful out there, sir. These streets can be a dangerous place for you."

"Don't I know it." He winked and walked away.

I shook my head and calmly drove the rest of the way to Nokea's house.

As soon as I turned into Nokea's subdivision, I saw Stephon's BMW in her driveway. I swung my car into her driveway and almost hit Stephon's car in the rear. I slammed my car door. I was about to get my clown on.

I didn't even knock on the door; I tried to damn near kick the motherfucker down.

Nokea pulled open the door.

"Jaylin, what are you doing?" she asked in a panic.

I pushed the door open and let myself in. I looked down at her stomach and was shocked at how round it was. Felicia wasn't lying. Nokea was for damn sure pregnant.

My fists were already gripped tight to do some damage. "So, what's up, Nokea? Who's the fucking father of your baby?"

Her eyes watered as she looked at me in fear. Just then, Stephon walked out of the kitchen.

"It's me, man. The father of her baby is me."

I looked back at Nokea. "Is this true? Is Stephon the father of your baby?"

She started crying, and Stephon walked over and put his arms around her.

'Jaylin, man, just go. Can't you see she's upset right now? Once I leave, I'll come over to your place and explain everything to you."

My eyes shifted back and forth from Nokea to Stephon; somebody was about to get fucked up. Wasn't sure which one it would be, but I wanted some answers.

"Nokea, how long have you been fucking my cousin?"

She ignored me and buried her face in Stephon's shoulder.

"Man, look, it ain't even like that. Why don't you just go home and chill out? I said I'll be over there to explain things to you in a minute."

"Shut the fuck up talking to me, you sorry motherfucker! You always had to have every damn thing I had, didn't you? Couldn't stand to see me with anything I called my own. Your ass had to have a piece of it, didn't you?" I said, laughing. "Even when we were kids, you had to take everything, just so I could be miserable. You and your fucking selfish-ass brothers. And your mother—aw, now, we ain't gonna talk about how she raised such a lowlife asshole when she was one her damn self, are we?"

'All right, man, that's enough!" Stephon said, grabbing my shirt and pushing me back. "Get the fuck out of here. And if I—"

I didn't give Stephon a chance to say another word. I slammed my fist into his jaw.

"Son of a bitch!" he yelled. "You wanna fight? Is that what you want? You want my lady to see you get your ass kicked?"

I punched his ass again. Without any hesitation, he punched back, and it was on. We scrapped so hard that we broke two of

Nokea's vases and her glass table. I wasn't letting up and neither was he. She tried to break us apart, but I pushed her down. I didn't give a fuck about Stephon's baby she carried.

When he saw her on the floor, the asshole really tried to get tough. He grabbed my waist and pushed me into the wall with every ounce of strength he had left. My body put a dent in the wall, and the picture above it came crashing down on top of Stephon. I picked it up and tried to bust his damn head open with it. He dodged it a few times and then tried to grab my legs and knock me on the floor. When he realized he couldn't do that, I pushed him back into Nokea's baby grand piano and flipped his ass over the top.

Nokea screamed and ran to the phone. As Stephon lay on the floor, holding his back, I ran over and snatched the phone out of her hand. I pulled the cord out because I knew she would call the police.

As I stood in front of her, she cried hysterically and shook like a leaf. I balled up my fist, just about ready to punch her in her damn stomach. She put her hands over her face and screamed.

"It's your baby, Jaylin! Please don't do this. It's your baby!" She fell to the floor and cried out loudly. I slammed the phone down, and it broke into pieces.

"You lying bitch! You'll just say anything, won't you?" I wiped the sweat from my face. "I hope you and my cousin have a happy fucked-up life together.

"You had me fooled, though, baby. I thought you had a bit more respect for yourself. But I guess you ain't no better than all the other fucked-up women in my life. . . . Excuse me, did I say women? Naw, you're not women. You all are undependable, unpredictable, and unreliable bitches. Every last one of y'all, including my damn mother, who left my ass years ago.

"Shit actually started with my mother. And then his sorry-ass mother stepped in and tried to pick up the pieces, when the only thing she could pick up was a crack pipe."

In a rage, I pounded my fist into the wall. Nokea screamed for me to stop, but I couldn't. I couldn't let the situation go. "Let's see who else there is. . . . There's Simone, who left town with the only fucking thing I had to love in my life. And let's not count out Scorpio. Boy, she was a charm. Had me paying for her shit—big dollars—only to find out she had other mother-fuckers paying her too. And now you, little innocent-ass, virgin-bodied Nokea. Pretending all along that she loves me so much she can hardly see straight. And now, 'Guess what, Jaylin? I'm pregnant and it's yours, but I'm fucking your cousin too.' Bitch, get real! You were the worst one of them all because you stabbed me in my back purposely. You were the worst and I expected so much more from you, Nokea. So, you know what?" I walked over to her and lifted her face with my hand. "If it is my baby, you raise it your damn self. I'd be too ashamed to tell it that it's got a whore for a mother."

Nokea rocked back and forth on her knees and covered her ears so she couldn't hear me. I wanted to kick her in her face, but I caught myself. I didn't want to hurt her. Instead, I knocked one of her expensive statues on the ground and jetted.

As I was leaving, I backed up my car then went full force into the back of Stephon's BMW. I saw the front end of my shit fold like a piece of aluminum foil. His car was severely damaged.

By the time I pulled in my driveway, my car was smoking and the front dangled off. Felicia came rushing out of the house.

"Where's Mackenzie?" I asked because I didn't see her come after Felicia.

"Jaylin, her aunt came over here and got her. I wasn't about to go to jail for your ass. You were wrong for keeping that little girl, and I did you a favor by letting her go."

"You opened my damn door and let her take Mackenzie? Is that what you're telling me, Felicia?" I grabbed her neck. "Where in the fuck did she take her?" I yelled, though I knew Felicia couldn't tell me because I had a strong grip on her throat and she couldn't talk.

She gagged and tried to pull my hands away. When I let go, she fell to the ground like a piece of paper. She lay there for a while and coughed. I didn't give a fuck. I shut my front door and turned off the light so she couldn't see.

In hopes that Felicia had lied, I went into Mackenzie's room, but there was no sign of her. I sat on the edge of her bed and dropped my head. Everything seemed to be hurting on my body, but nothing as much as my heart.

I didn't know how I got myself into such a fucked-up situation. I had depended on too many people for my happiness, and every last one of them failed me. I was so mad that I could have killed somebody. But wasn't no telling who I would go for first.

I lay back on Mackenzie's bed and felt very sleepy. It wasn't long before I was asleep and dreaming. .

During my dream, I looked up at Mama and apologized for disrespecting her. I told her how upset I was with her for making me go to an orphanage, only to hear her apologize for that. But then she told me she was unhappy with my behavior. I'd not only disrespected her tonight, but I'd been disrespecting women for a long time. She said it was only a matter of time before my shit caught up with me.

I told her about all the good fortune I'd come into by doing things for myself. She said that she was proud, but acknowledged that I still had a long way to go before she could say I was the man she wanted me to be.

When I tried to touch her, I woke up, and found myself still

lying in Mackenzie's bed. My mother had come to me in my
dream and tried to get me to see how wrong I'd been.

I lay still for a while, thinking about Mackenzie. My heart
ached for her. She was such a joy to be around, and I hoped
like hell that I'd be able to see her soon.

It was damn near light outside, so I pulled off my shoes and
lay across my own bed. I watched the early morning news and
dozed off again.

When the phone rang, it woke me, and when I looked at
the alarm clock, it showed that it was almost noon.

"Jaylin, Mr. Schmidt is really upset with you," Angela said
on the phone. "Why haven't you come in or called or something?"

'Because I don't fucking feel like it. Tell your father-in-law
to kiss my black ass." I hung up. She called back several more
times and I finally picked up.

"Don't you hang up on me," she said. "Now, if you're having
some problems, I'll cover for you, but don't go hanging up on
me "

'Sorry, Angela. I'm not in the mood for doing any work
right now. Tell Schmidt I'm taking a leave of absence. In the
meantime, ask Roy to handle all my accounts for me. Don't
call me unless it's a matter of life or death, please."

"Okay, but you know he's going to want to talk to you."

"Well, fine! Have the motherfucker call back soon so I can
tell him to go fuck himself."

"Jaylin, calm down. I don't know what's bugging you, but
nothing is worth losing your job over. So, when he calls, you'd
better change your attitude."

"Yeah, yeah, yeah. Whatever. Just tell him to call me."

Ten minutes later, Schmidt called from his office on speaker-
phone. Roy was in the office with him, and in so many words,
Schmidt said if I didn't come in to work, I didn't get paid. That
was quite hilarious because I had plenty of money stashed

aside from my inheritance. In addition to that, most of my salary came from Higgins and his buddies anyway. I told Schmidt I would be back in action within sixty days, and he agreed to let me come back then.

For the rest of the day, I chilled. Took my phones off the hook and watched Judge Joe Brown and Judge Judy as they showed no mercy for people in their courtrooms. My body was sore and bruised from fighting with Stephon; I relaxed in the tub about five times that day.

The only phone call I made was to my lawyer to find out if there was anything I could do about Mackenzie. When he said there wasn't, I told him to go fuck himself and then fired him. Then I called my other attorney. He said that if I could prove Scorpio was an unfit mother, I stood a chance of getting Mackenzie. I wasn't trying to hate on Scorpio, but I wanted Mackenzie back in my life. I told him I would think about it for a while and get back with him.

After lying across the bed most of the day, drinking shots of Martel, I found myself getting horny. Right about now, Scorpio was probably fucking a brotha and sucking him well. I kicked her out five days ago, and my dick was lonely. I looked in the pocket of the suit I'd had on at Aunt Betty's funeral and found that tender's phone number.

I called, and when she answered and realized it was me, she sounded excited. I talked to her for an hour and managed to coax her into coming over to see me. I jazzed myself up, knowing she'd give it up to me in a heartbeat.

When she rang the doorbell, I watched the last five minutes of a sitcom and made her stand outside and wait. Still, as she saw me approach the door, she was all smiles. I let her in and closely observed her to make sure I wanted to go there with her. She wasn't no dime, but her plump, juicy ass in a tight red mini-skirt kept her in the running. I noticed her fingernail polish was chipped, and I immediately knew she couldn't be in Jaylin's world if she tried.

She looked a bit young, too, but when I asked how old she was, she told me she was twenty-seven. As long as she was legal, that's all I cared about.

We chatted in the living room for a while, and then I escorted her upstairs to my room. I wasn't about to waste any time.

"Hey, uh, what did you say your name was?" I asked, already forgetting.

"Brashaney."

"Can I get you something to drink?" I poured myself another drink.

"No, no, thank you. But if you have some water, I'll take a glass of that."

"I don't serve water to my guests. If you'd like something else, let me know."

She cut her eyes and gave her lips a slight toot. "I'm good," she said. "Forget it."

I didn't care much for her attitude, but for the time being, it didn't even matter. I sat on the bed, put my drink on the nightstand, and asked her to stand in front of me.

"Why?" she asked. She was starting to become a pain.

"Because I want you to take off your clothes. You don't mind if I watch, do you?"

'No, but can we listen to some music or something before we get down like that? I mean, I haven't been here five minutes and you already talking about taking off my clothes."

"Brashaney, I don't have time for games, baby. I invited you here tonight because a brotha liked what he saw. If you want to sit here all night and listen to some music, fine, go right ahead. But I asked you to come here so I could make love to you. So, what's it gonna be?" I stood up and started to remove my pants. "Are you taking off your clothes too, or do I put on some music?"

Brashaney gazed at my dick and started to remove her clothes. I could tell she was young because she had young, fresh titties. Nipples didn't even look full-grown yet. But when she got on top of me and swallowed my dick like a shark, I wasn't really sure.

I slid on a condom and just lay there as she put an arch in her back and tried to put it on me. I rubbed her ass a few times, and that was it. She took my hand and tried to make me feel her insides, but I couldn't get with it.

The thought of Stephon fucking Nokea was fresh in my mind. I remembered how he told me he be airlifting women, sucking their pussies, and I wondered if he'd done that to Nokea. I also wondered if she liked the feel of him better than me. How or why would she bring that much hurt to me, I didn't know. And Stephon's backstabbing ass . . . I couldn't believe he had gone there when I simply told him not to.

I was unable to focus on my intimate time with Brashaney, so I stopped.

"What's wrong, Jaylin? Aren't you enjoying yourself?" She took my hand and rubbed it on her pu-tain.

"Yeah, I'm enjoying myself. Let's get this over with so I can go to sleep, though."

I flipped her over and took control. I banged her insides just so I could have the pleasure of hearing her say my name. When I heard that, I cut her short and came. She was all up on me, trying to get close, but I wasn't having it.

"Say, baby, I'm really tired. Why don't I call you tomorrow?" I said.

She yanked the covers back, put on her clothes, and left without saying goodbye. I wasn't sweating it. I got what I wanted, so what the hell?

I woke up in a sweat as I dreamed about my Aunt Betty. The

thought of her beating me and throwing me into a dark closet wouldn't leave my memory for shit. I prayed many nights for Mama to come back and save me, but she never came. I hoped Daddy would come and take me from that orphanage, but he never showed.

I lay across my bed, and a few tears rolled from my eyes as I thought about my horrifying past. To me, women were only good for one thing.

Wasn't no telling when I would feel any differently, but I knew that treating them the way I'd been doing wasn't going to make my life any better. Changes had to be made, but I knew that would take some time and willingness on my part.

29

NOKEA

Stephon and I cleaned up the place as best as we could, and then I asked him to leave for a short while so I could be alone. He called J's Towing Service to come get his car, and they took it to Al's Body Shop.

I was sick about what happened. I didn't intend for things to go as far as they did, and I really didn't expect Jaylin to be that upset with me about Stephon. I mean, they'd shared plenty of women before. Wasn't no biggie for them, so why did he trip with me? And the baby? I wondered if he believed me when I told him the baby was his. Maybe that's why he calmed down a bit and left. Either way, I'd never seen him that angry with anyone. I didn't like the fact that it was me who had upset him the most. I was the one who was always there for him, and for him to call me those names was extremely hurtful.

Ever since I saw him, I couldn't get him off my mind. The look on his face was terrifying, and I could only imagine how hard he was still taking the news. I'd known Jaylin for a long enough time, and I knew he'd shut out everyone and try to face this all alone. And, even though I enjoyed being with Stephon, I hated to admit that Jaylin still had my heart. Just having him in my presence did something to me.

Maybe I was wrong for sleeping with Stephon, but I had needs. I'd already gone thirty whole years without sex, and nine years without having sex with the man I loved. Since Stephon was the one who was willing to take care of my needs, I had to go with the flow. And Stephon wasn't there only for my physical needs. He'd been there for me: cooking for me, massaging my body for me, listening to the baby's heartbeat, and feeling the baby move—everything Jaylin should have been doing. It wasn't my fault he decided to be with Scorpio.

I guess things didn't work out with them either. He sounded upset with everybody, and I guess in his mind, he had good reason. But when was Jaylin going to realize that life didn't revolve around him? He had his own little messed-up world, and if people didn't do things his way, then there was no other way.

I sat around the house for hours and thought about Jaylin as I took care of the damage he'd done to my place. I had insurance on my piano, so the company I bought it from would replace the smashed one. I told them someone had vandalized my place. This guy Pat knew came over to fix my drywall. Pat came with him because I didn't feel comfortable letting a strange man in my house.

When she walked in, she was stunned. Plaster was all over the floor, my table was without glass, and one of my expensive statues was without a head.

"Girl, what the hell went on up in here? I know you told me it was bad, but this is ridiculous. You need to send that mother-fucker a bill. He can't be coming over here tearing up your stuff like this."

"Come on in the kitchen, girl. I know Jaylin was wrong for

messing up my things, but if you think about it, he kind of had good reason to."

"So if he would've punched you in your stomach, he would've been right? Is that what you're saying, Nokea?"

"No. All I'm saying is maybe, just maybe, I was wrong for not telling him about the baby to begin with. And then, to turn around and sleep with his cousin? I . . . I'm not sure if that was the right thing to do."

"I can't believe that after all this fool done to you, you still sticking up for him. Now, you did what you had to do based on the situation he put you in. If Stephon—or anybody, for that matter—stepped in and picked up where Jaylin left off, then, hey, his loss. Although I'm not saying sleeping with Stephon was the best thing to do, because I think he's a bigger ho than Jaylin is. If not a bigger ho, a smoother ho. He knows how to charm a woman out of her panties just like Jaylin. The problem is both of them fine, and now you've got your work cut out for you."

"Pat, I don't care about who's the finest between them. All I care about is who's going to be there for Nokea and her baby. That's it. I want a man to love me and to be a good father to this baby. And if that's Stephon, then that's what I want. I can't see Jaylin loving me like I want him to. Right about now, he wants to kill me. I don't stand a chance with him anymore," I said, looking down at the floor.

"Nokea, forget about who loves you for a minute. Where's your heart? Who do you really want to be with? Now, I can tell you who I want you with, but you got your own mind. So, make your own decision."

"What's your recommendation, Pat? Who do you want me with?"

She looked at me and crossed her arms. "Neither one. Personally, I think you were wrong for sleeping with Stephon, but since I hate Jaylin so much, I went with the flow. You need to get rid of both of them and move on. You're a beautiful person, Nokea, and you won't have a hard time finding somebody who will truly love you."

'But it's not that easy. Being with Stephon is great, but my heart still belongs to Jaylin. I don't know what I'm going to do. I'm worse off than I was before." I put my head on the table and started to tear up again. Pat tried to console me, but even she said I messed up.

She stayed with me until Stephon came back over. When she opened the door, she stared him down like a bloodhound. I rushed her out the door because I didn't want her starting no mess with him over the baby.

'Look, Nokea, you don't have to push me out the door. I'm leaving. He already knows he ain't got no business over here."

' Pat, I got plenty of business over here. I got a baby on the way and a woman I love. If that ain't enough business, then I don't know what is."

"Negro, please. Spare me the lies. Save them for Jaylin so he won't whip your butt again. You know darn well that ain't your baby, because if it was, you wouldn't even be here. And love? Don't make me sick. I think it's pathetic and absurd you call yourself in love with Nokea. Too bad she don't know any better because—"

"Pat, stop! I've had enough drama already. Please don't do this, okay?" I asked politely.

She threw up her hands and walked out. "Call me later, girl. Love ya," she said.

I shut the door and looked at Stephon. "Tell me, am I wrong for wanting to be happy? Can't I be with who I want to and leave it at that?"

Stephon came over and held me in his arms. "Nokea, we both knew this wasn't going to be easy. Baby, this is just the beginning. Hell, you haven't even told your parents about us yet. I'm not sure how they're going to feel about me being Jaylin's cousin. But when all is said and done, we're going to be happy together. You, her, and me," he said, rubbing my belly.

"No, it's a boy. I want a boy so I can name him—" I was about to say Jaylin, but I stopped myself. "A girl will be just fine."

"No, no, now, if you want a boy then pray for one. And when he comes, we'll talk about what to name him then."

"I said a girl would be fine, Stephon. I don't ever want to think about having a boy again."

We sat on the outside deck and chilled. Stephon wanted to make love to me, but I couldn't get with it. After he jumped in the swimming pool naked, I joined him. I wasn't even ashamed of my fat stomach because he made me feel like I was the most beautiful woman that walked the earth. He held me in the swimming pool and rubbed every part of my body.

Mentally, I still wasn't there yet, so I hopped out of the pool and lay on a beach towel while looking up at the sky. Stephon played in the water and did all kinds of crazy flips, trying to make me laugh. Thoughts of Jaylin, however, continued to occupy my mind. When my laughter went away, Stephon came over and laid his wet body beside me.

"Shorty, I know you're still in love with Jaylin, but just think about what we could have for a minute. I'm not trying to make you love me, but it would be nice if you would be willing to give it a try."

I turned on my side and looked into Stephon's eyes. "I'm trying, Stephon, but it's so hard. Seeing Jaylin again kind of brought out some feelings I didn't know were still there. So, be patient with me. I want this to work between us too, but it's going to take some time."

He kissed me from the top of my forehead to the bottom of

my feet. He made love to me like this was the beginning of something special.

I was there with him for a while, but when I closed my eyes, I saw Jaylin. I squeezed my eyes tighter until he went away. I didn't expect him to be away for long, and deep down, I knew the drama was just beginning.

30

JAYLIN

Since I'd last seen Mackenzie, it had been almost a month. I felt like I was in another world, and only left the house when it was necessary. I knew that leaving a lot would cause me to do something stupid, like go cuss out Nokea some more or provoke another fight with Stephon. I decided to let them have each other. As a matter of fact, they deserved each other. I was truly bothered by their relationship, but with Nokea being pregnant by him, what could I do? I knew her parents would want her to be with the father of her child, and Nokea would do anything to please her parents. It was over, and once again in my life, I had to accept the situation and move on.

Other than Nokea, Scorpio's pussy was heavy on my mind. Since I was occasionally sticking my dick in Brashaney, the rest of my time was dedicated to finding Mackenzie. I'd been to one law firm after another trying to find out what I could do. After paying big dollars for consultation after consultation, I gave up. The only thing I heard was that if I wasn't her biological father, there was little I could do.

I knew so little about Scorpio that I didn't even know where to begin to look for her. I called her house, but the number had been disconnected. I even drove around Olivette to see if I saw her car parked somewhere, but no luck. I was starting to give up on them too, but something wouldn't let me.

Since Ray-Ray's party was that night at his cousin's house, I stopped searching and went home, showered, and changed into one of my favorite outfits. I put on my black Armani wide-legged linen pants and my black-and-off-white, thick-striped linen shirt with an oversized collar. Then I put on my off-white gangster hat and tilted it to the side. GQ magazine didn't know what they were missing. My Rolex was on one wrist, and my thick gold diamond bracelet was on the other. I was bling-blinging, ready to get my party on as soon as I sprayed on some Clive Christian. I put twenty hundred-dollar bills in my money clip and stuck it in my pocket.

I knew I'd see Stephon tonight, but I wasn't backing down or going. I had other friends who would surely be in attendance, so what the hell?

As I was preparing to leave, Brashaney rang my phone. I had to answer because I didn't want to mess up the only booty I had lined up, especially since I knew I'd probably want to get my sex on after the party tonight. The last time we hooked up, I went through her purse while she was asleep and peeked at her driver's license. She didn't lie about her age; she was actually twenty-seven, and I felt bad about not being able to trust her.

I ended the conversation with Brashaney and told her to meet me at my place around two in the morning. I told her to make sure she called before she came just in case I wasn't home; then I jetted. I was looking good, feeling good, and smelling good, so I decided to drive my Boxster for the night.

Ray-Ray's bachelor party was at his cousin's mansion in Ladue, and I was dying to see what it looked like. I heard it was banging, but I also heard it wasn't banging better than mine;

however, when I pulled up, I knew I had some competition. I had to push an intercom button and announce who I was just for the gates to open up and let me in. Then, I drove up a long driveway lined with waterfalls and marble rock landscaping. And when I saw the house—damn! It was bad. Twice the size of mine, with big white columns in the front, like the White House.

When I pulled up in my car, one of the valets parked it alongside the other cars. Mercedes, Lexus, Lincoln, Cadillac, Jaguar, BMW; you name it, they were there. But I was glad to see that nobody had a Boxster like mine. The lot also had its share of fucked-up cars too, so I knew it wouldn't be all good inside.

There was already about a hundred brothas outside, so I imagined what the inside would look like. As I walked past them, they checked me out from head to toe.

As soon as I hit the door, I saw men all over the place. There was a double staircase cluttered with people. Mesmerized, I stood in the spacious foyer, which was covered with green, black and white marble. Shit was off the hook. Whoever told me I could compete lied like hell.

I walked through the place, and I tried to figure out how I could be down. I was more infatuated with the house than I was with all the ladies that flounced around butt naked.

I finally stepped into the room where the party was actually happening. It was packed with fellas and the music thumped loudly. I bounced my head to the rhythm and quickly scoped one of my boys from the barbershop. He came up with a couple other brothas and asked what took so long for me to get there.

"Man, I was trying to hurry, but perfection takes a little more time," I boasted. Yes, I was arrogant, but I didn't give a damn.

"I heard that," Ricky said, giving me five. "You know you

clean, though, bro. And where in the hell did you get that shirt? It's off the chain."

I usually didn't tell anybody where I got my things from because I didn't want nobody trying to look like me. So, I pretended that I didn't hear him, and then stepped away from Ricky to get a drink at the bar.

My eyes searched the crowded room for Ray-Ray, but I didn't see him. I knew he was somewhere, but finding him would be like searching for a needle in a haystack.

As I tipped the bartender, the lights flashed on and off, which meant a stripper was on her way out to entertain. The floor cleared, and all the brothas, including me, watched as this dark chocolate sista came in and danced her way to the middle of the floor. She danced to a slow, funky song as we all watched and waited for her to take it off. She had on a red leather shorts outfit with her cheeks hanging out. Her tinted blonde hair was straight and hung down to her butt.

When she sat in a chair and stretched her legs straight out in the air, motherfuckers hollered like they ain't never seen no pussy before. She grabbed this one brotha on the floor and put her goods all in his face. She tied him to a chair and pulled out some whips. Now, this shit was too damn freaky for me. Not interested in that kind of action at all.

I went back over to the bar and got another drink. A stripper who had already performed came over and stood next to me. She wiped the sweat from her forehead and threw a towel over her shoulder.

"So, are you having a good time?" she yelled over the music.

"Yeah, it's cool. But have you seen the groom yet?" I asked, leaning down toward her.

"The last time I saw him, he was in one of the rooms upstairs." Made sense. That was probably where I should've looked for him.

I smiled. "So, what's your name?"

"My real name or my play name?"

"Whichever one you want to give me," I said, really not giving a fuck.

"It's Nicola. What's yours?"

"Jaylin," I said, looking to see what all the hype was about because the men were hollering again.

"So, Jaylin, did you see my performance tonight?"

"No, I just got here. I must have missed you."

"Well, if you'd like, I can give you a private show in one of the rooms upstairs."

I looked down at Nicola and set my drink on the bar. No doubt about it, she was fine. But since I thought about how Scorpio probably put herself out there like this, I had to turn her down. She didn't give up, though. She stood next to me while we both watched Dark and Lovely entertain.

When she finished, Dark and Lovely walked out of the room with all kinds of dollars stuck in her thong, down her top, and in her hand. I slid her a hundred-dollar bill because the sista worked hard for it. She smiled and whispered that she would be back.

Since Nicola hadn't budged, I had no choice but to pay her some attention. I wasn't sure what she wanted from me. Even though I knew I had it going on, I hadn't paid her nearly much attention as the other men.

I finally saw Ray-Ray. He came down the steps with two chicks on his side. Stephon was right behind him with another chick.

I excused myself from Nicola and met Ray-Ray at the bottom of the steps.

"What's up, playa?" I said and then gave him five. Stephon and me eyeballed each other as he walked away.

"Man, man, man! Where have your ass been? I've been

bragging to all the ladies about my partna Jaylin and you just now getting here?"

"Fool, I've been here. Since I got here, I've been trying to find your ass. But you can't be found if you don't want to be," I said, looking at the two chicks.

He laughed and took his arms from around them. "Hey, let me holla at you for a sec," he said.

We walked into another room where just a few people were chilling on a circular leather sectional.

"Listen, I'm not going to hold you up, because I know you want to get your party on like I intend to do. But Stephon told me what happened. I'm hurt, man, because we've been boys for too damn long. And to let some bitch come between y'all, that ain't even cool. I'm not saying y'all need to squash things tonight; all I'm saying is y'all need to get together and talk this shit out."

"Ray, thanks for trying, but this shit goes beyond him fucking my woman. If you're worried about me tripping tonight, then don't. I don't have any intention of messing up your night."

I grabbed Ray-Ray on his shoulder and we walked back into the other room. Stephon stood next to Nicola, but when he saw her look my way, he moved away. She walked back to me. I looked at him and he looked at me.

"Say, did I interrupt something?" I asked.

"Naw, seemed like she was hollering at you, dog."

"Right, right. But you know if you want her, I ain't got no problem with that."

"Nope, ain't interested. Besides, I already got my shit off tonight with that sista right over there," he said, pointing to the chick he came down the steps with.

"Well, I got two questions for you: Was it good, and how much did it cost you?"

He laughed.

"Aw, it was good. And so was I. So good that once I was finished, she gave me fifty dollars back."

"That's how you do it," I said, giving him five.

Stephon reached over and gave me a hug. I hugged him back. It felt good that my cousin and I were on our way to settling our differences. He was way more important to me than Nokea, and we were both wrong for allowing a woman to come between us.

Nicola had worked her way over to some other brothas, so Stephon and I talked about the fine-ass ladies in the house.

"Man, I can't believe you haven't found you no shit up in here yet," Stephon said, gawking at everything that walked by. "It's all kind of ass floating around here."

"Yeah, I've been checking it out. I'm just waiting for the right one. There ain't no question in my mind that I'll be fucking tonight. The only question is, who's going to be the lucky woman?"

After scoping the set with Stephon, I thought about my conversation with Brashaney tonight. I pulled out my cell phone and called to cancel our plans. I knew there was no way I would be home by two. She didn't answer, so I left a message and told her I'd call her tomorrow.

When Stephon walked to the bar and got another drink, the lights flashed again. The floor cleared and the fellas made room for the next stripper. Nelly's "It's Gettin Hot in Here" started playing.

I almost spilled the drink in my hand when I saw Scorpio enter the room. She had on some thigh-high white leather boots with spurs and a cowboy hat. As she walked in and swayed her hips from side to side, the white tassels that covered her ass also moved from side to side. Her top was a strapless corset with fringes dangling from it. She strutted around the floor in circles and the men went crazy. She tossed her hat into the crowd, and her long, wavy hair fell down over her face.

Stephon looked at me and pointed. "Is that—?"

"Yes, but don't say anything. I don't want her to see me." I ducked behind Stephon and this other dude who seemed to really be enjoying the show. I had to see for myself how nasty she could get at one of these parties that she claimed were so innocent.

When the music changed, she pulled not one brotha, but three on the floor. She sat one in a chair and the other two on the floor. As they eagerly waited for her to get busy, she removed her top, swung it in the air, and tossed it on the floor. Then the money came in. It covered the floor. When she slid out of her shorts and draped them across the face of the brotha in the chair, I cut my eyes and shook my head with disgust. She was left standing with a sheer white thong. Wasn't no need for her to have it on because everyone could see the smooth hairs on her pussy.

My heart raced as I continued to watch. Stephon and the rest of the motherfuckers stood with their mouths open, mesmerized by her trashy perfomance. And when she flipped her body over the chair and wrapped her legs around the brotha's face, with her face in his lap, I had seen enough. I put my drink down and headed for the door.

Stephon grabbed me. "Come on now, Jay. You better than that, ain't you? Don't let this woman ruin your night. Besides, it ain't nothing but a show anyway."

He nudged me back into the room, and I sat in the corner where I couldn't see what went on. The noise was distracting because brothas screamed and hollered more for her than they did anybody. It was a good thing I'd ended it with her before tonight, because if I hadn't, I'd be up there kicking her ass.

After Scorpio racked up the dollars, she blew kisses at the fellas and swished her ass out of the room. I at least wanted to

find out where Mackenzie was, so I told one of Ray-Ray's part-
nas to stop her when she came out of the bathroom. I told him
to tell her that if she was willing to come to the room at the
end of the hall, it would be worth a thousand dollars.

After I paid him a hundred dollars for doing it, he stood by
the bathroom door and waited for her to come out. I ran upstairs to the room at the end of the hall and took off my shirt
so she would think I was naked. Then I turned off the light,
hopped in bed, and waited for her to enter.

The room had an odor like somebody had already been
there fucking, but it was still a bad-ass room. It was gold and
white, had mirrors on the closet doors that went from one end
of the room to the other. The wallpaper was gold-and-white-
striped, and the rugs matched the white curtains that draped
the windows. The bed had gold satin sheets, but I threw them
off, not knowing who had laid their ass on there tonight.

I sat up with my arms folded, my legs crossed, and leaned
back on the soft pillows as I waited for her to come. It was dark
as hell, but I could see a sliver of light coming through the
window.

When the door creaked, I took a deep breath. She walked in
and shut the door behind her. I knew it was her because I
could smell her perfume.

"Excuse me, are you going to turn the light on?" she asked,
still standing by the door.

"Are you going to take off your clothes for me like the song
said?" I asked in a deep voice.

"No, I'm not. I came in here to tell you I don't go out like
that. If sex is what you want, I'll set you up with one of my girlfriends out there. As a matter of fact, she's waiting for you
now."

"I'm not interested in her." I made my voice deeper. "I got a
thousand dollars right now that got your name all over it."

"Sorry, sir, that ain't my style," she said, turning to open the door.

"I said that I'm not interested in her. I want you."

I reached for the lamp and turned on the light.

Scorpio turned and looked at me. She cracked a tiny smile. "Jaylin, what are you doing here?"

"I came here to party, just like everybody else," I said, admiring her sexy body in her tight blue jeans and matching jean halter-top.

"Did you try to set me up or something?"

"No. I liked what I saw downstairs and wanted a sista to come shake a brotha down. But since you don't get down like that, I guess I'll have to settle for your girlfriend."

She smiled. "Well, I can always make an exception for a man like you."

"Naw, naw. Don't do me any favors. I'm sure your girlfriend wouldn't mind shaking a brotha down tonight. Go ahead; call her in here so I can get this party started."

Scorpio turned around and threw her backpack with her clothes in it over her shoulder. "Well, you have a good time. I came here to do what I had to do tonight; now I'm going home."

I gazed at the gap between her legs where I used to lay my dick, and I couldn't let her walk out. I jumped out of the bed and put my hand on the door. As I pressed my body up against hers, I moved her hair to the side and whispered in her ear.

"Don't go, baby. Let's make love. I'm sorry for not trusting you. I'm sorry for putting my hands on you. Just . . . just make love to me right now. I miss you beside me. I miss having your body next to mine."

She turned around and put her finger on my lips. "Jaylin, that all sounds good, but all I want to know is do you love me? If you miss me so much, then tell me. Do you love me?"

"Baby, you know how I feel."

"No, I don't. Tell me how you feel. If you can't tell me you love me, then ain't no sense in me hanging around."

I took a few steps back and looked her pretty self in the face. I rubbed her cheek and then kissed it. "Where's Mackenzie?" I asked, as I wasn't about to tell her something I didn't mean.

"Jaylin, is loving me that hard for you? All I'm asking is for you to love me, that's all."

"Scorpio, I can't. I'm sorry, but I don't feel that right now. Why do you want me to lie to you? What's the big deal? My feelings don't get any stronger for you than they are right now. If this ain't enough, I'm sorry. So," I said with a sigh, "where's Mackenzie?"

"She's at my sister's house."

"Bring her over to my house tomorrow so I can see her."

"I'll try. I have a few things I have to do tomorrow, but I'll try."

"Try hard." I opened the door so I could let her out.

She walked down the steps in front of me, and brothas pulled on her like she was a piece of gold. She smiled as a couple of them stuffed money into her back pocket, then she walked out the door.

Stephon stood in the doorway to the party room. I walked up to him. "Come by my house tomorrow so we can talk," I said.

"Fo' sho'. Any particular time?"

"Anytime. I'll be there."

He nodded.

I saw Dark and Lovely, who performed earlier, grabbed her hand and told her let's go. Maybe a little whip action was what I needed. She put her drink down and didn't waste any time getting in the ride with me.

As we were leaving the premises, I saw Stephon getting into

his car with the sista he'd been with earlier. He pulled his car in front of mine and cut me off. He got out of his car and came over to my window.

"Hey, man, I got something for you," he said, giving me a piece of paper.

I looked at it. It was a bill for $11,386 for the repairs to his car.

"Pay the bill, motherfucker," he said, laughing. "Pay the bill."

I ripped it up and threw it at him. "Negro, please. If I pay your bill, you can pay mine. If you don't move your car so I can go home and make love to this woman, I'm gonna tear your shit up again."

Stephon hopped back into his car, still laughing, and sped off. I zoomed past him on Lindbergh Boulevard and blew the horn.

I wanted to ask him about Nokea, but I was staying my ass out of it. She was sadly mistaken if she thought Stephon was any better than I was. He was slick, and knew how to charm the hell out of women. I didn't have time for that shit; I was the kind of man who always told it like it was, no matter what. I guess that's why Scorpio couldn't stand me. But I wasn't changing my ways for nobody.

When I pulled into the driveway, Brashaney's car was parked in front of my house, even though I'd told her not to come over. Either that or she didn't get my message. I stepped out of the car, and Sexy Chocolate got out on her side. Brashaney stormed up the driveway and positioned her hand on her hip.

"Say, baby, I called and left you a message. You didn't get it?" I asked.

"No, Jaylin, I didn't. So, what's up? Are you kicking it with her tonight or what?"

"Well, since both of y'all here, why don't we make the best of it?" I said, thinking that a threesome would be good right about now.

Brashaney smacked the shit out of me. I could only smile. I knew I'd played her, but, hey, at least I tried to call.

She walked back to her car, threw her purse inside and sped off.

I worked Sexy Chocolate all night long. I put on a condom three different times, but my big dick and all the pressure I put into this woman caused the damn thing to slide off. I hated using condoms, but under these kinds of conditions, what else could I do? I wished they'd come out with something special for a brotha packing it like me, because this shit just wasn't working.

I pulled off the torn condom and we went at it again. After I made her come six times, I'd had enough. All the moaning and groaning, screaming and hollering, and "oh, baby, this is the best dick I've ever had" bullshit worked my nerves. Been there and heard that shit before. I rolled my happy ass over and went to sleep.

After Sexy Chocolate left, I laid my lazy butt around the house all day doing nothing. I waited for Scorpio to call and tell me when she would bring Mackenzie over, but it was almost three o'clock in the afternoon and she hadn't called yet. Brashaney did, though. She called and cursed my ass out for playing her like I did last night. I didn't say a word. Wasn't no sense in me getting all hyped up about a woman I really didn't care about. She went on and on about what a dog I was, and I just agreed and then ended the conversation.

Women are just some crazy creatures, I thought. They like too much fucking drama if you ask me. If somebody played your ass like I did last night, why would you still want to be bothered? She was actually calling here to try to fix shit. If I was such a dog, then why waste the time? Never could figure some women out—and wasn't trying to either.

I lay back on my bed with my hands folded behind my head and laughed at the situation. The phone rang again. This time, it was Stephon. He asked if I wanted to catch dinner at Applebee's, or order some Chinese food from the hood. Since I figured our conversation would get pretty deep, I suggested he come to my place and I'd have some Chinese food delivered. He agreed and said he was on his way.

I went downstairs to the kitchen and tried to find something to snack on because I was starving. When I realized I hadn't been grocery shopping in a while, I picked up the phone and quickly ordered our Chinese food. I ordered Stephon some house special fried rice with extra shrimp and bean sprouts because it was his favorite. Then I ordered the same for myself, minus the shrimp and sprouts. I threw in an egg roll just to be greedy.

My place seemed to be a bit out of order, so I called Nanny B and arranged to have her come over the next day. I'd been in a slump, and cleaning up my place was the last thing on my mind. I asked the nanny to do everything from washing the windows to scrubbing the floors. She gave me a price, and I was all for it. Told her I'd see her at nine in the morning.

Finally, Stephon showed up, as beat as I was from last night's festivities.

"Damn, I thought I looked bad. What happened to your ass? Did you at least brush your teeth this morning?" I asked, laughing as he strolled in.

"Fuck you, man. I got a damn hangover. Hangover from drinking and from that pussy. Couldn't get that woman out of my place until an hour or so ago." He plopped down on the couch.

"Yeah, I know what you mean. After fucking, you just want to say, 'Get your shit and go,' don't you? But you know how it is; gotta play the nice, 'Oh, I really want you to stay here with me,' role just in case you might need that ass another time."

"You got that right," Stephon said, slamming his fist against mine.

"So, uh, I hate to ask you this, but do you want something to drink?"

"No, thank you! A tall, cold glass of ice water will be just fine."

"Just in case you forgot, I don't serve water to my guests, so get your ass up and go in the kitchen and get it yourself."

Stephon went to the kitchen, and I went to the bathroom. "Say, man, I ordered us some Chinese food," I yelled.

"Oh yeah?" Stephon yelled from the kitchen. "What did you order?"

"I ordered some—ahhhhh, shit!"

"Some what?" he yelled back.

"Damn! What the fuck!" I yelled, leaning my hand up against the wall and holding my dick in my other hand.

Stephon rushed to the bathroom door. "Man, what the fuck you doing?"

"My dick is on fire! This motherfucker straight up feel like fire shooting out of it."

"Fool, quit playing."

"Playing? Do I look like I'm—ahhhhh, shit!"

The doorbell rang, but I was in no condition to get it. "That's probably our food. Get the money off the table and give it to them. And don't give him a tip because he late. They told me ten minutes and it's been thirty-five."

"Man, you knew they weren't going to get here in no ten minutes."

"Well, they shouldn't be lying to people by telling them that bullshit all the time then. So, whatever you do, don't give him a tip."

Stephon laughed and went to the door. I slid my thang back into my pants, flushed the toilet, and washed my hands. I took slow steps entering the kitchen. Stephon cracked up as he removed the boxes from the bag.

"What in the fuck is so funny? I need a doctor," I said, looking for my doctor's number on the refrigerator.

"Jay, it ain't like you gon' die or nothing. I know her office closed today, so you might as well wait until tomorrow. Sounds like you might have a STD."

"Damn, does it have to burn like that? I ain't never got caught up with no shit like this, and if that's what it is, I'm gon' mess somebody up."

"Yes, it burns like hell. Happened to me a couple of times. That's why I be telling you to strap your shit up. Ain't no telling where some of these tricks been."

"I do strap myself up—most of the time. I've had two women within the last week, and the condom ripped with the one I had last night. I guess I know where to place the blame."

"You gotta take responsibility too if you want to continue getting down like you do. It's too much shit out there now. And since motherfuckers dropping off like flies, I make sure I strap my ass up no matter what."

"I know, but the condoms just don't fit right. They be sliding off and everything. I'm gon' have to strap up my handler with a trash bag or something."

We cracked up, and then started to chow down on the rice.

"So, what was up with Scorpio last night? Are y'all still kicking it or what?"

"Nope. Not right now anyway. I'm sure I'll be back in them panties soon."

"What happened? I mean, I didn't even know she could get down like that."

"Shit, I didn't either. That's why I kicked her ass out of here.

She lied, man, flat-out lied about her occupation. I didn't want
to tell you the details because I didn't want your ass to tell me
how badly I fucked up."

"Well, you did. But we all fuck up sometimes. I hope you
learned from your mistakes.

I feel you, though, about a woman who lies. Ain't nothing
worse than a lying-ass woman. It's all right for us to lie, but
women are supposed to be better than that."

"I agree. And it sure in the hell hurts when they do," I said,
thinking about Nokea. I wanted to ask Stephon many questions about their relationship, but I didn't want him to think
that I was interested in getting Nokea back. I knew if I said the
wrong thing, that would spark an argument between us. I definitely wasn't trying to go there.

"So, my brotha, how are things going with you and Nokea?
She's just about ready to pop that baby out, ain't she?"

"Yeah, just about. She's getting pretty big, but she looks
good, though. Cutest little pregnant woman I've ever seen,"
Stephon said, smiling.

I chewed my food and tapped my fork on the table. "Tell me
something . . . when was the first time you had sex with her?"

Stephon was silent for a while and then cleared his throat.
"About two weeks after you did. Remember when you went
over to her house—had sex with her after you had been with
Felicia in your office?"

"Yeah, I remember. Remember well."

"Well, she found out about that. She was upset and came to
me crying. After that, one thing led to another, and then she
told me she was pregnant."

I thought about our conversation at the funeral. "So, you
had sex with her before Aunt Betty's funeral? Don't you remember our conversation at the funeral? Just to jog your memory, I told you then that Nokea was the exception. You knew I

didn't want the two of you getting involved. I made that quite clear."

"Yes, I remember what you said, but she was already preg- nant by then."

I thought about how thick Nokea's breasts looked at the fu- neral, and my comments about her thickening up a bit. Stephon wasn't lying. "Okay, but if we had sex with her only a few weeks apart, how do you know it's your baby and not mine? After all, she did tell me it was my baby too."

"First of all, she lied. She told you it was yours because she didn't want you to punch her stomach. How I know it's mine is she had her period after she had sex with you. And when she went to the doctor, he pinpointed her delivery date nine months after the last time we had sex."

Stephon was unable to look me in the eyes. I wasn't sure if it was because he felt guilty or if he was bullshitting me.

I took a bite of my egg roll, folded my arms, and looked at him. "So, do you love her?"

"Yeah, I can pretty much say I do. Nokea's been in my heart for a long time, Jay. I know that's not what you wanted to hear, but she has. Problem was she could never get over you. But when she did, I saw an opportunity and took it."

"But the door wasn't open for you yet. She was still with me and still in love with me when you took it upon yourself to fuck her."

"I know, but she was tired of all the bullshit. After that inci- dent with you and Scorpio in the shower, that did it. She might have slept with you after that, but her feelings were fad- ing."

"Man, you know better than I do a nine-year feeling don't go away just like that. If I had to place a bet on it, I'd say you were the one who approached her and went after her vulnera- bility."

Stephon wiped his mouth with a napkin and rubbed his hands together. "Actually, it worked both ways. She came to me, and I was willing to comfort her."

"If you don't mind me asking, how often do you comfort her now? I mean, since you out kicking it with other women and everything. Is she shaking a brotha down like she supposed to?"

Now, Stephon looked me straight in the eyes. "Not a day goes by that I don't make love to her. Lately, it's been here and there, but that's because of the baby. But I do enjoy every moment I spend with her."

My throat ached, but Stephon would never know it. Hurt me like hell that I'd waited nine years to make love to this woman, and now she was giving it to my cuz every time he wanted it. I wanted to stop torturing myself with the questions, but I had a few more for Stephon.

"So, if you say you love her so much, why you cheating on her?"

"Because I'm a man and that's what I do. These other bitches out here don't mean nothing to me. They just something to play with."

"Then why can't you be honest with Nokea and tell her you got other people in your life? I think she's going to be more hurt by you lying to her than she was by me being honest."

"And I disagree. I think what she don't know won't hurt. Eventually, I'm going to cut the shit anyway; and when I do, I'm going to be with her and only her. So why mess that up by bringing all this drama to the relationship?"

"Okay, man, your call. I just hope you can live by your words."

"You know I'll do my best," Stephon said. He reached out and slammed his hand against mine.

Stephon chilled at my place for a while. We played several games of pool and hooked up my video game to my theater-

sized TV in the bonus room. He left the room a couple times
and called Nokea. I don't think he told her he was at my
house, but when I heard him tell her he loved her, his words
stung like hell. Maybe asking him all those questions wasn't
the right thing to do. I'd never felt jealous before when it came
to him, but realistically, he had my woman.

As I thought about Nokea, my heart went out to her.
Stephon and I were damaging her. Now, it was all up to him to
make things right. At the rate he was going, I didn't think he
was capable of doing that. I'd definitely have to sit back and
watch him try.

When Stephon left, I hurried to the bathroom and almost
fell to the floor, trying to stop the pain as I urinated. I couldn't
wait to go see my doctor the next day. I truly had nobody to
blame but myself for settling for any kind of woman and not
fully protecting myself.

I finished up in the bathroom and the doorbell rang again.
Damn, can a brotha get some peace around here? I thought.
But when I saw who it was through the window, I jetted down-
stairs to open the door. It was Mackenzie and Scorpio.

When I opened the door, Mackenzie jumped right into my
arms.

"Daddy!" she yelled as I hugged her and swung her around
in my arms. She gave me a big wet kiss on the cheek, and then
wiped the spit off with her hand. "Why did you make me
leave?" she pouted.

"Mackenzie, I didn't make you leave. I had no idea your
aunt was coming to get you that night."

"Mommy said you made us leave, and when I asked why, she
said because you were mad at us."

I put Mackenzie down and cut my eyes at Scorpio. She shut
the door and tooted her lips.

"You were mad at us, weren't you?"

"I was mad at you, not her." I dropped to one knee and looked into Mackenzie's eyes. "I'll tell you the truth one day when you're old enough to understand. But for now, please know I would never do anything to hurt you."

She smiled. "Can I go up to my room? When I left, I forgot to get something."

"Sure, baby. It's just like you left it. And you don't have to ask if you can go up to your room because it's yours. Okay?"

She ran up the steps to her room. I looked at Scorpio, wanting to kill her for lying to Mackenzie.

"Why did you tell her I put her out?"

"Because you did. When you kicked me out, you kicked her out. You didn't think I would let her stay here, did you?"

"I don't know, but I'm glad you brought her over here to see me. Has she missed me?"

"Jaylin, I don't know what you've done to my baby. She's been crying almost every day, talking about how much she misses her daddy. Why did you tell her that you were her father? You're gonna confuse her, and she don't need that right now."

"Scorpio, look, I explained to Mackenzie what type of daddy I was. She knows I'm not her biological father."

"No, she doesn't. She really thinks you're her daddy."

"Well, I'll have a talk with her later so she'll understand."

Scorpio walked further into the house and her eyes scanned the rooms. "Have you had company lately?"

"Why?"

"Because I want to know who's been getting what I've been thinking about every day since I left. Excuse me; I mean since you kicked me out."

"Get over it, would you? You know damn well that I had a good reason. Now, I was wrong for putting my hands on you, but I apologized for that."

"Naw, baby, you apologized with your mouth. I was hoping

you would apologize with something else." She stepped up to me and placed her hand on my goods. Burning and all, my thang had the nerve to get hard. Since she had come over looking very good, I had to make sure I kept my distance and focused my mind elsewhere.

She placed her arms on my shoulders. "You know what I want?" she said, kissing me on the lips.

I eased my arms around her waist. "What do you want, baby?"

"I—you don't mind if I'm blunt, do you?"

"Be as blunt as you'd like."

"I want to have sex—fuck you, right now. I'm in no mood for those five-minute, I'm-too-tired fucks, but one of those all-nighters you give me when you're at your best."

My dick throbbed. I wanted to strip her ass naked and wear her out right then and there. But how was I going to get myself out of this one tonight?

I kissed her forehead and massaged her butt. She backed away and led me up the steps. When we got to my room, I was able to come up with an excuse to save me for a while.

"Scorpio, you know I can't make love to you with Mackenzie still wide awake."

"Oh, I know. But I kept her up all day so she'd go to bed early tonight."

"You just knew you could bring your little sexy self over here and use a brotha for his thang when you wanted to, huh?"

"Yeah, pretty much; especially when he be using a sista for hers when he wants to."

I hopped off the bed and got me a shot of Remy. I almost didn't care about my little problem. All I wanted was to feel her insides. I tried to talk about something else, but no matter how hard I tried, she kept bringing me back to having sex with her tonight.

I was glad to see Mackenzie come through the doors. But

when she came in and rubbed her eyes, I knew what time it was. She yawned and walked over to the chaise to sit next to me.

"Daddy, I'm sleepy. Can I stay the night with you?"

"Of course, Mackenzie. You can spend as many nights as you want with me."

"So, what about Mommy? Can she stay the night too?"

Scorpio interrupted. "Just one night, Mackenzie. After that, we're going back home. I'll bring you over next weekend to see Jaylin."

Mackenzie leaned on me and started to cry. "Daddy, why can't I live with you? I don't want to go to Aunt Leslie's house anymore."

I held her in my arms and wiped her tears. I knew how she felt; it was the same way I felt when I had to go live with my Aunt Betty. I carried Mackenzie to her room and told Scorpio we'd have to talk when I came back.

I read a bedtime story, and Mackenzie was asleep in less than ten minutes. I was so glad she was back in my life. There was no way she was leaving me again.

Scorpio had already taken off her clothes and was under the covers. She had the blankets up to her neck and a wide smile across her face. I sat on the bed and pulled the covers off her, just to get a good look at what I couldn't have. I rubbed my hand on her breasts and wiggled my hand down to her belly button. I lowered my hand again and cupped her pussy. My fingers slowly entered her wetness, and she widened her legs so I could dig deeper. Touching her excited the hell out of me, but I could go no further.

"Baby, I can't . . . I can't make love to you tonight," I said, removing my fingers.

She squeezed her legs together. "And why not, Jaylin?"

I thought about telling her the truth, but I couldn't.

She picked up Sexy Chocolate's business card on my nightstand and tossed it to me. "Is this why you can't make love to me? Did you have sex with her last night?"

I crumbled the card in my hand and massaged my goatee. "Yeah, baby. I did. I, uh, brought her here last night and things happened."

"Do you want to tell me about it, or should I call her so she can tell me like she told me this morning after she left?"

Damn, I was busted. Didn't even dawn on me that she knew Scorpio. She used what Sexy Chocolate told her to attack me even more.

"Yeah, that's right, Jaylin. I knew she wasn't lying to me because she described your 'million-dollar mansion' to a T. She told me how you fucked her so good and made her come six times. Said you banged her on the floor and in the shower. And then told me how good your dick tasted. When she gave me the exact measurements, I had to hang up on her. But the killing part about it was she said another bitch was waiting for you when you got here. When she described her, it didn't sound like anybody I'd ever seen you with, so I guess she's a new bitch, huh?"

I couldn't do nothing but sit there and listen. Seemed like if I tried to open my mouth, she already had the answer.

"You really don't waste no time, do you?" she said. "Kicked my ass out just to let somebody else in. I offered my body to you tonight because I wanted to see if you'd allow me to go behind her. I guess I should pat you on your back for backing out of it, huh?"

"Hey, it was the least I could do," I said in a sarcastic tone.

"You're pathetic, Jaylin, and you seriously need to cut the bullshit before it's too late." Scorpio pulled the covers back over her and turned away from me.

That was fine with me. I went downstairs and lay on the couch so I didn't have to hear any more of the drama. I knew I

wasn't right, but I was my own man. I didn't have any ties anywhere and was free to do whatever I wanted.

But when I thought about it more, I realized Scorpio was
probably hurting the same way I was when I found out about
Stephon sleeping with Nokea. I went to sleep thinking of a
way to make it up to her.

I sat on the examination table and waited for my doctor to
come back in with the results. She was a beautiful and classy
forty-seven-year-old woman, and if she wasn't married, I would
have tried years ago to knock her. When she walked in, she
lowered her glasses and peered over them.

"Jaylin Rogers, you know better. How many times have I
told you to use a condom? You're a grown man and you shouldn't
be naive when it comes to sex."

"Doc, I'm still a young man," I joked. "I'm only thirty-one."

"Well, you'll be thirty-two soon. You need to start being responsible for your actions. So, how many girlfriends do you
have now?" she asked.

"None."

She chuckled. "You wouldn't be all messed up down there if
you didn't have any."

"Doc, I've been waiting on you. Waiting for you to tell your
husband you're marrying a young man like me."

"Jaylin, please. I wouldn't trade my monogamous husband
in for something like you to save my soul. You need to get your
mind out of the gutter and start putting it to work like you did
when you landed your job. Leave all these fast-tail women
alone and start taking care of yourself. This time, your test
shows positive for gonorrhea. Next time, it might be something else. And you know what I mean."

"I got you, Doc. But you act like a brotha forever coming up
in here with these kinds of issues. This was my first time, and
as many—" I paused.

"Go ahead, say it. As many women as you've slept with, you could have had something a long time ago, right? But having unprotected sex one time is too many, Jaylin. And who says you don't have anything else? Gonorrhea is just the first sign. If you've been messing around for a long time without using protection, I suggest you get an AIDS test done. Today."

"Are you serious? You know I ain't got no damn AIDS."

"I'm just trying to be on the safe side. Go get yourself tested, and when your results come back, we'll talk about it then. Before I forget, make sure you contact your recent sex partners and tell them to get checked out. I know that might be a difficult task, but they need to be tested too."

"Trust me; I am not out there as bad as I could be. I've made some mistakes, and I promise you I'm going to correct them."

My doctor tooted her lips then gave me a shot and a prescription. When she said I couldn't have sex for two weeks, I placed my hand on my chest.

"Damn, you're breaking my heart. Two whole weeks? Why two weeks?"

"Because I said so. And you should be ashamed of yourself. Get your butt out of here and go take that test like I told you to," she said, hitting me on the butt with a towel.

"Now, you know that turns me on," I said, holding my behind.

"Jaylin, go! Get out of here before I have you arrested for statutory rape."

I was laughing as I left. I went down the hall and took the AIDS test. They told me my doctor would be in touch.

By the time I got home, Nanny B was there cleaning up the place—with the help of Scorpio and Mackenzie. Just to make sure the cleaning was to my liking, I helped too. I was delighted to have Mackenzie back in my life, and seeing Scorpio again was a good thing too. I just wasn't sure if we'd work on our relationship again, and I didn't know if I had what it took to give it another try.

31

FELICIA

Jaylin didn't have to worry about me calling him anytime soon. After he choked and damn near killed me, I'd had enough. I hadn't called him since then, nor did I intend to.

My ex-boyfriend, Damion, was back in my life. No matter how hard I tried to pretend Paul had set it out for me, I couldn't. Dick just couldn't do the job I wanted it to do. And after I made it perfectly clear to Damion that I wasn't going to put up with his baby mama's drama, he promised me there would be no more confrontations.

When Friday night came, I didn't feel like being bothered with Paul or Damion. I took a hot shower and decided to go to The Loft. The women at work bragged about how they be having so much fun there, and this one lady named Shirley invited me to her birthday party. It was time for me to get out.

I put my braids in a bun and let two single ones dangle on the sides of my face. Then I slid into my coal black satin mini-dress with a V-dip in the back. I added silver accessories and put on my high-heeled black satin sandals that tied up just below my knees. My eyebrows were a little bushy, so I quickly arched them, and then put on the new Oh Baby lip-gloss I picked up at the MAC counter. I looked so good I couldn't even stand myself.

The Loft was packed, and I had a difficult time finding a parking spot. When I did, I looked in the mirror and slid some more lip-gloss on so I wouldn't have to keep running to the ladies' room. I made my way to the door, and this attractive older man with gray hair stopped me.

"Say, beautiful, are you coming in?" he asked.

"Yes, I'm supposed to meet some of my girlfriends from work."

"Then you don't mind if I escort you in, do you? I have a VIP card, so you don't have to pay. And when we get inside, if you'd like a drink, let me know."

He walked to the door with me, and I was flattered to enter the club with this man. He had clout, and, I could tell, money. Not only that, he must have had every woman up in there before, because when we walked in the door, many eyes started to roll.

I went right over to the bar with him, told him my name, and got my drink. After that, I planned to stay away from him for the rest of the night. I had enough drama already and definitely wasn't looking for more.

I found my girlfriends in the party room, sitting at some tables that were reserved for Shirley's party. When they saw me, the fakeness began. I'm sure they really didn't expect me to come.

"Felicia!" Shirley said, running up and giving me a hug like we were the best of friends. "I'm so glad you came. And your dress, girl, where did you get it? It is nice."

I hugged her back and didn't tell her nothing. She introduced me to some of her other phony friends, and they all gawked at me with jealousy in their eyes. I pranced over to the buffet table to get some chicken wings.

After I sat at a table and talked to this brotha whose breath smelled like garbage, I searched the dance area for a dance partner. The DJ was on point with the latest hits, and I was ready to get my party on.

The floor was crowded, hot, and musty. Somebody had definitely forgotten their deodorant before they came, but the brotha I danced with had his act together. He broke it down to the floor, and I tried to keep up with him. I could tell he was a little younger than I was, but what the hell? If he was setting it out like that on the dance floor, no telling how good he was in the bedroom.

We laughed with each other as we left the dance floor. I danced so well that several men grabbed on me for another dance. I declined, and my dance partner went to the bar to get us some drinks. I checked out his front and backside and surely thought about taking him home with; however, when I looked up and saw Stephon at a table with some of his boys from the shop, my plans changed. He looked downright workable. He had it going on way more than my dance partner.

I went to the ladies' room to make sure everything was still in place. Then, I freshened my make-up and hiked my dress just a tad bit higher. When I came out of the bathroom, I headed straight to the table where Stephon sat. I swayed my hips from side to side and worked my ass so they'd be sure to notice when I walked by. I saw them checking me out from a distance, but I continued to look forward as if I wasn't paying them any attention. As I neared the table, one of Stephon's friends grabbed my hand.

"Say, baby, why you moving so fast? Why don't you have a seat and holla at a brotha for a minute?"

I smiled; my plan was already working well. I eased myself between Stephon and his friend.

"What's up, Felicia?" Stephon said, smiling at me with his pearly whites.

"Hey, Stephon," I said then quickly turned to talk to his friend.

His friend gazed at my breasts and licked his lips. "So, uh, what did your mama name such a pretty woman like you?"

"My mama wasn't the one who named me; my father was. My name is Felicia. Felicia Davenport."

"Felicia, huh? I got one question for you Felicia. How does a woman get as fine as you? You are definitely a sight for sore eyes."

He put it on too damn thick for me, and I tuned him out. I tried to figure out how I could kick up a conversation with Stephon, who sat next to me smelling like Gucci Envy. When he got up to dance with this other chick, I gazed at his tall, nicely cut body that showed through his light blue silk shirt and jeans. The front of his shirt was unbuttoned just enough to reveal the thickness of his chest. The light-blue round glasses that covered his hazel eyes had me melting like butter. Brotha had it going on, and it was hard for me, along with many other females, to keep our eyes off him.

The brotha I danced with earlier came over to the table and handed me my drink.

"I was looking for you. Why did you leave?" he asked. As I put the drink on the table, I noticed the crookedness of his teeth.

"Sorry, my man came in," I said, rubbing my hand on Stephon's partner's back. "I'll pay you for the drink if you'd like."

Cheap motherfucker stood and waited for me to give him the money. I reached into my purse and gave him ten dollars. He snatched it and walked away.

After he left, Stephon came back to the table with this light-skinned chick who wasn't giving him any room to breathe. There wasn't any room for her to sit, so she stood behind him and talked. I could tell he wasn't interested because he conversed with other women as she stood talking to him. She finally got the picture and walked away.

And when she did, I picked up where she left off.

"So, how have things been going, Stephon?" I crossed my legs so he could get a glimpse of my oily thighs. His eyelids lowered and he looked at them like he wanted to see what was between them.

"It's going pretty good, Felicia. Can't complain."

The DJ was right on time with a slow song. I interrupted as Stephon talked to one of his boys.

"Say, Stephon, would you like to dance?" I already pulled the chair back because I knew he wasn't going to turn me down.

He didn't say yes or no. He just got up and followed me as I strutted with sexiness to the dance floor. When he put his arms around me and leaned his head down close to my shoulder, I lowered his hands and slid them over my butt.

"Felicia, what you doing?" he said, grinning and keeping his hands where I'd put them.

"What do you mean, what am I doing? I like for a man to have his hands on my butt when we're slow dancing. Not on my back."

He gave my butt a squeeze and pulled me closer to him. I felt his goodness press against me. "Is that better?" he asked.

"Yes. A whole lot better."

"So, what are you doing here? I didn't even know you still hung out at places like this."

"I don't. I came tonight because it's my co-worker's birthday. And now that I'm here, I'm so glad I came."

"And why is that? Would it have anything to do with me?" he whispered.

"As a matter of fact, it does. I got a feeling something good . . . very good is going to happen to me tonight."

"Oh yeah? Something good like what?"

"Something good like my place or yours."

"Felicia, are you trying to get me in bed with you?"

"Stephon, I don't try at anything I do. I'm known for being a success. So, like I said, my place or yours?"

Stephon quit dancing before the music stopped and looked at me.

"Meet me outside in five minutes. I have to take care of something before I leave, so just give me five minutes."

I walked off the floor and went back to the table to get my purse. His friend asked where I was going, but I kept on walking.

I was outside talking to a police officer when Stephon came out. "Come on," he said, grabbing my hand and walking me to his car.

When we got in, he sat for a minute before he started the engine.

"Are you having second thoughts or something?" I asked, rubbing his bald head.

"Nope. Just thinking about something." He backed up.

"May I ask what?"

"No, you may not. And put your seatbelt on. I don't like people riding with me without a seatbelt on."

I buckled myself in, just so I didn't have to hear his mouth. "I guess since you're driving, we're going to your place, huh?"

"Yes. Do you have a problem with that?"

"No. I didn't know if you wanted to take me there since Nokea might decide to show up."

"Felicia, if you came with me tonight to talk about Nokea or Jaylin, I can drop you right back off at the club. I don't play games like that, baby, all right?" he said sternly.

"I didn't come with you to talk about them, but I thought it was a legitimate question. And since you don't want to answer it, then so be it. Ain't no trip."

We were quiet the rest of the way to his house. By the time we got there, I'd almost fallen asleep from boredom. I hoped his sex was good, since he seemed to have no conversation.

As soon as we got inside, Stephon picked up his phone and checked his messages. I stood by the door until he gave me the go-ahead to have a seat. When he came back, he'd already taken off his shirt.

"Come on, let's go downstairs," he ordered. I walked behind him as he led me to the basement. He had the damn hook-up downstairs. It looked like a nightclub, unlike his upper level that wasn't much to brag about. His basement had a beige leather sofa that circled the room, huge beveled mirrors that covered the walls, a diamond-shaped bar in the middle of the floor with wine glasses that hung down above it, and beige leather bar stools surrounding the bar. The floor had shiny beige, black and white tile that looked like it had never been stepped on before. His entertainment center covered one complete wall. Jaylin's name was written all over his basement. I knew he had to be responsible for financing this sucker because there was no way Stephon could afford to live like this.

Stephon went over to the bar, while I took a seat on his sofa, which was amazingly comfortable. When he walked over to me, he didn't waste any time. He set a bottle of Moët on the floor next to him and kneeled in front of me. He rubbed his hands on my hips and slid them up the sides of my dress, raising it up a bit.

"Felicia, I don't want you having no regrets after I fuck you," he said, already pulling my dress over my head.

"No regrets for me." I started to unbuckle his pants. "And definitely no complaints," I said as I got a glimpse of what was seconds away from going inside me.

After he took off the rest of my clothes, he picked up the bottle of Moët and poured it all over my body. I trembled as he had the pleasure of slurping it up. It burned a little between my legs, but he had no problem cooling it off with his tongue. Then he stood up and flipped me upside down so he could get a better taste of me. I wrapped my legs around his head so I wouldn't fall. He held me tight around my back, and I worked his goodness on the other end.

My hair fell down as I pulled it from the excitement of him working me so well. He backed up to the couch and lay back with my legs still straddled across his face. He fondled me with his fingers, and I slid my body down and sat on top of him. I put my pussy to major work, which caused him to tighten up and grip my butt.

"Felicia! Slow down, baby. I ain't ready to come yet."

I cut Stephon no slack. I was showing him something Nokea probably didn't know how to. He squeezed my hips tightly and eased himself in deeper so I could feel the full effect of him. I was in another world with him. We seemed to click so well together, almost better than Jaylin and me—but right now, Jaylin was the last thing on my mind.

Stephon and I finished up in the middle of the bar. He had emptied the second bottle of Moët on his body, and this time, the pleasure was all mine. I hopped down off the bar and plopped my naked body on the couch. He joined me, and I lay against his chest.

"I had no idea you had it in you, Stephon. I mean, I've always noticed how nice looking you was, but I guess I couldn't see past Jaylin."

"Well, I knew it was good because Jaylin told me it was. But he didn't tell me you could work it like that."

"I only work it like that when I have to. Besides, it was hard for me to keep up with you. You're packing a load down there, aren't you?"

He laughed. "Something like that. But I'm sure you'll be good company for it."

"So, does this mean this isn't a one-night stand? I know you told me not to ask about Nokea, but won't this interfere with your relationship with her?"

"Nope. Because what she don't know won't hurt her. Besides, I'd like to keep this on the down low as much as I can. Jaylin and me kind of just settled things after what happened with me and Nokea, and I don't want to do anything to mess that up."

"Stephon, please. If Jaylin finds out we're sleeping together, he'd laugh. He doesn't care about me. He could care less who I have sex with.

"I was really surprised to find out you and him went at it over Nokea. Her friend Pat told one of my girlfriends at work what happened and she told me. I knew he liked Nokea, but I thought I'd never see Jaylin fighting over a woman."

"Well, he's happy now, Felicia. He's doing what he wants to right now, and so am I." Stephon rose up and moved me away from his chest.

"Where are you going?" I asked, not wanting him to leave my side.

He turned on his CD player and sang a song by Luther Vandross. He moved from side to side with his hands on his chest like he was slow dancing with himself. His eyes were closed as he sang, "Let me hold you tight, if only for one night."

I laughed, as his voice didn't sound anything like Luther's.

Stephon grinned and held out his arms for me. There was no way I could resist holding a sexy naked body like his. This man had charmed the hell out of me, and had me leaving with a serious smile on my face.

32

NOKEA

I was so ready to have this baby. My doctor had me on maternity leave early because my blood pressure was high. I tried to remain calm and focus on the positive things, but I was worried about how all of this would work out. Stephon told me about his conversation with Jaylin, and I felt bad that he had to lie to Jaylin about us having sex right around the same time as him. But I guess everything was for the best.

Jaylin's birthday was just around the corner, and no matter what, I always spent it with him. Even when he was in the orphanage. My mother and I went to see him and took him some toys both years he was there. As we got older, we met each year at Café Lapadero, where we laughed and talked about the crazy college life. When I turned twenty-one, he was all mine. I always went out of my way for his birthday, just to let him know that somebody still cared about him.

This year would be different. I wanted to do something nice for him, but things were going so well with Stephon that I didn't want to go behind his back and cater to Jaylin. Stephon was a charm, just what I needed during my pregnancy. He satisfied all of my physical and mental needs. Problem was I still didn't love him. Couldn't kick these feelings I still had for Jaylin.

Every time Stephon left, I cried. He had no clue how I felt, and I hoped to overcome my misery soon.

I wondered if Jaylin would show up at Café Lapadero on his birthday. Then I thought about calling him to make sure he would be there. Finally, I decided to just show up without calling.

The morning of Jaylin's birthday, I searched my closet for the nicest maternity outfit I had. I decided on a pink blouse with big white flowers on it. My white linen shorts were loose enough for me to get my fat butt into, but my hair wouldn't cooperate. I put on a white straw hat with a pink ribbon around the rim, and dolled up my face to perfection.

We usually met up around 1:00 p.m., and I got there an hour early so I could make sure we had a seat, just in case he showed up. The sun shone brightly, and there was a nice comforting breeze, so I asked the waiter if he could seat me outside. I asked him for an ice-cold glass of water with a lemon, and some rolls. I hadn't eaten anything all day because I was so nervous.

I pulled out the Black Expressions card I had bought him and signed the inside. I still had thirty minutes, so when the waiter came over again, I went ahead and ordered a salad. I didn't want to sit there doing nothing and looking anxious.

By quarter after one, my stomach felt queasy. Another fifteen minutes zoomed by, and I felt like a complete fool. Why would I think Jaylin would put forth any effort to meet with me? Especially on his birthday. He probably had plans with his other woman. Plans to make love to her and make her smile like he'd done to me over the years. Stupid me, I thought. Always setting myself up for disappointment.

Almost in tears, I stood and dug in my purse to pay the waiter. I wiped my eyes and hurried to leave the restaurant.

Then, a soothing wind picked up and blew my hat off my head. I quickly turned to pick it up, and that's when I saw Jaylin behind me with my hat in his hand.

'Were you getting ready to leave?" he asked, handing my hat back to me.

"Yes," I said, still wiping my eyes.

"Why are you crying?" He put his hand on my cheek.

I sat down in the chair and chuckled. I wanted him to know how happy I was to see him, but didn't want to go overboard with expressing my feelings. "Since I've been pregnant, I tend to get emotional for no reason."

"I wouldn't know nothing about that." He pulled back a chair and sat next to me.

He looked amazing, and those addictive grey eyes behind his tinted glasses pierced my heart. His glowing tan was in full effect, and his tailored suit had me screaming naughty things silently to myself. No doubt, life seemed to treat him well.

I wasn't sure how well I looked; I'd gained so much weight since the last time I'd seen him. I hoped my look was to his satisfaction.

"So, were you getting tired of waiting for me?" he asked.

"Yes. I was about to leave. I . . . I didn't think you were going to come."

"I always come, don't I? No matter what, I always come." His eyes dropped to my stomach, and I saw his Adam's apple move in and out.

"I thank you for coming. You don't know what it means to have you in my presence right now," I said.

"No, I don't know. I really didn't think you were going to show. That's why I took my time."

"Really? I've been here. Been here since noon." I wanted so badly to talk about the baby, but I was unable to look him in the eyes. He lifted my chin and made me look up at him. My eyes watered.

"What's wrong, Nokea? Why do you keep crying? I thought you'd be happy to see me."

"I am very happy to see you, Jaylin. I just didn't think it would be this hard for me seeing you again. The last time we spoke, you were pretty upset with me, and—"

"And I'm sorry. I should have never come to your place and disrespected you like that. I was wrong. That's what I wanted to come here and tell you today. I'm sorry for everything I've ever done to you. I've had a lot of time to think about my mistakes, and what can I say other than I fucked up? I have to move on and stop thinking about what could have been."

"Do you ever think there might be a chance for us down the road? I mean, right now, you're happy, I'm happy." I was trying to convince myself that I was, and I didn't want Jaylin to know that I wasn't. "But . . . but is there a chance we can be happy together?"

"Honestly, Nokea, I don't think so. You have my cousin's baby on the way, and you shared something with him I will never be able to forget. And as much as I thought that maybe someday we would be, that dream ended when you got pregnant. I'm not saying I don't still have feelings for you. All I'm saying is I got to take my feelings elsewhere."

My throat ached; that was definitely not what I wanted to hear. I dug in my purse and pushed his birthday card to him. "I wanted to do something else special for you, but I decided to keep it simple."

He picked it up, read it, and smiled as he closed it. Then I reached into my purse and pulled out the teddy bear he'd given me on my birthday. The front of the shirt still said: HAPPY BIRTHDAY, NOKEA YOURS FOREVER, JAYLIN. Printed on the back was MY HEART BELONGS TO YOU FOREVER, LOVE NOKEA. He smiled again and gazed at the teddy bear.

There was silence for a while, and then he said, "I guess sometimes people who love each other just can't be together."

I blinked several times and fought back my tears with every-thing I had. "Yes, they can. Love can conquer anything. If you love me, we can make this work, Jaylin." I reached my hand out to touch his. He eased his hand away.

'Nokea, it'll never work out. There's too much damage that's been done. And I'm not talking about with just you and Stephon. I'm talking about all the damage I've done to you, too. You deserve better. Much better than I can offer you." He stood up and reached into his pocket. He tossed a fifty-dollar bill on the table and put his teddy bear under his arm.

"Listen, I'm not going to be able to stay for lunch. I have some business to take care of. This should take care of lunch and then some. Good luck, baby. And I wish you and Stephon all the best."

He leaned down and gave me a lengthy kiss. Touching his lips and tasting his tongue felt so good to me, but he backed up as he felt me getting deeper into it. I took off his glasses so I could look into his eyes.

"I love you so much," I said, unable to get any other words to come out of my mouth.

He stared deeply into my eyes. "I know. And you know how I feel." He took his glasses from my hand and walked away.

I was crushed. I felt my entire body shake. I hurried to my car and cried like a baby. I cried because reality had set in. What we had was over, and I'd have to let go and make the best of my life with Stephon. Maybe Jaylin was right. After so much hurt, how could a relationship between us ever make any sense?

When I got home, Stephon was there. He was in the baby's room, putting up some wallpaper I'd picked out at Lowes. I felt guilty as I stood in the doorway and watched him go out of his way for a baby that wasn't even his.

He climbed down the ladder and came over to give me a

kiss. "Hey, baby, are you okay? You don't look so good. Why don't you go lay down for a minute? I'm just about finished and then I'll go whip up something in the kitchen."

"I'm fine. I went to the mall with Mama this afternoon and she had me doing a lot of walking."

"Aw, so, what do you think? It looks good, don't it?" he said, looking around at the wallpaper.

"Yeah," I said dryly. "It looks perfect. Just how I imagi—" I grabbed my stomach because I felt a sharp pain.

Stephon reached over and held me. "Baby, go lay down. You look tired."

"All right. I think I will go lay down for a minute."

I felt faint walking into my bedroom. I lay across my bed and let out some more tears as I thought about Jaylin. When another pain hit me, I yelled for Stephon to come help me. If the pains were contractions, the baby was early.

Stephon ran into the room. "Nokea, are you okay?" he said, bending down on the bed to hold me.

"Stephon, I think I'm in labor."

"Well, come on! I . . . I'll go get your things for the hospital and get the car." He rushed around the room in a panic. "I'll come back and get you in a minute."

"Hurry!" I yelled as I continued to hold my stomach.

Stephon zoomed around the house and gathered my things. Then he came back into the room, picked me up, and carried me to the car. I couldn't tell who was more nervous. He kept asking me the same questions over and over: How are you doing? Can you feel the baby yet? By the time we finally got to St. John's Mercy Medical Center on Ballas Road, I actually could.

The emergency room crew rushed me to the delivery room and called my doctor to come immediately. I asked Stephon to call my parents to let them know. But when I told him to call Pat, he cut his eyes at me. I begged until he said he would.

Once everyone was notified, he came back in the room with me and held my hand for support.

I lay there in so much pain. My doctor asked me to push and I gave it everything I had—but I couldn't force this baby out for anything in the world. Stephon bent down and tried to coax me, and after he squeezed my hand tighter and yelled at me, I pushed harder and the baby came out.

It was a boy. A six-pound, five-ounce baby boy. After the nurses cleaned him, they put him in my arms. He was handsome, with a head full of curly, coal-black hair. He was light-skinned, and when he forced his eyes open, I saw that they were a beautiful grey like Jaylin's. The baby looked just like him.

I was filled with joy as I rocked my baby in my arms. Stephon reached out, and I gave my baby to him. He smiled and rubbed the baby's tiny fingers.

"You did good, Shorty. I'm really proud of you," he said, bending down to give me a kiss.

"Thank you. Thanks for being there for me. I don't know what I would have done without you," I said, feeling exhausted.

Stephon gave the baby back to the nurses. They cleaned me up and took me to the private room I'd arranged for.

Mama and Daddy rushed in a few minutes later, anxious to see the baby.

"Where is he . . . she?" Mama said.

"It's a boy," I said softly. "Your grandbaby is a beautiful, handsome boy."

Mama started crying, and Daddy held her in his arms. She made me cry. I knew from the beginning that my parents would be elated about this moment.

While Mama and I talked, Stephon stared out of the window like he was in deep thought. Daddy walked over to him and shook his hand.

"Man, thanks. Thank you for being there for my baby. I was a little worried about her, but I'm glad she and the baby have you."

"You're welcome, Mr. Brooks, but you don't have to thank me. I wouldn't have had it any other way."

I was relieved it was all over. I couldn't wait for the nurses to bring my baby in to see me. When they did, we spent the next few hours showing nothing but love to our new arrival.

I became tired and asked everybody for some alone time with my son. Stephon walked Mama and Daddy to the car, but Pat hung around so we could talk.

"Girl, you got yourself a fine young man there. He's got to be the cutest little baby I've ever seen, and I'm not saying that because you're my best friend."

"Isn't he beautiful? I feel so blessed to have a healthy, beautiful baby, especially since he came early."

"You mean especially since he came on Jaylin's birthday. Ain't that something? When Stephon called me, I damn near died because I remember you said you were going to see him today. So, how did that go? Did he even show up?"

"It was okay. He came, but he was late. Bottom line, he never said he loved me, and he said we could never be together." I started getting choked up.

"Nokea, let it go. Stop trying to chase him. If he hasn't come back to you in all this time, forget it. I hate to see you keep torturing yourself like this."

"I know. The baby is born now, so it's time. I think I'll be much better anyway knowing I have him in my life."

"Good. I'm glad to hear that." Pat gave me a kiss on the cheek. "Get some rest and I'll call you later."

As she headed out, Stephon came in with a balloon and some flowers he'd picked up at the gift shop.

"Take care of her for me," Pat said, stopping him at the door. "She's a good woman and she deserves a good man in her life."

"I got her back," Stephon said.

Stephon put the flowers and balloon on my windowsill. I smiled and scooted over so he could sit next to me. He rubbed my hair back with his hand.

"I know. It looks a mess, doesn't it?"

"Naw, Shorty, you look beautiful. I can't believe you're a mother now. You're going to be a good mother. I know you will. Your mama and daddy did a good job raising you. I would've given anything to have parents like yours." Stephon looked a bit sad.

"And you're going to be a good father. My baby is going to have a daddy in his life that he can be proud of. Thing is, I don't know what to call him. Would you help me name him?"

Stephon walked over to the baby and picked him up again. He brought him over to the bed and sat next to me. He stared at the baby for a minute and then looked at me.

"He really doesn't look like you, you know?" he said.

"Yes, he does. He's got my nose."

"No, he doesn't. Actually, he has my aunt's nose. He looks like his daddy. Don't you, little man?" He rubbed his nose up against the baby's nose. "You look just like your daddy. I say we name him after his daddy . . . Why don't you call him Jaylin?"

"Stephon, I don't think that's a good idea. I mean, if we're going to raise him together—"

"Yes, we're going to raise him together, but ain't nothing wrong with me naming my child after my favorite cousin, is it?"

I wasn't sure about that. Naming the baby Jaylin could be full of future consequences. Too many people would question it, and I wasn't prepared to explain myself each and every time. Jaylin might see this as an insult.

Then again, what if he found out the baby was his? He would want his child named after him, so maybe I should go with what Stephon suggested.

"No, I guess there's nothing wrong with you naming your child after your cousin. Jaylin it is."

We both held little Jaylin in our arms for a while, and after he went to sleep, Stephon called the nurse to come get him. He climbed sideways in bed with me and stared into my eyes.

"I love you, Shorty. And every chance I get, I'm going to make you the happiest woman in the world. Your worries are over. So, no more tears, no more arguing, and no more disappointments." He reached over to hold me, and I kissed his cheek.

"You are so wonderful. Why couldn't you have come into my life before Jaylin? This would be a lot easier for me if you had. I just don't know when or how I'm going to be able to move on."

Stephon climbed out of the bed and stood next to me. "You're going to move on right now. It's time. I have always been in your life since you and I were kids. Unfortunately, you just recently started to notice. Life is so unpredictable, and sometimes we have to go wherever it takes us. I never thought in a million years I would be here with you, loving you like no other man in this world can love you. And asking you to . . . to be my wife." He reached into his pocket and pulled out a small black box.

I was too nervous to open it, so he opened it for me. I looked at it and blinked my eyes so I wouldn't cry.

"Shorty, will you marry me? I don't want to waste any more time being without your love." He took the ring out of the box and waited for an answer. Must have paid a fortune for it because the diamond was huge!

"When, Stephon? When do you want to do this?"

"Whenever you want to, baby. I want to give you time to get things situated with the baby, and also time to share the news with your family. After that, I want you to be my wife, and I'm not taking no for an answer."

I took the ring from Stephon and slid it on my finger. I looked at it and smiled, as it weighed down my finger. Again, I wasn't sure about this, and my feelings for Jaylin definitely hadn't all gone away. I had feelings for Stephon, too, and it was now time to choose one versus the other.

I couldn't deny how much Stephon had made me happy, and being happy with a man that I loved had always been my goal. How could I walk away from something that felt so right?

' If I never loved you before, I love you now. There is no way I'm going to let you walk out of my life when you've been so good to me. Six months, Stephon. In six months, you'll have your wife." I gave him a juicy wet kiss that showed him just how excited I was.

Stephon stayed in the room with me all night. He fell asleep in the bed next to me. Feeling slight pain, I eased out of bed and sat in a chair by the window. I raised my hand several times and looked at my ring. I was happy, and all of this started to make sense to me. I stared up at the sky and thanked God for my healthy baby boy and my new handsome fiancé.

33

JAYLIN

Meeting with Nokea was one of the toughest things I had to do. I'd been thinking about her a lot, but I figured it was because I had been missing her so much. During our brief lunch, something else hit me and surprised the fuck out of me. I realized how much I loved her. Chills ran through my body, and when I looked deeply into her watery eyes, my heart felt as if it jumped out of my chest and into hers.

I wanted to tell her how I felt, but seeing her pregnant brought so much hurt to me. Damn, why did she have to be pregnant with Stephon's baby? She looked so beautiful. A part of me really wished she were having my baby.

I couldn't stop thinking about what she'd said during my fight with Stephon. Maybe she was truthful about me being the father, but if I dug deeper to find out, Stephon would think I was desperate to get his woman back. I didn't want either of them to think I was desperate. If the baby was mine, I was sure the truth would come to the light.

For now, Mackenzie and Scorpio had moved back in, and their presence helped me cope with my thoughts of Nokea and

Stephon. I'd forgiven Scorpio for lying to me about stripping, and since I saw for myself that she was all about the money, I felt at ease with her. She promised me that she wouldn't lie to me again and said that taking off her clothes for men was history. That was fine with me, as there was no way for me to accept a woman with that kind of profession. She had to do better.

When I got back from meeting with Nokea, Scorpio and Mackenzie were in the kitchen baking me a Black Forest cake for my birthday. My favorite. It was a bit lopsided, but I appreciated their efforts.

I sat on a stool in the kitchen, and my mind drifted back to my day with Nokea.

"Baby, you seem kind of preoccupied today," Scorpio said. "Does your birthday always get you down? You know, since you're getting older and everything." She laughed.

"Don't go calling me old until this motherfucker here can't rise anymore," I whispered, grabbing my thang.

"Jaylin, watch it. Mackenzie's in here."

"I'm sorry," I said. I walked over to Mackenzie, who was standing by the counter and putting more icing on the cake, as if it didn't already have enough.

"Daddy, do you like it?" she asked, licking the icing off the spatula.

"Like it? I love it! And since you made it, I really love it."

She scratched her head and whispered, "I really didn't make it. Mommy did. If it's not good, blame her, not me."

We all laughed. One thing I like is an honest woman. She wasn't taking credit for what she did or didn't do. I gave Mackenzie a wet kiss on her cheek and she wiped it off.

"Yucky." She smiled.

Mackenzie put the finishing touches on the cake. She and Scorpio stuck some candles in it and sang "Happy Birthday" to me. It was so sweet, I damn near wanted to cry. Later, they took me to Morton's Steak House in Clayton and we got down on the food.

On the drive home, my cell phone rang. It was Stephon. I hadn't heard from him all day, which was quite unusual, since it was my birthday.

"Say, man, happy birthday. Sorry I just got around to calling, but I had a busy day," he said, sounding like he was out of breath.

"Well, I'm glad you found time in your busy schedule to call a brotha."

"Listen, what's on your agenda next weekend? I have something really important I want to holla at you about, but it'll have to wait until then."

"Nothing much. I signed Mackenzie up for ballet classes, but that's at nine a.m. After that, I don't have any plans."

"Good. Then I'll see you Saturday afternoon. I'll call before I come to make sure you're there because it's important that we talk."

"If it's that important, why don't you meet me at my house tonight? I'm on my way there now."

"Naw, it's got to wait until the weekend. Besides, I want you to enjoy the rest of your birthday with your fine-ass woman tonight."

"All right, man, if you insist. I'll be by the shop this week anyway to get my hair cut, so I'll see you before then."

"Okay, that's cool."

He wished me happy birthday again then hung up.

By the time we got home, Mackenzie was sound asleep. I carried her to her room and kissed her for at least the hundredth time that day. I really appreciated her and Scorpio as they tried to make sure I had a good birthday.

I shut Mackenzie's bedroom door, and I saw Scorpio standing in the foyer, looking upstairs at me.

"Oh, Jaylin," she said, smiling and motioning with her finger for me to come to her.

I smiled because I knew what time it was. She was butt-ball naked and headed toward the Jacuzzi.

By the time we got outside, I had dropped my shit off in the living room. And since I'd kept sex between us on the down low because of my burning ordeal, I was ready to tear into her. And that I did. Loving was so good, made me wanna fuck all night long. She was definitely in it for the long haul, and I couldn't find it in my heart to kick her out again, no matter what.

I'd hired a private detective to keep an eye on her, though. She promised me that she would leave all the bullshit behind. According to her, her main focus was finishing school, but I had to know for myself if she was still lying to me about stripping. I knew that if she was, it was all about the money. Had nothing to do with trying to get her fuck on with somebody, because I was doing that and doing it well. It was strictly about making sure she kept some money in her pocket, and the best way she knew how to do it was by showing men her sexy body.

I wanted to believe that she wasn't doing it anymore, but last week, she came in at two in the morning. She claimed she and her sister went out with some of their girlfriends, but I wasn't no fool. I'd been a playa for many years and definitely knew the game. Knew it well.

After I finished making love to her, we went to the kitchen and warmed up our leftovers from Morton's. I sat on a stool while Scorpio stood her naked body in front of mine and stuffed some potatoes in my mouth with a fork. I rolled the potatoes around in my mouth and opened it wider for some more.

"Wow, I didn't know your mouth could get that wide," she said, holding back on giving me some more.

I slid her closer between my legs and held her ass with both of my hands.

"Where do you see us in five years?" I asked.

She laid the fork on the plate and gave me her full attention. "I see us standing here in the kitchen doing the same thing we're doing right now. I see me loving you more and more each day. And maybe, just maybe, some more kids in our future."

I nodded and thought about what she'd implied. Since Nokea had moved on with Stephon, that didn't sound too bad. But we still had some major work to do with our relationship. My feelings weren't quite there yet, and if Scorpio wanted that kind of future with me, she'd have to do a better job of showing me. Lying to me wasn't helping at all, and my gut told me she might still be up to her old tricks. My loving Nokea wasn't helping the situation much either, but I hoped to overcome my feelings.

"Do you ever think you'll get tired of making love to me?" I asked. "Not only that, do you think you'll always be willing to put up with my sometimes fucked-up ways? I can be a mother-fucker when I want to, you know."

"Oh, trust me, I know. Probably better than anybody does, because I'm the one who lives with you. But it's okay, baby. I know how to deal with your mood swings. I just get out of your way when you don't want to be bothered. Eventually you come around, don't you?

"Anyway, why are you asking me about the future? Are you planning on keeping me forever?" She rubbed her fingers through my hair like she always did.

I took her hand and kissed it. "Baby, I have a serious problem with loving women. I told you this before, and I don't want it to damage our relationship. It's not that I don't love being with you, but something inside just won't let me get too attached. And every time I feel as if I'm getting too close, I back off. I go find myself another lady to occupy my time . . . to take away some of these feelings I have for you."

"But in due time, Jaylin, that will change. Those days I was away from you were hell for me. But it took that for me to realize I couldn't lie to you if I wanted to be with you forever. I had to do whatever it took to get you to trust me again, so now I'm working on proving to you that you can trust me. And once you realize you can, all of this is going to change. You'll be able to love me like I want you to. You'll see."

I turned Scorpio around and pressed her butt against my thighs. "I'm tired, baby. I'm truly burned out. It's time for me to get back to business. I've focused too much of my time elsewhere. After tonight, I don't know how much time I can offer you. I mean, I still want us to be together, but my work is going to take priority over everything. By not working, I'm losing money, and I don't like to lose out on money. I'm a brotha who likes the finer things in life, and I know what I have to do to make sure that continues."

"Jaylin, by all means, handle your business. You've been more than a blessing to Mackenzie and me, and there's no way I'm going to stop you from doing what you need to do. All I ask is that you don't forget about us.

"Maybe some day I'll be able to handle it if you do, but Mackenzie won't. She's so crazy about you it scares me. I really think she wants to be with you more than she does me. But you do have a way with the women, so I know exactly where she's coming from."

"I will never forget about you and Mackenzie, especially her. She's made me realize so many things over these past months, and most of all, she's shown me how to love somebody. In a different way, of course. And for me, that's a big step. I don't think I've ever loved anybody in my entire life except for her and—" I paused.

"Her and who, Jaylin?"

"My mother. Her and my mother," I said, backtracking my thoughts, as Nokea was on my mind.

"Well, I'm at least glad you love a part of me. That makes me feel special right there. And I know if you can love my daughter the way you do, then you will eventually find a way to love me too."

"Maybe so," I said, kissing her on the neck and getting ready to stick my thang where it belonged.

Scorpio and I got down in the kitchen, but I cut it short because I had to get up early and get back to work.

Shit was crazy back at work. The market had dropped to a five-year low and everybody lost money—including me. Roy tried to keep up with all my accounts, but the way things were, we were all lucky to still have jobs.

No sooner had I plopped down in my seat than Schmidt rang my phone.

"Jaylin, welcome back. Hope you're ready to do some work around here today because you have it cut out for you."

I laughed and hung up on his ass. That's what I always did when I felt pressured: just laughed and did what worked best for me.

My first call was to Higgins. Even though I spoke to him occasionally from home, I wasn't really able to handle my business with him like I was at the office. He was cool. He understood the ups and downs of the market, and didn't blame me at all for losing thousands of dollars in his investments. My suggestion to him was to buy while the market was low and wait to see what happened. Didn't expect much to happen anytime soon, but a year or two from now, we could all be back on the right track. He went with the flow, and so did his buddies.

Roy had seen how well my plan worked for me, and he got on the phone and started to do the same. We called people we hadn't talked to in years and tried to get them to invest. Drove around visiting companies that didn't have pensions or any type of retirement plans set up and talked to them about investing.

By day's end, we cooled out in my office and I kicked off my shoes. Schmidt came in and congratulated both of us. He told me he was glad to have me back, and frankly, I was glad to be back. Not once did I think about my crazy life outside of work, because that's truly what it was—crazy.

After my conversation with Scorpio, I couldn't deny or ignore my love for Nokea. I knew she was the one who'd kept me going all these years. And as much as Scorpio fulfilled all my other needs, my heart was empty because Nokea hadn't been there to fill it for a long time.

But wasn't a damn thing I could do about it. I was hurt too badly by Nokea being with Stephon. I just had to play it cool and focus on the good things I had in my life, like Mackenzie and my job, my obscenely wealthy status, and even my woman's pussy. Now, that was getting better and better each day. Too bad it wasn't filling that emptiness inside of me.

Things started to calm down by the end of the week. Everybody went with the flow of the market and waited for something positive to happen. Angela and Roy became my right-hand team. They had things under control and made sure I didn't feel much pressure. It didn't dawn on me that the reason they were so close was because Roy was banging her.

When I left the office on Friday, I had to go back and get my keys because I forgot them. I passed by Roy's office, and the lights were out. I knocked because I could hear a bunch of rumbling going on. The only thing I could do was smile. I had been there and definitely done that before. Roy didn't know what he was getting himself into. And to think Roy and her husband were supposed to be friends.

It made me think about who I truly considered to be a friend of mine. I really didn't have many to begin with, because it was too many brothas hating when I inherited my grandfather's estate and started making money years ago. I had to leave behind motherfuckers I'd known for years. Not because I was big-balling, but because they tried to take me for everything. When they came to my house, shit always came up missing. I learned my lesson early on and decided to limit myself to just a few friends. Actually, Stephon was the only person who was close to me. Our bond was pretty tight, and no matter what, I wanted to keep it that way.

When I pulled in the driveway, Scorpio's car was gone, as usual. Sometimes she was there when I got home, but usually she wasn't. When I met up with the private detective yesterday, he said she was definitely still in school. He also confirmed there was nothing going on with her and the guy who read her scripts. But he did tell me she still stripped at parties. Showed me pictures of her entering and leaving motherfuckers' cribs—and even tried to defend her by saying she always left alone. I paid him for his time and thanked him for what he called "easy work."

The thing about it was I didn't even trip. Pretended like I didn't know nothing about it. And I for damn sure didn't ask her any questions when she came in that night. She always gave me excuses anyway, like she went somewhere to study, or she went out with her sister. Explanations sounded pretty good. And if I was a brotha who didn't know any better, I'd probably have believed her. Sad thing about it was she thought I was stupid enough to believe it. Puzzled the hell out of me, but what the fuck? Arguing about it wasn't even worth my time—for now.

The only reason I kept my mouth shut was because of Mackenzie. I told Scorpio I wanted to adopt her, and without any hesitation, she agreed. Once everything was settled with the courts, I would do what I had to do to have shit Jaylin's way. I didn't hate Scorpio for what she did because after all, money was the name of her game. I knew people out there who would do anything for money, no matter who got hurt. But she was a sista who could have had it all. Didn't even have to go out like she did. Looks, charm, personality, and a little more willingness on her part could have gotten her anything she wanted. She wasn't even smart enough to realize that, and that's why I couldn't love her like she wanted me to. Besides, there was no way to forgive a woman who lied to me as much as she did.

Mackenzie always waited for me when I came through the door. I sat her on my lap in the living room as I rummaged through my mail. There was a letter from my doctor, and I figured it had to be the results from my AIDS test.

I tapped the envelope against my hand and let out a deep sigh. I unfolded the letter, and when I saw the word "negative" and read the comments from my doctor, I jumped for joy. She'd tried to reach me by phone, but the letter said her attempts were unsuccessful. Either way, I was ecstatic.

Mackenzie jumped for joy with me. She didn't even know what I was happy about; she was just happy because I was. Now, that was the kind of love I needed in my life, I thought as I swung her around the living room.

I paid Nanny B for watching Mackenzie and called Stephon to make sure he still planned to come over the next day. When a very familiar voice answered his phone, I thought I'd dialed the wrong number.

"Felicia?" I said.

"Hold on," she said.

He immediately answered. "What's up?"

"Man, was that Felicia who answered your phone?"

"Yeah." He was to the point, but didn't have much else to say.

"I just called to see if it was still on for tomorrow. But, uh . . . what is Felicia doing answering your phone?"

"I was asleep. She wasn't supposed to answer it. If Nokea had called, I would have been fucked."

"No doubt. When did this shit between you and Felicia—"

"Man, I don't know. It's been a while. I was going to tell you, but I didn't want you tripping like you did when you found out about Nokea."

"Man, whatever. That's your prerogative, so, hey, go for what you know. It ain't nothing but some pussy." I heard Felicia in the background moaning.

"Right, right. But, uh . . . I'll give you a holla tomorrow. This one here just can't seem to get enough."

"Tell me about it. I definitely know how that is."

I hung up and didn't even sweat it; wasn't even worth me stressing over. Stephon was just too much, and so was Felicia. She was nothing but a whore who I'd seen through from day one.

I put Mackenzie on my shoulders and carried her up to my room. When I put her down, she laughed so hard that spit dripped down her face.

"Mackenzie, that's nasty," I said, tickling her.

"Daddy, stop tickling me," she said, grabbing her stomach. "Stop before I tickle you back."

"Okay, give it your best shot." I flexed my muscles and tightened my six-pack. She ran her hands across my stomach. When I didn't laugh, she stopped. She sat on the edge of my bed and pouted.

"Mackenzie, what did I tell you about pouting? What's wrong with you now?" I asked.

"When I tickled you, you wouldn't laugh. Mommy said when you stopped laughing and smiling, it was time for us to leave. I don't want to leave, Daddy. I want to live with you forever and ever and ever." Her eyes were watery.

"Mackenzie, how many times have I told you you're here to stay? Wherever I go, you go. I don't care what your mommy says to you. You're my little girl, and I'm never going to let you leave this house again until you get married."

"Like you and Mommy. She said you were going to marry her."

"No, no, Mackenzie. I told you that you'd be the first to know when I decided to get married. And right now, I'm not ready for a wife."

"But I'm ready for a husband. Can my husband come live here with us too?"

I laughed. "Baby, you're much too little to be talking about having a husband. Daddy's going to have to screen these young men out here for his baby." I hugged her. "When the time comes, he'd better have it going on like your daddy does, and be able to buy a beautiful home for you so you can live there with him."

Scorpio walked in. "Or be able to afford one yourself," she said, taking her jacket off and laying it on the bed. That still bugged the hell out of me, and after my look cut her in half, she picked up her jacket and hung it up in the closet. Mackenzie ran up and gave her a hug. She walked out of the room with Mackenzie, and I went into the bathroom and shut the door.

I ran some steaming hot bath water and hung my clothes neatly in the small closet in the bathroom. I slid my body deep down in the tub and closed my eyes. Scorpio knocked on the door and cracked it open so she could see me.

"Hey, you got a minute?" she said, walking into the bathroom.

I kept my eyes shut. "Always. I always got a minute for you."

"Jaylin, why do you be telling Mackenzie all that crazy stuff? I want her to grow up being independent. I don't want her to think the only way she can make it is if a man takes care of her. You're giving her the wrong impression about life."

I opened my eyes and looked up at her. "Scorpio, almost everything you tell Mackenzie has been a lie. If anyone is giving her the wrong impression about life, it's you, not me. I make a decent living; you don't. Well, in your mind it's decent, but I tell you what: I'm going to make damn sure, whether you like it or not, she don't have to go through life shaking her ass just for a fucking dollar. Now, if you got a problem with that, that's too bad. I'm not going to sit here trying to convince somebody who thinks I'm too damn stupid to realize she's still taking her clothes off for money." I closed my eyes again.

She left the bathroom. I could see her in the mirror as she sat on the bed with a sad look on her face. I wasn't in no mood to comfort her. After a few minutes, she took off her clothes and re-entered the bathroom.

"Can I join you?" she asked.

"I'd rather you didn't. I'd like to enjoy my bath alone, if you don't mind."

"Sure." She covered herself with a towel and went back into the bedroom, where she lay across the bed and turned on the TV.

When I got out of the tub I flaunted my big dick in front of her. I walked into the closet and pretended to look for something. I stood right in the doorway and dried my body with a towel, then grabbed the *St. Louis American* newspaper off the nightstand and pimped out the door. I lit up a Black and Mild, and after I closed the door to the bonus room, I laid my naked body on the floor with my feet propped up on my leather sofa. I opened the newspaper and started to read.

Scorpio came in and locked the door behind her. She took the newspaper from my hand, straddled my chest, and then squatted down on it. I got a glimpse of her good stuff, as every bit of it stared me in the face.

She rubbed her clitoris and allowed her fingers to find a way inside of her. As her juices flowed, she placed her fingers on my lips because she knew that was definitely how to turn me on. I sucked her fingers into my mouth and continued to lay there and watch. Her attempt was to fuck with my mind, and just for the hell of it, I took my fingers and teased her walls. But when she turned around and put her ass in my face, how could I resist?

I took a few puffs from the Black and Mild, and then blew the smoke out of my mouth. I scooted her down on my face so I could lick her at the right angle. I tore her insides up, but when I thought about my weakness—and my love for Nokea— I stopped the action. I moved her over to the side and stood up.

"Jaylin, why . . . why did you stop? Don't you want to fuck me?" she said, kneeling down in front of me.

I rubbed my hand on her cheek. "Baby, sex doesn't solve everything. I'm not saying that I don't want to have sex with you. All I'm saying is it's not going to keep us together forever. I find it funny how easily you can make me love your pussy. Question is, can you make me love you? For that is the only thing that counts." I picked up my paper, grabbed my Black and Mild, and went to sleep in one of the guest rooms.

Scorpio didn't bother me for the rest of the night. I actually got up in the middle of the night to make sure she hadn't left with Mackenzie. When I saw both of them still there, I went back into the guest room and went to sleep.

Mackenzie and I rushed to get her to ballet class on time. I bought her pink shoes instead of purple, and she made a big deal about it. We had to stop by the store to exchange them before we went to ballet class. I made it perfectly clear to her there would be no more complaining from her. And even though she cried again, I felt good about standing my ground for the first time.

After seeing her twirl around the floor, I couldn't do nothing but smile. I stood and watched as she took charge and learned everything that the instructors taught her. I was proud of my baby girl, and I didn't care what anybody said.

Before going home, we stopped at McDonald's on Olive Street Road. Mackenzie took about ten minutes deciding what she wanted, only to play with the toy that was inside of the Happy Meal. She didn't eat a thing. When I tried to make her eat it, she did her normal routine and pouted. I reminded her about our conversation earlier, and when I told her I would give her hamburger to Barbie, she ate it.

I was surprised to see Scorpio's car still in the driveway when we got home. Usually, on Saturday mornings, she'd find somewhere to go, like to the gym or to Chesterfield Mall or Saks Fifth Avenue to spend my damn money. But I guess that since I'd gotten a little tight with the money, she had fewer options.

She must have heard us pull up because she came outside and asked how Mackenzie's ballet class went. I felt like if she really wanted to know, she would have gotten her ass out of bed and gone with us. But what the hell? I couldn't make Scorpio do what she was supposed to do, and I wasn't trying to kick up an argument with her today.

I went into my office to turn on my computer. My intentions were to catch up on some work before Stephon came over, so I closed the door so I wouldn't be interrupted. No sooner had I taken off my jacket than I saw him pull in the driveway. He was outside talking to Scorpio—probably trying to coax her ass in the bedroom too. I did promise him a while back that as soon as I was finished with her, he could have her. Again, it didn't matter to me either way.

They were outside for a while, so I pulled my curtain to the side to see what was taking them so long. Scorpio held a baby's car seat in her hand, and Mackenzie jumped up and tried to look at the baby.

I guess Nokea finally had it. I was nervous about seeing the baby. My palms had already started to sweat. Stephon, of course, couldn't wait to bring it over here and throw it in my face.

I heard them coming through the front door, so I rushed to my desk and pretended to be occupied. Scorpio peeked in and told me Stephon was here to see me. When I told her to let him in, he walked into my office with the baby in his arms. I lowered my head and rubbed my goatee. Couldn't even get up enough nerve to look at the baby. Frankly, I didn't know how to respond.

Stephon cleared his throat and got comfortable in a chair. "Say . . . say, man, I know I'm a little bit early, but I figured you and Mackenzie was probably back from her ballet class."

I looked up. "I see you got yourself a son there, huh? Can't help but notice all the blue and white he got on."

"Yeah, I got myself a son."

"How's Nokea? I didn't think she was due so soon. I just saw her on my birthday and she didn't mention anything about her delivery date being so soon." I knew Stephon had no idea we'd seen each other on my birthday.

"So, you saw her last week? What did she say?"

"Nothing much. She just wished me well and we talked, that's all."

"Aw, okay. But, uh, she's doing pretty good. She hasn't been getting much sleep because of the baby, but her parents and me been trying to help out."

"So, I take it you had a night off last night since you were at your place with Felicia."

"Aw . . . yeah, that. Well, ah, Felicia and me, we cool. But I didn't come here to talk to you about her. We've shared plenty of women in the past—eight of them, to be exact—and we never made it a big issue, so I don't want to do it now."

"I'm with that. And actually, it was nine, to be exact. I counted them myself just last night."

"Well, nine then. I'm just glad we don't have a problem keeping it in the family."

"Naw, no problem. But there was one exception. One I sure regret not keeping to myself, and one that I told you was off limits," I said bluntly.

"I know, Jay, but things happen. I couldn't control my feelings for her, and I really thought you had moved on with Scorpio. So, what I'm about to tell you, I want you to listen and listen good. If you get upset with me, just know I didn't come here to fight with you again. I think it's time this came out in the open so we both can get on with our lives."

My voice rose. "That's all I'm trying to do. But every day, it's something new. I don't know how much of this back-stabbing, playa-hating bullshit I can take."

"It ain't even like that, Jay. Just . . . just let me start from the beginning. As you know, when we were growing up, I always liked Nokea. You never paid her any attention, and I think that's why she liked you so much. When y'all started dating, I was really disappointed. And then when you kept fucking around on her, seeing all these other different women, Jay, it bothered me. All I wanted to do was see her happy. Year after year, same ole shit.

"And each time y'all got into it, she came to me for comfort. This past year was the first time she ever said it was over between y'all, and I truly felt it was time for her to move on."

Stephon moved around in the chair and tried to get more comfortable. He could see the daggers in my eyes ready to do damage. "So, anyway, I stepped up," he said. "I tried to show Nokea what a good man could really be like. But she still wouldn't love me like she loved you. No matter how hard I tried. So, a part of me felt like if I saw other women, maybe her feelings would change. Maybe she did want a bad boy in her life.

"She doesn't really know about the other women in my life,

but I think she suspects something. And just that small suspicion is bringing her closer to me. Making her want to be with me more and more. I know it sounds crazy, but it's the truth. She seems to like me more because she thinks I'm a challenge for her now."

Stephon took a deep breath and looked at the floor. "When I told you I made love to her a few weeks after you did, I lied. When I told you we'd had sex before my mother's funeral, I lied about that too. I lied to you because I wanted this baby to be mine. I wanted Nokea to be happy and I wanted him to be raised by me. I know it was wrong, my brotha, but I felt like at the time, it was the best thing to do."

He stood up and carried the baby over to me. He took him off his shoulder and laid him in my arms. "This is your baby, Jay. I took it upon myself to name him Jaylin because he looks just like you."

Since I'd obviously been lied to so much, I hesitated before accepting the baby in my arms. Stephon laid him in my arms and pulled the blankets back so I could get a good look at him. My eyes searched his head full of curly black hair and the shape of his eyebrows. Stephon rubbed his cheeks, and as he squirmed around a bit, his eyes started to open. When they did, I could see myself written all over this baby. Wasn't no denying him. My baby picture was almost identical.

I looked at Stephon as a tear rolled down my face. I hadn't cried in a while, but having my son in my arms just did something to me.

"Did anybody ever think about what I wanted? This could have changed things for me a long time ago. Why in the hell would you and Nokea lie to me about something like this? Maybe I didn't have my head on straight, but . . . but this is something we could have worked through together. You all I got, man, and I thought our bond was much stronger than that."

"It is. That's why I couldn't go another day without telling you. It's been killing me not being able to, but I did what I thought was best."

"So, when was he born? She had to have just had him."

"He's a week old today. She had him on your birthday. I guess after seeing you last week, it was too much for her."

I smiled and thought about my conversation with Nokea at the restaurant. God surely had a way of making a way out of no way. As stubborn as I'd been, I didn't know why he was looking out for me. "On my birthday, huh? She had him on my motherfucking birthday?"

Stephon nodded.

"So, now what, Stephon? You seem to be the man with all the answers. Where do we go from here?"

The grin on his face vanished and he walked back over to the chair to take a seat. "I've asked Nokea to marry me. She accepted, and in less than six months, we're going to be married. I don't want to keep you from seeing your son, but I want to be a part of his life too. He will definitely know who his father is, and I will never do anything to keep him from you."

I could have damn near died. I shook my head and even had to chuckle a bit from the bullshit I'd just heard. "So, now you're going to marry her? Just like that. Walk her down the aisle knowing damn well that she still loves me. Man, that's crazy. How can you be with a woman knowing how she truly feels? Don't make any sense, and neither does your plans for my baby."

"Well, it makes sense to Nokea and me. She's different, cuz. Ever since she's had the baby. She wants a family. She wants to set the same good example her parents set for her. And personally, I think she is starting to love me. I didn't expect you to be happy for us, but this is what we want, and nobody is going to stop us.

"I would like for you to get on board and be my best man. I really wouldn't have it no other way."

I stood up and put the baby on my shoulder. Did the best I could, anyway, because I really didn't know how to hold him. 'You have got to be out of your fucking mind," I said, not knowing any other way to put it.

I looked out the window to see where Scorpio and Mackenzie were. They were outside washing the cars, so I turned my attention back to Stephon. "You expect me to stand there and watch you marry the woman I love? Man, please. I don't even want to talk about this shit anymore. My mind is going a mile a minute."

"Jay, man, don't be like that. We can put this behind us. You can accept this situation for what it is and move on with Scorpio and Mackenzie. Please, man; be there for me. You don't have to give me an answer today, but think about it."

He picked up the baby's car seat. "We gotta go. I told Nokea I was taking him to the barbershop to brag on him, and she's going to be looking for us, so I'd better go. I didn't tell her I was coming by here, so if you could keep this quiet until you decide what to do, I'd appreciate it."

I looked at the baby and kissed his forehead. My mind was so messed up, I didn't know which way to turn. I gave him to Stephon and watched him lay the baby in the seat. This motherfucker had my son and my woman, and it was actually the first time in my life I felt as if I'd lost control.

He slammed his hand against mine, and before heading to the door, he turned. "Just think about being my best man. Call me when you've made up your mind."

"I already gave you my answer, Stephon. Ain't much to think about. But you can do me a favor and tell Nokea to call me. I want to talk to her and make sure this is what she wants to do."

"No problem. Will do. I'll ask her to call you later." He shrugged and left.

I figured Stephon wasn't going to tell Nokea nothing. I looked out of the window and watched him put my baby in the car.

I couldn't blame anyone but myself for fucking Nokea over like I did. I never thought my mistakes would cost me a son and the only woman I'd ever loved. But no question about it, what goes around definitely comes around, and I was starting to feel the effects of every bit of it.

I sat in my office all day long with the door locked. Scorpio hollered in and told me she and Mackenzie would be at her sister's house. I guess she figured I needed time to myself since I'd refused to come out of my office when she asked me to.

It had gotten late, and I was still in my office. I didn't turn on any lights, just lay on the couch, sleepy as ever, and thought about my child. During my dreams, I called on Mama and she encouraged me to go get my son. She said she was finally proud of me for realizing the mistakes I'd made. Claimed it was not always about me, even though I wanted it to be, and yelled at me for not respecting her wishes by being with Nokea. When I tried to touch her again, I woke up. It was another dream, but it seemed so damn real.

I wiped my face with my hand and the tears just kept on coming. No one was there to stop my pain. No one was there to hug me, and right about now I needed that more than anything in the world.

As I soaked in misery, there was a light knock at the door. "Daddy, are you in there?" Mackenzie whispered. "Come out. You haven't played with me all day."

I chuckled and felt a sudden sense of relief. I went to the door, and then locked it after Mackenzie came in. We remained in the dark because I definitely didn't want Mackenzie to see I'd been crying.

"Daddy, why are you in the dark?" she whispered as she hopped up on the couch and turned on the lamp next to it.

"Because, Mackenzie, I'm thinking." I held my head down.

She got off the couch and stood in front of me. Then she lifted my head like I did hers when she felt down.

"Have you been crying?" she asked. "It looks like you've been crying." She wiped her hands on my face. "Don't cry. I'll take care of you."

I held Mackenzie tight and we rocked back and forth together.

"I love you, Mackenzie. I really and truly do love you."

"I love you too, Daddy. But I'm hungry. Would you make me some of those pancakes you made me last week?"

"Pancakes at this time of the night?" She nodded. "Sure, baby. You can have anything you want."

I led her into the kitchen. Scorpio came in and sat on one of the stools. Mackenzie didn't waste no time telling her I'd been crying, and she looked at me with sympathy in her eyes.

"I know that was your baby Stephon had today. I want you to know that I will be here for you if you need me. Whatever you decide to do, I'll back you all the way. Even if that means you want me to move out. I talked to my sister about moving back in with her, and she said it would be okay—"

"Scorpio, I don't know what I'm going to do. I haven't asked you to move anywhere, so don't go making plans to move out just yet, all right? Besides, I need you right now. Need you more than I ever have before. You and Mackenzie both."

Scorpio gave me a hug and placed her lips on my ear. "I love you," she whispered. "More than you will ever know."

34

FELICIA

Stephon and I were having sex every chance we got. He crept into my place and I crept into his. But when he told me he had proposed to Nokea, I was devastated. It didn't stop him from putting it on me, so I tried hard to get him to change his mind. But no matter how hard I worked him, he stood his ground. I thought about calling Miss Homebody and telling her the news about her so-called fiancé, but knowing her, she'd probably try to kill her damn self. I didn't want to be responsible for nobody taking their life over a man who wasn't worth it.

Nokea was a fool, though, a prime example of every stupid woman who puts all her trust in one damn man. I knew better. And even though I had kicked Paul and Damion aside for Stephon, the door was always open so they could come back. I made sure of that, because I kept our conversations going, the dinners going—and even the money. Anything I needed, they gave, even though I'd cut off all the sex.

Wasn't no need for me to be screwing three men when Stephon tore it up like he did. He was definitely better than

Jaylin. Besides, who better to replace him with than his own cousin?

When Stephon and I got together, we were like two dogs in heat. He couldn't stay away from me for two days, so I didn't know how he thought this marriage thing would work itself out. If it did, he knew damn well that as soon as the honeymoon was over, he'd climb right back into my bed. When I brought that to his attention, he laughed. Laughed because he knew I wasn't lying. He knew Nokea couldn't satisfy his physical needs like I could. So, I knew for sure, if I wasn't a pain in her side now, I'd sure as hell be one in the future. The Jaylin drama was over for us, but her husband drama had just begun.

I'd called ole Jaylin a few times to try to explain the Stephon situation, but he blew me off. I knew he wouldn't trip, but to hear him say, "A dog might get into a little trash sometimes," it kind of messed me up. I asked if the dog in him was up for dinner, but he hung up on me. I was a little hurt even though I wasn't expecting him to embrace me with kindness.

Stephon promised to be at my place no later than nine o'clock. When he didn't show until eleven-thirty that night, I was pissed. I had put the food back in the refrigerator, and I sat on the couch with my arms folded while he tried to explain why he was so late.

"Look, Felicia, I told you I had to work late tonight. A couple of fellas called the shop and told me they needed their hair cut before going to this concert tonight. Since I need the money, I stayed and cut it for them."

"Well, you could have called. I cooked all this food for you and you didn't even have the decency to call and tell me you were going to be late. And when I left you a message, you didn't even call back."

"I don't know what else to tell you. I'm answering to you like you're my woman or something. Let's get an understanding

now, before this shit starts to get out of hand. I don't answer to
no motherfucker! I've told you where I've been out of the
kindness of my heart. But if you don't believe me, that's your
problem, not mine." He stood up and got ready to leave.

I grabbed his hand. I didn't want him to leave without giving me something hot and heavy. "Stephon, I'm sorry. You're
right. You don't owe me an explanation. I appreciate what you
told me, but I get upset when I think about you being with
someone else."

"Well, ain't no need for you to think about it. I am with
someone else—and not just Nokea—so make up your mind
about us, because I'm not going to be dealing with this bullshit
every time I come over here. Either you're with it, or you're
not. If you decide to deal with it, then I don't want to hear
anything else about my delays, Nokea, or anything else, all
right?"

"Ain't no trip. You do you and I'll do me. But don't get upset
with me when I get back to business with some other men who
I've put on the back burner for you."

"I never asked you to put anybody on the back burner for
me. You did that yourself. So, don't be mad at me about your
own decision."

"I'm not. I thought it would make things easier for us, that's
all."

"Naw, baby," he said, standing and unbuttoning his pants.
"Do what you want and with who you want. I ain't got no control over it."

Stephon took off the rest of his clothes and undressed me as
well. He fucked me good. So good that I realized even though
his mouth said he had no control, his dick showed me he did.

After he left at three in the morning, I put on some clothes
and took a late night drive by the St. Louis Riverfront. I
parked close to the river and laid a blanket on the ground so I
could sit and think for a while.

For a sista to have it going on like I did, I was a bit disappointed in myself for settling for less when it came to men. I knew I could have always had one to call my own, so I couldn't figure out why I had to have somebody else's man. Paul was the only man I ever had that I could call my own, and I treated him like a pest. I knew if we got together, there would be nothing in the world I couldn't have—with the exception of a big package. I was smart enough to know a good man when I had one, and going forward, I intended to focus on trying to improve my relationship with Paul. Stephon's good loving might set me back a few times, but since he had plans to move on with Nokea, it left me with few options.

35

NOKEA

Nobody in the world was happier than I was. I still had my moments of Jaylin withdrawal, but slowly but surely those were fading away. My baby showed me how important it was for me to be there for him. I loved him more than life itself. I wouldn't let anyone or anything stand in the way of our happiness.

Not even Stephon. I could feel something wasn't right with him, and when Pat told me she saw him at the Old Spaghetti Factory with another chick, it confirmed my suspicions. He said she worked at the shop with him, but I knew better.

I started having trust issues with Stephon, but didn't really give our relationship much attention. The only person who needed that kind of attention from me was little Jaylin.

I still planned to marry Stephon because there was no solid evidence that he had lied to me about who the other woman was. And after being with Jaylin for so long, a part of me felt that cheating was in a man's nature. Sometimes, no matter how hard they tried not to, they just couldn't be right, even if their lives depended on it. As long as Stephon gave little Jaylin and me what we needed, and he hadn't brought any chaos to our relationship, I accepted his explanation. Yes, he made a mistake by not telling me about his lunch plans, but I'd made plenty of mistakes too. He'd forgiven me for mine, so how could I not forgive him for his?

When the phone rang, I was rocking LJ to sleep. Mama was supposed to come over and watch him while I went to the gym, but she was late. The call was from Jaylin. I was surprised to hear from him, but it was good to hear his voice.

"Can I come by to see you?" he asked.

"That might not be a good idea."

"Please. I really need to see you."

I knew Stephon had told him about the engagement, so I figured I needed to explain my reasoning. "I'll come to your place. Mama should be here soon, so give me a few hours, okay?"

"All right," he said and hung up.

I put on my lime green fitted dress that hugged my petite body, which was already back in shape. My hair had really grown since I had the baby, but it was styled with one side short, and the other side long and swooped above my eye. I sprayed my body with perfume. When Mama got there, she could tell I wasn't headed for the gym.

"Actually, Mama, I'm going to see Jaylin. He called and wanted to talk to me about something."

"Do you feel comfortable about going to see him?"

"Yes. It's been a while since we've seen each other and we really need to have this discussion."

Mama didn't say another word. She gave me a hug and told me she loved me.

I was nervous about going to see Jaylin. My stomach turned in knots and my sweaty palms kept the steering wheel wet.

Every time we got together, something always seemed to go wrong. This time, I kept my head up and prayed for God to give me strength.

I rang his doorbell and took deep breaths as I waited for him to answer. He opened the door wearing only his blue jeans with the top button undone. His body was so perfect. I had a vision of rubbing my hands all over his bare chest. When I saw that he wasn't smiling, though, my heart beat faster.

"Have a seat, Nokea," he said, leading me into the living room. "Can I get you anything?"

"Yes. Some water. My throat is very dry." I was testing him because I knew Jaylin never served water. He went into the kitchen and came back with a glass of water in his hand.

"Here," he said, sitting on the table directly in front of me. "Take your time because you won't be getting any refills."

"And why not?" I said, laughing.

"Because I ran out. Besides, there's something in that water I don't want anyone to have but you."

"Oh yeah, and what's that?" I asked, holding the glass to my lips.

"It's called love. And since I never knew how to love anyone before, it was hard for me to do. Today, there are so many things I want to tell you, but first I want to tell you I love you. I don't know what that means to you, but it means a whole hell of a lot to me."

I uncrossed my legs and put the glass of water on the table next to him. He took my hands and held them together with his.

"I want my son, Nokea. I want him in my life twenty-four/seven. Not only that, but I want my woman back."

I couldn't believe the words that were coming from Jaylin's mouth. Just to hear him say that he loved me released a lot of pressure that was inside of me. I'd waited years to hear those words, and I tried hard to fight my emotions.

His timing couldn't have been more off.

"What about your other women? What about Stephon? I can't turn my back on him after all he's done for me. I'm finally happy, and he's part of the reason why. Things can't just happen when you want them to."

"I know, but there aren't any more women. The only person I've been chilling with for a while is Scorpio. I realized that I couldn't ignore my feelings for you, and using her to help me cope with my situation wasn't fair. A few weeks ago, we decided that she would move out. I bought her a condo, had my interior decorator hook it up for her, and we're trying to move on. I won't lie to you and say that we've stopped having sex, because sometimes we do. But she and Mackenzie are all that I have right now.

"I love Mackenzie with all my heart, and she visits me twice during the week and spends the night here on the weekends. Right now, I'm going through the channels to adopt her. But it's still not enough, especially since I know I have a son now.

"You can't lie to me anymore, Nokea. I know that the baby you had is mine. I saw so for myself." Jaylin was almost in tears, and so was I.

"He is yours, but I—"

"Don't say a word. Let me show you something."

He led me up the steps and took me to one of the guest rooms he'd converted into a baby's room. It was to die for—better than the room I had for the baby at home. It was blue, yellow and white. The walls were painted with white clouds and had yellow birds drawn on them like they flew around the room. The crib was round, with a sheer blue canopy above it that draped to the floor. It was white and matched the dresser and the changing table that had light blue handles on them. The closet was filled with baby clothes: T-shirts, pants, jogging suits, and tennis shoes. Like LJ was really going to be able to wear all these things.

I was taken aback by the room, and observed it in tears. When I looked in the baby's bed and saw the teddy bear Jaylin and I had exchanged on our birthdays, I lowered my head. Jaylin came over and held my waist from behind.

"I feel you, baby. I know exactly how you feel." He turned me to face him. "Tell me, do you still love me?"

I wanted to scream "yes" at the top of my lungs, but I knew that revealing my feelings would be a big mistake. Jaylin would take my words and run with them, and Stephon would be left brokenhearted. I was confused and needed to speak with Stephon before I told Jaylin how I really felt.

"Jaylin, I can't answer that. I'm confused right now. I . . . I don't know how I feel. I need to go—"

He pulled me closer to him. "Then don't answer me right now. Just let me make love to you today. I know it hasn't been that long since you've had the baby, but I promise you this will feel different. It will be everything you always wanted it to be, and I'll show you nothing but love. And if you don't feel my love, then you leave here and go marry Stephon. I won't interfere with your relationship with him anymore."

I shook my head. "I . . . I do still love you, but I don't know if making love to you is going to solve my problems. I don't know if it's going to answer all these questions I have. In fact, I think it's going to complicate things more if—"

He put his fingers over my lips, and then took my hand and escorted me to his bedroom. He pulled my dress over my head and smiled at my naked body. At that moment, I wanted Jaylin just as much as he wanted me. Maybe even more. I eased back on the bed and watched as Jaylin removed his jeans. He got on the bed and held himself up over me.

"Don't think about anything else right now but me. Clear your mind right now, and think about how good I'm going to feel inside of you."

I got a jump start and stroked his dick as he circled his

tongue around my nipples. He pressed my breasts close together and massaged them. When he went down and licked my navel, I ran my fingers through his wet, curly hair.

I couldn't wait for his tongue to enter me, and when it did, it caused a high arch in my back. My legs trembled, and I felt my insides vibrate. A tear rolled from the corner of my eye. The love he had for me was truly being displayed.

"I'm so sorry for causing you any hurt," I said. "You have to know that I never, ever stopped loving you."

Jaylin kept working between my legs, and I put my hand down there to stop him.

"I don't want to come like this. Give me what I really want and I'll come as much as you want me to."

Jaylin licked my taste from his lips and placed my legs on his shoulders. He went inside and worked me in a smooth, circular motion. My eyes shut, and I sucked on my bottom lip from the feeling. It had never felt like this before, and I came quickly. He turned me on my stomach, and a few minutes later, I came again. His hands rubbed almost every part of my body, and as I gave him a ride, his thickness rubbed against my clit.

I was on the verge on coming again, but Jaylin hadn't come yet, and I wanted to satisfy him as well. I lowered myself, but he stopped me.

"What's wrong?" I asked.

"Nothing. I'm just loving the feel of you, and I didn't realize how good you look from the back."

I took that as a hint and a compliment, and turned my backside to Jaylin. He lay on me and nibbled on my ear.

"That tickles," I said, moving my head so he would stop.

"Oh, I plan to make it tickle. But you aren't going to want me to stop."

He held himself up with his strong arms and rolled his tongue down my back. After he kissed my butt cheeks and massaged them with his hands, he reached underneath me and

304

BRENDA HAMPTON

fondled my clit while inserting himself back inside. The only thing I could do was lay my head on his pillow and somehow prevent myself from trying to pull out my hair.

Minutes later, we released our energy together, and he continued to kiss the back of my neck.

"I love you, I love you, I love you," he repeated, and then turned me to face him.

I held his face with my hands. "You have no idea how good I'm feeling right now, but where do we go from here? Do we now just say to hell with everybody who's been there for us? Do I go home and tell my parents I've changed my mind, I'm not marrying Stephon?"

Jaylin rubbed his nose against mine and kissed my forehead.

"You don't tell anybody anything," he whispered. "You go home and hold our son in your arms and think about what's best for him. You think about who you want in your future. Think about where your heart truly is and where it's always been. And when you get your answer, you come over here again so I can make love to you like I just did and we can talk about putting our relationship back together.

"If there is any doubt in your mind, I want you to be honest with yourself. I don't want you to have any regrets. I would rather you stay with Stephon if you think I can't be everything you want me to be.

"The last time I told you to go home and think about it, I didn't give you time to think. I decided for you, and I quickly moved on. This time, I'm not. If you want to be with me, I'm here. I'm not going anywhere until I hear from you."

I nodded. "Just give me some time, okay?"

We got out of bed and took a shower. As he washed me, the thought of him being with Scorpio was in my mind. I wouldn't doubt if the thought of me being with Stephon had crossed his as well. But in an effort to clear my thoughts, I asked Jaylin to make love to me again. He honored my request.

* * *

Jaylin sat in bed and watched reruns of *Good Times* as I put on my clothes and got ready to go. He said Scorpio was on her way to bring Mackenzie over for the night, so I hurried as fast as I could. She was the last person I wanted to see. She had a way of making me feel insecure. I really felt none of this would have happened if she had never met Jaylin. But the more I thought about it, I realized someone else probably would have interfered.

Jaylin walked me to the door and kissed me goodbye. No sooner had I got in my car than Scorpio pulled up. Surprisingly, she spoke to me. I responded politely. She really was an attractive woman, and I knew Jaylin had to have a difficult time keeping his hands off her. As much as he claimed to love me now, a part of me knew she would remain in the picture no matter what.

I watched Mackenzie run up to Jaylin. He picked her up and was all smiles. As he waved goodbye to me, she waved with him. I waved back and swallowed the lump in my throat. I really knew that no matter how hard I tried, this just wasn't going to work out.

As I drove away, Luther sang on the radio "I'd Rather." I listened as he said he'd rather have bad times with the one he loved than good times with someone else. I didn't quite know why, but I definitely understood his message.

36

JAYLIN

I could see the hurt on Scorpio's face when Nokea pulled off. And when she went up to my room and saw the bed all messed up, she sat on the chaise and held her temples with the tips of her fingers

"So, is it over between us, Jaylin? Is this as far as we go?" she asked.

I went over to the bed and sat in front of her. "For the most part, it is. But I don't want you to ever think you didn't mean anything to me. These past months with you have been the most exciting time in my life. You've taught me a lot—more than I thought you would when I met you. I was in it for one thing and you knew it. Never in my wildest dreams did I think I would come out of this with a daughter who I love with all of my heart—and with so much respect for you. So, don't walk away from this feeling empty-handed. If there's anything, and I mean anything, I can do for you, I will."

Scorpio sighed and moved her head from side to side. "I never wanted anything from you but for you to love me. I was so sure we were moving in the right direction, and I'm not giving up on you that easily. I was always taught to fight for what I wanted, and I intend to do just that."

"Baby, I'm in love with someone else. I don't know what good fighting is going to do you when my heart is with her. I'm just telling you this because I don't want to see you continuing to hurt yourself over something that will never be. Besides, I want my little girl growing up with a mother who is sure of herself. One who knows she shouldn't fight a battle that can't be won. Don't make her suffer through watching us tear each other apart because we can't get along, okay?" I handed Scorpio the Kleenex box on my nightstand and she wiped her watery eyes.

"So, what about just last week? You made love to me like you wanted to be with me forever. You can't tell me you were thinking about her when that was happening. You seemed to be right there with me. Am I wrong?"

"No, I was there. I'm always there, but . . . but there comes a time when sex just ain't everything. I know coming from me you might not believe that, but I'm at a point in my life when I want more than just sex. And I can't get that from you. Not to say you're not good enough, but there are some things that, over time, I know only Nokea can give me."

"See, Jaylin, this is all messed up, because I know you. You're saying these things today, but tomorrow you'll have a new attitude. You'll come over to my place and strip me naked, convince me to make love to you, and be right back there again two days later.

"In the meantime, what do you want me to do? I love you and I don't want to deny you. I can tell you no all I want, but we both know I'm going to give in to you. How can I not set myself up for disappointment when I know this is going to happen?"

"I'm not going to deny what you're saying, because you're right. But I'm going to need you to stand your ground. Depending on what Nokea decides, the future might be different for me. I probably will be knocking at your door some lonely nights, but be woman enough to stop me, especially since I've told you where things stand.

"The harder you make things for me, the easier you're going to make things for yourself. I have a sexual passion for you that I've never had for any other woman. Including Nokea. But the love I have for her goes deeper than that. I admit that the passion we have for each other may send me your way again, but you know where my heart is, because I've told you."

Scorpio went into the bathroom and splashed water on her face. She looked at the shower that still dripped from my recent encounter with Nokea. I didn't like myself right about now because I'd for damn sure hurt too many women. I always thought it was about me, and felt bad for not recognizing their needs and feelings too.

I tried to make Scorpio laugh before she left by playing Twister with her and Mackenzie. Scorpio seemed out of it, and I saw her biting her nails. I knew she was hurt, and I was glad she agreed to remain friends. When she got ready to leave, I gave her a hug and patted her ass.

"If you decide to give yourself to someone else, don't let him get it from behind, because that's my place," I said, laughing.

She found no humor in my words. She gave me a blank stare. "See, Jaylin. That's what I'm talking about. Don't be saying things like that when you know the only person I want behind me is you."

"I'm sorry. I just wanted to see a big, bright smile before you left."

She gave me a fake grin and showed her pearly whites. We both laughed and rocked back and forth with a tight hug.

"Thank you for being you," I whispered in her ear.

"Anytime," she said and walked out the door.

* * *

The next several weeks were hell. I was sure I'd hear from Nokea, but she never called. Didn't come by either. I promised myself I would give her time to think about what she wanted to do; however, when Stephon called and asked again about being his best man, I knew the wedding was still on. I made it clear that it wasn't in my best interests to be there for him like that. When he mentioned they'd made plans for their honeymoon, my heart ached. I wasn't about to tell him how hurt I really was, and continued our conversation like I wasn't even tripping.

After our conversation was finished, I got back on the phone and called Scorpio. She'd made herself available to me whenever I called. And when she did try to tell me no, I went to her place anyway. I had a key to let myself in, and fucked her like fucking was going out of style. Couldn't help myself.

Nokea didn't even have the decency to call and tell me she'd made her decision. That really fucked me up. Tore me apart. I couldn't concentrate on anything but the last time we were together. She had to know how deep my love for her was. If not, she had to feel it.

I went into my son's room and looked around. He was growing fast, but he didn't even know I existed. He'd never spent one fucking night with me, and if it were left up to Stephon and Nokea, he never would. Stephon promised he wouldn't keep him from knowing who his real father was, but every time I talked about bringing LJ over to see me, Stephon always made excuses. If he did bring him by, they only stayed for a few minutes then he said they had to go.

The only reason I hadn't interfered was because I gave Nokea my word that I would allow her time to make her decision. It looked as if she'd already made it. I just truly wished it had been different.

37

JAYLIN

A week before the wedding, I had mentally prepared myself for it. Everything else in my life was going smoothly. The market was on its way back up and my adoption of Mackenzie had gone every bit of my way. I spent every moment I had with her, and tried to ease some of the pain I felt. Without a doubt, she helped me cope very well. I'd even changed the baby's room back into a guest room. Gave all his clothes to charity and sold his furniture to my neighbor who was pregnant.

Nokea never did call, and I made no attempts to call her. It was obvious who she wanted to be with, so I left things as they were. Scorpio didn't lie, though; she wasn't giving up on me. She did everything in her power to win me over. Even had Mackenzie begging me to get back together with her. But even though Nokea had moved on with her life, I still wasn't ready for the type of relationship Scorpio wanted.

One thing that fucked me up was that, according to Stephon, he still saw Felicia and screwed around with his ex-girlfriend. And if that wasn't bad enough, he planned to get up

on this new chick that started working with him several weeks
ago. So, Nokea really had her work cut out for her if she
planned on marrying him.

Me, I pretty much chilled. I was down to fucking Scorpio
about twice a week and that was it. That was good for us, considering the fact it used to be twice a day. I'd met a few other
ladies from time to time, but wasn't nothing but phone conversations going on. I hadn't invited anyone over yet, and I
wouldn't until I knew for myself this marriage was actually
going to happen.

The night of Stephon's bachelor party was like any other
night to me. He'd invited me and so did our other boys, but
again, I told everyone that I didn't want to have anything to
do with his marriage to Nokea. Stephon called during his party
and mentioned all the fly women and fun they were having. I
wasn't in the mood, so I told him to knock one out for me and
hung up.

I lay my head back on the pillow, tired of flipping from
channel to channel, when the phone rang. When I heard
Nokea's voice, I quickly sat up on my bed.

"Jaylin, I'm sorry I haven't called you until now, but I felt
this was the only way for me to figure out what I really wanted
to do. I had to give Stephon at least six months to show me
how much he wants this, and he's worked hard at proving himself. And even though I know there's a possibility he could be
with someone else, I truly don't believe it's going to be any different with you. You told me if I had any doubts, to marry him,
so . . . so that's what I'm going to do."

I had finally heard it straight from her mouth. I cleared my
achy throat.

"So, have you prepared yourself for the storm? It's headed
your way. And it's nothing like what I did to you either. It's
worse." She didn't respond. "My storm is over. I'm not saying

I've been celibate, but it's been different since I've been in love with you." I could hear her sniffles on the other end of the phone.

"Stop torturing yourself and let this happen with us, Nokea. I won't get another chance to ask you before the wedding to-morrow, but think about it. Close your pretty eyes tonight and think about us—"

She hung up the damn phone on me. As I sat for a moment and thought about why, she called back.

"Hey," she said, sniffling. "I love you."

"Right back at you," was all I could say before she hung up again.

I turned on the radio to listen to the Quiet Storm. The lights were off, and I lay in bed with my eyes closed and one hand resting on my chest. I hoped that Nokea realized how much I loved her. As Gerald Levert sang "Made to Love Ya," the words to the song took effect and tears welled in my eyes. My heart felt like somebody was squeezing it in their hands and wouldn't let go. To help ease my pain, I reached into my drawer, pulled out a picture of Nokea, and laid it in bed next to me. I couldn't really see her picture in the dark, but I rolled my fingertips around it thinking that I could feel her and wishing I could have her in my bed forever. I fell asleep hoping she'd do the right thing the next day.

While I was in a deep sleep, Mama stared down at me and smiled. She told me to go get my woman and my son, and told me to never lose them again. When I reached out to touch her, Aunt Betty touched my hand and told me it was too late for me. Said that Stephon was the one for Nokea and I didn't de-serve her. As I started to dispute that with her, they both faded and I woke up.

The sunlight beamed through my room, and I sat up on the edge of the bed with my face resting in my hands. I wiped my

hand down my face and got out of bed to prepare myself for a
long day. I went back and forth about attending this wedding,
and came to the conclusion that we all needed closure. I had
to go, just to see if Nokea would truly go through with it. If I
were there, it might be the perfect time for her to realize what
a big mistake this was and come to her senses.

I was running late for the wedding messing around with
Mackenzie. She acted like she was the one getting married.
We dressed alike in our cream-colored outfits; mine a suit and
hers a dress. We accented the cream with royal blue because
that's what she wanted. But when I tied the bow around her
waistline, she insisted it didn't look right.

She pouted all the way there because I wouldn't stop by the
store and get her a new color. Once again, I reminded her of
our previous conversation and she perked up.

Mackenzie and I sat in the last pew of the church because I
really didn't want to be seen; however, Stephon spotted me
and came over to take a seat.

"Thanks, man. Thanks for coming. I know how hard this is
for you, but you always had my back when I needed you to—
even when you refused to be my best man. It was foolish of me
to ask, knowing how you felt. I just hope after today, this will
all be over and we can go on being like brothers again. I miss
kicking it with you, dog, talking about the ladies. . . . You
missed a live party last night. I'll tell you all about it, but now
ain't the time. You can't tell me you don't miss us kicking it,
Jay, and—"

"Of course I do," I said, interrupting his bullshit talk. "After
today, I'll be fine. I came here not only for you but for me as
well. I need closure. I need to put this shit behind me and get
on with my life. Today, after I see how happy you and Nokea
are going to be, then maybe I'll be able to do that. So, go do
your thang, man. Don't let me stop you."

Stephon smiled. "You don't know what it means to have your support. And Nokea and me are going to be very happy. She's made her choice, Jay, and all we can do is accept it."

It was a good thing that Mackenzie was by my side because this would have been the perfect opportunity for me to knock the shit out of Stephon. Instead, I reached for his hand and shook it. "Good luck. I hope everything works out for you."

"Likewise," he said and then made his way to the altar.

I looked at the front pew and saw Nokea's mother holding my baby. I wanted to at least hold him, but I was sure the last person her mother wanted to see right about now was me. So, Mackenzie held her arm around mine and held it tight. It was as if she could feel the pressure I was under and was acting as my support system.

When the music started, I took a deep breath and watched as the bridesmaids started making their way down the aisle. The maid of honor came in, and I knew it was just about Nokea's time. The slower the maid of honor walked, the better off I was, but it seemed like the music was on fast forward, and then the pianist broke out with "Here Comes the Motherfucking Bride."

I dropped my head. I couldn't even stand up to watch Nokea as she walked down the aisle. Mackenzie stood up because everybody else had, and she claimed the bride was the most beautiful person she'd ever seen. I finally stood up and straightened my jacket.

When Nokea turned the corner right by my pew, she looked at me with her eyes filled with water. Mine were filled too, but I nodded and gave her the go-ahead. She cracked a tiny smile and slightly nodded back.

As she got closer and closer to the altar, I looked at Stephon. He was all smiles. Definitely knew he was getting a jewel. He'd promised me he would make her happy. Did I believe him? Hell no, and I had to do something about it.

When Nokea made it to the altar, everybody took a seat. The minister prepared for the exchanging of vows. But before he did, he asked if there was anyone who knew any reason why these two should not be joined together in holy matrimony. "Speak now, or forever hold your peace," he said.

I dropped my head again, covered my face with my hands, and then watched my legs as they trembled. I knew damn well that this was something I couldn't let happen. I knew that Nokea loved me. If I put her on the spot, she'd have to come to her senses and do the right thing.

I cleared my clogged throat and stood up. I stepped into the aisle and watched as many heads turned to me. Mackenzie grabbed the back of my jacket and asked where I was going. I touched her soft cheek and whispered, "I always told you you'd be the first to know, baby. Daddy's going to get married."

As I proceeded down the aisle, I could feel Mackenzie close behind me. Everybody watched and whispered. I stood at the altar with my hands behind my back. The entire church was in disbelief. I looked directly at the minister.

"I, uh—" I cleared my throat again. "I don't mean you any disrespect, sir, but I have love for this woman who stands before you today."

I held out my hand for Nokea to take it and looked into her big brown eyes. "If love for me is not a good reason to stop this wedding, then I don't know what is." I continued to hold out my hand for Nokea.

Stephon's mouth was wide open, and Nokea's father looked like he wanted to tear me apart. Nokea, though, forced out a tiny smile as she dropped her bouquet on the floor. . . .

Later that night, I stood looking over my balcony, drinking a glass of wine. My eyes searched the stars as a south wind blew, and I lifted my glass to Mama. Nokea had made her choice, and now I'd made one. I'd come to realize how important it is to treasure the one you love, and I now knew how easily a good thing can slip away. I tilted my wine glass upside down, poured some of the wine over the balcony for the people who weren't with me, and thought about where I'd go from here.

A tear rolled down my face while I stared at the curvaceous silhouette lying sideways in my bed. She was my rock. From the day I met her, she had always been in my corner, and she was my shoulder to cry on. She put up with my attitude, and had loved me during the times I felt as if I had no direction and didn't love myself. I looked at her in bed, swallowed the huge lump in my throat and thought . . . *is this really what I want?*

To be continued . . .
Naughty 2: My Way, No Way

Coming May 2009

NAUGHTY 2

My Way, No Way

1

JAYLIN

I had crashed out in a lawn chair on the balcony, and was awakened by a kiss on my lips. Scorpio rubbed her fingers through my naturally curly hair and straightened my thick eyebrows. I slowly opened my eyes and just stared because I was in no mood for fucking. All I wanted to know was why? Why didn't Nokea give me what I wanted? She said that she loved me and for damn sure knew how much I loved her, so why? Why did she just walk away from the altar?

I was humiliated. Downright pissed off. And I was seriously ready to kick somebody's ass. After she left me standing there looking like a fool, I didn't know what else to do but walk away myself.

I sat with no emotions as Scorpio stared deeply into my gray eyes. She leaned in for a kiss, but I turned my head to avoid it. All I could think about was how the atomic dog in me was getting ready to come out, and whoever crossed me this time was going to pay. Stephon was at the top of my list, and Nokea was close behind.

Scorpio wanted my attention, so she rubbed her fingers

along the sides of my neatly trimmed beard. "Say, I know you're
hurting, but can I at least get a smile out of you? If you didn't
want to be bothered, then why did you call me to come over?"

I moved Scorpio away from me and went into my room.
While loosening my tie and unbuttoning my shirt, my throat
began to ache from the tears I held back. I didn't want Scorpio
to see my hurt, so I went into the closet.

She followed me. "You haven't said anything to me since I
walked through that door. Whenever you want to talk, just let
me know. I'm not going to pressure you," she said.

She helped me out of my shirt and laid it across her arm.
Then she removed my belt and unzipped my pants. When she
squatted down to help me out of them, a pleasant thought
came to mind.

"Give me some head," I asked softly.

"What?" she said, looking up.

"You heard me."

"Jaylin, you know better than to come to me like that. You
haven't said anything all night, but you have the nerve to ask
for some head."

I looked down at her still squatting in front of me. "Listen!"
I yelled. "Are you going to do it or not? If not, then get the hell
out of my closet! I'm not in the mood for any bullshit!"

Scorpio stood up, laid my shirt on my shoulder, and left the
closet without saying a word.

I quickly grabbed her arm. "Where do you think you're going?"
I asked.

"I'm going home." She snatched away and snapped, "You
are one crazy high-yellow Negro. I'm not going to curse you the
hell out, because I'm trying to be patient and understand what
you're going through. Mackenzie told me about what happened at the wedding, and I didn't want you being alone.
That's why I came. But I'm not going to let you dump on me
because some other bitch fucked up your day."

"She's not a bitch, so watch your damn mouth, okay?"

'Defend the B-I-T-C-H if you want—that's your choice But I call it as I see fit. In the meantime. I'm getting the hell out of here. Call me when you're willing to get your act together."

Scorpio grabbed her purse off the chaise and headed toward the bedroom door. I dashed out of the closet and stood in front of the door so she wouldn't leave. "Hey, I'm sorry. Don't go. It's been a messed up day, and I really need you to stay." I gave her a quick peck on the lips, but when I tried to get some tongue action, she wouldn't open her mouth.

"Jaylin, kissing me doesn't make up for how you've treated me. I'm sorry too, but I'm going home tonight, so please move out of my way."

She pulled on my arm, which was blocking her from leaving the room. I didn't budge.

"I said stay. Please," I begged.

"And I said I'm leaving. Now, move your arm so I can go."

I lifted my arm and let her pass by. When she reached the stairs, I ran up behind her and begged again. "Don't go, Scorpio. Make love to me on the stairs, like you did when we first met. Please . . . I need you to relax me and put my mind at ease for the night."

She ignored me and kept on moving down the steps. I hurried in front of her and carried her back up the steps. She kicked her legs, trying to make me lose my balance.

"Put me down, Jaylin," she yelled. "I said I'm going home!"

When we reached the top step, I dropped her to the floor and kneeled between her legs. I eased my boxers low enough to expose my dick and massaged it to make it hard.

Scorpio sat up on her elbows and moved her head from side to side. "Not tonight, Jaylin. I don't feel comfortable letting you do this to me, especially after how you've treated me."

"I'm sorry! Damn! How many times do I have to say it?"

She backed away from me and crawled her way to my bedroom door. As she neared the bedroom, I grabbed her ankles and lifted her skirt. She rested on her stomach, and I laid my body on top of hers.

"I told you I didn't want this," she said. "Why are you forcing yourself on me?"

I squeezed her hands together with mine and placed my lips on her ear. "Because I need you, baby. Can't you see how much I'm hurting? You said you'd be here for me, didn't you?" I lowered my hand to rub her ass, then moved her panties to the side.

I rotated my fingers inside of her and the juices started to flow. "Can I have you now?" I whispered in her ear. "I'm dying to feel the inside of you."

Scorpio's eyelids fluttered, and when she nodded, I went for it. I inched my way into her wetness and took deep strokes. The feeling of her juicy and warm pussy always had a way of relaxing me.

I moved her long hair away from her back and pecked it with my lips. "Damn, you're good," I said. "Too, too good."

She backed me up and got on her hands and knees. That was even better, and as I slammed my hardness into her from behind, we started to sweat.

Scorpio took deep breaths and dropped her head in defeat. "Let's go to the bed, Jaylin. You're hurting me on the floor, and I really need to get comfortable."

I removed my nine and made my way to the bed. I sat with one leg on the floor and patted my lap so she'd know I was ready for a ride. She stood at the door and worked her skirt over her curvaceous hips.

"I told you not tonight, but why do you always insist on having your way?"

I winked. "Because my way is the only way."

"Not always, Jaylin. Good night, and I love you." She blew me a kiss and flew down the stairs so I couldn't catch her. By the time I got out of bed and made it to the stairs, she had closed the front door behind her.

I was left holding a hard dick in my hand. I had to resort to the *Black Tail* magazine in my closet. I couldn't believe Scorpio had played me, but I'd for damn sure make her pay for it later.

After lying across my bed for hours, sulking about Nokea, I finally got up to take a shower. The water sprayed on my body as I pressed my hands against the marble wall and thought about my dramatic day. Nokea had looked so beautiful, even though she was standing at the altar getting ready to marry my cousin Stephon. I knew she still loved me. When I interrupted their ceremony, all she had to do was say yes to me, and we would have been celebrating our honeymoon right now, but instead, she showed what a coward she was by running out the door.

Stephon was foolish enough to run after her, but I had already made a complete fool of myself by showing up and walking up to the altar. Every eye was on me, and when Nokea's father yelled for me to leave, that was enough. Mackenzie took my hand, and we walked out together.

I saw Nokea drive off, leaving Stephon with his hands in his pockets and shaking his head. I wanted to run his ass over, and if Mackenzie hadn't been in the car, I probably would have. She really helped me keep it together, but I was glad to drop her off at home with Scorpio. She had too many questions, and I wasn't in the mood to answer them.

When Scorpio came over later, I thought it was to comfort me. But at a time when I needed her most, she had the nerve to play games and walk out on me. It surely wasn't like the old days, when I had multiple women giving me whatever I wanted or needed. Nokea had always been there for me in the past. That was one of my many reasons for loving her so much— but not anymore. And then there was Felicia. Even that hoochie gave me what I wanted. I just had to cut her loose because I couldn't deal with her whorish ways. She wasn't nothing but a freak. I found out recently she even had the nerve to be sexing Stephon after all that good-ass loving I kicked down. I chuckled as I realized that I had taught her well.

Saturday night was working on Sunday night by the time I moseyed out of bed. The phone woke me several times throughout the night, but I ignored it and took my butt right back to sleep.

After a while, my stomach was growling, so I went into the kitchen to look for something to eat. It was pathetic—couldn't find much of nothing in the fridge. There was a small container of strawberry ice cream in the freezer, so I reached for it. I straddled a stool in front of the kitchen island and started to eat in the dark. I licked the ice cream from the spoon wishing it were Nokea.

The last time we made love felt so right. All I could think about was her bright smile, her scent, and her silky-smooth, petite body. We had both been so emotional, and I just knew she'd do right by me and our son.

Speaking of my son, I wasn't sure how I was going to approach my situation with him, but some serious changes had to be made soon. Simone had already taken my daughter away, and I'd be damned if I let another child slip away. I might not be prepared to talk to Nokea or Stephon after how they betrayed me, but I'd make them regret ever stabbing me in my damn back.

I finished my ice cream and reached for the phone to check my messages. There were seven messages. Scorpio had called to explain why she left me hanging last night, and then she called again and reminded me about picking up Mackenzie today. I had so much shit on my mind that I had forgotten. My secretary, Angela, had called, telling me she wasn't going to make it into work on Monday because she was ill. Brashaney, one of my fuck buddies, had called, telling me how badly she wanted me to fuck her, and Stephon had called, insisting that we needed to talk. Calls seven and eight were Nokea. She felt like she owed me an explanation and wanted to come by.

I deleted each message. The only person I wanted to talk to was Mackenzie, so I called Scorpio's place and asked for her.

"I was wondering when you were going to call," Scorpio said with a bit of snap in her voice. "Mackenzie has been asking for you all day long."

"Then cut with the attitude and give her the phone."

"I will. Before I do, though, I want to talk to you about last night."

"There's nothing for us to discuss. Now, put Mackenzie on the phone."

"Jaylin, you know you were wrong for—"

"Woman! Didn't you hear what I said? I don't want to hear your mouth! Put Mackenzie on the phone so I can apologize for not picking her up today."

Scorpio hung up and I called right back.

"Helloooo," she said in a sarcastic tone. I didn't find any humor in her games.

"Don't make me disrespect you, all right? Now, I'm asking you nicely to give the phone to Mackenzie."

"She's asleep right now. I hope you didn't expect her to stay up all night waiting for you."

I hung up on Scorpio, and prepared to go over to her place.

Scorpio refused to open the door, but when I reminded her I had a key to let myself in, she opened it. I walked by her and went into Mackenzie's room. I climbed into bed with her and rubbed my nose against hers to wake her. She slowly opened her eyes, and I turned on the lamp so she could see me. I could see the dried-up tears on her face.

"Why were you crying?" I asked, tickling her to make her smile. She gave me a hard time like Scorpio had. She wouldn't even crack a smile. "Okay, then I won't tell you what I have planned for us next weekend." She folded her arms and pouted. "I guess I'll just have to take Barbie to the circus with me, since you don't want to go."

She revealed her pearly whites and gave me a hug. "Are we really going to the circus, Daddy?"

"Yes, and after the circus, we're going to stop at McDonald's for hamburgers." She pouted again. "Jack-in-the-Box?" I said. She rolled her eyes. "How about Burger King?" Her eyes looked like they rolled to the back of her head. "Okay, what about one of my favorites? Outback Steakhouse." That got her to smile. No doubt about it, I was teaching her to have the best. At five years old, I'd been lucky to get a hamburger from White Castle.

Mackenzie took her arms from around me. "Daddy, why didn't you pick me up today? Did you spend the day with your wife that left you at the church yesterday? You were so mad it looked like you wanted to cry."

Damn, I thought. *Now, why did she have to go there?*

"No, Mackenzie, I didn't spend the day with her, and she's not my wife. Daddy was just tired today. I kind of . . . got my feelings hurt and wanted to be alone. I know I should have called you, but I slept most of the day."

"Did you cry when you got your feelings hurt?"

"A little bit, but, uh . . . let's talk about something else, okay?"

"Okay, but your wife looked really pretty yesterday. Will you buy me a dress like hers?"

"Mackenzie, I told you that she's not my wife. And yes, she did look pretty. I promise you I'll buy you a dress prettier than hers when you get married."

She hugged me again and scooted underneath the covers so

she could get back to sleep. Bottom line, she kicked me out after I told her I would buy her a dress, but I didn't care; she was definitely one person that could get anything she wanted from me—maybe the only person.

After I closed Mackenzie's door, I went into Scorpio's bedroom. She was lying naked across the bed, flipping through a cookbook. Her sexiness always gave me a rise, and the well-shaped mountain on her backside couldn't be ignored. I gazed at her perfect, moisturized body, but played down my desire for her.

"Hey, I'll let myself out. I just wanted to say thanks for not making a big deal about me coming here to see Mackenzie."

She pulled her long hair over to one side and teased it with her fingers. "You're welcome. I'm glad you came, because she was really upset when she didn't hear from you today."

"Well, we worked it out."

Scorpio closed the book and rolled on her back. She bent her knees and rubbed her thighs. I awaited her next move, and when she massaged her breasts together, she looked in my direction. "Are you possibly in the mood to work out something else before you go?" she whispered.

I folded my arms, enjoying her performance. "What kind of workout do you have in mind?"

She turned sideways and slid her hand between her tightened legs. "Do you have to ask? I was hoping to get one of those all-nighters that I haven't had in a long, long time."

"Um, I see where you're going with this. But, uh, I don't have all night. I gotta get up early for work because my secretary ain't going to be there. So I'll take a rain check."

"You're just saying that because I left you hanging—aren't you?"

"You're damn right I am. And you know what else?"

"What?"

"I'm going home to call this sweet young tender who's been

begging me to fuck her, so that all-nighter you just asked me for, I'm going to have the pleasure of giving it to her."

"Yeah, right. You're crazy, but you're not that stupid to rely on somebody else to give you what only I can."

"You're not as good as you think you are, Scorpio, so don't be so sure of yourself. As a substitution for the night, you might want to make sure the batteries in your vibrator are working, because my dick has other plans. Good night, and I'll see you whenever."

Scorpio turned her back to me and I left. As soon as I got home, I called Brashaney and she was there in a flash. I couldn't give her that all-nighter I'd told Scorpio I'd give, but I damn sure made Brashaney's visit worth it.

Scorpio rang the phone several times throughout the night, but I was busy fucking and sleeping. It was almost six o'clock in the morning when I asked Brashaney to reach over and answer the phone.

"Hello?" she said in a soft tone. Her eyes widened and she grinned as she gave the phone to me.

"What?" I yelled.

"You are one low-down, dirty, ignorant, stank Negro, Jaylin. I can't believe how trifling you are. If you want to play games, then hey, let the games begin. I guarantee you—"

"Some other time, Scorpio," I said casually. "I'm sorry that your vibrator didn't do the job you thought it would do, but I'm busy. A trifling man like me doesn't want to disrespect my company, so I'll get back with you when I can."

I gave the phone to Brashaney and asked her to hang up. Scorpio called right back. I snatched the phone and told Scorpio if she wanted to listen to what was about to go down, she should feel free. I laid the phone on the nightstand and rolled on top of Brashaney.

"Jaylin, why don't you hang up the phone? I don't care to let another woman—"

"In a minute," I said, placing her legs high on my shoulders. I inserted myself and Brashaney let out a loud moan. She closed her eyes and sucked in her bottom lip.

'I . . . this would be so much better if you'd just hang up on her."

I dug deeply into Brashaney. When I felt that Scorpio had heard enough action, I reached over and disconnected the call. Then I quickly wrapped up my business and tried to get some rest before going to work.